MESCALERO BLOOD

MESCALERO BLOOD
by Dennis A Nehamen

Published by Golden Poppy Publications™
Los Angeles, CA
www.dennisnehamen.com

ISBN: 978-0-9890572-7-1

Library of Congress Control Number: 2016904523

Cover and Book Design by Nick Zelinger, NZGraphics.com

Nehamen, Dennis A Author
Insatiable Hate
Dennis A Nehamen

1. Fiction
2. Adventure
3. Suspense

Printed in the United States of America

First Edition

A ZACH MILLER ADVENTURE: BOOK 3

MESCALERO BLOOD

DENNIS A NEHAMEN

Golden Poppy Publications™
Los Angeles, CA

This book is dedicated to the Mescalero Apache Indian people. The richness of their culture and traditions inspired me from the inception of The Zach Miller Adventure Series to infuse their history and way of life into my stories. I am eternally grateful for all that I have learned through my study of this heroic tribe. I would only hope that my readers take to heart the important lessons I've outlined from these people, especially regarding harmonious transformation of values and beliefs, as well as honor and pride.

No work of art can be accomplished without the support of loved ones. For each and every moment of patience and tolerance, I thank my wife, Bernice.

PROLOGUE

THE STATE OF NEW Mexico hadn't seen anything like it since it served host to the Manhattan Project and the development of the first atomic bomb. You might have thought Einstein had been reborn and was visiting. Instead, it was Stevie Green of LIVE.

For the past seven years, the iconic leader of his band had owned the world of music; he was the world of music. It was all about Stevie, as much a wonder as a new planet never before discovered. Then, to top it off, he was playing a one-night-only show in Albuquerque at Isotopes Park—he was an isotope, a divined element recently greeted into the periodic chart that had his fans dancing ecstatically to the magic and spirit defining the miracle.

This genius had literally branded a novel movement in sound. He borrowed from his training as a classical composer á la Beethoven, infused it with hip-hop, and then bestowed it with as revolutionary and energetic a pulse as Presley did for rock and roll.

Thanks for a father-in-law who was eager to babysit. My wife, Preeti, and I were enjoying a night out in heaven. It's doubtful that one more seat could have been packed into the stadium. The stage had been temporarily constructed in the center of the area, what would normally be the territory of a deep-playing second baseman if the field were being used, as it typically was, for baseball—an actual theater in the round.

We were sitting high up in the bleachers above the right field line, which were ideal seats that a friend of mine had acquired by way of her special status at the University of New Mexico, where the park is located. All was going well and the group was halfway through what they usually perform as a twenty-minute piece, "You Can Do the Same Thing Too." Then, the unexpected happened. The forecast for the early spring evening had called for a few clouds with no rain, but the weatherman must have had plans to attend the concert and suffered from an unforgivable case of wishful thinking— it started to pour. Most everyone has been in a rainstorm, but this was a New Mexico deluge, a genus unique to the region. On this evening, the act featured an unthinkable array of luminosity.

Lightning bolts, so dense and thick they might have passed for brightened torpedoes, struck like warriors' weapons on the sky's breast. Gods hurled exploding light patterns mimicking upside-down trees pointed at the earth like spears. Then, dancing stick figures of persons and animals stepped on stage, replaced by broad panoramic views of a globe outlining the borders of continents and countries in white—all electrical activity showing off its immense power.

But that was not the main attraction. Rather, it was that the rainfall had a mind of its own, splitting the stadium laterally from just behind the infield such that it heavily soaked the half with the playing field and all the boxes, booths, and seats wrapping around from the first base line to home plate and to the third base side. There were fans sitting literally two seats from me getting drenched while my wife and I were dry as unused Pampers.

The band was facing home plate and Stevie was in front, receiving his full share of the rainfall while the musicians standing behind him could have been dying of thirst. Remarkably, the legion refused to acknowledge the unexpected act of nature and went on singing, sopping up water like a gutter. In fact, Stevie was entranced, seeming to be brought to an unimaginable outpouring of emotion and energy, as if the heavens above were breathing through him.

To make matters more bizarre, there was no wind and the storm idled for almost a half-hour in one spot. Then, just as Stevie was finishing another piece, "Boo Hoo Bitching," the tempest exhausted itself, the beast packing up the show as if it had been waiting for its limousine.

Most of the concertgoers who had the misfortune of being seated in the downpour left to seek shelter. Their wet clothing and the coolness of the air precluded many from returning. The second portion of the program was viewed by about half of the beginning audience, but the star never mentioned a word about it.

While listening to the rest of the music, I couldn't help thinking about the incident, especially how life has a way of randomly slicing and dicing, cutting and lacerating, severing and disjoining, slitting and splitting, fissuring, parting, abstracting, divorcing, segmenting, subdividing, and fracturing us along an infinite number of planes and angles.

The wrong side of the tracks, the right side of the law, the right side of an investment, the wrong side of bed; we wake to uncertainty, live it out every minute of the day, and go to sleep, never sure if we're about to find ourselves on the wrong side of life when we rise the next morning.

A sick child, a spouse seeking love in the arms of a stranger, a lost job, an accident killing an innocent person crossing the street, a freak murdering for joy, a sad soul preferring suicide to facing another disappointment, winning a lottery, moving into a new dream home, making the basketball team, finding a new best friend, falling in love for the first time. Every second of every day we're turned like flapjacks on a griddle…one side cooling while the other burns.

That night, I, Zacchaeus Miller, known as Zach to my friends, was on the right side of the stadium. I hadn't always been as fortunate as on this concert night and wouldn't always be in the future.

The worldwide following of this man of unparalleled musical greatness was going to be on the wrong side of the news the next morning. Stevie Green's career slithered to a dead stop that evening and with it went the man himself— never to be seen or heard from again.

What happened? Well, that's the question hundreds of millions of people were trying to answer. It's also the mystery I was called on to investigate—and I begged not to take the job.

I will divulge that this adventure I'm about to scribe speaks to destiny's mercurial trickery and how human will is contested by folly. It seems that things just don't always turn out the way man plans. Some people get lucky and in the end find their way home safely. Some aren't so fortunate, and the load of dung they leave along one of their past roads traveled turns up at the most unexpected time and place—and stinks worse than a busted sewer pipe. This story speaks to the magical and maddening power of fate; one of life's inevitabilities that bullies you…more so if you try to toss it in the trash.

Welcome to Mescalero.

1

LIVE AND IN PERSON

HISTORY DOES HAVE A way of repeating itself. A few years earlier, it was my closest friend Preston who enthusiastically called me one cheery morning to suggest that I visit a boy named Jivin on a Mescalero Indian Reservation. He was supposed to be a mystic. I traveled seven hundred miles out of the way. Then I was sent on a journey to Israel that nearly cost me my life.

Since returning home from that harrowing experience, I'd married and had a child. Temporarily I'd put aside my career as a writer and was finding contentment running a restaurant called Kuruk that my wife had opened before we met. Now out of the blue, Preston calls with a hair-brained story about the Stevie Green band members believing that Stevie intentionally disappeared. Then he informs me that they want to employ me to find him.

It seems that Preston was hired by LIVE to handle their sound engineering. As he became better acquainted with the members of the group, he heard one theory after another being proposed about what happened to Stevie. Plus, not a day went by when the media didn't report somebody swearing they'd seen him or knew where their beloved idol was hiding away or being held captive. The band members finally decided that they needed to conduct an independent investigation.

From the onset, I disputed Preston's judgment to propose me as the man to locate the band's leader. Even more, I questioned these musicians' collective wisdom in allowing Preston to sell them on the idea that I could accomplish what no law enforcement team had come close to doing. Still, he was thrilled to break the news to me. Making my best effort to quash his excitement, and willfully preclude the aphorism of historical repetition coming true, I hung up on him. I thought the firm action might punctuate the point that I was at peace with my dull life as a husband, father and small business owner. It didn't.

"Zack, if this goes where I'm thinking it might…you'll soon be writing the story of the century," Preston cheered the next morning after flying into town to surprise me. "The boys say Stevie was very depressed before he disappeared…they're absolutely sure he's alive. He could be wandering in one of those fugue states—"

"Preston, what are you talking about?"

"A state…like when you lose your identity."

"I know what a fugue state is," I answered impatiently, "but for Christ sakes, has the world gone nuts? If Stevie Green couldn't find his self, I promise you there would be about a billion people who would point it out for him in the time it takes to burp—the guy couldn't walk out in public to buy a soda without being swarmed by fans."

"Well, maybe that's not the answer. But he's alive. Now, I told them you'll get to the bottom—"

I cut him off with a derisive chuckle. "I wouldn't know where to start."

"This is a short assignment, I promise." He tightened his lips and nodded his head to assure me that his words were true, totally ignoring my objection. "I've already talked to Preeti and she's excited for you."

Preston pulled two airline tickets from his pocket, flashing them as if they were passports to heaven.

"Preeti has you packed and ready to go," he laughed, taking me by the arm and leading me toward the house.

Two hours later, we were in the air and an hour after that we landed at the airport in Los Angeles. After exiting the plane we made a near one mile-long trek down the corridors of the terminal. At last, a suited man holding a white placard with black lettering that read "Zach and Preston" met us.

My friend stood by my side beaming. "Hold your horses, Zach, my man. The fun is about to start."

We were taken by limousine, but not as I anticipated to the hotel. Rather, the driver used a side road out of the main section of the airport, and in moments we entered a zone I never knew existed. It was a small heliport. In an instant we, along with our travel bags, were hoisted into a waiting copter. It was just turning dark, and whirling east from the airport made my first ever ride in a whirlybird one of the coolest experiences I'd ever had.

It took no more than ten minutes before we descended onto a landing site on the roof of the Staples Center. Two men from the band's security team greeted us. They escorted us through the interior arteries of the building. Gradually, I felt the floor rumbling and the ceiling vibrating. The noise increased with each step, breezing through the hallway like a chemical blast.

The concert was beginning. In a moment, we came to a door where another security officer was stationed. Without a word spoken, we were taken to two seats on the floor directly in front of the performance. Preston looked at me with a signature mischievous smile as wide as a politician's. He gently tapped me on the shoulder, leaning to yell in my ear over the deafening sound of the frenzied crowd.

"How's that for VIP treatment? And the best is yet to come."

I didn't want to damage his delirium by telling him I wouldn't be shacking up that night with one of the beautiful women he'd already promised me were as plentiful and diverse as jelly beans in the fan-world of music. I didn't have to. My wife had cast a spell on me and Preston knew it. "The best is yet to come" was never designed to tempt my fidelity.

The concert was insane although I would be a lying-out-of-the-side-of-my-mouth fibber if I said the group was anywhere near what it had been with Stevie. No, it wasn't so much the performance as it was being there front-stage-center with every one of the almost 20,000 seats filled with screaming fans that put me on a high. No wonder the guys comprising LIVE were smiling as if they were on drugs (remarkably, they weren't). I imagined if I were singing to a maniacal crowd that size, I'd be ecstatic too.

When halftime arrived, the lights went on and I gazed about for the first time. I'm not going to be a name-dropper—and after spending time with presidents and ministers of countries in Israel I'm not impressed with stars—but within twenty feet of me were some of the biggest names in sports, music, and film.

Preston quickly grabbed my arm and led me back to the door from which we had entered. The guard now greeted Preston like a good friend, and they exchanged a couple of words before he took us through another entrance and into a large room. Just as we arrived, the rock group came in through a separate door.

This space was sparsely populated, obviously designed for the artists to relax and work out any last-minute kinks for the second half. We stood talking off to the side for a moment.

"How do you rate this kind of treatment, Preston?" I queried.

He looked at me as if he were about to disclose a top security matter of national concern.

"Cameron Wilky, the new guy stepping in for Stevie, what do you think?"

"He's as close as you could get to looking like Stevie and he's definitely able to mimic his style on stage," I acknowledged, aware that I was hedging my position.

"Right. But his singing, what about that?"

I grinned, ready to admit a truth my close-up observation post permitted.

"Fair. It was the sound that carried the stand-in Stevie into the performance. His voice is—"

"Anyone ten rows back and further from the stage can't tell and most of the people closer don't care to think about it," Preston asserted. Then proudly he added, "So you ask why I have the privilege of walking in here uncontested—"

"I didn't ask," I teased.

"Well, I'll tell you anyway. It's because I make Cameron sound like Stevie to millions of people. Zach, I'm the best at what I do."

Preston wasn't boasting. It wasn't in his makeup. He was the best sound engineer, and LIVE was desperate for his talent. As we were talking, from across the room, one of the members I recognized, Arnie Manzano, waved to Preston and moved in our direction.

"Zach, you know who Arnie is, right?"

"Sure," I responded. I knew the names of each member of the prestigious band.

Arnie was the keyboardist. He was also an arranger and composer. In the absence of Stevie, he had picked up much of the slack: in his own right he was an accomplished artist. He was using a towel to wipe himself, still sweating profusely. Drying his hands, he shook with Preston and then with me.

"Zach Miller, right?" Arnie stated breathlessly, as if he'd just jumped off an elliptical machine.

"I am he. Good to meet you..." my mouth forming an "M" sound but freezing, not knowing what to call him.

"Call me Arnie, please. I think we'll be getting to know one another quite well."

"We'll see. I fear my best friend here oversold me," I responded humbly.

"Preston doesn't make mistakes. He's one of the few men I've met who knows when he's right and won't compromise when he does." He turned respectfully toward Preston. "He and I have gone head-to-head a few times about getting Cameron's sound squared away. Your friend here had it balls-on right."

"His expertise is music, not investigations," I said, intending to further depreciate my stock in a proposition I truthfully had no interest in pursuing.

Arnie laughed, treating me like a prankster.

"You're not the only great man to refuse praise." He let the comment float like a musical note. "Preston explained to me how close the two of you have been, but in case you didn't recognize it, let me assure you your friend's best expertise is neither music nor investigations…it's people." He nodded his sharp-pointed chin up and down like a hammer nailing a point. "If he told me my father had been Genghis Khan in a past life, I'd listen."

"He is a fairly good judge of character," I concurred.

"Damn right he is. Anyway, I'm not going to make you uncomfortable prying into the details about what you did in Israel, but your credentials are impeccable to me and the rest of the group," Arnie complimented. "If it's agreeable with you, after the show we'll all meet back at the hotel and talk out our business."

In an instant, Arnie broke into a slow jog. The door he had entered opened to the undifferentiated clamor of the awaiting audience. Immediately, he and the rest of the group made their way onto the stage to deliver Part Two.

The show ended and we hooked up again with the band. We were ushered into a limousine and shuttled away like dignitaries. The vehicle was surprisingly quiet. Except for a few depreciating comments about the performance, none of the boys talked. They seemed morose. By the response of the audience, they were a smash hit—I wondered if Roger Federer went into a slump each time he won Wimbledon because he thought he could have played better.

They certainly couldn't have been in a funk about the meager quarters they were going to have to settle for at the Ritz. They had taken a whole floor of nothing but suites. I deliberated: *If Stevie were here, would they have cut to the chase and taken over the entire hotel?*

We settled in Arnie's suite. I noticed immediately that there were no drugs and no women. Preston had assured me none of the members used. It had been a strict code established by Stevie that nobody would be part of the group who employed substances or abused alcohol. He was serious about his craft and recognized the ingredients most likely to lead to trouble—shooting, snorting, and smoking were taboo. The rest of the group knew the rules.

Stevie had been an avid health enthusiast, but one would have never recognized it while sharing a meal with him; he ate heartily. Still, it appeared that if gaining weight had been his mission, he'd failed terribly. Furthermore, from the rail-frame figures composing his group, it was apparent that they were emulating him—and likely starving to do so—together they might have fit into one pair of my pants, and I'm not a heavyweight.

Women were another story. What the fellows were known to lack in appetite, they famously redeemed for themselves in the area of carnal lust. Stevie had no objection to his group members screwing their proverbial brains out as long as they were never late for a rehearsal or missed a performance because they were up too late or slept away for the evening. He, on the other hand, was known to abstain from woman. Was he gay? There was no shortage of rumors speculating on his sexual preference but all it amounted to was grist for the media mill. Some less charitable ponderings suggested he was virginal.

On this evening, the ladies eagerly anticipating partying would have to wait for the esteemed guest of honor, Zach, to be prepped about his requested assignment by the group before performing their own service to the band. I would find out the next day when Preston discussed the festivities after I left that orgiastic celebrations included several of the stars I had witnessed sitting near us at the concert.

"Zach, you could have balled Brenda Verity. She was so stewed she would have whacked the bellman," Preston shared excitedly.

"Not too flattering, Preston, if you're telling me you nailed her," I needled him.

"She's beautiful," he giggled like a high school kid celebrating his sperm count. "I'll never forget it."

"The question is, will she?" I couldn't help ribbing him.

That evening, it was clear to me Arnie had established himself as the new leader of the fractured legendary band— he took the reins for my initial briefing. As he was about to begin, I surveyed the performers sitting around the room with me. I noticed the ordinariness each projected. On stage, their wardrobes suggested purchases from charity shops or vintage used clothing stores. Their hair was unkempt. They looked like...musicians.

But in the brief few moments they had before gathering in Arnie's suite, they had put on pricey tops and pants and combed their hair. When they talked, there was no mistaking that they were finely educated. In all, they could have passed for members of the Board of Directors of IBM.

"You can forget all the nonsense you read about in the press. Most of it is bullshit. We're all willing to bet a fortune that Stevie is alive...disappeared of his own volition." He scanned the room of silent partners. "We've discussed this between ourselves and believe you're the person we've been looking for to try and find him."

"I still have to caution you—"

"We know all about it, you're not admitting to being an investigator. That's not what we need. You've had your life on the line, nearly died several times, right?"

"Yes, but I never intended it to happen," I responded earnestly. "I'm not actually an adventurous man."

"We know that too. But you don't have fear like most of the people we've interviewed for this—in this case, the critical issue we're concerned about is *not* danger but being bought off. We know you won't compromise if you get close," Arnie praised.

"The bottom line is it's our belief that Stevie staged this...and he had help," interrupted Sonny Boy Blue, the bass guitarist. "We know who assisted him and he's as wily a son-of-a-bitch as you'll come across."

"I'm confused," I interjected. "Why would he want to do this in the first place?"

Collectively the group chuckled, as if the obvious answer was an inside secret.

"Surely you noticed how Stevie leaned toward dark skin," Arnie pointed out. "He and I spent a lot of time together, but he wasn't inclined to talk about his past. Still, occasionally he'd drop hints, and less frequently he would discuss his background in more detail. The story is that his parents were Sephardic Jews who came here from Israel not long before Stevie was born. He was an only child. By the time he was two, his mother had a life-altering stroke.

"The mother had worked as a pharmacist and his father was a physicist. It seems after the stroke, not only was she unemployable but also what was needed to care for her kept the family near the poverty level. From what he described, these were very religious people. Stevie was raised with a huge dose of guilt.

"No matter what happened, however, his education was the priority. At sixteen, he was sent to the Royal College of Music in London and then graduated from Conservatoire National Supérieur de Musique in Paris. It might impress you if I mentioned that Debussy and Bizet both went there."

"I think he had it with all of us, to tell you the truth," Rudy Dee, the group's drummer broke in. I discerned his voice as dissenting. "None of us wanted to face it, but my analytic take is he transferred his shame to us. Hell, he knew he was carrying the group." Rudy spoke matter-of-factly and without abasement. "Each of us is damn good at what we do—Stevie was extraordinary and needed to move forward on his own. Frankly, we were holding him down."

"That's your opinion, Rude," countered Arnie, who clearly disagreed. "Stevie needed us as much as we needed him."

"Then why was he so depressed?" Rudy shot back.

"All that started after his parents were killed. You know that," Arnie retorted.

"No, I don't. That's what I mean about none of us being willing to face it. He was depressed long before, but he got worse after the tragedy, Arnie," Rudy insisted.

"Come on, guys. This poor man might think our family needs a good therapist," Sonny said, employing humor in an attempt to lighten the mood.

"What happened to his parents?" the budding investigator in me piped in.

"Believe it or not, neither his father nor mother had ever come to one of his concerts. They were disappointed that after all the training in classical music, he bonded to rock. 'They were pissed' would be a more apt description of how they felt," Arnie explained. "Finally, he talked them into coming to Telluride, Colorado to see one of his shows. Stevie had hired a private jet..." Arnie stopped, angling a look of regret my way. "You get it."

"When was that in relation to him disappearing?" I asked.

"Two months later, we did Isotope in Albuquerque and," Arnie paused for a sigh, "you know the rest."

"But you forgot to tell him, Arnie, that if what we believe is true, he had to be planning his escape long before that," Rudy asserted, unwilling to let what he considered vital information escape me. "Mr. Miller, as close as you and Preston here have been throughout your lives, that's how it was for Stevie and his attorney, Jay Weiner—he's the guy who knows the truth, but he'll never talk."

"Jay Weiner is in Beverly Hills. He handled literally everything pertaining to Stevie's affairs and now he manages the trust under the conditions of the will—it's very complex," Arnie clued me in. "That's where I'd start if I were you."

"What am I supposed to do, just show up at his office? If he's sworn to silence, he'll refuse to see me," I reasoned out loud.

"We have rights to much of the material he's collected. It will be arranged by our counsel for you to have access to all the information that has to be shared with us," Arnie guaranteed. "You understand that money is not an issue. We want to know the truth. Then, if Stevie wants out, as Rudy argues, we want to give him our blessing. Everything you need, we'll provide. When you travel, you'll be booked first class all the way—our staff will arrange everything, or if you need to expend something on your own, we'll reimburse you immediately."

"You on board, Mr. Miller?" Sonny asked, as if tossing me the hot potato that nobody else wanted.

"I'll tell you what. I'll give it two months," I proposed. "If I come up empty, I'm finished. Is that a fair deal?"

"Good," Sonny responded. "I want to add one other personal observation about Stevie. Especially within the last several months, I noticed that he made a radical transformation. He came to hate what he stood for and the glorification that had been heaped on him. Even more, he hated the fans and was disgusted that they could deprecate themselves by bowing to another mere mortal."

"You know where he came up with the simple name LIVE?" Rudy tossed out. When I didn't respond, he answered his own question. "Stevie loved playing with words. Just reverse the letters and see what you get."

I did, quickly recognizing that L I V E became E V I L.

"His success ended up being evil for him. It became increasingly more evident when he was on stage. We all noticed a drop off in energy. Then Isotope. He was more dynamic that evening than he had been in at least a year." Now Sonny Boy, who had jumped into Rudy's disclosure, paused and looked at his fellow band member. "I don't proclaim to have an answer to all this, but Stevie was not killed and isn't entertaining extraterrestrial creatures on one of our cousin planets. We'd all love some facts, Miller. Good luck."

All I could do was turn to Preston, who had not said a word but sat by my side during the entire briefing.

"You're one hell of a friend."

"Just helping out the little dude by getting you a story," he quipped. "That's why I had to fly into town to bring you the news."

Preston was referring to Jivin (my wife's deceased son who was seen as a boy mystic by his people) on his deathbed promising me that future stories for me to write would arrive at Kuruk. By coming to my home, Preston reasoned that he was validating Jivin's prophecy.

My friend was correct. I'm not sure it's what Jivin had in mind but this time the tales were to come in a batch, three stories at once. I had my hands full, assigned the task of sorting out the twists and turns and then ultimately twining the separate cords into a single unified rope that I wondered along the way might in the end be used as a hangman's noose.

2

BIFURCATION OF THE TRIBAL COUNCIL

I HAD SCHEDULED A return flight to Albuquerque the following afternoon and had reserved the morning to visit with my mother and her husband. When I arrived, the lady seemed the happiest I had ever seen her. Why wouldn't she be? She had recently married a man she loved, her son was safe and happy, she adored her daughter-in-law—and she was now a granny.

When I was ready to leave, I called for the town car and was taken to the airport. After setting down only fifty-five minutes late in Albuquerque, I grabbed a cab to Kuruk. The biyearly restoration of the dining room had been ongoing for several days and when I walked in to inspect it, I saw Preeti directing her crew.

She didn't notice me entering. I stood for a moment observing my wife. Her beauty was calming. She may have had a pregnancy but her physique showed no signs of mother-hood. She was as lovely to me as the day I first set eyes on her.

She had one pair of tan, white, and pastel-blue buffalo hide moccasins that were calf-high, and she wore them religiously, as she did a pair of old jeans with the bottoms tucked into the leather. With a white sleeveless summer top she was in uniform—her wardrobe fit into a closet sized for a water heater. If she thought her dress was going to bore me to indifference she was going to need more than the lifetime we were allotted together.

I adored her face. Often in the morning, I'd watch as she lit up her skin by applying a lotion she concocted from local plants. If she noticed me staring at her, she'd giggle the sweetest expression of bashfulness while she brushed her long brunette hair. She wore it straight down, and I marveled at its insistence to rest over the left shoulder and then drape her breast.

These images so forcefully dominated my senses as I watched her from near the front door, that I hardly noticed her turning around and running over to embrace me.

"Come on, darlin'" she smiled as she took my case and placed it on a table. "We have lots to do today."

We spent the rest of the day at Kuruk. All the furniture, walls, and ceiling beams were being refinished. With the exception of rust-colored chair pads, the interior of the restaurant was comprised entirely of dark and light varieties of wood that required sanding, staining, and varnishing every few years. The job had been ongoing for several days, during which time we were closed.

The task should have been done during the winter but we had been too busy to take it on then. The only benefit of closing in the springtime was that the staff loved having time off during one of the most beautiful periods in Mescalero. Each morning during this season of splendor the sun torrentially poured down indiscriminant and blinding rays of light—treetops, roofs, plants, and groundcover basked breathlessly like lazy vacationers indecisive about how to spend the rest of their day. The explosion of brightness burst indoors. They were like silent atomic pulses deafeningly louder than an alarm clock.

Although erupting with brilliance inside and out, springtime had a slightly different effect in our immediate home. At the first sign of dawn's glorious light, Preeti would frequently open her almond eyes and smile sadly at me. It might have been nothing more than the dewy orbs glistening from the beams rushing into the room, but her tears were more plentiful the further into April and May we descended, more so than during the previous months. I'd ask her what was wrong, and while the sorrow would stream down her cheeks like tiny falls, she'd hug me but say nothing.

I knew it was Jivin. She could never get over his passing. Her son had been born with weak lungs. During childhood, he suffered consistently from episodes of shortness of breath and a hacking cough. Preeti assumed Jivin's condition was some sort of asthma, and she treated it with a potion made from local plants. Applying it with a cloth over his mouth and nose seemed to do the trick—at least until his symptoms worsened. Later he was diagnosed with a rare respiratory illness, depriving the special child of even reaching pre-adolescence.

Spring had always been Jivin's favorite season. It was a time of joyous anticipation for the boy wonder, knowing that the treasured tribal Puberty Ceremony would be coming in early summer. This annual event was considered the most sacred tradition for his people. It was the time when young girls assumed their esteemed position as women. The highlight of the festivities for Jivin was his dance. During his performance, Jivin was transported from a world of physical reality to a land of magic.

My wife's early-morning sorrow would be curtailed after only a few moments, for we'd invariably hear Souche calling from her room. Preeti would then jump out of bed and skip down the short hallway, never pausing for the rest of the day to overtly memorialize her lost son. There was delight for both of us when the little one announced her awakening.

Preeti's first tender words to our daughter were always the same. "Has my sweet White Painted Woman brought the sun out for us today?" Then Souche would let out a giggly screeching response that would out-duel any past sorrows either of us faced upon waking. So it was most every morning.

The final coat of varnish was drying when Len Cloud, Preeti's father, arrived. Preeti was an only child. As a passenger in her intoxicated cousin's car, Preeti's mother had been killed when the youth drove the vehicle off a cliff. Alcoholism was and remained a big problem on the reservation, and Preeti was no doubt relieved that I rarely drank—and even then in moderation. Len had never remarried, opting to raise his daughter by himself. They had a very strong, but at times acrimonious, bond.

Len (I never got into the "dad" thing with him, and I think he was relieved I hadn't, though he treated me with fondness in spite of the fact I was not an Apache) stood about my height but was broader and frankly more powerful than me. His face was firm and rarely openly joyous, but he always exuded a kindness and gentleness of demeanor.

Almost without exception, he wore a long-sleeved flannel shirt with the hem hanging out, hiding the waistline of his faded heavy blue jeans. He also was never seen without his brown boots. Even on hot afternoons, I'd gaze at him bundled up the same as on a cool winter day; observing not a bead of sweat on him put me in awe. His chest rose high and protruded a tad further than his barely extended belly. When I looked at Len—and even more so when I listened to him speak—the word "pride" always came to my mind.

His paid vocation was as a furniture maker. Len Cloud could recall the lathe, saws, and drills used to construct each and every chair at Kuruk—and if the conversation were to come up, he'd boast that there was not a single nail, screw, or drop of glue used to join the pieces.

"Zach went to see Stevie Green's band members, yesterday," she announced proudly to her father.

"Who's that?" Len asked naively.

"Shitaa (father in Apache), stop acting dumb."

"Your father never acts, you know that," Len countered with what I thought was a grin. "I don't know this Stevie fellow."

If he was jesting with his daughter, there was no way to know. Len would have made an excellent poker player. It was as if his features had been chiseled out of stone. The form of his mouth, eyes, cheek, brows, and forehead were impervious to the normal muscle grimacing, squinting, and tautening that causes creases and lines in most people his age. Len Cloud's face, old and wise, was still smooth enough to evoke envy in many women who glanced apprehensively into an unsympathetic mirror, reminding them that the forties had descended upon them.

"That's because this tribe is your whole life. The world is bigger than Mescalero." Preeti's deferential tone couldn't mask her annoyance.

"When your daughter becomes a woman you'll be grateful I protected our traditions," Len Cloud admonished his daughter with words and gesture, flicking his long, straight, and shiny silver-colored hair like a gown; it parted naturally down the center and then descended like a shawl, reposing confidently on his shoulders.

"Well, for your information, Stevie Green is probably the greatest musical artist to ever live," Preeti instructed. "And Zach is going to look into why he disappeared."

Reuben, our chef, by chance was standing next to Preeti. The down time afforded him an opportunity to organize his kitchen but he'd come out to survey what we wanted for dinner. It was strange how the man landed into our life. Just at the moment we needed a cook, Reuben had passed through Mescalero on his journey to . . . nowhere. He fell in love with the country, heard we had a position open, and has been with us ever since.

"Reuben, do you know who she's talking about?" Len queried the cook whom he seemed to hold in high esteem for reasons we all assumed were related to his appreciation of Reuben's culinary skills and fine manners.

"Of course. But greatest of all time...that may be over-stating it a bit."

"My daughter mocks me Reuben, but she was brought up a strong Apache woman. I know she will do the same for Souche." Still addressing Reuben, and using the topic of Stevie Green to edify our cook regarding his tribal culture, Len continued. "Zach was brought into our life by Jivin. No, my son-in-law is not a Mescalero but he has the same courage as our ancestors. We have always been brave people, the greatest of warriors."

"Father, we have a proud heritage but some people think of us as dishonorable raiders," Preeti said with a comical shrug.

Len would have no part of the humor.

"That's the coyote filling your tongue with foolishness. Would you set my suitcase outside your door?"

I had heard the phrases and metaphors many times but was aware Reuben would be at a loss to interpret. I stepped in to clarify for him.

"For the Mescalero, women have most of the power. In past generations, all a woman had to do was place her husband's goods outdoors and the man was out of her life."

"Yes, dear Zach, there are some traditions that should never be compromised," Preeti mischievously lobbed my way.

"You taught me well. That's why I refuse to possess a suitcase."

"Perfect solution, my cowardly husband," she teased.

"With the power of generations at your disposal, you still wouldn't be able to get rid of me," I promised her.

Secure that our bond was good for at least one lifetime, Preeti then turned to ease the tension with Len.

"Daddy, I love you. We come from different generations but I am as Apache as any of my ancestors. Souche? She's going to have a little bit of lots of cultures, but I promise my warrior father she will be OUR White Painted Woman."

Again, I perceived the need to enlighten Reuben.

"To the Mescalero Apache, Reuben, White Painted Woman symbolizes the life spirit of The People. She circles eternally through the feminine side of the tribe so that the loss of one individual will never threaten the elasticity and viability of the group."

A tad awkward being the teacher of Mescalero tradition, I eyed Len for approval.

"Zach is right. White Painted Woman is the force that directs the elements necessary to secure the inherent balance and harmony of our existence. If she were to lose faith, disengage from her people, we would disappear with the swiftness of an owl taking his prey." Len leaned over to kiss Preeti. "This is why the Puberty Ceremony is the most sacred tradition of our people. No devout Apache would dream of not having their daughter assume her womanly role."

I had forgotten that a Tribal Meeting had been called for the next morning. After dinner, Preeti reminded me. Being married to Preeti qualified me to attend these formal gatherings that were called periodically by the Tribal Council, when a matter of concern to the full membership at large was at stake.

An issue had been brewing for months. On the surface, it appeared benign. The number of non-tribal people coming to Mescalero to witness the tribe's sacred Puberty Ceremony had been increasing year after year. The festivities took place over the course of *four* days and coincided with the Fourth of July Independence Day celebration—some of the members of the tribe would not speak on the point to strangers but considered it thumbing their noses at the United States by encroaching on such an important holiday for Americans.

Each year, the props and attractions used to bring in tourists multiplied. The prior year, for example, enough bleachers had been installed so that one might have mistaken the affair for a professional football game. Banners advertising everything from Google to Apple computers distracted from the dancing and singing as offensively as promo campaigns at Dodger Stadium assault the fans' senses away from baseball. Concessioners were granted rights to sell food items, memorabilia, and clothing with the tribal logo—it was a mob scene. But the more people who came to camp out and party, the more dollars that were stuffed into the tribe's bank account.

The Mescalero Apache Indians were as clever in commerce as they had been defending themselves against foes. Now, however, there was a schism, a portion of the devout members were not only disgusted with the fanfare but genuinely worried that the very existence of the Mescalero tribe was in peril. Many of the young girls were abstaining from participating in the Puberty Ceremony either because their parents objected to the "prostitution" of the ritual or they themselves saw no purpose to the "public circus."

The latest plan was to incorporate a huge fireworks show on the Fourth. The subject had edged its way into informal discussions between tribal members—often generating acrimony. The commercial success of the ceremony had butted up against tribal traditions, and for some, like tribe council member Len Cloud, it was time to declare war.

I had attended several of these large assemblies since marrying Preeti. The meetings were conducted in the sacred main hall, a rounded space with an enormous glass window facing north, inviting a view of the 12,000 foot-high Sierra Blanca mountain peak. My wife had educated me about the formal procedures I would observe and their significance. Each time I was impressed by the orderliness. There were designated procedures used to both express disagreement and resolve conflict—the latter typically by consensus.

Crucial to the Mescalero people, was the concept of Life's Circle. The world was basically divided into four parts, since there are four seasons and four directions. The principle of the circularity of life was symbolically represented in almost everything pertaining to the life of the Mescalero people. For example, the arrangement of the auditorium dictated that the council members sit at the south side, with the general members across, facing the council, but in the north portion of the space.

The council is composed of ten members—the Mescalero believe that odd numbers inherently represent imbalance. Every two years the group-of-ten stands for re-election. Last year, I witnessed Walter, a man about my age, elected for the first time. It was actually Walter who had befriended Preston and taken him to Kuruk, where he first saw Jivin.

In fact, it was Len Cloud who spoke for Walter to be a council member and he had since served as his mentor. Both were seated as the tribe president, Bernard Platta, started the meeting by making a formal statement regarding the controversy that necessitated this gathering. As was the custom, a hierarchy dictated who spoke and in what order, commencing with the council officers, followed by the remaining council members, and then the audience at large.

There were fairly rigid rules determining who had priority within each category of membership and how long they might speak—elders were religiously and respectfully deferred to. What always intrigued me was the prescribed period of silence following any person's speech. It's a time of contemplation, soft voice consultation with fellow members, and hopefully perspective leading to closure.

This was to be the first meeting I witnessed that would end chaotically. It was also the first time that Preeti, or anyone else attending, had ever seen it end in the manner it did. It's said that the natural direction of the circularity of life is east to south to west to north. Thus, a speaker would be expected to move directionally in that pattern when approaching a microphone to address the rest of the tribe.

When Walter—outraged by the acquiescence of passive members to the position advocated by Platta of endorsing fireworks—stood and deliberately strode west to east to scream into a microphone his opposition, his behavior abruptly ended the meeting. Collectively, the tribal members were nonplussed, as well as mortified. The reversal of a formal pattern heralded a certain disruption and instability—harmony and balance had been broken.

After Walter's performance at the meeting, the tribe's hope to restore the order he had single-handedly dismantled rested either through Jivin from his perch in the cosmos birthing a new uniformity out of chaos by invisibly dancing at The Puberty Ceremony or his backup White Painted Woman stepping in to spiritually guide the people out from the frightful abyss. Sadly, both must have been on vacation.

As I was soon to learn, the enmity and divisiveness running through the tribe, like nuclear dye injected into the human venous system, was lethal. There was to be death by killing, not the most natural way of parting. As for my father-in-law, it was to be the trusted messenger, Mr. Owl rather than the trickster, Mr. Coyote, bringing him life-shattering news. They were tidings that would put wrinkles on his youthful complexion.

3

JAY WEINER, ATTORNEY AT LAW

IT WAS SHORTLY AFTER meeting the band when I received a call from Gip Wilsey, the manager of LIVE. He had arranged with Jay Weiner's office for me to begin my investigation into Stevie Green's disappearance. I was in no hurry. I agreed to come back to Los Angeles in three days. Wilsey assured me that he'd have me booked "to my satisfaction." I refrained from mentioning to him my negative sentiments about flying, as well as suggesting that a private jet might improve my attitude. I had been treated once to a ride in one of those sleek rocket-like, rich-man crafts, and I'll be the first to admit it's the way to travel…when somebody else is paying. I didn't have the nerve to mention it…and he didn't offer.

For the next couple days after the council proceedings, the daunting feeling within the tribe had not let up a notch. There were many informal gatherings. Kuruk was buzzing with worrisome gossip, especially during breakfast and lunch. Thus, the three days until I returned to Los Angeles passed briskly. Before I knew it, I was again in flight.

My hometown was usually behind the curve getting summer off the ground. It was dewy and cool when I jumped into the cab. The driver spoke absolutely no English but was a master with the GPS hanging from his car's sun visor.

"9701 Wilshire Boulevard," I called out.

In forty-five minutes, there I was in front of a fancy Beverly Hills office building. If Stevie was alive, he was taking good care of his friend. This was as swanky a Beverly Hills law office as the swanky city had to offer. Mr. Weiner had the whole penthouse floor. The secretary was prepared for my arrival.

"Mr. Miller?"

She didn't wait for me to confirm her suspicion, rising from her chair and personally walking me down an interior hallway to Mr. Weiner's office—or should I say mansion. No wonder he needed the whole floor. He could have set up a volleyball court and still have had room to meet with the directors of Starbucks, Stevie's main ex-sponsor.

I had gone to school with several Weiner-rich-kid types. You look at them and know in an instant that they've never in their life looked at the price of a menu item in a restaurant. Jay was about five nine and his hair was light brown, rich and healthy looking, but cut in a crew. He was in his mid-thirties. In the corner of his office were both a treadmill and stationary bike exercise machine. From his appearance, I'd bet he used them routinely—he epitomized a well-conditioned assassin.

He introduced himself in a patronizing manner, almost to the point of obsequiousness. But he failed to omit a note of condescension to make sure I would never forget that to him my assignment was a big joke.

"Anything you want," he generously offered. "My staff is at your disposal." His graciousness didn't stop there. "And if I can help you in any way, let me know."

Throughout my dealings with him, he adhered to all of his declarations. He never reneged on his word and provided anything that I requested. He was the consummate gentleman, and as I got to know him better I found him increasingly loathsome. For underneath the smooth, dandy veneer, I smelled a rat. But did he know what happened to Stevie Green? I guess my job was to find out whether my initial assessment that Weiner had a stench was a bad first impression or a clue from which I might sniff an answer.

"I received a call from LIVE's people, as I'm sure you know," Weiner informed me. "They wanted you to have everything and that's what you'll get."

He then motioned for me to follow him. We went back past the reception area where I'd initially entered and into another short hallway. Then he led me only a few feet further to a door that he politely opened for me. We entered a large office, definitely twice the square footage of a good size hotel room. I noticed upon passing the threshold that through the only window, one covering almost the entire outfacing side of the rectangular space, there was a view of the Neiman-Marcus department store. As I scanned the rest of the office, I saw boxes nearly piled up to the ceiling on the other three walls.

"May I call you Zach?" Weiner asked. Before I could answer the obvious, he offered similar informality to me. "Just call me Jay, please."

"What is all this?" I asked, arcing both of my hands tenuously in a semi-circle toward the cases.

"Everything. Every detail I have on Stevie's disappearance."

I looked at him with a smirk, knowing this gag was on me.

"What am I supposed to do with all this?" I questioned, murmuring more to myself than expecting an answer from him.

"Zach, these people who hired you are..." Jay swirled his right index finger around his ear, "just a bit wacko. I know they're convinced that I know something about Stevie and I won't disclose. They've had access to all of this before and can't find a thing. Now it's your turn to try."

"I'm not the first person they hired?" I mumbled less as a question than an exclamation.

"I don't know if they were paying the clown they sent in here several months ago. If there was anything to discover that I haven't already disclosed, he was not the man for the job—he couldn't have found himself in a mirror." Weiner paused for a timeout, finally adding what I perceived as a disingenuous attempt to stir emotion into the subject. "Stevie was my best friend. They may have been his band mates, but I've known him since he was a boy."

"I was told there were some unusual conditions in his will."

"Just one," Jay admitted, shaking his head in consternation.

"The boys will fill you with more aspersions about me than Lilly makes Prozac pills."

"They just told me to ask you about the will."

"There was one clause Stevie invented." Jay laughed at what he labeled as an absurdity. "I'd never seen it used myself. It stipulated that in the event there was suspicion of wrongdoing toward him—if he went missing under dubious circumstances and his body could not be found—then his assets would be frozen for seventy-five years. By that time, if he were alive, Stevie would be well over a hundred.

"The legal complications to accomplish what he was requesting were overwhelmingly complex. In the end, Stevie had to agree to clauses that left numerous loopholes… I think it would take quite a bit of time for me to explain them and I doubt it would serve your assignment. Your employer doesn't even understand most of it; unintentionally, all Stevie did was fuel their wild imaginations," Jay said derisively.

"When did he draw up his...I guess, 'living' will?"

"The will was drafted initially a year after he started to generate income from his career. He might have modified it once or twice a year, but that condition I just mentioned was put in about two years ago."

"Like he might have anticipated he'd drop off the face of the earth?" I flippantly queried.

"I asked him about that when he first presented the idea," Jay said, moseying circularly as if inspecting the boxes I was soon to begin addressing. "All he said was that he recognized he was a renowned celebrity and wanted to account for any conceivable contingency. At the time he asked me, 'What if someone kidnapped me and five years later, after I was assumed dead, I was discovered?'"

"I can see why the rest of the band would find that suspicious," I affirmed.

"I can too," Jay quickly agreed. "But that doesn't mean I know if he is alive, and if he is, where."

"Right."

"This office is yours as long as you want it. The boxes are all numbered and follow in chronological order," Jay mentioned as he exited, seeming to have lost interest in our conversation.

Later that afternoon, we talked further. He then mentioned that Stevie's assets were being held in several institutions and allocated to innumerable investments. His estimated worth was in the hundreds of millions, "approaching a billion," Jay mentioned matter-of-factly.

Weiner withdrew funds only for expenses but acknowledged they had several investments that were comingled. All of the financial transactions were being certified through the Wells Fargo Bank Trust Division.

He also outlined more thoroughly the content of the cases it was my job to examine. Due to Stevie's international status, it was considered to be appropriate that a full historical accounting of his affairs, both before and after his disappearance, be collected. It was determined that these should be kept in anticipation of possible museum exhibits. All of the data composing that record, pertaining to the search for the missing icon, reportedly lined the perimeter walls of my new office. Also, since the star's absence, literally thousands of reported sightings and explanations of his whereabouts had been submitted. Weiner assured me he had also archived that mass of speculation.

I was staying down the block from the office at the Beverly Wilshire Hotel. After several hours familiarizing myself with my assignment, I went back to my hotel for dinner. After I ate, I made two calls. The first was to Preeti, who assured me she missed me but knew it was the right thing for me to be in Los Angeles. When I told her I would need at least a week, she offered no objection.

The second call was to Arnie. It was brief because I reached his cell phone. I left a message letting him know the status of my investigation. Then I went back to Jay Weiner's office to begin the real work. In fact, for the next week I had the restaurant pack breakfast and lunch so I didn't have to lose time going out for meals. The turkey was so fresh I wondered if they decapitated the birds in their kitchen at the hotel. Not sure when I'd be back to stay at this pricey spot, I ordered the same Thanksgiving sandwich every day.

Jay was forthright in his suggestion that most of the reports by fans claiming to have seen Stevie were absurd. Local police had filed reviews on the claims and dismissed them as bogus. There were 218 cartons in total, and in each were numerous files and individual sheets of paper as well as an unbelievable number of magazine and newspaper articles. As I proceeded with my reading—which went faster than I expected—I began to suspect my two-month commitment to the assignment would in the end be shortened, unless the band provided me with additional research projects.

That said, on the fourth day while eating my lunch, I gazed out the window, leaning back in my fancy leather desk chair. I spotted a man I would have bet my future lifetime Israeli pension to be 50 Cent going into...Neiman-Marcus! *Al Michaels, the sports announcer, okay, but 50 Cent? I would have thought he bought his t-shirts at Target. If it's not him, it has to be his brother,* I mused.

I was about to pick up the phone and break the bad news to Preston, another fan of the hip hop artist, when I glanced down at my work and realized I was getting sloppy...and bored. I started over with the box I had been working on to be sure I hadn't missed something consequential to my assignment. As I did, sure enough I came across a single sheet of paper that had the same stamp I'd already found on thousands of similar documents. It designated the date the material had been recorded, who had reviewed it and put it in the file, and what, if any, action had been taken.

What stood out was that no comment had been made regarding the disposition of this particular claim. As I read the contents, they intrigued me. I decided to make a copy. My assumption at first was that this document had been neglected due to an innocent mistake, which would have accounted for the missing details as to how the claim had been resolved. I might add that due to the volume of reports, I understood that resources had to be allocated selectively toward the most promising claims.

Over the course of the next couple of days, however, I came across one additional item that I determined should have been more carefully explored. Given the mass of material I had reviewed, two pieces of data represented a fraction of one percent. Still, it was the content and tone of the persons sending the reports that tweaked my imagination that perhaps Jay Weiner or someone in his office intentionally decided not to pursue them further.

That afternoon, my last scheduled day at his office, I decided to gently push the matter. I walked down the hallway and noticed his door was open. However, as I was about to pass the reception area, I was stopped abruptly by his secretary's militant voice.

"Mr. Miller, can I help you?"

"No, I want to ask Jay something, if he has a few minutes to talk."

"Please have a seat and I'll check if he's available," she said in a tone suggesting I was being scolded.

A second later she waved to me that I had been granted permission. I strolled into his office.

"I hear you're leaving."

"For now anyway. I think I've gone about as far as I can."

"I hope you found everything in order. You need anything else...don't hesitate," Jay assured me.

"I do want to thank you for your graciousness having me in the office," I informed him while contemplating that he had never asked me to lunch or initiated a single conversation the entire time I was a guest in his domain. "By the way, I did find everything meticulously well-organized," I praised him so as to not set off an alarm that might cause mistrust on his part. "If I need to return to look up any specific references, I'll let you know."

Jay stood up in anticipation of my leaving. I was certain that when he stretched his arm, he had in mind to shake me out of his life forever. That was the moment I chose to pose the question I had planned to test his credibility.

"I'm awed how you waded through the voluminous material," I complimented to kindly disarm him. "By the way, how did you determine which reports you wanted to investigate further and which to dismiss?"

Jay smiled as if he was about to reveal the secret formula for how to make Coke. "I made the final decisions on every single claim—and I assure you I've seen every one of those files you just went over."

"Well, I can attest to the fact it was no easy job."

"We spared no expense. If there was any chance of credibility to any of those claims, it was examined thoroughly," he boasted.

He had to be lying. He couldn't be stupid. He was not a man with poor judgment. Yet, what I thought were the two most promising statements made by disinterested parties had been ignored.

What confused me was why he'd done what he had. If, for whatever reason, he hadn't wanted those two narrative stories addressed, why hadn't he just tossed them so they'd never be found? More perplexing was that I now was aware that I was, at the least, the second person that might have seen them, yet he had brashly left the two items to be discovered. Why?

That's the question I kept asking myself while getting ready to leave—and what also kept pestering me on my way home. I finally dismissed the query with what I posited to be the most logical explanation, carelessness.

I shook hands with him, thanked him again, and left. Of course, I never mentioned what I had come across. Truth be told, it was proof of nothing. I was well aware that these two leads would most likely turn out to be dead ends. Still, I owed it to LIVE to stay the course as long as I perceived that there was a possibility I could help.

I went directly to the airport. At the bookstore, I purchased a road map to help me plan my next trip. I would head to Vaughn, New Mexico, about a hundred miles east and slightly south of Albuquerque. I wouldn't be able to fly the hypotenuse of the triangle. Instead, I'd have to head back north to Albuquerque and then follow the right angle east. Still, it wouldn't be too long of a drive—even with me having misread the map.

I thought I'd spend a few days at home before leaving. Unfortunately, I wouldn't be in Mescalero for even two hours before tragedy would strike. White Painted Woman had been shoved from a northerly to westerly position—it wasn't going to be pretty.

4

LUCKY TO BE HOME... SORT OF

SOUCHE WAS THE FIRST to greet me when I arrived home. She was digging in a dirt planter and looked up as the cab parked in front of our house. When she saw me, she let out a gleeful shriek. The single blast was delight to my ears. After paying the driver, I dropped my bag and ran to meet the waddling midget who streaked joyously across the lawn. The excitement was intoxicating and Preeti, standing off to the side, smiled approvingly; moms love watching their little girls as they learn how to dazzle their dads—it keeps the household happy.

After being away for a week, it amazed me how quickly things had returned to a normal routine. Preeti was relieved that everyone seemed to be calming down from the tragic council meeting. As soon as I was settled in, we ran over to Kuruk. Preeti wanted to tend to her garden, and I needed to see what work awaited me after a week's absence.

My desk was piled high with mail and reports, tasks I knew would take most of the next few of hours to address.

Sitting atop the stack was a proposal by Reuben for modifying the summer menu. I glanced at it before picking up the phone to place a call to The Prairie Motel in Vaughn. The stopover joint was owned and operated by Bill Cooley, a man shameless with expletives.

"My fuckin' lord, where the hell were you when I needed you?" he hollered. "I shit you not. Your boy blew his ass in and out of here like a goddamn fart."

"If it's okay with you, Mr. Cooley, I'd like to come meet you this Friday."

"Fuckin' A. I'll be here all day." Then he let out a bruising bellow of laughter. "Can't miss this shithole. There ain't nothing but that rotten rascal bastard Emmett Roach's shop and my place out here on hell's acre."

"I'm sure I'll find it."

I hung up, making a note to take my *Cursing Is Cool Dictionary* with me. I sat back, appreciating the peacefulness of a land I now called home. A moment later, I heard Preeti calling from outside. I ran to where I gauged the sound had been coming from, and there was Reuben looking like he'd had a squabble with one of our English holly shrubs.

Reuben was a conscientious man, never negligent of a commitment and as averse to tardiness as rattlesnake venom. As my wife tended to his wounds, he was more worried about arriving late to the kitchen.

"What happened to you?" I asked while inspecting his bloody frame.

"I went out hiking today. I don't know how, but I got lost and before I knew it the sun ducked behind a cluster of trees.

I realized it was getting late. Maybe I panicked that I wouldn't be here on time for dinner." Reuben's head bobbed to punish an unforgivable error. "Anyway, I decided to shorten the trip by cutting through the woods and while I was going up an embankment, I slipped on a mossy stone. I must have tumbled down fifteen feet into the bramble."

"I can see who won that battle," Preeti joked as she poured a drop of iodine on one of the deeper gashes.

Reuben grimaced from the pain but was a good patient and held steady while he continued recounting the story.

"I pulled myself together. I was trying to double-time back, but down the road a couple miles there was a pickup that was stuck. There was a lady in it, and her right front tire was blown. She was crying her eyes out. I couldn't help asking what was wrong. She said she had to get something—parts for a car, I think—for her husband. He was going to beat her silly for being late."

"And you stopped to help her? Looking like this?" I asked in amazement.

"I didn't know how I looked, and she must have been so upset she didn't care to notice," Reuben answered. "I guess I was a little in shock and really wasn't feeling anything," he added.

Preeti continued to minister to Reuben, deftly employing one article after another from the first aid kit. I was snickering to myself and wondering how this puny specimen was able to change a tire. Reuben was built like a matchstick, lacking much in the way of a figure. He was narrow at the shoulders, narrow at the chest, narrow at the waist, narrow at the legs.

His profile was so spindly that on a bright afternoon, he might be mistaken for the trunk of an adolescent tree.

He wore his hair in a short ponytail, which only tended to accentuate the flatness of a face made all the more unremarkable by its small features. Overall, he looked babyish, innocent, and anemic.

He proceeded with more details of his adventure. "After I finished with the tire, I looked at my watch and panicked a second time."

"You were already worried you were going to be late, so why stop?" Preeti posed to him.

"She was there, helpless, and I must have forgotten everything else for that moment."

"Very chivalrous of you, I must say," Preeti complimented.

Instead of acknowledging the praise, Reuben narrated the final leg of his journey.

"I knew there was no way I would have time to shower and change and then supervise preparing for dinner. But I figured that if I rushed, I'd be in the kitchen when the crew began serving."

"Got to have a little more confidence in your staff," I gently chided him.

"They are pretty good, aren't they?" Reuben admitted.

"You trained them—I'd say they're excellent," I commended.

The worst laceration was on the left forearm. Preeti must have wanted to test his resilience because she poured hydrogen peroxide on the wound as if it was tap water. That did get a rise out of him.

"Hold still," Preeti sternly instructed. "I hope you don't need a stitch in this baby."

"It'll be fine. Thanks, Preeti."

"I'm not so sure, but we'll see. Next time, use the main trails," she advised him.

"Poor lady. Good thing I came along," he said compassionately.

Preeti couldn't help adding some motherly advice. "Be careful with that come-to-the-aid-of-a-distressed-lady nobleness. If I may warn you, whatever you do, DO NOT get involved with a woman whose husband has promised her a beating. The damn fool girl will be looking forward to it, and while he's knocking the crap out of you, she'll be forever resentful of your efforts to defend her honor."

Preeti's life philosophy was the type that reduces human interactions to simple motivations. Formal study in psychology would have enlightened her theoretically but left her ignorant about how normal human beings react under real life conditions—my wife understood the nature of the human animal and that can take a person a long way in life.

Unfortunately, in a matter of moments, and before Reuben had the opportunity to respond to my question, she would join the rest of humanity in pure humility. Reuben was about to go to his room to clean up when a vehicle we all recognized as belonging to Len Cloud screeched to a dusty halt in the parking area. Preeti's dad jumped out. His face remained expressionless but his eyes spoke, "the words of a thousand skies."

"You better come with me, daughter."

Sensing disaster, Preeti shrieked. "Shitaa?"

"Nascha Clearbrook's girl, Ila...she was just found murdered."

Preeti looked at me and literally fell to the ground. I stood over her helplessly while she wept a puddle in the ground below her.

"Daddy, what happened?" she finally muttered, her lips nearly kissing the earth.

When she finally looked up at him, Len just shook his head, letting her know he didn't have many details.

"All we know is that she was strangled on her way home. No Apache would use his hands to do that."

He motioned for her to come along.

"I'll take care of Souche and everything here—go with your dad and call me as soon as you can," I instructed.

There's no good time for murder and no victim is better than another. Still, this was the daughter of a very close friend of Preeti's since grade school, a woman who displayed undying devotion toward Preeti after Jivin left us.

To make matters worse, Preeti was godmother to the girl and had treated her as her own daughter. My wife would never recover from losing Jivin, and now this? I knew we were in for hell, but even with that terrific wisdom, I never would have calculated how much suffering was soon to come our way.

That evening, I drove to the Clearbrook home. Understandably, business was lighter than usual at Kuruk. One of the waitresses volunteered to look after Souche.

It had been an extraordinary event for the tribe after Jivin passed away. Their undisputed greatest asset had been lost.

He had been only twelve when he transferred to The Real World of Truth, Potential, and Power. However, he was the only being I have ever met who came close to the designation of a saint, guru, or shaman.

Even with the enormity of the loss to the tribe after Jivin passed just two years earlier, the second I arrived at the Clearbrook home I knew this experience was much more horrifying—Ila Clearbrook had been murdered. Nobody knew much, other than the fact that Ila Clearwater's death had been the result of a vicious act of violence that none of the tribe members could recall ever witnessing in their lifetimes. Following on the heels of Walter's ominous act at the tribal meeting, superstitions long ago laid to rest were unpacked at the Clearwater home like artifacts from a sealed trunk.

Elderly men were seen wearing eagle feathers and speaking stories of the tribal heritage—and the younger members were listening as they wept. Len huddled with a group of saddened friends of Ila.

"In four days, the Great Spirit, God, created life. First, He made the sun and Mother Earth. On the second day, He made everything in the sky—wind, Old Man Thunder, Little Boy Lightning, and rain clouds. Then on the third day, He made all the animals walking on their legs, the birds using their wings to fly, and the creatures crawling on their bellies. It was not until the fourth day He made man. He made Apache.

"Then He instructed the Sun to be His representative to man. He told the Moon to be man's eyesight at night, the Stars to guide man in travel, the Wind to carry man's word, and the Rainbow to remind man of God's own beauty. Then He called the Eagle, who He let know He favored, and told him he would be all knowing. And He instructed the Eagle, 'My Creation, Man, will have autonomy to live as a people, but only through your authority.'"

Len paused to stare at each of the sad faces looking at him. "In the beginning, Mother Earth had two sons, twins. Their father was the Sun. It was a glorious time because all creatures spoke the same language and could understand one another. The firstborn twin of the Sun killed evil and the second born brought abundance. There was happiness. Then something happened. There were enemies." Len spoke slowly as he pronounced each word of the next sentence.

"Then came...killing...loneliness...brutality...grief...and heartbreak. But we were now a People, brave and able to fight for our way of life."

I had just arrived and was listening to Len from the right side of the room. When he noticed me interloping on his talk, he turned toward me. His penetrating stare alerted me that he was laboring as he conducted his assigned role of the brave Mescalero warrior.

"Today, I wear the feather of the Eagle," Len continued his talk to the children seated on the floor around him. "As long as he looks over us, we will live as a people. Later, I'll take all of you outside so you can thank the Moon and Stars for their guidance and light. Tomorrow we will prepare to send Ila on her journey. We will speak words so the Wind will breeze along with her while the Sun protects her as she travels to The Real World where she will meet our fathers."

One of the little boys began crying and came to Len. While still seated, my father-in-law reached out and grabbed the standing boy by both arms, gripping them to the sides of his tiny chest and lifting him like a mirror in front of his own face. "The Owl has arrived, delivering death. We are in the Land of Sorrow. Be strong. Do not fight with death. He has spoken His will."

He put the boy down. I estimated him to be about eight. The kid's face tightened, and for a few seconds he was a warrior. Moments later, I witnessed him sobbing together with his mother. The boy, Elan, was Ila's brother.

I spent little time with Preeti that evening. She was already involved in planning for the burial that would take place in four days. As I awkwardly wandered through the house and grounds, I frankly felt out of place—I had no role. My responsibility was at home. Out of respect, I spent a couple of hours at the Clearbrook home before leaving.

On my way to my car, I saw Len standing in the driveway, talking with two other men. I noticed Walter first, and then Bernard Platta, the tribal president. Their voices were raised. Platta had made an accusatory comment to Walter, essentially blaming him for the disaster, due to his foolish and reckless action at the council meeting.

Walter despised Platta, a fact evident to me not only based on observing them interacting at the council meeting but through discussions I had listened to between Len and Walter at Kuruk. It was Walter's position that Platta was the devil and would ultimately drive the tribe into extinction.

It went deeper than fireworks on the Fourth of July. The tribe was becoming wealthy. Each member shared in the accumulated assets derived from the reservation and received regular distributions from the various tribal enterprises. It was Walter's position—and Len's as well—that the people were getting fat on greed, and the more they had, the easier they bent under the influence of an unconscionable man like Platta.

My car was parked only feet from the men. What I overheard was not pleasant.

"There's nobody to blame for this but you, Walter," Platta shot his words at the younger man.

"Accuse yourself. Go and beg forgiveness from this family. You're as guilty as if you murdered her yourself," Walter spit back, taking an aggressive step closer to Platta.

"Chick!" Len cautioned. He was referring to Walter by a nickname derived from an abbreviation of his surname, Chicory. "An evil spirit has come to Mescalero. The White Man has already descended on our land, looking at each of us as murderers." His words were bitter. "He will probably never find who did this."

I couldn't compute if he was assuming ineptness on the part of whoever would be investigating the crime or subtly suggesting that the tribe would quash any clues regarding the act so that the unwelcome party would be powerless to successfully solve the mystery. It was a matter of pride and a feeling that ran deep for many of the Mescalero Apache. It was humiliating to have a murder occur on their land, but to have outsiders have legal authority over the tribe, on tribal land, was an indignity of unendurable painfulness.

Len picked up a weed from the ground and tossed it into the breezeless evening air. "The White-Eyed Spirit is here. We must speak the message that will allow the Wind to take him. Then we will settle our business."

As one of the wise elders, Len had learned that physical violence was never a solution to a problem. Reason would always prevail if given time to work its magic. He sensed that at least for the moment, he had quelled the hostile impulses of the other two men. The larger issue looming for him was Gabe Kershaw, the FBI agent assigned to the Mescalero reservation.

Len was the legal advisor to the tribe. However, his jurisdiction was for internal matters only. He did not handle the legal affairs of the tribe as far as its dealings with federal and state statutes, or outside business entities. Matters of those sorts were contracted out to hired attorneys, most of whom were not tribal Indians. I can attest, nevertheless, that he was knowledgeable on all matters pertaining to the legalities of the tribe. Once, after a discussion involving a contract dispute between the tribe and an outside vendor, he explained why the conflict was being handled through a state court.

After we talked, he lent me a book entitled *American Indian Law* by William C. Canby, Jr. He suggested that I read it, which I did. It was fascinating. The legal intricacies between the American tribes and various United States agencies and administrations are complex. I'd often discuss points with

Len, finding him able to reference passages from the law and speak extemporaneously on areas of dispute off the top of his head.

Generally, the tribe handled both civil and criminal internal affairs. Len was the most knowledgeable elder in the field of legal history and also the tribal judge. If the crime just committed had been theft by one tribal member toward another, instead of murder, jurisdiction would fall to Len's court. On the other hand, had a crime of similar severity been the act of a non-tribal member toward a tribal member, the matter would be referred to the federal government and if the injustice were committed by a non-Indian against another non-Indian—on the property of the reservation—the state court would be called upon to handle the matter.

This was murder and the tribe would surrender jurisdiction, like it or not. The agent assigned, Gabe Kershaw, had the reputation of disinterest in tribal matters. "Don't ask, don't tell," the previous official U. S. Government policy on homosexuality in the military, would have described Kershaw's attitude toward the tribe. As long as he wasn't informed about indiscretions or unacceptable conduct or actions on tribal land, they didn't exist. It was a favorable working relationship for both parties, and the tribe knew it. The thought that the agent could be reassigned and his replacement turn out to be more of a hand's-on guy was dreadful to the locals.

"Kershaw and his people were swarming over the place in minutes," Walter disclosed with disgust. "We could have handled this ourselves."

"How, Walter?" Platta made no attempt to mask his condescending attitude toward a man he saw as ignoble. "We haven't seen anything like this in all of our lifetimes added together."

"The Clearbrooks need us right now. We can address how we handle this later." The words angrily expressed by Len were the last I heard.

I saw him walking back to the house. I tiptoed to my car and started the engine. I went home to check on my sleeping princess. I quietly peeked into her room. Souche was lying on her back, breathing silently. She was my world. I wept for the Clearbrooks—the next few days and the coming years were going to be torment for them. I sensed I needed to do what my daughter was doing—build up energy and strength to face the ordeal of the next few days.

I doubt Preeti slept more than a couple of hours. Len brought her home at about two in the morning. I listened as she cried herself to sleep. She instinctively jerked up at the sound of Souche, but I was on the task before she had a chance to react. Still, she couldn't fall back asleep.

Later that morning, I called Mr. Cooley at the Prairie Motel in Vaughn and asked if I could postpone my visit with him until early the following week.

"Fuckin' A! You'll find my bony ass right where she sits at this moment."

The man definitely had a way with words.

The next three days were uneventful, at least for me. For Preeti and the Clearbrooks, the tribal singers and medicine spiritualists, it was a busy time. The body was stuck between This World and The Real World. Energy had to be allocated toward assuring a safe and favorable passage. I used the time to take care of as much business as I could. In a flash, it was time for the funeral.

The Clearbrooks were Catholics. The Coyotes were Baptists. The Thunder family was Mormon. The Rockfishes were Dutch Reformed Christians. It always amazed me that a relatively small group of people could adhere to so many different faith orientations. Then again, it was my impression that the religious lake they fished from had been packed with a wide variety of types that they caught randomly. If choosing a western theological orientation had not been the thing to do, they would have been just as content to "cut and release"— their souls were native Apache, and while they were reading The New Testament, it was The Wind turning the pages.

Preeti had no religion, which suited me fine. She would argue with her father regarding tribal rites, rituals, and traditions, but she was pure Apache in her heart. My wife could taste salt in the air, smell the scent of roses before they bloomed, feel the coming of rain by reading the sky, and trick a trout by hearing his movement through a shallow stream. However, she couldn't anticipate murder, she couldn't stop it, and she couldn't hide the horror she was living through on the morning of the burial.

The Circularity of Life dictating behavior under normal conditions has to be modified for death. The passing of life to The Land of Ever Summer takes into account that harmony and balance have already been disrupted. The ceremony is ordered to try and restore equilibrium. Stones are placed around the burial site, and rather than the expected first stone being in the east, it finds its home to the north. Eulogies do not follow the four-part pattern; instead there are only two sections.

Many brief speeches were made at the burial site of Ila Clearbrook. The affair moved faster than I anticipated, likely due to the unfamiliarity of dealing with a murdered victim. Funerals for children are the worst under any circumstance. For murdered children, they are the worst of the worst.

Speeches were unprepared. The tribal custom dictated bad omens for the deceased if comments were planned ahead. Many of Ila's friends spoke, highlighting her fine qualities of bravery, competitiveness, strength, honesty, and dependability. I had met the girl a few times but knew little about her. It saddened me that it was not until her funeral that I came to appreciate what a fine inspiration she had been to others. I tucked a note into a my-life-would-be-richer-if storage area in my brain that I needed to be mindful to at least try to take the time to get to know better the people passing into and through my life.

Before I knew it, spades of dirt were being tossed. Family members went first, followed by the others in attendance with the most highly esteemed taking their place directly after the family of the deceased. At the conclusion of the ceremony, everyone went home to cleanse. Preeti explained it was a ritual to bathe immediately after the funeral, including washing one's hair. A fresh change of clothing was also required. The customs were established to separate living beings as quickly as possible from anything related to death.

That evening we ate alone, and quietly. The Clearbrook clan also dined alone—when a child dies only the family members take food in the home. Preeti would be with her friend the next day.

While the funeral was being conducted, Kershaw and his people remained at the crime scene. The FBI had erected an impenetrable security barrier around the perimeter of the area. The Mescalero themselves were initially prohibited from entering. Nobody knew if any clues had been uncovered, but what's a clue anyway, especially where you couldn't find a soul eager to help you convert it into a fact? Most of the Mescalero people were not going to be cooperative in Kershaw's investigation.

The weekend passed. By Monday, when I was scheduled to visit Vaughn, New Mexico, the thought of a day's break from Kuruk felt right. I could have made a longer trip out of it and looked into both leads I had amassed at the same time, but it would have necessitated a lengthy drive and more days away—I had a better plan.

I was going to take a few days after coming home from Vaughn and then fly out of El Paso or Albuquerque. From there, my destination would be Kansas City, Missouri. I calculated that at most it would be an hour's drive from the airport in Kansas City to get to my second destination, Topeka, Kansas. Ah, but first…

5

VAUGHN, NEW MEXICO

I SET OFF FOR Vaughn at six in the morning, hoping that an early start would beat any traffic I might encounter, offer a cool drive, and optimize my chance of returning without having to take a hotel for the night. Immediately upon leaving the sorrow that had settled over Mescalero, I noticed a lightening of my disposition. However, descending onto the desert floor, I couldn't help but observe that gradually the force of gravity overpowered my fine mood, permitting the endless sand to suck it up like a sponge absorbs water.

I could run away yet never really escape. My heart was in Mescalero—it was broken no matter where I took it. I wasn't an Apache, but the balance and harmony of my home had been disrupted. I cursed that White Painted Woman was proving to be as busy as most gods, boasting a long waiting list.

As I motored on my journey, the thought struck me that many times in my life when I had headed west to east I ran into trouble. That certainly had been the case as I traveled to Israel. I was then able to check off numerous other examples of similar outcomes when I had reversed what the Apache considered life's natural circular direction. Here I was again, only a few miles from Albuquerque and about to make another hard right, eastward, onto Highway 40 and then south onto 285, into a land that reminded me of California's Mojave Desert.

The highway was in great shape, courtesy of recent grants from the Federal Department of Transportation. It only took an hour-and-a-half from Albuquerque to reach near Vaughn—even without speeding. On both sides of the highway, I noticed in the still dim early morning light nothing remarkable other than reddish brown soil and a scattering of low shrubs. My guess was that if Vaughn were famous for anything, it would be iron dust.

As I came closer to the town, I found intrigue in clusters of cottonwood trees. These samples were small and reminded me of dancers that were old, crooked from injury, and tired. Yet they retained dignity and an embodiment of strength, as if they had suffered damage but could still live through whatever hell a desert storm or intense heat could dish up. So remarkable were these crippled yet humble specimens, they would have given cause for any heathen son-of-a-bitch passing through to wonder if God might have assigned himself duties 24/7 at this outpost in Vaughn, New Mexico.

Cooley had warned me that I had to pass through town and then go about two miles east before I'd see the Prairie Motel—within five minutes it came into view. Closer to town were two or three other small, clean-looking, inexpensive stopover spots. The clientele of Mr. Cooley's establishment had to be people who had lost claim to the down-and-out-club—they were plain out. If his report were true, Stevie Green had moved counter to life's natural circularity and this dump would have been his first punishment.

I pulled into the parking area, spotting the "rascal bastard" Emmett Roach's place. I couldn't imagine what the two businessmen might butt heads over; their respective businesses were separated by enough worthless desert land to charter a city. Roach ran an auto body shop, and the number of vehicles at his place was about equal to those in Cooley's parking area, three.

I wasn't even out of the car when I saw a man approaching from the office. He was wearing a soiled, tan, western hat over brownish-grey hair that straggled several inches down on the sides and rear of his neck. His blue jeans were worn thin, faded and soiled; a white tank top undershirt hanging out failed to conceal a small beer belly. He stood tall and strode in an erect posture. Covering his eyes were tiny, tinted spectacles that looked like they had been left over from a sixties Doors' concert—he later removed them for a moment, revealing still youthful bluish irises.

"Got my best fuckin' suite waiting for you," he clowned. "Would have given the mother fucker to Stevie but all he asked for was a goddamn room and that's what I gave him."

Good thing I brought the dictionary. I knew this was going to be fun.

"How's the car running?"

"Just fine," I answered, perplexed why he'd ask.

"Good, 'cause if you got a problem don't stop in at that asshole Emmett's place. He'd steal the dress his mom was buried in—lousy hopeless bastard."

"No, I wouldn't dare," I assured him. "Now I read the report—"

"I suspected something right off...but who the fuck am I?" Cooley took off his hat to wipe the sweat off his brow, rubbing his hand on his pant leg to dry it. "What am I doing? Come on inside where it's cooler."

He headed toward the office, a small area at the west side of a single-wing dilapidated structure. I wouldn't have expected anything other than what was inside his quarters, a mess. He lived and operated in what I estimated to be a few hundred square feet of space, not dissimilar to a Manhattan apartment with a kitchen space hardly large enough to drop a pot. There was a sitting area with two maple rockers with seat and back pads of a filthy maroon color. On the wall opposite was a large screen television, the muted sound leaving the pharmaceutical ad for an anti-diarrhea drug looking like a promo for a tooth brightener.

"Probably a shithole by your standards but after living with my bitch wife for five years it's a happy fuckin' home for me."

"I understand, Bill. Now getting back to the report you filed—"

"Twice I tried to get someone to listen," Cooley expressed with consternation. "Actually three times, if you include our genius fuckin' state police trooper, Corbin. Asshole damn near laughed me off my own place."

"I don't recall seeing anything about that in your report," I informed him.

"Informal. Corbin showed up right after it happened." Cooley kicked his feet up on a small table, displaying a new purchase, shiny brown boots. "He stops by when he's got nothing to do, which is about every fuckin' minute he's paid for. I talked to the asshole about it, including that I damn well knew Stevie Green spent the night at Prairie Motel."

"What did he say?"

"Told me if I kept drinking he'd be calling the paramedics soon." Bill smiled, his teeth surprisingly straight and in good order other than showing a disgusting amber film, no doubt due to decades of tobacco use. "He didn't really listen. Then I saw in the paper all the to-do about Green going bye-bye.

"You know, you don't need to be some highbrow to appreciate Stevie. I'd walk through the whole fuckin' desert to Albuquerque to see him perform—the little shit spoke to me, spoke to everyone." He stopped to deliver his words of wisdom. "That's what made him a goddamn saint."

"So you wrote to the newspaper—"

"Emailed to that site they set up to try and find Stevie but never heard a thing. Then I wrote to the editor of the Albuquerque Journal, not a fuckin' word back, ever." He shook his head, expressing disbelief. "I gave up. 'Fuck 'em,' I said to myself. 'Leave Stevie alone; if he wants to go away and never be found, it's his damn right.' Besides, maybe he gave us everything he had," Cooley added reverently.

"That's a good point," I sincerely concurred. "Would you mind going over everything that happened with me, in detail?"

"There's no details, um..."

"Zach, my name's Zach," I said, anticipating the nature of his pause.

"Zach, young fellow, I'll tell you everything because I recall it as clear as the day I kicked that bitch out of my life. It's about two-thirty in the morning after the man did his last concert at Isotope. This guy pulls up in a car. I'm still awake, had a couple beers, and I'm watching Platoon...you ever see it?"

"I have. Wonderful movie."

"Closest fuckin' thing to Nam you'll ever get without going there, which I'd strongly advise against."

Cooley slowly lifted himself out of the chair, pulled off his glasses and tossed them on the table. Then he grabbed his undershirt and pulled it up. A large gashing scar ran laterally across the chest and down to the abdomen, left to right. He strained to straighten his body and walked over to a wood cabinet, opening a drawer. He took an object out and carried it like a newborn for me to witness.

"Ever hear of Son Toy?"

"No, what is it?" I questioned.

"Special troop operation to recover prisoners of war in Vietnam. This here," displaying the Medal of Honor like the treasured object it is, "is what President Johnson gave me in '67." He lifted his shirt again, staring down at himself mournfully before looking back at me. "I was a fuckin' wild kid who knew no better. My parents never talked about wars worth dying over and wars worth evading."

"But that's the greatest honor a serviceman can get," I said respectfully.

Cooley wanted no part of the praise I was bestowing upon him.

"Fucked up my head. I haven't slept a wink since without drinkin' a damn pint first."

We sat for a few minutes, not a word passing between us. Cooley drifted into a reverie. I thought I witnessed him wanting to cry, when abruptly he pulled out of it.

"So you came to hear about Stevie, right? Okay. I get up to see who pulled into my parking lot. There's a man with a black cap and long-sleeved shirt getting out of a vehicle. So I shove that baby," pausing to point to a .357 Magnum loitering a few feet away atop his kitchen countertop, "in my belt behind me and go out to see what he wants.

"It was still pretty fuckin' hot out. When I saw how he was dressed, I knew I was dealing with a wacky dude. Anyway, the guy's frame was about as intimidating as a popgun. He asks if he could get a room for the night and after registering him I took him to Number Seven, right over there," pointing to the second to last in the row of rooms.

"So what alerted you that it might be Stevie?" I questioned.

I knew from his report that there was more information, but I wanted him to recount it. My reasoning was not only that I needed to be sure the story was consistent but also to see if by chance there might be other clues he had omitted.

"At that point, all you knew was a man checked in late who was dressed peculiarly."

"I know what the fuck you're doing," Cooley quickly confronted me. "We used to do that shit too when I was in Nam—make sure the bastard's not changing the story each time he tells it," he laughed knowingly, but dismissing my maneuver without insult. "It was noon the next day. I heard a loud sound like a gun firing. Shit, I yelled to myself. Then, I rushed out to see what the fuck was going on. There was nothing there. I figured that bastard Emmett finally did the world a favor and shot himself. Anyway, my car was parked across the lot and I'd had a freakin' flat the day before. I wanted to see if the mother fuckin' spare was holding air.

"I'm standing at the opposite side of the car, furthest from the rooms, and as I glance over I notice the door to Number Seven opening. But instead of the fellow just leaving, he hesitates. Then he pokes his impish head out, inspecting before he leaves the room. When he comes out, he's wearing the same cap and long-sleeved shirt—it's fuckin' sweltering outdoors. He walks over to his car and starts it up. Then I notice he pulls off the cap and the outer shirt before taking off. That's the last I saw of him. Never did find out what that noise was that got me outside in the first place."

"I'll tell you the truth, Bill. I drove out here because I've been hired to look into the disappearance of Stevie Green. After I saw your report and noticed nobody had come over to talk with you, I thought it might be a good idea for someone to interview you face-to-face."

"Damn straight it was."

"Okay, but the question I have is what leads you to be so sure it was Stevie Green?"

Cooley for the first time seemed uncomfortable.

"I didn't get that medal-of-fuckin'-honor for being a moron," he delivered lyrically. "I know things. I just know. Corbin thought it was a big joke. I'm sure you do too, but I—"

"I know you believe it, and you may be right, but I wish you could give me something concrete."

Cooley forced himself upright again, signaling that I was to leave. His patience for trying to convince me had run a short race.

"I'll take it to the grave. Like I said, at this point I say leave the little man be."

"I'm inclined as you are," I earnestly agreed a second time.

"If you want, young fellow, you can take my file with you." Cooley grabbed a few pieces of paper sitting on the table in front of us. "I won't be needing it now."

He handed it to me. I thumbed through quickly while we were standing, Cooley seeming eager to get rid of me. I started to accommodate his wish to leave but noticed a small drawing, rectangular in shape, with three letters followed by three numbers written within the heavy perimeter, drawn with a black marker. Cooley went to his refrigerator and took out a beer, turning to me while I was gazing at the symbols. "One for the road, partner?"

"Bill, what is this?" I asked, pointing to the drawing and ignoring his offer of the drink.

"License plate for the car he was driving," he shrugged matter-of-factly.

"This wasn't in your report, and you never mentioned it to me today."

"What the fuck's the difference? Nobody's gonna listen," Bill said dismissively.

"They won't listen if you don't tell them everything you know," I admonished. "You're sure this is the license number of the car that the man was driving?"

"Yeah. Land of Fuckin' Enchantment, New Mexico. I learned to make notes with symbols in Special Ops."

"You have my word I'll check out this car and let you know if I find out anything," I promised. His response, however, surprised me.

"Don't let me know a mother fuckin' piece of what you discover. Last thing I need is a bunch of cock suckin' news people coming out here and spoiling my peace." Cooley smiled, adding what I perceived as a proud disclosure. "I have a pension from the service, a little social security—I don't give a crap if anyone ever stays here. I just like being alone most the time.

"Once in a while, my little girl comes to visit and I load her up with whatever money I have left." His next words were delivered like bullets aimed at the heart of an enemy. "Her man ever lays a fuckin' hand on her while I'm alive and he'll have breathed his last breath—he damn well knows it too."

I held out my hand and with a wide smirk he took it. "It ain't what it looks like. Nothing is what it looks like."

I walked to my car with my emotions in a tangle—there were elements of trauma in this man left over from Vietnam.

He'd never achieve a full recovery. When the soul has been battered, it steps out of line from the rest of humanity.

I couldn't help feeling terrible for the man. He'd given a huge chunk of his life for his country and lived to regret it. In the car, I journeyed back to murder, a family suffering, a tribe of friends in disarray—it wasn't likely to be a pleasant drive home, but I assumed at least I'd be sleeping in my own bed.

6

BEGINNING THE INVESTIGATION

IN ADDITION TO GRIEVING, the drive home offered me time to formulate a plan on how to proceed. While my sentiments regarding Stevie Green were not dissimilar to Cooley's—let sleeping dogs lie—I did make a pledge to LIVE that I would find out what I could for them about their leader. Thus, the vehicle corresponding to the New Mexico license, LKB 374, had to be identified. This sort of work was all new to me. *How does one run a check on a license?* I deliberated.

I made a mental note that once I returned home I'd call the AAA office in Alamogordo and see if they could help. I left the windows to the car open and turned up the volume on the radio to let the sounds sizzle in the hot desert air. After a few minutes of my ears burning, I reversed the conditions of the ride, shutting off the radio and substituting air conditioning for nature's punishment.

As I was headed down the highway, I had an idea. Why not use the time driving back to Mescalero to double check if Cooley was being forthright? It may have been an oversight that he had never disclosed he had a license number. It might also be that the license was a random number he wrote down. Most likely, I surmised, it belonged to a '97 Chevy pickup retired to a junkyard months before Cooley claimed it was on his property.

That's when I wondered if I might reach this State Trooper Corbin. As another possibility, might Cooley have forgotten that he told Corbin about the license plate? In that case, the officer might have already checked on the car corresponding to LKB 374 and found it to be unrelated. There was one way to find out if I even needed to investigate further.

I was only about twenty minutes outside of Vaughn when I decided to call the closest office of the New Mexico State Troopers to see if Corbin could be reached. It must have been fate, because the man was standing next to the receptionist when she took the call. In an instant, I heard a voice.

"Corbin. What can I do for you?"

I explained I was investigating Stevie Green's disappearance and had just left Cooley at the Prairie Motel.

"Bill Cooley gave me some information. I just wanted to verify it with you," I said respectfully.

I heard a chuckle. "The word 'verify' fits with Cooley about as well as Perignon champagne on the shelf with Ripple wine."

"That's why I called you, sir. He mentioned that he told you everything about the evening he claims Stevie Green stayed at the Prairie Motel."

"Where did you drive in from?" he inquired.

"I live in Mescalero," I responded.

"No shit! We heard about the murder."

"It's been very difficult. The girl was my wife's godchild," I shared.

"Sorry. You an Apache?" he asked without hesitation.

"No. My wife is. We run a restaurant, Kuruk."

"No shit, again! My wife's Apache. We ate at your place for our anniversary last month. Wow, we loved it."

"I'm glad you had a nice evening. Well, about Cooley—"

"Where are you now?" Corbin inquired in a friendly manner.

"I'm on the 285 heading north. In a few minutes, I'll be transitioning west on to the 40."

"Perfect. Meet you in twenty minutes. You'll be getting to Moriarty and you can't miss the exit. Turn right off the highway. On your right, you'll see Tammy's Café. I'm stopping for a snack. We can talk."

The line went silent again, this time owing to the trooper hanging up.

When I reached Moriarty, the first thing I saw was State Trooper Corbin's vehicle parked in front of Tammy's. The hostess greeted me warmly. When I mentioned I wanted to see Corbin, she immediately pointed to a uniformed officer sitting alone at a table, reading the newspaper.

I walked over to introduce myself. As I approached he looked up, then he rose to shake hands—he was a giant. He looked about thirty-five years old. His hair was a beautiful auburn color and cut short. If I'm six one he had to be six ten, at least. Carrying an extra fifty pounds, he couldn't have weighed himself on a standard scale—he was a huge specimen of mankind...like a giant.

He motioned for me to sit.

"You're not shitting me about owning Kuruk?"

"No kidding, it's ours."

He kept bobbing his head, trying to shake out the disbelief. "Best meal I've ever had. Your wife is Mescalero. You told me that."

"What about yours?" I asked in return.

"Chihuahua. Same difference, huh?"

"I think so," I agreed, recalling Preeti telling me their tribes were closely related.

"Look now, I know you didn't come here to talk about our ladies. You got worked over by old Cooley, did you?"

"I don't know what you mean by worked over," I sighed, "but he did tell me his story about Stevie Green staying overnight at his place."

Corbin grinned, obviously entertaining himself. "He never shuts up about it. He's so damn crazy, he even has a few locals out there believing him—the few willing to listen to him."

"He certainly didn't have any solid proof that it happened," I responded.

"That's because it never did. You've been out there. Why the hell would Stevie Green head out in that direction? He'd have stayed on the 40 if he wanted to make a quick getaway from Albuquerque."

"I wondered about that myself. I actually made a mistake going out to see Cooley, assuming Vaughn *was* on the 40."

The waitress came up to take the order. Corbin responded. "Same as yesterday, dear."

I asked for a cup of coffee. We chatted casually. Corbin informed me that Cooley had been hospitalized several times for mental problems. He also let me know that rarely did a customer stop to stay at his place. He referred to it as "eerie at night," adding with a grin, "like the Bates Motel in that *Psycho* movie."

It seemed only a few minutes before his lunch arrived— half-pound burger with cheese, a large mound of steak fries, and a malt served in a glass container large enough to be an aquarium. Snack? Maybe it was. A man of his size wouldn't be settling for a boiled beet salad with ginger for lunch.

"Cooley's not a bad fellow," Corbin said charitably. "What else did he tell you?"

"When he made the report or talked to you, did he ever mention a car license plate?" I asked.

"No way. I even asked him if he got a description of the car and he didn't say a word." Again, he chuckled. "Then again, with Cooley it's hard to catch him sober. But I saw what he wrote to the newspaper and no reference was made to a car."

"That's funny," I said. "He had a diagram he'd drawn of what he identified as a New Mexico license." I handed him the piece of paper I had written on. "Before I called you, I was contemplating how to find out who the owner of the car is."

Officer Corbin was swallowing a mouthful of his sandwich. He completed the task before he broke into unrestrained laughter, nearly gagging as the chewed beef descended down his throat.

"One hell of an investigator those boys hired," he teased.

"It's a long story, but I agree. I'm hardly up to the task."

Corbin reached for his phone. "Hey there, Dolly. Willy here. Can you do a plate for me? Home state, Larry, Ken, Bob 3 7 4. Take just a second," he winked.

We sat silently about a minute or two before he began scribbling on a piece of paper.

"Thanks, love. Call if you need me."

He sat for another moment, taking the time to neatly write out for me the information he had just jotted in shorthand.

"It's all right here. The car is owned by Gateway Auto Rental, that vehicle assigned to their Albuquerque office."

"That saves me a lot of trouble. Thanks."

"Look here. You have my number, right? Well, you call me if you need help with anything—we understood on that?" he bellowed kindly to me.

When a state trooper, who might be taller than Shaquille O'Neil, and definitely broader than a full-grown oak tree, asks if you understand what he says, believe me, you understand, even if you haven't heard a word he said.

Corbin promised he'd call next time he came to Mescalero, and I vowed in return to comp his dinner if he did. Nothing wrong with having friends in the right places, I reasoned, particularly given the fact I didn't have much of a background in squeezing out facts from clues.

I jumped back on the highway, figuring that even after

stopping in Albuquerque at the Gateway office, I'd still easily make it home in time for dinner. In less than an hour, I arrived at the auto rental agency's district office located about a mile from the airport. I walked in, told the clerk that a car with license number LKB 374 was registered to their office and that I needed the rental history for the vehicle for the week of March 26 of this year.

"Sir, we can't give out that kind of information," the young man informed me.

"All I need to know is who the car was rented to during that timeframe." A stranger would have described me as pleading. "It's a long story, but I promise nobody will ever know you gave it to me."

"Sorry, sir," he insisted in a whisper, "but that's against company policy."

There was another customer waiting. I looked over my shoulder at the man and noticed him impatiently gritting his teeth while staring my way. I walked away from the window, defeated. What was I thinking? They're going to give information about a customer to a total stranger? I had to laugh at my own ignorance.

Before going to my car, I sat down on the top of a retaining wall used for the landscape of the building, contemplating what to do next. I knew I could call Corbin right back. I assumed if he walked into the office, the same employee would dish up the answer to him faster than he could blow his nose—but I didn't want to impose on my new friend unless it was absolutely necessary.

While I was deliberating my next move, the clerk who had just refused me walked out for a break. He didn't look up, his chin dragging dolefully toward the ground. He ended up sitting only a few feet from me on the same wall. From a paper sack, he produced a reddish apple. He took a bite, the loud cracking sound confirming a hard, fresh Fuji, Delicious, or similar variety. The noise offered me an opportunity to address him.

"That's a genuine apple," I chuckled. "Get one that snaps louder than a Rice Krispy and it's a winner."

"At least I got one thing going right," he said despondently.

I estimated him in his early twenties, probably his first full-time job.

"Girls can tear your life up," I said knowingly.

"It's not girls," he assured me.

"That leaves only one thing," I said wisely, but not sure if what I was about to say was true. "Money issues, huh?"

He sighed to let me know that I had shot a bulls-eye, moving his head back and forth repeatedly as if plagued by a problem weighing on him for some time. I was thinking that put both of us on equal terms, problems we couldn't solve. But might there be something that could help both of us at the same time, even if not a total fix I wondered? Then without further conscious consideration, I reacted.

"I have a problem, you have a problem. What if I could help you and in return you do me a favor?"

"Great. But how?" he queried dejectedly.

"Look, I need that information on the car I mentioned to you. Nobody is going to get hurt. I've even talked already with a state trooper I know, but I don't want to ask him for another favor."

Then I did something I had never done in my life. I took two one hundred dollar bills out of my wallet, made sure he saw them, folded them tightly in one hand, and reached over to where he was sitting—I knew as I placed them into his palm that I was guilty of bribery.

He looked toward me, a sad expression on his face as his hand grasped the money tightly.

"I'm the only one supporting my family. My mom is sick and needs medication." As he spoke, I noticed the young man squeeze the money even tighter. "Wait here. It'll take me about ten minutes.

I might have been proud. I was acting like one of those hotshot investigators I'd seen in a movie or on television that make a career of bribery. But I felt like crap. It seemed dirty to me, and to boot, this was a kid who impressed me as being pure as rainwater—and I had just corrupted him.

It took almost fifteen minutes before he returned. During that time, I deliberated getting into my car and leaving, without the two hundred or the information on the rental car. I wondered if the boy was too straight and I'd soon be having a different encounter with Corbin—being arrested for an action that detectives do routinely with snitches.

When he did finally return, he handed me a piece of paper and said something I'll never forget.

"We're not poor enough to qualify through the state for her treatment and not rich enough to buy it. This could save her life."

He went back to work. I never asked his name and I never saw him again.

My first informant was thorough. He provided the name of the renter of the vehicle, the dates the individual had the car, the credit card used in order to secure the vehicle, where and at what time it was picked up, and the driver's license used for the rental—enough information to guarantee that if Stevie Green was driving that car at the Prairie Motel, he had been using an assumed name.

"F. Artanis," I murmured to myself as I started my car. Before putting it in gear, I glanced to be sure the same name had been used on the rental application, credit card, and license—it was. I was aiming for Mescalero; I'd definitely be home before Preeti put dinner on the table.

As I was driving, I realized that in reports made by Cooley to the Albuquerque Journey, as well as what he sent to the website set up for information about Stevie Green, he had never mentioned the name that the man whom he insisted was Stevie Green had registered under, and he never told me. Predictably, the blundering investigator never asked him either.

Then again, as Corbin stated, nobody believed Cooley. I might have instinctively measured him up as lacking credibility as well. Still, I wanted to confirm it was F. Artanis—I knew I'd have no problem reaching Cooley.

"Mr. Cooley, Zach Miller again."

"Wrong fuckin' guy to invest in stock, partner. Just filed for bankruptcy."

The line went blank, Cooley obviously mistaking me for a salesman. I liked his counter-pitch—bankrupt. I asterisked it, thinking I might borrow the strategy next time an annoying con artist called to sign me up for a cheap plot in a cemetery— what sort of moron at thirty-four wants to plan his funeral?

I called Cooley back immediately.

"Bill Cooley. It's Zach. I was just at your place earlier."

"Why the fuck didn't you say so?"

"Bill, I had a question I forget to ask you. Got a moment?"

"A goddamn lifetime...or whatever's left of it. What is it, son?"

"I can't see where you ever mentioned the name Stevie Green used to register," I said, trying to make him feel good that I believed it was actually Stevie.

"Shit, why should I? Nobody gives a fuck anyway." I heard Cooley shuffling about his tiny home. "Got it right fuckin' here in the log for that day—F. Artanis. He made up a doozie, huh? F. Artanis. Guess he was in too much of a hurry to give himself a proper damn first name."

"Thanks for everything. You've been very accommodating."

"That's it. You come back here again, don't be mentioning Stevie to me or I'll ream your fuckin' asshole with a billiard stick."

He hung up—the Mouth at Prairie Motel had spoken. The Man from Mescalero had no intention of taking him up on his offer.

It was only fair that I made an attempt to find the real F. Artanis and to confirm it was not Stevie. That was to be the next, and likely last, part of this investigation. The problem was I had no idea how to go about finding him.

My next call was to Arnie Manzano of LIVE.

"Got me at a great time, Zach." Arnie sounded winded. "Just jumped off the treadmill. What do you have for me?"

"I'm not sure it's anything," I said blandly. "But I do have a request."

"Anything you need, you have it," Arnie said breathlessly.

"I know you said I had an unlimited budget, whatever I need, but I still wanted to check before making a major purchase."

"You want a James Bond Ferrari?" he quipped. "My Lord, Miller, Preston said you had an imagination."

"Not my style. But I would like to employ an investigative service to help me get some information I can't attain on my own," I informed him.

"Expense it to us, pay for it and itemize it to us and we'll pay you back...however you want to handle it," he offered as if I was requesting bus fare.

"Okay. I'll get back to you in a couple days," I apprised him.

I pulled off the highway to collect my thoughts about how I would find a credible investigative service. Then I remembered in Jay Weiner's office that there had been several reports assigned for further exploration to P. A. Farley Investigations in Albuquerque. The reports I'd read from that company were intelligent and thorough. In a matter of a few seconds, I found the number and was on the phone with the owner of the one-man shop.

"Farley Investigations," the male's raspy voice shouted.

"I'm hoping to talk to Mr. Farley. My name is Zach Miller."

"Mr. Miller, P. A. Farley here—investigator, secretary, receptionist, and pinball wizard at your disposal," he clowned.

"I'll take the investigator only," I quipped back at him.

"Fine with me, but I'm one hell of a master with a pinball machine."

"Maybe next time," I humored him. "Right now, I need someone to research a couple of things for me."

"No freebies on the phone. P. A. Farley is an equal opportunity employee. I'll work for anyone with cash on the barrelhead."

"That's not a problem. You'll be paid. How soon can you see me?"

"Come on over now and let's make you a deal," he sang out like a television show host.

Farley gave me his address. I reversed direction, back to Albuquerque. It was only a short drive, and within moments I was sitting across from the man. When he said he was the secretary, receptionist, investigator, and pinball wizard, he was not off the mark. His office was on the second floor of an old building serving as headquarters for several tiny businesses. The front door of each set of offices opened to a poorly maintained wooden outdoor balcony.

The window in Farley's suite was on the opposite wall from the entrance—as I entered I was looking straight at it and noticed it was covered in dust and looked ingloriously onto an apartment building with several units using their porches to string clotheslines to dry sheets and garments the old-fashioned way—what matter was it to Farley? His desk, the only one in the space, faced the door on the opposite wall. A single chair for his clients was across from where he was seated. I sat down. Off in the corner, nearly hidden by several old oak cabinets was...a pinball machine.

Farley was wearing a white-and-pale-blue stripe suit, slightly soiled and grossly more than slightly wrinkled. He also had on a white cotton shirt with a black bolo tie, held together by a silver horse pendant with the inscription, "Colt Firearms."

His hair was grey, thick, overgrown at the sideburns, and randomly pulled back from the forehead before being tied in a ponytail hanging down below the neckline. The most outstanding thing about his face was a large chip that had been broken off one of the top front teeth. Every time he smiled, it announced personal neglect and sloppiness—the sly smirk seemed to be a serial habit for the man.

"Now, Miller. One fifty an hour," he announced without shame. "I'll need a retainer of five hours. Of course, anything I don't use I'll return."

"That's fine, but don't you want to know the assignment first?" I asked.

"Don't matter much. I've done about anything you can imagine—'cept I don't do murder or any criminal acts." He laughed boisterously. "I'll cut a corner if necessary, but it may cost you extra if I have to pass some green to get a favor."

"I doubt that will be necessary. My need isn't that complicated. I just can't do it myself."

As Farley stood up to grandly reach his hand out to shake, I noticed he was carrying extra weight, nearly all of it firmly protruding from the belly like a pregnancy. He was slovenly. I felt repulsed by his overall physical presentation.

"We got us a deal then," Farley elated. "Let's get down to work."

"There's a man, F. Artanis. I want to find him."

"Can do. If he's alive, I'll find him," Farley boasted as he sat down on his desk. "Anywhere in the world—I've been to 'bout every country on earth. It may not look like much of an operation here, but anyone in town who needs a job knows P. A. Farley is the man to get it done."

"Here's the information I have on him."

I handed Farley the credit card number, driver's license, and information regarding the rental car at Gateway. Farley glanced at it casually.

"Piece of pie—do this all the time." He picked up the paper again, staring more attentively. "New resident, I suspect."

"Why do you say that?"

"Driver's license number is a recent one." He stood again, indicating he was dismissing me. "I'll have this for you in a day or two."

I gave Farley my contact information and a check. Then I turned for the door.

"You just want the address for this clown? Or you want me to take pictures?" Farley picked up a pair of cheap reading glasses and a pen from the desktop. He leaned down, poised to write. "I need to know what you want, young man."

"I want to know who he is, where he lives, where he works—pictures would be great too," I instructed. "Mr. Farley, I simply want to know if the guy's for real."

He scribbled a couple notes and tossed the pen heedlessly so it rolled across the tabletop.

"I'll have a detailed report prepared for you."

"Thanks."

I left the office and noticed it was getting dark. I called Pretti and told her I'd be home first thing in the morning. Hotel Andaluz, a pricy spot where my mother had taken Preeti and me for lunch during one of her visits, was only about a mile away. I called ahead to be sure they had a room. I took a deluxe king—LIVE wasn't volunteering to buy me a Ferrari but fine accommodations were a given—then went down for dinner. It wasn't on the level of Kuruk, but it was a hell of a lot more expensive. I could see why people drove hours to dine with us.

A few minutes before I was about to fall asleep, my cell rang—it was Preston.

"You talked to Preeti tonight, I'm sure," he said with a tone of urgency.

"A little while ago," I informed him. "Why?"

"She didn't tell you about your buddy, Reuben?"

"Reuben?" I remarked curiously. "What about him?

"She probably didn't' want to upset you—"

"Uh, but you do!" My reaction was mixed between alarm and irritation.

"Zach, she treats you delicately, that's all. Anyway, I told you something was off with the guy, didn't I?" Preston's voice took a more humble tone than when he'd spoken about Reuben in the past.

From their first meeting, Preston had expressed vehement

mistrust toward this man he barely knew. Even when I highlighted Reuben's strong traits of honor, honesty and reliability, Preston balked. His argument was that Reuben was a drifter and I had no knowledge about his background. Unabashedly, he accused me of carelessness in allowing a stranger to occasionally look after Souche.

"The guy could be a sadistic killer!" he reminded me nearly every time he found an excuse to bring up Reuben's name. Then he'd nag me to research where Reuben came from, his references from prior jobs, any criminal history… he'd rattle off a list of items for me to look into and while a few times I was inspired to do as he was insisting, I'd soon conclude the task to be a senseless exercise.

"What happened with Reuben?"

"Nothing really happened. You left right after the funeral, right?"

"I did, Preston, right."

"Well, about the same time the reliable and trustworthy Reuben," Preston now spoke with an air of mockery, "or whatever his name is, comes down with a case of depression. Preeti's had her hands full—the guy's weeping like a child, despondent to the point he's practically dysfunctional."

"What's it about?" I presumed it was some sort of crisis in his family.

"That's what she can't figure out. Came to work this evening but Preeti said he's in a daze."

"I'll talk to him in the morning after I get back," I promised.

"I knew the guy was nothing but trouble," Preston said.

"Before you get too excited about being right, Preston," I said to slow down his glory, "let me tell you that if Kuruk loses him we're in deep trouble—he's practically become an acclaimed chef."

"I'll be visiting soon," Preston stated, ignoring my concern for our business.

"Just what I need, you in the kitchen," I said to tease him.

"Better than having a damn mental case working for you," Preston said mercilessly, an attitude I still couldn't completely compute.

"Preston, what if someone close to him died and he has nobody to talk to? How are you going to feel then?" I said purposefully to evoke guilt.

"I'm getting called. I'm in Chicago for a concert." Preston wouldn't bite on my shame-on-you warning.

"Anyway, thanks for the heads up," I said as we hung up.

I considered calling Pretti back but thought better of it— she always made an effort to protect me, and I appreciated it. I knew if she couldn't handle it, she would break down and call.

I flipped off the light on the nightstand, and with the tender thought of Preeti's concern for me fell into a deep sleep.

7

TIME WITH REUBEN

I AWOKE THINKING OF the second lead I wanted to investigate and how soon I'd hear back from Farley. My mind was jumbled. In that state, I failed to recall that I was coming home to the aftermath of murder and that I might have another crisis with Reuben awaiting me at Kuruk. I took a deep breath. As I exhaled, the sad realities I must have been unconsciously avoiding popped out like cue cards for an actor. I called Preeti to tell her I'd be home in a couple of hours, but I didn't mention that I had spoken with Preston—that could wait.

Approaching Mescalero, I couldn't help noticing that both coming down the hill and ascending up were numerous state trooper vehicles and unmarked plain cars, the latter no doubt belonging to FBI agents. Murder had inspired an about-face for Agent Kershaw. He was employing every law enforcement official he could grab into his investigation—not a welcome development for the Mescalero Apache people.

When I did finally reach my home, Preeti looked exhausted. Still, she insisted I get settled before she would talk to me about a subject that, unbeknownst to her, Preston had already prepped me about. Finally she related what had happened.

"Zach, he came into the kitchen to supervise but he was out of it. He just sat there inspecting nothing, gazing at space."

"Did he say anything about what was troubling him?" I asked.

"I was up until two in the morning with him, Zach," Pretti disclosed. "On top of trying to comfort Nascha all day, it was over the top for me."

"Let me see if I can get anywhere with him," I suggested. "He's usually comfortable talking with me."

Preeti paused, as if hesitant to make the statement she knew she was going to regardless. "Honey, he reminds me of Jivin."

Then she stared at me. I read the look as imploring me to shake her to her senses, to discredit her perception as foolishness—I didn't. At times, I had also found his behavior reminiscent of Jivin but could find no value in mentioning it to Preeti. I shook my head, acknowledging that I had heard her but giving no clue if I agreed or not.

"He did something odd," Preeti added, overcoming greater levels of reluctance to talk. "He walked outside the kitchen for a while, and when I looked for him, he was dancing a slow rhythmic movement just like Jivin might if he were the Libaye." (Libaye was the term used for the boy clown who at a ceremony moved between the two worlds of dreams and reality.)

I took Preeti in my arms, realizing how much she had suffered the past evening.

"I know how you miss your son. You're going through a lot right now. Let this all settle down," I advised. "Things will get back to normal, you'll see."

I felt badly for my wife—death, murder—losing two people so precious to her in such a short period of time. Reuben was not Jivin returning in another body, but he was every bit as odd a creature as the boy had been. That presented a mixed blessing for Preeti.

I left immediately to go to Kuruk to check on our chef. When I arrived, I knocked on his door but there was no answer. I waited a few minutes, assuming he was showering. Then I tapped again. A couple minutes later, he responded. When I saw his condition, I understood her alarm. He was trancelike, his eyes glassy and remote. All he had on were the bottoms to his pajamas, his partially developed chest void of manly hair. He hardly acknowledged recognizing me but did finally invite me in.

There was a nice living area in his apartment. It was decorated with a sofa and two soft chairs. All the furniture Preeti had when she and Jivin lived there was set out exactly as she had left it. It was obvious that Reuben knew how to take care of his possessions. He applied the same standard of cleanliness to his personal living space as he insisted his staff maintain for Kuruk's kitchen. I sat while he put on clothing.

"What do you think about us taking a little walk?" I suggested. He said nothing, but a moment later he came out of his room dressed in hiking shorts and light boots.

His face was sunken more than usual. He marched to the door like a robot. I followed in his steps. Across the parking lot was a path that accessed the forest. After a short distance, it began crisscrossing and intersecting with numerous other trails used mostly for jogging or walking. As we proceeded, I couldn't help thinking that it was a journey as benign as this one that Ila Clearbrook set out on days earlier before she was killed.

We must have traveled half an hour, all the while angling from footpath to road and back to trails—I hoped Reuben had memorized the direction we were headed because it was not unfathomable to get lost. He said nothing. I followed, assuming eventually he'd walk himself out and stop to talk— I was correct. As if he had taken the trip many times in the past, he led us to a spot where there was an old decaying bench, the wonder of which was how it ever found its way to this remote site. Reuben sat and I did the same.

How he had discovered this lovely and inspiring resting place I didn't know, but I hadn't been there before. It was about thirty yards off the designated path and situated in the tiniest grassy meadow. The wood structure upon which we rested was situated to the east end of the opening and had tangled itself tightly with the surrounding plants and shrubs. Approaching this object from only a few feet away it looked like an architectural wonder, as if it were naturally constructed from the outgrowth.

To the right was a clearing where bright sunlight was nurturing a clutch of prickly pear cactus. They were rose-colored and had tulip-like cups that seemed to lift their small canister shapes to proudly soak in the morning rays. But the best of the attractions I nearly missed, and would have had I not followed Reuben's gaze directly across from where we sat. A rock wall rose about fifty feet and the face was home to milkwort plants that had matted themselves against the surface. They had lightly scattered pink flowers, but the real show were the thousands of triangular-shaped butterflies resting on the vines and leaves. I had never seen this variety, but they were black with two rows of bright yellow dots along the two equal sides of the triangle—they looked like advanced experimental spacecraft.

Reuben seemed transfixed, but finally after several minutes he spoke.

"You want to know what's happening to me, right?" He continued without pausing for my answer. "I don't even know—I don't know why I'm feeling the way I am. All I'm aware of is that I feel like I don't know me, like I've lost my sense of self. How would that make you feel?"

"Mixed up," I assured him, for I was familiar with that exact experience. "But Reuben, this couldn't have just appeared like clouds breezing in for an afternoon storm."

"That's a good way to say it. It was exactly like a cloud... a dark, gloomy one. It settled over me about the time of the funeral. Since then, it's gotten worse."

"But you didn't even go to the funeral," I imposed on his thinking.

"I didn't know the girl either," Reuben quickly submitted to the inquiry.

Nothing was making sense. I decided to try another tact.

"Reuben, we've talked often, about all sorts of things. I'd like to think of you as a friend, not only an employee. What I'm asking is, are you sure something didn't happen and you're ashamed...embarrassed, or you just don't want to bring personal affairs to work with you?"

"I don't have much that could go wrong in my life along the lines you're referring," he sadly responded. "My parents died years ago. I have no brothers or sisters, or other relatives that I know about. My father was Mexican and my mother was French Creole—see the darkness in my skin? I could pass for a Native American Indian if I had to."

"Come to think of it, I do," I acknowledged, as if seeing the man for the first time.

"I couldn't even talk last night. I hope I didn't upset Preeti," he said remorsefully. "There it goes," he sighed, his eyes watering with tears.

"There what goes?"

"It takes me over—this feeling I have. It's guilt about the girl."

"You have no reason to feel guilty—you did nothing," I foolishly reasoned with his stubborn neurotic line of thought that was hell bent on displacing blame unfairly.

Reuben dropped his head into his hands and rested them on his lap. He was deep in sorrow. Then he began sobbing. I might have thought he was possessed if I believed in evil spirits or the devil.

"Zach, I did nothing—I couldn't have stopped it, right?"

"Not unless you knew something nobody else but the killer did, that it was going to happen," I affirmed his reasoning.

Reuben picked his sagging head up, looking at me imploringly.

"I didn't do it."

I had no idea at the time he and I were talking what the specific details were pertaining to the killing of the young girl. When I did later become apprised how Ila Clearbrook was murdered, I would have given the weakling sitting next to me as much of a chance of slaying her as becoming a professional football player.

"Reuben, sometimes we have a tendency to put on ourselves responsibility for events or conditions that have nothing to do with us," I explained mercifully to a man I had never witnessed expressing anything other than sound reason and good judgment. I further cautioned myself about rashly drawing conclusions about his mental state based on a depression that was all of one-and-a-half days old. "This murder is crushing for the whole community, Reuben," I continued my pep talk. "Truthfully, I think everyone feels responsible but doesn't understand why."

"I just feel like I know something. It's very heavy on me, like I need to expel it and I can't."

"Like taking a good crap," I jested.

"I wish it were that simple," Reuben responded.

I glanced at the weepy man sitting next to me. I was trying to grasp him, feel what he was going through. His eyes were wide open and he was looking my way. It was then that I realized he wasn't there; he had dissolved in front of me into a vast ocean of nothingness. Then, within a few minutes he transitioned again. I could tell that the old Reuben had reemerged.

"Ready to go back?" I tentatively asked him, reasoning at that moment that just as a person might catch a cold from airborne germs, Reuben had been temporarily infected by a tragedy in Mescalero.

"Don't worry," he assured me, "I'll never let you down at Kuruk." A notable hint of lightness in his voice encouraged me that this would be a brief depressive episode.

"I wasn't worried about it." I lied. Quickly, I corrected the mistruth. "Well, that's not entirely true. You've done something for Kuruk that we can't replicate...it did worry me."

"Zach, a good leader prepares for his departure as much as his role in the here-and-now. I'm more confident now that there are people in that kitchen who are trained adequately to take over for me."

"But they don't have the imagination," I contested.

"That's what you think. I wouldn't have hired them if they didn't."

We wandered back to Kuruk. Reuben strolled silently most of the way, never looking up, yet directing us home without one detour.

When we went inside, the staff was already preparing for lunch. Still, they collectively paused, eager to drop a surprise on their leader. Soeze Willitts, our manager, had received a call from the secretary to New Mexico Governor Kyle Rossiter informing her that Reuben had been selected to be the chef for a dinner the governor was hosting to honor U. S. President Harold Cross' visit to the state.

Frankly, the employees were more thrilled than Reuben seemed. It was bad timing. While he had momentarily refreshed himself talking to me, he was not out of the soup—his depression had the legs of a marathon runner.

Still, the fact remained that our chef at Kuruk was becoming a celebrity cook. Periodically, guests would announce that they had flown to New Mexico for no purpose other than to taste the cooking of Reuben Zapata.

After the excitement settled, I walked Reuben back to his quarters at the rear of the restaurant. He invited me in, another tear forming.

"Sometimes I think part of it is loneliness. I'll admit I've felt depressed before. I have had bouts of unhappiness, but this one is worse." Reuben waved his hand around the room, directing me to nothing in particular, but just the same guiding my eye purposefully. "I have nothing, nobody. I did it to myself, but that doesn't make it any easier."

"No girlfriend?"

Reuben smirked shamefully. "Never. I've never...it's never been my thing. I remember a song with lyrics that refer to how sooner or later it happens to everyone, but I don't know its name or the group that did it. They were talking about falling in love, but it's never happened for me."

"I'm sorry."

"But I love to see you and Preeti and Souche together— you earned the love and companionship you have."

"Someday I'll tell you how it happened." I laughed reflectively. "I didn't do a thing."

"I hope we can keep this between us—I'm a bit embarrassed, as you can understand."

I nodded to assure him that his secret would be well kept.

Then my cell rang. When I looked, I noticed the call was from my hired investigator, P. A. Farley. I was surprised to hear from him so quickly. The man wasted no time delivering verdicts.

F. Artanis never existed.

8

WHO IS F. ARTANIS?

REUBEN MOTIONED FOR ME to take a seat on the couch, which I did. Then he handed me a pad of paper and a pen— I had no idea how he knew I'd need it. Then he walked into his bedroom and shut the door.

"Know why P. A. Farley has been in business for over thirty years while dozens of other guys couldn't make it?" Farley's voice proudly questioned.

"No, I don't. But congratulations."

"Never string a client along. If I can do it in an hour, I'll do it in an hour. That's all you'll be charged. None of this billing mill crap for me," Farley noted with disgust. "Once I worked for a big-shot lawyer and he wanted me to jack up the charges so he could make his clients think he was doing more than he was. Lawyers are the biggest crooks—"

"What did you find?" I asked impatiently.

"Your boy, Artanis, pulled one of the oldest tricks in the books," he howled. "He takes out a Social Security number using his fake name and phony personal information. Then he goes to the bank, makes a hefty cash deposit, gets a checking account, and starts spending. When all that is set, he applies for a credit card through the same institution."

I pictured Farley at his desk, his upper left lip packed with a plug of tobacco, spitting filthy saliva through his broken tooth into the wastebasket, his makeshift spittoon. I witnessed him practicing the habit in his office.

"What's next? Driver's license for the State of New Mexico and you have yourself a proper citizen," he giddily disclosed. "Lots of petty crooks do it."

"So F. Artanis is a real guy but just a common criminal?" I posed to him.

"Don't be slow on me," Farley gently ridiculed. "Artanis is a shell—he never existed," Farley informed me. "Like a whistle in the night. He's gone forever."

"How do you know there is no real person with that name?"

"I checked every possible listing. The man you're looking for existed for just a brief time and then evaporated." I could hear a splashing sound I was sure came from Farley ejecting a shot of spittle against the metal bucket. "One thing was strange, and I'm not going to charge you extra for the insight," he bellowed.

"I appreciate it," I responded.

"I don't think he's a weasel, swindler, or felon. When he dropped off the car in Topeka, Kansas—"

"Where?" I blurted out.

"Yeah, I know. Who the hell goes to Topeka these days?" Farley concurred, but he had no idea what had shocked me.

"No, it's not that. It may be a coincidence but Topeka ties into something else I'm looking into," I informed him, realizing what an amateur investigator I was for not asking the fellow at Gateway Rental where the car was left off.

"It didn't matter to me what city the car ended up in but the fact he paid off in cash?" Farley questioned. "Then, I found out somebody using the name F. Artanis checked into the Fairfield Inn in Topeka using the same credit card but paid...again, in cash."

"What's the point?" I eagerly queried him.

"Crooks don't pay—they don't use precious dollar bills when they can leave a load of debt on an unpaid credit card. That's why they go to all the trouble to build fake identities," Farley spoke saucily. "This Artanis character went so far as to pay off the credit card of all charges with a check from his bank account, closed the checking account, and said *au revoir* to the identity he worked so hard to build—there was even a balance of several hundred in the regular bank account, which is being held to this day under his name."

"I don't get it," I responded with perplexity, just as Reuben walked back into the room. When he saw I was still talking he turned to go back out, but I motioned him to stay. "Is the guy a prankster?" I asked Farley.

"You are green," he laughed boisterously. "I see why you came to me. My bet, your man is a runaway."

"A what?"

"People do it all the time," he explained, now trying to be respectful of my naivety. "They want to disappear. Get it?"

"Mr. Farley, I presume you couldn't find out why Mr. Artanis... or whomever he really is, wanted to disappear?" I glanced up at Reuben, who was now listening to the conversation.

"I don't think we'll ever know that, because he used Artanis as his getaway, a transitional name. By now, he's taken another assumed name, the one he'll take with him for the remainder of his life, or until remorse, shame, or loneliness drive him back to the hell hole from which he needed to escape." There was silence for a brief period. "No, that's as far as we can go and probably as far as you want to go. Unless it's some wealthy entrepreneur, politician, or celebrity, it's a chapter in the madness of mankind that will close and never be reopened."

"I want to thank you. I presume if I need you again, I can call?"

"I'll have to send you a check for the time I didn't use. But sure, call me anytime. P. A. Farley gets his man," he boasted. "Actually didn't get your man but I did get you what you were looking for, didn't I?"

"I couldn't have asked for more, really," I said to express the appreciation he deserved.

I hung up the cell.

"I was talking with this investigator I had help me get some information about Stevie Green," I mentioned to Reuben, who knew I was hired by LIVE to find him. "Everything the guy told me fits perfectly with what you'd expect for Stevie Green if he were trying to disappear," I voiced thoughtfully to Reuben. "What do you think?" I asked, intending to focus his mind on something other than his own woes.

"I know you're getting paid for this, but why do it? Kuruk is doing well. Frankly, I've questioned why a man like yourself wants to get involved with this type of affair."

"I'm not sure I understand what you're saying," I posed to him.

"I told you I liked Green too. He was a great talent. But let's say all this you're digging up confirms he's alive. What have you done other than give his fans hope for something that will never be satisfied, his reappearance?" Reuben posed back to me.

"At least they'll know he isn't dead—that he wasn't killed or abducted," I answered.

"So you'll...or the guys in LIVE...will instigate an endless series of magazine and news articles, all producing more speculation on a subject Stevie Green would likely puke over."

"Why do you say that?" the choice of word, "puke," fused with disgust, tweaking my interest.

"Zach, the guy was sickened by his fans. That's why he would have taken off in the first place."

Reuben had drawn a conclusion commanding my attention. It was similar to what Stevie's band mates had related to me. I kept the awareness of what I thought to be an odd likeness of mind to myself. Reuben's irritation heightened. I let him talk.

"How would you like having hundreds of millions of fans all over the world treat you as if you were a god? At the same time, how would it feel being aware that none of them knew you as a person, could relate to you intimately or could feel your pain?"

"I get it. I'd start to hate it, feel...alone."

"Zach, that's what I think. He was sick of it and fell into a state of disdain for the fans that idolized him. The only hope he had of finding genuine companionship and love was to leave it all behind."

While Reuben was talking, I was half-listening and half-doodling, playing mindlessly with Artanis' name on the pad of paper that Reuben had handed to me.

"Personally, like I said, I cared for his music, but as a person I don't know a thing about him...and could care less. Do you think he'd grieve if I was sick and dying, if one of his fans was hit by a car and killed, or if a devotee's father lost his job?" Reuben sneered. "Why should he? And why should his fans bow to him, except that they are weak followers, people I imagine Stevie would look down on as ignorant fools?"

While he prattled on, I continued playing with the letters of Artanis' name like a Jumble Puzzle in the newspaper. All of a sudden, I made a word. I didn't think much of it, but it nearly distracted me from hearing Reuben's final thoughts on the subject of Stevie Green, the man considered a prophet-to-the-people.

"And what would you think of your great worth if you were Stevie Green and you knew your iconic image had been purchased by a mass of morons who would rather try to live through your life than live their own?"

Reuben stood up and went to open a window, seemingly unaware that he had worked himself into a steam that needed a cool down.

My attention was split between two equally demanding matters. The word I had scrambled was probably a meaningless one, but I still found it interesting. Reuben's statement about Stevie despising his fans was mere speculation on his part, but I had to question him because I perceived him to be proclaiming it as fact.

"Reuben, you said the guy was sickened by his fans—"

"That's just my opinion as I try to put myself in another person's position. You don't agree?" Reuben questioned me.

"It makes sense but you seemed so certain."

"I think about things like this...sort of like a philosopher. You know, how would I handle this or that situation? In honesty, I think the best I could say is it probably all comes down to projection, how I would respond if I were in that situation."

I looked down on the name of another famous star I had created out of the letters of Mr. Artanis.

"I met a man once who risked his life—and suffered a serious injury—to save a famous dignitary," I shared with Reuben. "The last thing he wanted was to be designated a hero. I think his abhorrence at the thought of being publicly recognized as such an important person was for the reason you're suggesting."

"It's our responsibility as humans to retain our dignity. The Jews refuse to bow. I'm not born a Jew, but I respect why they would give their lives for the principle. Every man can have only one hero, one divinity," Reuben proclaimed, holding up the index finger of his right hand. "He must have one god," and then with greater force he asserted. "There is only one god."

Religion, god, and faith. These were subjects I preferred not to discuss with people. They were divisive. Unless the participants in the dialogue were in total accord with one another, there would be enmity, hostility, and all too frequently, violence. Reuben's proclamation of "only one god" smacked of the irreverence I associated with how so many people relate to organized faith. It alarmed me, setting in motion a flight instinct, but there was nowhere, nor any time, to run.

"That god better be inside each person. If you're not god, if your god is not you, you're the Tin Man in *The Wizard of Oz*—you have no heart and you'll revere people like Stevie Green because you want to live through them." Reuben whispered. "Let this guy disappear. Yeah, it's my impression his fans fleeced him of his lifeblood like the sun dries grapes to raisins. If he survived, the only meaningful thing for him now is to find peace in his own god."

I hugged Reuben. Then I tore the single piece of paper from the pad that I had been scribbling on and shoved it in my pocket. I waved to him as I strolled out.

I thought it might be a good idea to call Arnie and brief him on what I had discovered, which up to then wasn't really earth shaking. There was still no evidence to suggest that whomever had used the name F. Artanis was in any way connected or related to Stevie Green. At the same time, the limited amount of data I'd collected did excite my curiosity.

When I called, I reached him immediately. In fact, Preston

and he were together. They were in Seattle, preparing the venue for a performance.

"Mr. Miller, got your best friend Preston right here," he yelled out over loud sounds shooting through the facility where they were working. "Any news?"

I explained to him what I had just related to Reuben. He listened attentively. Then the conversation took a fortuitous turn initiated by way of a quirky, seemingly ridiculous question I posed to him.

"The name Sinatra mean anything to you?"

"No, Miller," Arnie said sarcastically. Then he yelled rhetorically. "Preston, you've never heard the name Sinatra, have you?" Arnie paused before playfully delivering his next statement. "Miller, acting dumb is not going to get you off the assignment, if that's what you're thinking."

"I was playing with the letters of the name Artanis, the one I just told you about. I was randomly shifting them around to see what words I could make. It's probably nothing, but I wrote them every which way and came up with no words using all the letters. But when I reversed them it spelled—"

"Why the fuck didn't you say so?!" he cried excitedly. "We told you where the name LIVE came from, remember? Well, it's common knowledge that Stevie's mentor, at least the person he believed was the greatest singer ever, was Frank Sinatra."

"It was F. Artanis," I mumbled. "Frank Sinatra!"

"Miller, you're a genius. He's alive," Arnie hollered out.

"This doesn't confirm it, but if you can give me a little

more time, I think I can get you information that might point us closer to the truth."

"Of course. Money…time. Take whatever you need," Arnie cheered.

"I want to make something clear, just so there's no disappointment," I proclaimed. "It seems I might round up the evidence to prove he is alive, but I won't promise, or even suggest, that I'll actually find him—this very well might be the end of the line as far my participation in this matter goes."

"We'll see. Miller, you underestimate yourself," Arnie admonished.

"I don't think so."

"I believe at this time it's best that we keep this between the two of us. Is that okay with you?" Arnie proposed.

"I don't plan to participate in any disclosures about Stevie Green to anyone at any time," I again declared. "I'll leave that to you and the band members. Is that agreeable?"

I wanted to confirm that I wished to distance myself from any fallout if the world were to find out their hero was alive somewhere. F. Artanis was dead. Frank Sinatra was dead. I had one more trip I needed to make before my investigation of Stevie Green would hopefully be dead as well.

Ila Clearbrook was dead too. The examination into her murder was just beginning. FBI Agent Kershaw, unfortunately a man who would have played out his tenure as an FBI agent handling Mescalero by avoiding as much as possible any direct contact with tribal affairs, was finally left no choice but to take a very active role. He was now epitomizing everything a group of proud and brave Mescalero Indians had worked to minimize in their affairs for decades, the involvement of White Eyes in their business.

9

NOT A PRETTY START TO
AN INVESTIGATION

INVESTIGATING A MURDER IS complex. Investigating the murder of a youth has twice the complexity. Investigating the murder of a youth on an Indian reservation has triple the complexity. Investigating the murder of a youth on a Mescalero Indian Reservation quadruple the complexity.

Gabe Kershaw had been assigned to the Mescalero reservation because his boss, Hal Rizzo, despised him. Kershaw had the reputation of being an aggressive and bright agent. He was forty-two at the time of Ila Clearbrook's murder and had been designated the agent for the reservation, but never once had he been involved in any type of enforcement or action. It was precisely how Rizzo wanted it, punishing Kershaw into obsolescence and hopefully early retirement from the bureau.

Kershaw's first appointment with the agency had been to an office in Chicago, Illinois, where he was placed under the direction of Rizzo. For the preceding three years, while Rizzo had been running the office, virtually no large cases had been prosecuted. It was gossiped by some of Rizzo's colleagues that he was incompetent, or worse, corrupted.

Along came hotshot, super-energized, tall, slender, athletic, and sharp-looking young Agent Kershaw. Within a year, Kershaw busted a major money-laundering ring and then the leading counterfeit operation in the nation came under the radar of the new agent, who was subsequently successful in dismantling it. Rizzo took offense.

The association between Rizzo and Kershaw seemed to end swiftly after the latter was duly recognized and promoted to the classification of special agent. Rizzo never let go of his urge for vengeance and would have died trying to satisfy it, had it not been for the fact that Rizzo's brother-in-law, also with the bureau, had been appointed to the position of assistant director. It would prove to be the demise of Kershaw. A decade later—after having worked directly under Rizzo—he was relocated to New Mexico. It was not by chance that his assignment was to again be placed under the supervision of Rizzo.

It was a simple deal for the boss. Assign Kershaw to Mescalero and watch him dry up like mud in a desert. Rizzo knew the ways of the Mescalero and was further aware of no other tribe as savvy in depreciating the worth of the White Man—Kershaw was going to suffer for at least two years under Rizzo.

It was only about a year into Kershaw's unfruitful commission, when Ila Clearbrook was murdered. The sad news had an upside for Rizzo; he was already giggling deliriously thinking about how the tribe would make a fool of the agent he resented.

Rizzo was actually an expert in Indian history and knew more about the Mescalero than almost any scholar. He liked the people, respected their culture, and appreciated the progress they had made—he also had no interest in feuding with them. Prior to Ila's murder, Rizzo assumed that proactive Kershaw would mix it up with the tribe and then he'd be forced to discipline him. Instead, Kershaw followed his instincts and managed to stay one step ahead of his boss.

Kershaw reasoned that New Mexico would be a wonderful place to raise his two children for two years—a fourteen-year-old son and an eleven-year-old daughter. He loved the outdoors, and it suited him fine to spend this assignment with his family. It took him no time to outline the wonders the state had to offer him—teaching his children to raft the Rio Grande River, hunt elk, deer, quail, and dove, ski in Taos or Red River, or fish the Rio Chama or Pecos Wilderness.

He carefully plotted his strategy, showing up at the office, seeming to be dejected and sullen, leaving within an hour and repeating the same routine five times a week. It was obvious to Kershaw that Rizzo was ecstatic watching him deteriorate, while in truth Kershaw was having a swell time.

Then came the murder of Ila Clearbrook. On prior occasions, Kershaw was required to make cursory visits to Mescalero activities. During those excursions onto the reservation, he was always received with politeness and subtly appreciated for his lack of enthusiasm to partake in matters of tribal interest.

While on the assignment, Kershaw did make an extensive study of the Mescalero tribe. He saw it as his responsibility to be prepared to understand the indigenous people in the event that he needed to interact with them. He was, therefore, aware that these Apache were in some ways typical of most American Indian tribes, yet unique in others.

They were people known to be kind to their own families and friends, but unimaginably cruel to enemies. They had fought the incursions into their land by the Americans, suffered betrayal and deceit in their negotiations with the White Man, and rebelled against abuses. In the end, they prevailed, insofar as they were able to secure nearly a half million acres of land for their reservation.

The Mescalero battled internally to balance the preservation of their cultural identity with the need to interact with the broader world around them. As a result, they behaved with wisdom, using money awarded to them to develop commercial entities from which a stream of revenue would pour into the hands of the tribal members.

With their own system of justice and the ability to administer it, Kershaw saw little need for his services on the reservation. That changed the moment murder was committed—Gabe Kershaw might have thought he'd be taking a two-year sabbatical, but he never hesitated to shift to active status when the beast within him was called to duty.

The man was a dogged agent. When it came to criminal investigation, there was no way to suppress the instinct. By the time I returned from my short overnight trip to Vaughn, he had made it known there was a new sheriff in town.

Roads had been closed temporarily for vehicle inspections, and tribal members had been contacted for interrogations, initially conducted on-reservation for purpose of convenience since the field office was in Albuquerque. Several other agents had been designated by Kershaw to help with the case. The state police were also employed—Rizzo wouldn't risk being accused of standing in the way of allocating resources toward a matter as serious as murder.

Since the FBI had to assume jurisdiction—at least until a suspect was charged, in which case the matter would be tried through the Justice Department in a federal court in Las Cruces by a U. S. attorney—there was little Rizzo could do to move Kershaw off the case. In truth, he wouldn't have had it any different, knowing that the Mescalero would find a way to handle the matter internally and make a mockery of Kershaw's efforts.

What was clear was that overnight the FBI agent had become an enemy of the people. I came to understand the depth of the conflict that evening after I arrived home from my layover in Albuquerque. Len Cloud had stopped at our house after dinner, accompanied by young Walter Chicory.

Len looked haggard. His upper lids were heavy, actually drooping puffy bags partially over his fully opened eyes. We were just about to put Souche down for the night, when they arrived.

He always called before visiting, this time just a few minutes before. When he saw his granddaughter, he smiled, but it was evident that he was troubled. He gave his head a firm flick, waving his long grey hair back over his shoulder before picking up the little girl. He held her high in the air, on the way down kissing her olive shaded cheek.

"Shitaa, what is it?" Preeti asked, recognizing strain on the part of her father.

"Take care of Souche and then we'll talk."

Preeti and I went to put our daughter to bed. During the ten minutes it took us to do the pre-sleep routine, I heard another vehicle pull up in front of the house.

"We're not expecting anyone else, are we love?" My question broke the gentle, soft singing Preeti was performing for Souche.

"Not that I know. Why don't you check?" Preeti suggested.

"Okay." I kissed my daughter and walked out of the room.

When I arrived back in the living room, Len had already gone to the front door and opened it. I could hear him talking to someone outside but had no idea who—Walter must have been with him.

When I looked over to where they were standing, I noticed three men next to a white sedan. As I studied them more carefully, I recognized the third man to be Agent Kershaw, who I didn't know except by physical recognition.

"I told you several times that I don't want tribal members coming into the investigation site," Kershaw curtly informed Cloud. "We're not finished looking for evidence, and I've got people chanting, dancing, and traipsing around like it's a picnic spot."

"It's our land—"

Kershaw aggressively cut him off. "I told you when we first talked that the crime scene is not your land again until I have completed a thorough forensic investigation." Kershaw toned down his voice, trying to appease Len. "I'll open everything like normal as soon as I can." Then to further ease the tension, he made what seemed like a reasonable proposition. "Mr. Cloud, I don't see why we can't work together on this."

My eyes had focused through the darkness by the time Kershaw made his appeal. I was close enough that I could see and hear my father-in-law. Len said nothing, but his eyes were harshly focused on Kershaw. The glare by Len Cloud didn't seem to intimidate the agent in the least. I knew that Len was not a man to back off from an unpleasant encounter either. The situation spelled future trouble in my mind.

"Have it however you want," Kershaw said firmly, "but I will take any action within my discretion against anyone tampering with evidence or interfering with my investigation." Kershaw offered a foreboding stare back at Len. "We have a long way to go on this one. It will be easier on everyone to get along."

"You have excluded us from your findings," Len countered disdainfully. "This is a tragedy for our people. We could track the killer, but you won't let us on our own land."

"We already went over this," Kershaw said kindly, again looking to placate Cloud. "As evidence becomes available that can be shared, you'll be the first to know."

"Huh!" Len shrugged with a smirk. "Your words are crooked like a broken arrow. 'That can be shared!' You decide what can and can't be shared." Len now puffed out his chest as a gesture of indignity, his awareness of Kershaw's duplicity allowing him a sense of superiority over his white adversary. "You swim like a guppy but filthy the whole pond."

"Sorry you feel that way," Kershaw said, showing not a sign of offense. "We'll get this matter solved with or without your help. In the meantime, I'll keep you informed as best I can."

Len stood silently. Walter was glaring with fury, but seemed disinclined not to step over Len's authority. Kershaw turned to walk around the driver's side of his vehicle, stopping for a last statement.

"She was strangled. It was a quick and brutal murder." Kershaw looked down before glancing up at the men. "I'm sorry."

Len's question to Kershaw perplexed me.

"Frontal or from behind?"

"Frontal," Kershaw informed him. "Why do you ask?"

Len resumed his silence. Kershaw recognized the discussion was going no further.

"The killer will come to justice if I have to search every leaf and inch of dirt on this reservation," Kershaw asserted.

"You'll never find your answer on our land," Len shot as his parting words.

Simultaneously, they each turned from one another. I couldn't help but notice that Kershaw circled his car to the east first before rounding the back of the vehicle to come west to the driver's side door. The front entrance of my home was a straight easterly shot from where Len stood, but he took several steps away from the house in a westward direction be-fore turning north and then circling east back to the house—Walter followed behind him. The unconscious route taken by Kershaw—opposite that dictated by the Circle of Life—did not bode well for him, at least not if you're looking at life through the mind's eye of a Mescalero Apache.

Len and Walter took seats in my living room. By then, Preeti had joined us. The soft music in Souche's room wafted through a monitoring system I had purchased. It was harmonizing with the last pulses of resistance from a little girl battling to embrace every second of glorious waking life she could grasp before sleep proved victorious.

"Father, now you look worse. I can't bear more sorrow," Preeti said, more pleading for relief than shaming him.

She was right. The encounter with Kershaw appeared to drain him.

"No man of my tribe would do such a crime," he evasively responded to his daughter.

"Why do you say that, Len?" asked Walter.

"Nobody is more avid about retaining our customs and traditions than you," Len praised Walter. "Think about it," he challenged the younger man.

"I don't understand myself," voiced Preeti.

"There are subtle patterns about our people you can only learn by paying attention," Len informed his daughter.

"I'm listening, shitaa."

"A Mescalero warrior would never kill with his hands, especially facing the other person. Even more impossible would be him murdering a female," Len explained with exhaustion evident in his words. "This is the work of a coward. We do not breed this type."

"There are lots of people coming here every day for vacation or to work at the hotel or in our businesses," Walter reasoned before Len interrupted him.

"It's nobody like that," Len grumbled. "It's a bum, a vagrant, somebody passing through who is gone and will never return."

"Then we'll never find him," Preeti lamented.

"I doubt it," Len opined. "Ila lost consciousness in a few seconds—thanks to god there was little suffering," he added.

"This FBI agent who came told you this?" Preeti asked.

"No. The government man is drunk on bringing us justice. We only want Ila's spirit to be at peace."

"But father, you didn't answer my question," Preeti reminded him.

"Oh, yes. I have people who will inform me faster than this agent can conceal the truth," Len boasted. "The hyoid bone, that's right here (pointing to the Adam's apple), was fractured. Once the blood was cut off to the brain, it was only a minute or so until she was dead."

"Father, was she...you know..."

"No, my daughter. This killer is not a sexual deviant. He's just a plain vanilla madman." He stopped to emphasize that by vanilla he meant white man. "Preeti, you must not speak any of this with anyone. If it comes out that this information was leaked, it might stop me from getting more data as it becomes available."

"I promise." Preeti said obediently.

"Was there anything else you found out?" asked Walter.

"There were no wounds other than bruises on the neck. Her body was dragged by the legs about twenty feet to the base of a tree and dropped—it happened late afternoon, and the heels of her shoes made indentations outlining the direction she was moved. It was a calm day. There was little wind to upset the scene of the murder."

"Did they find any evidence yet?" I posed as my first question to Len.

"Yeah. There was a chewed stick of gum on the ground they presumed to belong to the killer, but they have no proof that's the case." Len then closed his eyes and spoke from the blind light of his mind. "It's not worth our time to waste further thought on this matter—our people are in worse danger."

"I can't imagine what could be worse," Preeti responded sharply.

"We are on the edge of extinction as a people. Birth and death are transitory states. But history, even with customs and traditions evolving over time, must forever be preserved. There is no life after, no spirit to live on in the Real World, if our past dies here in the Shadow World." Len peered sadly at his daughter. "If we lose our roots, we break the connection between the two worlds. Then we will have lost our way forever. It would be as if we never existed and can never exist again. Your son will never find his way back to his people."

My wife began crying, both owing to the still fresh loss of her son as well as the finality her father's position put on the matter. The thought that the tribe would cease to be was in and of itself dreadful to Preeti. But the consequence, that Jivin could never find his way home, was beyond devastation to her.

Walter had not said a word. He was a man more than any other in the tribe who reminded me that I was largely amongst Indians. He stood well over six foot and was as broad and strong as the proverbial ox. More remarkable were his facial features. The man was very dark, and his thick jet-black hair was parted meticulously in the center, pulled taut and then tied in two long braids, each worn down the front of his chest.

His features were compact. They jetted out ever so slightly from the flatness a frontal view of his face presented. What I couldn't stop staring at was the angularity whereby the chin dipped proportionate to the forehead rising, not only creating length, but more outstanding, the perpetual impression that the man was torn between communion with the gods above and the hell of life below.

Rarely did he smile. He came off as having no sense of humor, which I knew was not entirely the case. He was frightfully committed to the preservation of his people and hateful toward those behaving contrary to his beliefs—paint his face and stick a long feather toward the back of his head and Walter was the classical Apache warrior incarnate.

The rising tensions between men like Len Cloud and Walter Chicory on one side, and a few other tribal members, most notably Bernard Platta, on the other, were potentially explosive. Walter having walked counter-circular at the last meeting was a warning to the others. "I'm willing to sacrifice myself for the honor and tradition of our people. But our whole tribe must not walk where one man is willing to tread or we will cease to be." That was the message he intended to send and the words that he was willing to die for.

Walter now volunteered to explain the potential tragedy to the tribe, embellishing on the crisis boiling within the tribal council.

"Platta is becoming the devil. He places money as his first and highest value. By promising wealth and riches to the people, he gains their respect and devotion, but what they don't know is that each day he is bringing them closer to destruction."

I'd been sitting like a mouse. Walter paused and looked directly my way. It was a gesture beyond merely acknowledging or tolerating my presence. He then glanced toward Len, who gave an approving nod.

"Zach, we need your help," Walter said humbly.

I looked at Preeti for assistance, not sure how to react. It was Len Cloud who formally handled the request. He had never commented, at least to me, regarding how he felt about his son-in-law not being an Apache. I knew it was important to him that his daughter and grandchild carry on the traditions of his people and that he was grateful that I was not going to be an impediment toward that desire.

How he valued me or didn't value me, he had never given a clue. He treated me respectfully, and I assumed he did so because Preeti and I were happy together. He certainly never expressed or showed objection to our union. This day would be the first he'd openly address his attitude toward me.

"You are husband to my daughter and the father of my only grandchild. I'm very proud to have you as my son-in-law. Jivin brought you to us. He knew looking at it from the Real World, before any of us could see it, that you and Preeti would love one another. It's all worked well. Now Preeti tells me of your great skills as an investigator."

He went on, unaware that I was ready to break into unrestrained laughter. *Will somebody listen to me? I don't know a thing about investigating,* I silently pled.

"What you're doing to discover the whereabouts of this movie star—"

"Stevie Green is a singer, father," Preeti admonished.

"And I have to add, I don't intend to even find out where he is," I clarified.

"Whatever this Stevie does for a living, or whether or not you'll find him, doesn't matter. I'm impressed by what you're able to accomplish." Then he waited to deliberate how to approach his hidden agenda. "There's something I believe is happening regarding the tribal finances. I would like you to look into it."

"You know I'd do anything to help you out, but I have to tell you that I'm getting concerned. I'm a storywriter, not a detective. I'm afraid that I'm going to get myself in trouble," I informed him.

"Trouble? You're not committing a crime," Walter objected.

"No. The trouble I'm concerned about is ethical. If I can't do the job correctly, then I'm cheating people. I might get lucky…but I more than likely won't," I argued.

"Zach, we deal with unethical people all the time," Len wryly countered. "Some of them aren't even competent."

The matter was closed. Len Cloud had slammed the tribal gavel—I was about to be delivered my second investigative assignment.

In the meantime, Preeti and I were soon to greet a guest we were both excited to have come for a visit. However, we didn't know how long our company would be staying with us, nor could we have anticipated all the shocking delights this treasured friend would bring our way.

10

VROOM, VROOM, VROOM

REUBEN CONTINUED TO DRIFT in and out of his funk but was diligent in his responsibilities. In fact, at one of the moments he was not contemplating exorcism to expel the evil demons rampaging freely through his superego, he proposed to me the purchase of a tandoori oven.

He was working up a new menu and mentioned that he had, for a period of time, worked in an Indian joint in Seattle (the first time he ever mentioned a definite fact about his prior experience as a cook) and thought he could take a few dishes to a new order of gustatory excellence. He had researched the exact type of oven he wanted, an all-clay model pre-fired to 1,000 degrees for maximum strength, heat retention, and durability. It was the cat's meow, the Rolls Royce of tandoori cooking. The thing was around two grand, including shipping.

We were doing extraordinarily well, and with the added income from the Stevie Green matter, this was not a huge expenditure. Reuben, nevertheless, was so enthused that he had already offered to pay half before I even ruled on the purchase—it was my first monetary dealing with him, convincing me he would make a lousy businessman. That inkling about him graduated far beyond supposition, by virtue of a second area of financial experience I had with him. He never haggled with me about salary when I hired him, and in spite of the acclaim he was aware he had brought to Kuruk, he had never suggested a raise—I had volunteered two already on his behalf.

Reuben might not have cared about money, but he sure did advocate for the oven, which I gave the okay to without a blink. While we were talking at one of the empty tables, my cell rang. It was Preston.

"Where are you this week?" I joked, knowing the band was still on tour for another month and that meant several stops all over the country.

"Boston—saw the Sox whip the Yankees at Fenway Park. Zach, I think it's the only park left where Ortiz can pop a homerun into a neighbor's kitchen sink."

"Very cool," I commented excitedly. Since my youth, I had been a baseball fan and would have loved to take in an afternoon at Fenway.

"Listen, the reason I called is about this Reuben guy working for you—"

"You won't let go of it, will you?" I expressed with amazement, careful not to let on in front of Reuben that he was the topic of the discussion.

"I really think you're off base this time," Preston reported. "Reuben Zapata, right? His middle initial you said was "R," am I correct? Well, I had a buddy of mine who can use the

Internet like a kid rides a bike research the name. There are four living people in this country with that name. One at this moment is in jail for armed robbery in Nevada; one is a welder living with his wife and four children in Dallas, Texas; another is ninety-four years old and in a rest home in Portland, Oregon; and the last one is a police officer in Phoenix."

While I was listening, Reuben stood up and walked back to the kitchen, allowing me to talk openly.

"That proves the point, right?" I expressed with intended sarcasm. "Reuben is a fake."

"I don't know what he is. Zach, Stevie Green may have picked up and left it all in the dust. Can't this guy be on the run too, but not like Stevie who is getting away from fame, he's escaping something far worse?"

"What do you have in mind, treason?"

"I wish you wouldn't make light of this," he barked at me, in no mood to mitigate his finding.

"I'm not. But consider this. What if someone was looking for Zach Miller? They might find out something similar to what you did about Zapata, but be off the mark because they should have been looking for a Zacchaeus Miller."

"Great. I'm following my gut here. I'm going to keep searching until I find out who the hell he is!" Preston assured me.

"I have a top-notch investigator if you need one," I jested, thinking of putting him on to Farley.

"You're the investigator—try taking a look in your own backyard," he shot back. "Zach, I'm your best friend, sworn to look after your safety by your mother, and you know what that means."

I knew what it meant. Kaye Miller, my dear mother, had worried since I returned from Israel that I might burst an emotional seam. She authorized tightening Preston like a tourniquet around my heart—the kid was earnest in his assignment, but prone to overreach.

"If I see, hear, smell, or sense the slightest sign of perversity or criminality in Reuben Zapata you'll be first to know," I swore like pledging my allegiance to the flag.

"How about instability? Wouldn't that qualify as cause for concern? The guy's as depressed as a bottle of fizzed-out champagne."

"I have been too, if you don't recall."

"Right, Zach. But would you not agree that the severity of what you went through makes a period of depression expected? Like there's a reason for what you were feeling. With this guy, you have no idea what is or what has been going on to promote his psychological problems. Maybe it was months in prison for him for burglary or rape," Preston proposed as a possibility.

"I'm getting a better idea about him by spending more time with him," I said tentatively.

"Well, I damn near lost you once and I'm not letting that happen again," Preston promised me.

As I was listening to my friend's declaration, Reuben reemerged out of the kitchen. I sensed he was ready to continue our conversation.

"Preston, can we finish up on this later? I have to go."

"Okay. Just one thing before you sign off. Your mom told me Josea is coming up."

"Yeah, actually any day now. I'll keep you informed. Be well." I suddenly felt a pang of guilt, as if I wasn't being appreciative. "Thanks for your concern, really."

We had hung up and then within a second my cell went off again. Preeti was on the line.

"I was on my way over with Souche when Josea called—she's here! She's coming to Kuruk in about ten minutes."

"You're kidding. I know she said she'd be here soon, but she never mentioned the exact time."

"My fault, Zach. With everything going on, I forgot to tell you I talked to her yesterday. She mentioned she planned on arriving either today or tomorrow. I'll be right there," Preeti announced excitedly.

Josea is the girl I went out with on my high school prom. We had no contact after that until we met up in Israel, where her actions saved my life. She was considered to be a national treasure due to her superior mental capability. While girls her age were playing Little League or giggling over diary entries about their first crushes, Josea was achieving degrees and commendations. As a young adult, she orchestrated strategies for the national security of America, and then for Israel.

With all that brainpower, this cute and sexy girl flunked the subjects of dating and sexuality. I had thought of helping her get on track but then I met Preeti. I did set her up with Preston but my friend was still a confirmed bachelor trying to convince himself that shacking up with a different lady every night was a grand lifestyle. Josea, during the phase of her life after the Israeli nightmare, was slumping, spending her time rummaging through encyclopedic volumes to discover invaluable facts.

"My god," she called breathlessly to wake me far too early one morning. "Did you know that masturbation is found erotically poised in the dictionary between manipulation and matriculation?"

For the first time in her three-decade life, Josea was confronting disillusionment in her faith, general sadness about longings unfulfilled, and confusion owing to what purpose she might have in the future. She wandered aimlessly trying to discover facets of her being other than intellect, which had been the dominating theme for all her conscious years. Finally, she took off on a spiritual journey that extended for several months.

With great excitement we were awaiting her arrival in Mescalero. We were in for a surprise.

I was close to completing the non-negotiation with Reuben over the tandoori oven when Preeti zipped into the parking area. Reuben, who could be depressed to a state of catatonia, would run a 10K race on broken glass to see Souche. Both of us rushed out to greet my wife and daughter. While I hugged Preeti, Reuben took his little friend out of her car seat. It was then we heard a loud *vroom, vroom, vroom* sound coming up the unpaved road that led to where we were standing.

Each of us looked up. A large motorcycle was thrusting ahead of a cloud of dust like a surfer riding a wave. The creature atop the two-wheeler was wearing a bright gold helmet, heavy black boots, black leather pants and jacket, and goggles. The bike was fully packed for travel with two rear carrying cases. On the "belly" the words BMW with R1200GS were painted in bright orange against a black background.

That's not all. There was also a curious basket sitting at the front of the bike, cinched in place with two straps, the content invisible under a tan blanket. Josea jumped off the bike. Preeti literally fell to the ground gagging from laughter.

"What will you think of next, friend?" Preeti finally screamed gleefully to her.

Josea hoisted her left leg counter clockwise over the abdomen of the bike. Before she had steadied herself on the ground, she was flipping off the helmet, a bright beam glistening off of it as the protective head gear fell freely to the ground, revealing her new short-cropped hair that was pitch black in color with narrowly discernable streaks of yellowish dye. She looked like a commercial for the release of a *Chopper Girls* movie.

Josea stood for a moment. The rest of us did the same, as if we were all statues carved in wax. Josea melted first, reaching up to wrap her arms around her head in a gesture signaling that she was overwhelmed at seeing us.

Shockingly, after getting oriented to Preeti's welcome, she looked at Reuben, staring at him as if she had unexpectedly bumped into a friend from a prior life. She looked at me, sensed she was alone on stage, and broke down in tears. I couldn't tell if she was weeping joyously or woefully, but she cried black rivulets of mascara that sinuously worked their way down to her cheeks, chin, and then tucked under before they terminated on her neck—the kid was at a loss for words.

Preeti and I ran the few feet between us as if we were racing for a finish line, our arms reaching out to embrace her. Josea grabbed on for dear life, and the three of us huddled for what must have been an eternity. The whole time Reuben held Souche, who joined the undifferentiated emotion with shrill sounds of delight.

Finally, we disengaged. It was then that the most peculiar exchange occurred. Josea went to hug Souche, but when she reached out to where Reuben was holding her, Josea stood facing him for several seconds while they stared at one another. Ever so gently, she finally nodded her head and reached out her arms to signal that he could hand the child over. To this day, I'll never forget the moment because both she and Reuben seemed to be role-playing a silent acknowledgment of a past acquaintanceship in a production neither could have rehearsed.

Preeti and I looked at each other, my wife as observant as I. We smiled, both of us aware that we had the identical thought without needing to say it. All the effort and worry I may have devoted up to this moment toward my pledge to get Josea prepped to join the big league of adult romance had been fruitless. Was this man—who confessed to being equally inept as she in carnal pleasure, a man self-professed as ignorant in the field of eroticism and love, this meek, skinny appear-out-of-nowhere cook—going to set my dear friend's oven on broil?

I would have concluded that the attraction I perceived between the two was pure fantasy, had it not been for Preeti having the same thought. After all, our love had been born in an instantaneous glance, one flash of awareness that we would be soul mates for life. Why couldn't that be the case for these two? Was Kuruk to be to the members of The Lonely Hearts' Club what Ponce de Leon's legendary Fountain of Youth was to the seekers of eternal life? We were going to have to wait on this one, but it would prove to be one of the most unimaginable journeys.

Josea, the girl I previously labeled as amateurish at tear shedding, had improved her skills—she must have had practice during her months living in an ashram, a fact she later confirmed to me. Holding Souche evoked a second round of sobbing, ending sharply with Josea taking the little one, placing her on the ground, and holding her hand as she guided her back to the bike.

It was then that the object secured in the basket was revealed—a tiny puppy. The second that Josea set the little pisher on the ground, he piddled a pool of pee. My daughter was no stranger to wild bears, coyote, and elk, but we had never owned a dog. I couldn't mistake this one for a spaniel of some sort, and Josea informed us that it was an English Cocker Spaniel, which would grow to about thirty pounds.

She quickly announced that she would never think of bringing the pup as a gift to our daughter. Instead, she exclaimed that the little lad was to be her companion. I still had my doubts as to her true motive. I would later confirm with my mother that it had been a contrived deal, the two of them devising the scheme to bring a pet into our home. I think my mother felt guilty, because when I was being raised we never had a dog. Regardless, it would take less than an hour before Souche would befriend the animal and Josea would back off her earlier pledge that the little guy was hers.

"Look, if Souche really likes the puppy...she really seems to, doesn't she?"

And there you have it, the introduction of the fourth member of our family, named Henry. As the head of our household of four, I was given the honor of naming him and chose to dub the new addition after the honorable Henry Higgins, from my favorite musical, *My Fair Lady*.

We all went inside, the restaurant still empty before dinner. Reuben, as if unable to handle the powerful instantaneous attraction, ran off to hide in the kitchen. Interestingly, at that moment not a sign of his lingering depression was evident.

Preeti and Josea couldn't wait to relive memories of their first meeting at this very spot one more time.

"Do you remember when I told you I hadn't dated since my first husband was killed?" Preeti reminded Josea.

Cheerfully Josea responded. "Oh, yes I do. But don't forget, I countered that I hadn't dated since going out with this man (pointing to me) for my high school prom."

Then they both did a duet.

"Which one of us is more screwed up, friend?"

The laughter was a needed relief from much of the weighty

business we had been facing. They continued, singing their words simultaneously while both pointing to Josea.

"You, definitely." Then the finger pointing shifted to Preeti. "At least I had the excuse of raising Jivin."

They roared, reminding me of my mother when she'd get together with friends who'd tease one another to tears—it was a great feeling watching them. When I glanced over a few feet to the side, I noticed my daughter with her new dog. She was playing water games in a pool of urine. It set me to deliberating how long it would take for this fellow to grow into a thirty pounder and how much damage he would inflict on our home in the process. I was thinking like a real family man.

That evening we did something we rarely did. We asked Len to babysit so we could go out for dinner. Wanting to have an uninterrupted meal, we dined at our main competitor, the Inn of The Mountain Gods Resort.

Josea brought us up to date on her adventures over the past few months. She had felt as if she were in a deep hole, unable to find direction or meaning. It's not an uncommon place to land for a person in their early thirties, but Josea was in all fairness not a normal person. Knowing she had returned from Israel overwhelmed with offers for jobs, it took great discipline on her part not to get lured into one of those opportunities. However, the longer she rejected the positions presented to her, the more confused she became. Finally, a friend introduced her to a yoga movement emphasizing both meditation and exercise and that resulted in the transformational experience she needed. She described a sense of liberation, offering her the opportunity to finally begin to explore other pursuits than those of a purely intellectual nature.

Most delightful for her was the discovery of her musical talent. Both of her parents were artists of one type or another, but Josea had never shown an inclination in those directions. That is, not until recently, when she began playing the guitar and then experimented with piano and keyboard. The next thing she knew, she was writing music and lyrics. By the time she reached Kuruk, she had composed an entire musical, including the lyrics and a book.

One afternoon she played it for us, and I was amazed. The music reminded me of hip-hop, yet it was more than that—the compositions were filled with melodious rhythms and peppy beats. It was the story, however, that had Preeti and me turning our necks several full rotations—it appeared to be a tribute to Stevie Green.

Thinking back on it, her choice of subject matter was not a particularly striking coincidence. Most people in the world adored the icon, so making him the central theme of her first artistic work was not shocking. It's just that his name kept popping up in my life wherever I turned. Having Josea lug him along with her seemed a bit much.

Contrary to the facts I was beginning to collect, Josea had built the arc of her script around the idea that Stevie had been killed. It was written like a fairytale whereby the make-believe Stevie had fallen in love for the first time. He kept his darling top secret from the world. At the same time, he was deathly afraid she would leave or be unfaithful. His jealousy had gradually turned to paranoia, leading in turn to him making outrageous demands on his sweetheart. At first, it was an honor for the object of his affections to be faithful to the oath of privacy she had taken regarding their affair, but as he seemed to lose his emotional balance, she threatened to go public with the romance, and even worse, his "domination" and "possession" of her.

The Stevie character of her piece was devastated. At a moment of torment, he ran to the estate where he had sequestered his love. It was there that he presented to her a final entreat. He begged her to drop the threat in return for a promise to take her away with him to a private island where they would live happily ever after. Realizing that Stevie had been driven crazy by his fans, fame and fortune, and that she had tired of his desire to possess her, she killed him and disposed of his body.

As she watched the world grieve, she became saddened. The guilt and remorse pained her so deeply that she decided to confess her crime. She went out into the world telling everybody what she had done, but nobody would listen to her. Unable to attain the punishment she sought for her crime, she gradually lost her mind—in the final scene she kills herself.

To me, it didn't seem to be Josea's objective to shed light on what fate Stevie Green met, so much as to point out that fame can take a toll on the most talented gifts a society possesses. That she would choose the topic she did for her artistic creation, and that her point of view would veer so close to the sentiments being expressed to me by others, was eerie and disconcerting.

I perceived projection in her writing, especially in the final conclusion. Had she come to the awareness that notoriety and talent were threatening to her life? Was she using the case of Stevie Green to express her own disillusionment, along with the accompanying sense of futility?

As the evening was coming to a close, I asked Josea about her plans for the immediate future. She appeared to have changed immensely, leading me to question whether she was going to return to an academic life or instead pursue music as more than a hobby. Her response was welcomed, but not expected.

"I'm hoping I can stay here for a while," she said with a tone of inquiry. "If it won't work for both of you I understand... please, you have to tell me the truth."

"No, I want to hear what you're thinking," Preeti encouraged.

"I just need more time. The world can live without Josea Roth, that's been demonstrated," she smirked, as if remembering a truth she once foolishly disbelieved. "I want to get up in the morning and meditate, work on projects during the day, help out if I can in the restaurant, babysit Souche—and just stay on my journey."

"We have several extra rooms," I announced.

"Yes, when we built the house, Zach must have had in mind a family of five children," Preeti teased. "Are we down to two now, my love? We did decide it wouldn't be just Souche, didn't we?"

"To be determined," I muttered, knowing I was fairly content with the way our life was, but there was no way the odd number was going to be accepted. "Point is, Josea, you can stay with us as long as you like."

"Then let's go home," Josea said with wet eyes. "I'm still tired."

As we walked to the car, I raised the subject of Reuben in as demure a fashion as one might approach such a potentially charged matter.

"How did you like Reuben?"

"Who?" she answered matter-of-fact.

"Our chef...who was there when you arrived today," I reminded her.

"I really didn't notice much about him," she commented breezily.

We continued walking and I dropped the topic. In fact, it wouldn't come up between us for some time. Josea would never lie to me. I was dead certain of that. She would lie to herself. Honest people seem to be flawed in that way.

Before going to bed, Preeti couldn't resist raising a couple of points that we hadn't had time to discuss earlier.

"Zach, Josea has changed … she doesn't even look like herself."

"I'm happy for her. She needed to grow," I said fondly. "The motorcycle! She's definitely exploring."

"Yes, definitely! And did you get Josea's response about Reuben?" she said with obvious amazement.

"Floored me too."

"No woman breathes fire and doesn't get a sore throat," Preeti reflected.

"It was hot," I agreed. "No doubt old Reuben was back in the kitchen icing himself."

"Well put. Now, are you iced tonight?"

Thankfully, the thoughts that her father had called and requested a meeting with me the next day to discuss my new assignment, and that Ila Clearbrook's murder had the potential to create a second calling of Geronimo had caught a riptide, pulling them out of mind and out of sight.

Ice melted; I was roasting.

11

STUCK IN THE MIDDLE AGAIN

THE NEXT MORNING, I went to Kuruk before heading over to my father-in-law's place. I still hadn't caught up on my paperwork. The accountant had been nagging me to forward my quarterly data. Plus, Soeze Willitts, our manager, wanted me to sit in on an interview with a prospective hostess.

I feared there was more she wanted to discuss. I had implemented a policy shortly before the murder investigation to make it affordable for the law enforcement personnel at Mescalero to eat at Kuruk, offering half price on their meals. It drove Soeze to rage, and it seemed any opportunity she could find, she brought the topic up for debate. While a magnificent employee, she was not as the phonetics of her name would suggest, so easy.

She scored profits at our restaurant like a running back gains yards—kicking, slashing, and banging for every last penny. As a corollary principle, she grumbled about anything that reduced revenue. However, she did faithfully but begrudgingly comply with my wishes regarding discounts for police and agents.

Now with the FBI investigation underway, it was a common occurrence to find her in her office cursing as she was forced to divide several breakfast and lunch tabs by two. I also found out that the locals didn't approve of my decision to extend the courtesy to the agents who'd come to investigate the murder. But I stuck to my guns. As a result, I wasn't surprised to see Kershaw, or any of his men, regularly coming in to eat.

When I arrived, Kershaw was having breakfast, sitting alone at a table. The windows surrounding the main dining room offered a full view of the forest. From where the agent sat, he could see the beads of heavy dew moistening the ground. The sky forecasted a warning that heaving volumes of water would soon be upon us. When I came in, Kershaw glanced up and motioned me to come over. As I approached his table, he asked if I would join him.

"Gabe Kershaw. I'm sure by now you know who I am," he said amicably, reaching out to shake.

"Of course. Good to meet you formally."

"I know this is your place. I also know that your wife is Len Cloud's daughter."

"That's right."

"By the way, I love the food," he complimented kindly. "I've been having lunch here every day. And I have to mention, real nice touch by you to offer the special deal to my people."

"My pleasure," I assured him.

"Helps. Well, that's not what I want to talk with you about though," a tone of gravity evident in his voice. "It's your father-in-law. He's a cranky, cantankerous man."

"Things are difficult here right now," I responded, preparing to defend Len. "My father-in-law is devoted to his people and their heritage. I don't have to tell you the humiliation he feels having you invade his turf."

"He knows better than anyone that I have no choice but to handle this matter," Kershaw mentioned with a tad of irritation. "I'm trying my best not to intrude unless absolutely necessary. Now I've asked for his cooperation and what have I received in return?"

Kershaw allowed me time to deliberate on his question. "I'll tell you what's happening. He's instructing as many tribe members as will listen to him not to talk to me." Kershaw began to finger a pack of cigarettes out of the left breast pocket of his shirt, but stopped. "Sorry, forgot. I'll go out in a minute for a smoke," he announced as the box mindlessly fell into hiding behind his pure white cotton shirt.

"What I'm thinking is maybe you could consider talking to him, or have your wife bring him to his senses. I can make it hard on these people," driving the point forward by tightening his lips. "If I want, I can force every last one of them to come to Albuquerque for interviews."

"As it turns out I'm going to see him shortly. But I'll tell you the truth. I have no influence over him." I hesitated before saying what was on my mind, but finally proceeded without caution. "I'm not sure I want to have any. He believes this is a vagrant and the matter will die its own dea—"

"Bullshit! Cloud may believe he knows everything but he's never dealt with murder. I damn well believe there's a killer in Mescalero." Kershaw paused a few moments for me to absorb the possibility. "That's what I'm thinking. Right in your backyard is a sick son-of-a-bitch and Len Cloud would just as soon let the animal go on and do it again because of his Apache pride."

Hearing Kershaw's words alarmed me. What if he was right? My father-in-law might be blinded by his wish to exonerate any Apache of the crime. With that attitude, he could impede an investigation that might curtail further similar tragedies.

"You've got a wife and child, right? You want to sleep at night with a shotgun by your bed?" Kershaw picked up his coat, readying himself to leave. "That's why we have peace officers. This is my business. I'm here to solve a murder and you might want to have a heart-to-heart with that man. I don't want to get nasty but I will do what it takes to protect these people."

Kershaw was as headstrong as Len Cloud. They both believed in what they were doing and just might be willing to die for those principles. I noticed goose pimples rising like an army of insects on my skin. I was shivering in horror. I had been schooled in Israel on what a collision of dogmatic forces could produce in terms of tragedy. Worse, I knew the sense of helplessness one experiences when he realizes he might not be able to do anything to avert crisis.

They were both absolutely-certainly-right, a guarantee that soon there would be at least one man—and likely two— asking his Lord how he could have been dead wrong.

"Mr. Kershaw, I'll do my best. Besides, not everyone in the tribe sees things the same way as my father-in-law."

"I know. But those that don't are less cooperative—they're scared," Kershaw lamented. "They should be."

"Well, it was good meeting you. I'm sure I'll see you again."

"You will," he assured me. "I'm planning to bring my wife and children for dinner to celebrate my wife's birthday next week," he smiled. "I know the rules. No half deals for dinner."

Kershaw stood up and was about to leave.

"It's on me. Come and have a nice dinner. Just try and be sensitive to these people, please."

He nodded, knowing he would do his best. In the end, though, he'd have to play rough.

I took off for Len Cloud's home, wondering if it was worth the words to tell him about my meeting with Kershaw. I concluded it was not. With a man like Cloud, at best you might have one shot at reaching him, and you better time it as well as a magician performs a trick. No, Len Cloud was not ready to listen to me. It would take a whole lot more hurt for that to happen.

Len lived and worked at the same location, a shack about ten minutes from our home. Attached was a good-sized barn that he used as his studio. He made his living, if you want to call it that, building furniture and wood artifacts that he sold—the truth was that most of his income was derived from his share of the tribal earnings.

As I pulled up to the front of his home, I realized I'd never been inside his work area. I opened the car door and noticed

Len emerge from the studio. He waved for me to come and meet him there. As I entered, I couldn't believe what I was seeing. The place was crammed full of items he had crafted—there were chairs, tables, and cabinets made from fir, alder, pine, oak, and cedar. Out of similar material, he had stacked piles of floor planks, wall coverings, and molding.

Then there were frames for clocks, pictures, and mirrors. As I wandered about, I noticed that the smaller items all had engraved patterns and each incorporated the circle of life broken into four equal wedges. Sometimes the symbol was artistically integrated into more intricate designs, while there were other examples where the symbol itself was the dominant focus of the piece.

I was awed by the vastness of what this man had labored to produce and create—a lifetime of accomplishment from an unrecognized artist who seemed to have no interest in claiming the esteem I perceived he had earned.

"I've never been here, Len. I just realized that," I shared with him.

"Preeti used to love coming here while I worked," he began with a gleam in his eyes. "See that eagle over there," he asked, pointing to a beautiful bird about a foot high and perched over the door of the structure. "Preeti was fifteen when she made that."

"She never mentioned woodworking to me."

"Zach, the kid she married before you, Jivin's father, was my apprentice. Hell, he couldn't make money and once he became a dad he wanted to do good by his family so he went to work building The Inn—that's where he was killed." Len solemnly continued.

"That's why she stopped working with wood?" I asked.

"I can't say that for sure but I believe it was a factor." Len peered upward toward the wood replica of the revered bird. "The eagles always came to visit her. Maybe someday you'll be honored to meet our authority."

"It must have been really hard on her, losing her husband so early."

"Indeed it was. Zach, she was a child herself, raising Jivin on her own. Wasn't easy but look what she did. She opened a restaurant and I did what I could to help. Every extra dime I had I used to assist her in getting started and then to keep the business going."

I strolled in and out of the piles of lumber and items of furniture, wondering what Len planned to do with it all.

"Zach, I said I have a request for you."

"I remember you and Walter mentioning it," I responded.

"Right," Len mumbled. I saw his mind shifting gears. "Walter means well, but his anger could stampede a herd of beasts. He was foolhardy at the council meeting." Len was facing me by the time he proceeded. "I try to guide him, but in the end he always acts out of passion rather than reason."

"Probably because he's young," I surmised.

"No. It's Walter. His spirit is mean but he doesn't know it. He thinks his devotion to our tribal traditions can justify his actions." This was not a man to speak mindlessly. Typically, he would choose each word he spoke like pieces of fresh fruit in a market. The delays in the presentation of his statements highlighted the attention he was devoting toward selecting his thoughts carefully. "Someday, he'll fly away and leave me weeping to our God to forgive his spirit."

When I asked him what he was referring to, Len told me that men who cannot control their emotions would eventually harm others. As he spoke, I thought about men like Len and Kershaw, men able to thoroughly dominate their emotions. I realized they, too, could inflict great pain onto others, more so to those they loved.

"Now, this business I want to discuss with you. I might be wrong about Platta. If I am, nobody will be the worse for it. On the other hand, if I'm right, there will be some changes around here."

"If I can help, I'll try. I still have to caution you that I'm not skilled at what you might be asking me to do."

"I know that. Preeti's proud as a princess of you and believes you can do anything you set your mind to. Let's face it, Kuruk is a lot more successful since you came."

"Preeti had it all in place," I laughed, a habit I hadn't realized I used repeatedly when mitigating an accomplishment. "I took it to the next logical step. Eventually she would have—"

"I don't care about that." Len flatly dismissed my perception of the role I'd played thus far in Kuruk. He was eager to keep the talk aimed in the direction he had in mind. "It's Platta." Len stopped for a moment of reflection. "If you have any thought that this is a vendetta I have against him, I promise you're wrong. I don't care for what he's doing. I'll oppose him with thunder, wind, and fire, but I'll not do anything wrongful to harm him." Again he ceased speaking, taking a moment before his assertion. "I think he's stealing from the tribe."

"But Preeti said every tribe member has access to the books and shares in the profits."

Len looked at me with a typical void expression. "That's lady talk. Preeti is very smart but she's too trusting. I taught her to be leery of people but her nature is kindly, generous, and innocent. Women can afford such luxury, but we as men will drown in the blood of our own hearts if we open ourselves too freely.

"The assets of the tribe are all handled through a trust. That's on the up and up. But like any enterprise, there are always ways to cheat. Bidding for contracts can be rigged, special favors can be allocated to those willing to return the good deeds with financial gifts, and...I think you can figure it out."

Len picked up a thin folder he had resting on a table in the middle of the room. He handed it to me.

"This will give you a basic outline of how the tribe operates administratively and financially. Spend some time acquainting yourself with it and then start snooping around as discreetly as you can. That's all I'm asking."

"There are tricks to this business of getting information that I don't know. I have a man in Albuquerque who might be able to help me—"

"No! Don't involve anyone in these matters. If what I suspect is happening, you may go for advice to someone who will tip off Platta. Then all the rivers will turn dry."

"I'll try to see how far I can get on my own," I said tentatively. "By the way, any more information about Ila Clearbrook?"

"Nothing. The FBI agent is like a dog trying to catch his tail," Len joked, but without an outward expression of humor.

Kershaw sure didn't look like a toy Poodle earlier in the morning when I talked with him at Kuruk—closer to a Doberman. I would never tell Len, but I was inclined to be rooting for Kershaw and a quick resolution of the murder. The FBI man was right. Everyone would sleep more peacefully knowing the killer was isolated in a place where he couldn't harm anyone else.

12

BUT FIRST A TRIP TO TOPEKA, KANSAS

THE MORNING AFTER I met with Kershaw, and later Len Cloud, I left for Topeka, a trip I had already booked. I spent some time the evening before browsing the file my father-in-law had given me, trying to outline a plan of attack for a project the nature of which I had little understanding.

My mind felt cluttered between all the endeavors I had committed to handle. However, knowing by the time I returned from Topeka that I'd be relieved of one project—determining the status of Stevie Green—helped ease my sense of being overwhelmed. I reasoned that if I found further evidence he was alive I'd be finished with the assignment. If, conversely, I found nothing additional regarding his state, I would still be able to conclude my commitment to LIVE.

I assumed that soon I would be thumbing my finger at Jivin, faulting him for his arrogance to predict all these grand stories that would be coming to me at Kuruk. Thus far, in truth, I was being tugged and pulled this way and that; there was a murder, Stevie Green was probably alive, perhaps there was indiscretion with the tribal finances, but there was nothing qualifying for more than a short story. In my preparation to leave on this brief trip, I concluded I would be just as happy to return to my life as a husband, daddy, and businessman, occasionally hobby-writing fantasy tales.

It was a beautiful morning. I recall as I left Mescalero marveling at a vast eternal blue sky hosting one lone hawk, the hunter resting gently on an invisible current as it scanned below for a careless rodent scampering too far from shelter. There was no wind and the air temperature slid over my skin without perceptible sensation. My only wish was to praise the moment for the glory bestowed on me, for at that fleeting instant I was a wealthy man.

I drove south to El Paso, Texas, the smaller airport allowing me an easier trip to my destination. On the plane, I carried with me my notes regarding the uninvestigated report of Delia Spruce, another idol worshipper with a story that in my opinion should have been thoroughly explored by Jay Weiner or one of his people.

Why I was going in the first place, given I had already acquired ample evidence that Stevie Green was alive, I can explain in two ways. First, I felt compelled to get double the level of assurance I had already that he was still living. Second, I was curious if her story could be true, and if so, what it might tell us regarding why Stevie Green had been in Topeka. I knew the tale would end there. Farley had assured me that after Stevie abandoned F. Artanis as his cover, he would have moved on to a new identity. There would be no way, according to Farley, I would figure out who that new persona was—nor did I want to know.

Delia Spruce had a doozie of an account. She claimed not only that she had "SEEN" her God, but more. "I saw what makes Stevie, Stevie." She also proclaimed to have "TOUCHED" the man in the flesh. How could I resist meeting her?

Actually, I might round out the reporting by adding that a couple of days before leaving, I called Arnie with LIVE. I was already preparing for the trip, and it was the statement by the woman in Topeka of "seeing Stevie for what makes Stevie, Stevie" that dogged my imagination. What might she be talking about? When I called Arnie, I posed the question. He mentioned that Stevie was not a "tattoo freak" but had a tiny hawk inscribed just above the right wrist. It did cross my mind after he told me this that Bill Cooley had been struck by the fact that the man he took for Stevie Green was wearing a long-sleeved shirt in a temperature normally calling for a t-shirt or tank top.

Arnie did have one other item to share with me.

"I doubt this will be of any consequence, and Stevie wasn't inclined to advertise it, though it was referred to on one or two occasions, but he was a major fan of Mickey Mouse," Arnie chanted, waiting for my response. I said nothing and he proceeded. "Well, he never wore anything other than briefs that said Mickey Mouse around the band." He giggled. "Stevie had them made. They were all black, with the bright yellow words going all the way around the elastic band."

"He never wore any other type?" I inquired dubiously.

"Never. That was Stevie. He was a freak in some ways; he'd get into a habit then suck it like a teat."

"By some crazy chance if I need a pair—"

"Tits or panties?" Arnie tittered.

"I was thinking of the briefs you say Stevie wore."

"You don't have to choose, you know. I told you first class all the way—just expense the tits and I'll send you the Mickey Mouse undies if you like."

"Just the underwear will do."

"If I had known you were turned on by that sort of thing, I'd have offered a box of them when you were here," Arnie joked.

"No fetishes for me, none that I'm aware of, at least. But can I get one sample?" I asked again.

"Not a problem. Not for me, anyway, but you'll have to ask Weiner the question." He increased his humor. "He'll love it."

"Very funny. I'll call him. Wish me luck."

I did get in touch with Weiner. When I brought it up, he addressed my request as if I were asking for his fax number. He turned me over to his secretary who assured me she'd go to Stevie's house and have one sent immediately. A day later, overnight delivery brought me a pair of Stevie Green's underwear, a keepsake I likely could have peddled for ten grand on the Internet—and that's if it had been laundered. I wondered what it would bring if Stevie had soiled them.

Delia Spruce was ecstatic that I had called. Similar to Cooley, she had told her story so many times to so many people—none believing her—that she had ceased talking about it for fear of alienating friends and family. She was so enthusiastic about my wanting to talk with her that she was willing to give up a whole day's pay to see me, suggesting several options for locations where we could get together. I assured her the best plan would be for me to come to her place of employment, where she alleged to have seen Stevie— the Fairfield Hotel—the bonus being she wouldn't lose time at work.

Thus, as soon as my plane arrived, I took a rental car and went directly to the Fairfield, a multi-story structure that must have tipped the "AAA" evaluator big to purchase the high rating it boasted. It was a no-frills joint with rooms whose only appeal was that they had been recently debugged.

Apparently, a recent infantry of bed bugs had invaded Topeka. The assault was so pernicious that a chemical company was called in to invent a substitute for DDT. The pest control company servicing the hotel suggested they advise their patrons to be sure and wash their clothing in water over 120 degrees before bringing them inside.

I looked at the small sign in the corner of the lobby prepared by the Delight people that outlined the above warning. I also prayed for the owners of the hotel that nobody paid attention. If they did, the place would be empty while the laundry down the street would have customers sleeping on the washers and dryers, assured of a bug-free night's rest. They'd also find their wardrobes heated to a temperature that would have melted the fibers.

Ms. Spruce had given me her cell phone number, and when I called I could hear her excitedly bouncing up and down. She immediately advised me that she hadn't taken a break for two days and made sure management knew it so that when I arrived we'd have ample time to go over every detail.

I had the impression from the brief exchange I shared with Ms. Spruce after notifying her I had arrived in town, that it was not only the disbelieved claim of having eye-witnessed Stevie Green that had been bottled up in this lady, but a lifetime of tales needing to be told. I wondered if she'd talk me through the dinner I was looking forward to at the bed and breakfast where I had booked a room. The woman running the inn informed me when I made the reservation that she was a gourmet cook. She explained that she prepared dinner Monday through Thursday evenings for her boarders and asked if I wanted the meal included. I assured her I did.

I might as well get it over with and tell the embarrassing tale now. When I finally arrived at her place after meeting with Delia, just moments before the feast was to be served, I had no time to put away my overnight case in the room. The lady of the establishment suggested that I go straight to the meal. As she served me one item after another of the seven-course extravaganza (excluding the homemade lemonade), I never gave it a thought that I was the only customer eating.

She began with a muse—two airy balls that tasted similar to the sweetest orange citrus flavor while dissolving in the mouth like cotton candy. She refused to even hint what it was, but she was eager to announce that it was first in the lineup and had the assignment of "pacifying" the taste buds. If that was the case, then this woman was not a lady to betray. She disarmed my senses to the point that the next course rushed past my peaceful little lips and down my throat like Sherman ravaging Savannah.

It was hot. It might have carried a sign saying, "I can make you sweat." At first I gasped, wondering if she had planned to kill me, why would she go to all the trouble of preparing the meal? Then, I thought of the second movie in the *Silence of the Lambs* series and had my answer. Some psychos like foreplay.

Rather than go through each of the courses, I'll abbreviate my version of the cooking by saying her cuisine was not for the faint of heart; only the brave would survive. She believed a meal was not complete until those at the table begged to be relieved of taking another bite. I can proudly report that I was still sitting after course six, but I could have beaten my gut in a concert like a drum skin—she still hadn't served the dessert.

That was part one of my saga staying with Ms. Tiffany Amy Funster—the best was yet to come. Madame Funster was about fifty. She was overweight but not grossly so. She had a pretty face with pure white skin, and she wore her hair in curls that dangled like New Year's Eve streamers below her neck. Her makeup was heavy but did not seem to conceal any deformities or imperfections; to the contrary, her skin appeared smooth. She spoke in a kindly manner and treated me like the son she never had. She informed me while I was eating that she had a house nearby where she stayed but she would be back by early morning to make my breakfast.

After dinner, she invited me to enjoy the big (huge) screen television in the den. She offered me an after-dinner cognac, and we talked a bit before I realized it was time for bed. I glanced at my watch and she took the cue, promptly announcing that she was leaving.

As she was about to go out the door, she pointed up a stairwell and informed me that my room was the first on the left. I grabbed my bag and began the short journey upward. It dawned on me then that there were no other customers at her bed and breakfast. Furthermore, the door to my room, I quickly discovered, had no lock. One might draw the quick conclusion that dear Ms. Funster was coming back to have a party with young, dashing Zach. That wasn't what went through my mind, however. I thought the sweet spinster was waiting for me to fall asleep, after which she would come back to kill me.

I know it sounds laughable, but the more I thought over the evening's events up to that point, the more convinced I became that staying there the rest of the night was a death sentence. I even called Preeti, who was in stitches listening to my wild imagination. She tried to reason with me that if Ms. Funster killed all her boarders, by now someone would have reported her. Made sense to me, for a minute or two. My "rational" mind countered her. "There's a first for everything and I'm the perfect opportunity for her to expand her offering to bed, breakfast, dinner...and death." We finally hung up. My wife was still laughing delightfully, shocking me that she could take so lightly the prospect of losing her second husband.

I also called Preston, who suggested I sneak downstairs, find her, and kill her before she had a chance to do me in— the guy was a wizard. Then he told me he was a lot more concerned about Reuben being in my life, to forget the nonsense and go to sleep.

My thought was to shove the wooden dresser in front of the door so she couldn't enter and then stay up resting in the chair until daylight. At that point, I noticed a set of glass doors that opened to a small wood patio. When I examined the doors, I observed that they had no lock either. That's when a more creative solution came to me. I packed my bag, snuck down the interior stairwell like a thief, and then went out the back door to my car. I loaded it up with my small sack of possessions and took off with the feeling I had successfully escaped a bullet. That's how I ended up spending the night at the Fairfield "Hotel," taking an hour before retiring to search for bed bugs. I know it's not the type of story most people would disclose, but I've graduated with age to a state of peaceful shamelessness.

Back now to my meeting earlier in the day with Delia Spruce. She invited me to the fifth floor. I took the elevator, and when it opened there she was, a bleached blond girl with the effervescence of liquid spraying out of a charged bottle of soda. I estimated her age to be close to twenty-five. Contrary to Ms. Funster, whom I knew for certain had put on her face heavily as a ritual before slaughtering me at her B & B, Delia spared no makeup for a different purpose. Even with the masking cover-up, she was pimply.

Her figure was impressive, and if she calmed down long enough to get to know someone, I imagined she'd be sought after by men smart enough to know that once the hormones rejoiced over a pregnancy, the facial imperfections would revert to no more than a blemish.

I liked her and could tell she was fun. She hugged me first thing and without abashment. Also without uneasiness, I hugged her back, smiling broadly but without explanation for my elevated spirit—she had a lot going for her in terms of an infectious giddiness.

Before I knew it, she took my hand like a schoolmate and led me down the hallway. As we skipped along, two other housekeepers ran out and Delia introduced me to her mates like I was a celebrity. When we arrived at Room 531, she took me inside.

"Sit," she instructed, motioning me to take my place on the side of the bed.

She had obviously rehearsed the scene. All I needed to do was follow her directions.

"So here's how it works," she began excitedly. "Do Not Disturb on the sign outside the door means we can't enter...we come back later. Now, if it's close to checkout time, we call the supervisor. But if there is no sign on the door and the guest hasn't officially left, we are instructed to knock hard on the door and wait. If nobody comes, then we knock again. At that point, if nobody comes, then we use our key and open the door."

Delia was smiling gaily. She was eager to tell a story that was going to take more time than she had patience. Periodically, she demonstrated her sense of exhilaration by launching herself upward, visibly bending her knees below her thigh-high skirt, allowing her to thrust herself into the air.

"That's what happened when Stevie Green was here," she continued. "Okay, if we open the door we then listen to hear if by chance someone is in the bathroom. We even call out to let anyone know we're inside." She paused for a deep breath, swallowing down irrepressible excitement. "My God, this is the coolest part. When I opened the door he was standing there—he must have just come out of the shower."

"Delia, why did you think it was Stevie?"

"Hang on!" Delia shrieked. Her exclamation was so loud one of the girls in a room a couple doors down looked in to make sure she was okay. "He was really surprised. He was also embarrassed." Delia was reliving the experience, a Blu-Ray frame-by-frame reproduction in real time. "He was wearing his underwear!"

She was breathless. I figured it was a good time to give her a break. I reached for the small case I was carrying that contained the file of notes from Delia and the underwear from Stevie Green's house. I took out the latter. The second she saw them the screaming renewed.

"That's what he was wearing! They're identical!"

"Take a moment, Delia. I want you to be certain," I said calmly, hoping to stem her enthusiasm.

"No, I'd recognize them in a second. The yellow Mickey Mouse words all the way around the band." She was winded. "That's what I kept telling everyone. See, I used to read everything I could about him. I love him."

"Right, but couldn't you be mistaken? Couldn't this man have been an impersonator? I'm not disputing you," I assured her. "I simply want to be sure."

"Mr. Miller, my father is French and I speak French, German, English, and Russian. I can read articles from around the world that none of my friends can." For the first time, her presentation stilled. It was as if a cork had popped from a bottle of fine champagne and she was pouring a taste of her fermented maturity and intellect.

"Well, there was a small magazine in Germany and they interviewed him. It was the only time he ever mentioned that he loved Mickey Mouse. He even off-handedly joked that he wore Mickey Mouse underwear. That seems like more than a coincidence, don't you think?" she confidently posed to me.

"It's pretty compelling I'd say. Still, I have to consider that you're not the only person who can read German and knew about the Mickey Mouse fascination of Stevie Green," I added soberly.

"Well, let me tell you the rest. Then we'll see what you think." I noticed again her emotions frothing, the restrained Delia still not ready to take command of her passion. "As soon as I entered, he grabbed a pair of pants and in a second slipped them on, as well as a long-sleeved shirt. I stood there amazed. I told him I could come back but he didn't say a word. I stood there staring. Then when he was dressed and looking at me I asked him—"

"Asked him what?" I knew her pause was a prompt for me to query her.

"If he was Stevie Green."

"You asked him?" I remarked incredulously.

"Why wouldn't I? I wanted to hear it. It was the only

chance I'd ever have to be able to say I met the greatest man to ever live."

"He's a great artist and I'm impressed with him too, but the greatest man ever?" I voiced skeptically, mindless to why I would even address a point so absurd.

"That's my opinion," she asserted. "Anyway, he just laughed and denied it. You know what he said to me after that?"

"No idea."

"Lots of people have commented that they see a resemblance between Stevie Green and me. My name is Artanis—"

"He told you his name was Artanis?" I asked with excitement.

"He's a liar. I don't care. He just didn't want a nothing like me saying I met him," she disclosed to me, unaware of her sulky tone. "But I did touch him."

"How did that happen?"

"I told him I knew he was a liar," she stated irreverently. "He started to laugh real silly, like a baby. So I just asked if I could touch him and he said it would be fine."

"Delia, I don't know if we'll ever have living proof of it but I believe you. You touched Stevie Green all right," I assured her.

Delia's eyes glistened. Then she busted into tears, a true act of cleansing relief. Being called a prevaricator by every relative, friend, and government official you turn to for confirmation can weaken your faith in mankind—one gesture of assurance that you're not crazy can mend the pain of a thousand rebuffs.

Delia hugged me again, this time without ecstasy. She was relieved that she could now go on with her life, no longer needing to prove a point others would never believe, even if Stevie Green were to return and admit he had stayed the night at the Fairfield.

"Delia, just for curiosity, did you notice anything else unusual or that would further validate it was him?"

"I did forget to mention that when I saw the Mickey Mouse underwear I told him that I knew Stevie wore them. He just shrugged it off and said he already knew that." Delia expressed her offense with a shrug of her own. "I think that's when I called him a liar, but I'm not sure that's exactly when I said it."

"Nothing you noticed about the right wrist—his tattoo?" I asked.

"It all happened really fast. He had his clothes on in a minute. I'm not sure I can say anything except it was definitely a long-sleeved shirt."

We loitered in the room for a few minutes, her standing and me sitting back down again on the edge of the bed.

"Want to know how it ended?" she volunteered, recognizing the story needed closure.

I nodded for her to proceed, curious how it did come to a conclusion.

"I told Stevie I'd come back later to clean. He said he'd be gone in about an hour. I went into one of the vacated rooms to start straightening up. Then about ten minutes later, I glanced back down the hall and noticed the door to his room was open. When I went to check, he was already gone."

"Thanks for telling me the story, Delia. You realize that you and I may never be able to actually prove Stevie Green is alive."

"It's okay. I don't need to do anything else with it now," she said resolutely.

I stood to go, but it dawned on me I wanted her opinion on one other matter.

"Delia, why do you suspect he came here, to Topeka?"

"I've thought about that a lot, Mr. Miller. I have an idea but I would rather you discover it for yourself."

"That's not fair," I said playfully.

"Try. If you don't get it by the end of the day, call me and I'll tell you," she promised.

Sending me on a seek-and-find mission seemed a sweet way to part. Before I set out on the journey, I needed to tie up a loose end with the business office of the hotel. The clerk was accommodating and within minutes I had confirmed that F. Artanis had stayed one night in Room 531. The room had been held with a credit card under the same name but paid for in cash upon checkout.

Who the hell comes to Topeka? I must have asked myself the question a load of times before my genius mind reconciled that I had no answer. Farley? Why pay for what you can get free?

13

WHAT'S TOPEKA BEST KNOWN FOR?

AFTER I LEFT THE hotel, I drove the short distance to the city center. I could tell immediately that Topeka was not a thriving economic regional force—whatever wealth oil had brought to the area had dried up. Thus, it seemed to me as I walked casually through the downtown streets that it was a depressed community. There were people out shopping and restaurants in full operation. But everything moved in slow motion. Still, there had to be some form of commerce. The people had to eat; they had to have jobs; they had to live in homes or apartments and had to pay rent or mortgages.

I sat down in a small diner to order a cup of tea. The waitress came over to me immediately. The place was nine-tenths empty...at noon...not a good sign. While I was waiting for her to bring my drink, a thought dawned on me. Why not poke my head into several businesses, go to the local chamber of commerce, stop a few residents, and ask what Topeka is famous for? I laughed because I anticipated that using the word "famous" might guarantee failure for the survey, so I amended the question by substituting "best known for" instead.

My first subject was the waitress.

"May I ask you something?" I posed to her as she set down a steaming cup of water with a Lipton tea bag on the saucer. She said nothing but gave no sign of refusal either. "I'm visiting and I'm curious about something. What is Topeka best known for?"

She was an elderly lady with her light brown hair fastened in a bun on top of her head. Her facial skin was loose, a condition that by the end of the day I could have recommended a fix for if she had the will and means.

"Menninger's Clinic," she proudly announced.

"Ah, that's right," I responded, recalling that I had heard of Menninger's from a friend who had done an internship at a mental hospital in Reedley, California, a facility referred to as the Menninger's of The West. He'd told me it was a satellite of the facility in Topeka, which was considered one of the most, if not the most, prestigious psychiatric hospital in the world.

The answer she gave and my recollection of the facility unfolded in a fraction of a second, allowing my mind the privilege of thrusting forward with the next thought. *"Holy Moly!"* I said to myself. *"Was Stevie Green right under my nose?"*

Then it dawned on me that if that were the case, I had just figured out the game Delia wanted to play with me. *"How simple is this going to be?"* my internal dialogue went on. All I needed to do was nose around the place.

"Excuse me," I addressed the waitress. "Would you mind telling me how to get to Menninger's?"

Before answering, she looked at me with puzzlement. "You hop on the freeway, the I-35 South. Simple as that." Then she smiled. "Just over 700 miles...take you about eleven hours."

"But you just told me—"

"That's what we are best known for, but few people are aware, young man, that we lost them two ought three," she cackled.

"What? I don't understand."

"Two thousand three. Menninger's moved to Houston, over in Texas."

I sat wagging my head like an imbecile. Stevie Green did not come to Topeka to check himself into the psychiatric facility. Besides, now stopping to reason more soberly, how could he have kept it a secret all this time if he had? I decided to pursue my study further, taking off to wander around the city.

I posed my question several more times before hitting pay dirt. As soon as I did, I placed a call to Delia.

"Okay, smarty. I figured it out."

"It's useless. I've tried and they nearly arrested me." Delia's tone was demure as she disclosed the rest of her story. "They threatened to have me fired from my job if I pestered them anymore. I have my parents to look after. I have to have work. I'm sure you noticed there's not a lot to look forward to here unless Shell oil comes back to drill."

"Topeka does seem a bit tired," I agreed.

"Let me tell you something else. I've been thinking about this since you left." Her tone was saddened, but resolute. "I'm done. I don't care where he is. If he's happy then I'm happy for him. I read a lot. People can burn out, especially those in the helping professions."

"That's true," I interjected, pleasantly surprised by how bright this girl was.

"Think about millions of people needing your help. What if you ran out of steam and couldn't do it any longer—or you needed a break from it but nobody would give it to you?"

"Funny you put it like that. That seems to be the prevailing view on the subject. I think I'm soon to be done also with this potential invasion of Stevie Green's wishes," I shared with her. But I had more to say on the subject. "It seems a lot of people really had love for him. Isn't letting him go the best demonstration of adoration that a person could offer?"

"That's exactly how I feel," she retorted solemnly. "I'm glad you came to see me."

We hung up, and I focused on one additional task to complete before my work was finished. At the far northwest corner of the city was a compound with seven small buildings surrounded by several acres of space. The discreet sign on the outside gate read: Howard Medical Clinic. There were at least a hundred cars in the lot. Some were fancy vehicles with names like Maserati, Mercedes, Rolls, and Bentley, many had the license plate covered or removed.

After I became aware that the clinic existed, the whole mystery of Stevie Green fell into place like the tumblers of a safe. I was given the number of the facility by a receptionist in the doctor's office where I had stopped in while pursuing my investigation of poor Topeka. I'm sure I would have been hung up on had I not played my ace in the hole, telling the receptionist I was a representative of the band LIVE and wanted a meeting with Dr. Arnold Howard.

I waited on the line about three minutes before she came back, informing me if I came right then the doctor could see me before his next surgery. I rushed over to take advantage of the opportunity, though I knew in advance Dr. Howard only wanted to lie me out of town. Still, this was the end of my investigation as far as I was concerned. I pursued the matter solely because I didn't want to be requested by Arnie to come back to Topeka to wrap up one last lead I'd neglected to fully examine.

I was directed to press the buzzer at the gate and I'd be let in. I did as instructed and pulled into the parking lot. Before I was able to get out of the car, a young lady came streaking across the asphalt ground to intercept me. She stuck out a long, straight, right arm to shake my hand and with a militant mug introduced herself.

"I'm Brenda Adams, Dr. Howard's assistant," she brashly informed me. "He's very busy today so let's get over there quickly."

She raced back in the direction she'd initially come from. I sprinted behind, not feeling particularly welcome. She opened the door to one of the buildings and held it for me to enter.

"If you'll have a seat here," pointing to a waiting area with a sofa and several chairs, "I'll see if Dr. Howard is ready for you."

I'll begin this important chapter in the investigation of Stevie Green by acknowledging that Dr. Arnold Howard had to be a great talent in his field, a fact attested to by virtue of the massive success he enjoyed. That said I found him to be the consummate arrogant schmuck.

I'm told plastic surgeons are a breed of their own, a blend of scientist and artist. The former is known as a servant to a body of knowledge similar in complexity to most areas of medicine. The latter is a maniacal master divining beauty on imperfect human specimens that a tired god has abandoned.

Howard had come to Topeka to open his clinic because it was out of the way, and private. He had a dream of setting up an exclusive facility catering to the rich and famous around the world, a place where they could come with a guarantee of total, unmitigated discretion.

A princess in Saudi Arabia might wake up and realize her face was beginning to sag. A famous actress might suffer chronic depression owing to the fact her nose was tilted slightly left and she believed everyone saw it when she was on a set. A playboy heir might believe he'd be even more handsome without the vertical lines channeling parallel to his nose when he smiled. The daughter of a great industrialist might acknowledge how much she hated looking at herself in the mirror because her teats were too small and the nipples located too low—she'd like a little smaller ass too.

Howard knew from experience that what most of these people shared in common was the need for privacy. Many, in fact, wanted the procedure and aftermath to be so secret that in the end even they wouldn't be able to admit they had been reconstructed. It was all about psychology—mostly psychopathology—or what some more generously would call make-believe.

It can be assumed that when he sat down to consider the options, it dawned on his humble mind that even deities are imperfect and could use a good plastic man. His thinking came together in his imagination as a pyramid, although a rather unique one. At the top was Dr. Arnold Howard, the genius of reconstructing faces, tits, butts, and if requested, buttholes—though usually he handed the latter category of stinky cases to an associate. Next would come gods and goddesses, followed by the wealthy and famous. Poor people were not permitted, unless they won lotteries. He estimated he'd have an inexhaustible stream of patients lining up to come to his clinic. It worked. The buildings and grounds were testimony to his vision.

When I was informed that he was ready to receive me, I was escorted down a short hall to his office. It was well suited for an emperor. In fact, most of the jabbering just presented about Howard comes from my first impression as I walked into his inner kingdom. If there was any doubt about who was more important, the king seeking salvation or the guy with the scalpel, it was dispelled the moment one sat down opposite Dr. Howard.

The space was elegant. Every piece of furniture and each item of decoration, looked to be a rare antique or collector's item. I'm certain the designer of his office spent the first five million on the furniture and then the real purchasing began.

I could tell the moment I set eyes on him that he viewed me as a rat and wanted nothing more than to set off a trap, snap my neck, and have his lovely sergeant toss me in the trash.

"Just have a few minutes, Mr...." he glanced at a note on his desk, "Miller. What can I do for you?" his voice trailed off, but not before conveying that he was nettled having to allocate precious time to a pest.

I could tell even while he was sitting—he never stood when I came in—that he was about my height with an average build. His hair was reddish-brown, thick and full, medium in length, wavy and combed straight back. He was younger than I expected, in his early forties. All the while he talked with me, he shuffled papers on his desk, feigning that he was only half-attending to our conversation.

"As I told your office, I'm working for LIVE, the band that Stevie Green started. I'm sure you know them."

"Sure. So what does this have to do with me?"

"I think Stevie Green is alive," I casually informed him.

I could see he hadn't planned to spend enough time with me to lose patience. He knew we were about to engage in a cat-and-mouse game.

"I don't mean to be rude, but Miller, you're way off track if you think I know about this man."

"Then why did you even agree to see me?"

I understood that my question would provoke him— exactly my intent. The truth is I wasn't sure why he met with me, except perhaps curiosity regarding how I came as far as I did in terms of finding Green. What I knew for certain was that it was going to be a short interview and I needed to shoot my load quickly.

His voice raised a notch but he tried to conceal it with a smirk. "The band is famous, with or without Mr. Green. My business is dealing with famous people, and frankly, I agreed to meet you to preclude any offense it might bring to your employers."

"Stevie Green left Albuquerque after his last concert. Do you know what happened to him after that?" I posed to him.

"How would I? Seems that's what the whole world is trying to determine," Howard said innocently.

"Two days later, he ended up in Topeka," I asserted while staring him straight in the face. "I know this for a fact. He had a rental car that he dropped off here. Now you tell me, Dr. Howard, because I may have missed something. What the hell would a man like Stevie Green come to Topeka for?"

Howard looked at me with puzzlement, attempting to make it appear as if we were sharing the same confusion.

"I don't think there's anything here for him. Seems from what I know about the star that he had about everything a man could wish for," Howard related.

"I've researched The Howard Medical Clinic. Want to know what I found out?" I lobbed his way.

Howard was more annoyed now than when I first walked in. I could tell my time was running short.

"I don't really care what you found out," Howard answered sharply.

"Most everyone who comes here has about anything a person could imagine, except one thing, right doctor?"

"What one thing is that?"

"Happiness," I informed him.

"I'll admit most of them are dissatisfied about something."

The longer he talked without throwing me out, the more certain I was that Stevie Green had come under his knife. I knew he'd never openly admit it, but I was going to absolutely confirm to Arnie and the band that Stevie was alive, had assumed a new identity, looked like a different person, and didn't want to be found—the rest would be up to them.

"Some are dissatisfied about their life, period," I shot at him. "They want a new identity and that's your expertise. You re-birthed Stevie Green, didn't you?" I passed my question to him as if offering a stick of gum from a pack.

"We're done, Miller." Howard was now standing and pressing a button on the desk. "Dream your little dreams. We all have them."

In a moment, the same woman who straight-armed me in the parking lot came in. In a matter of minutes, I was in my car. She spied me as I left the property.

It was still early, and I had the remainder of the afternoon free before having to check in for the bed and breakfast experience I've already described. My heart was pumping a bit harder and faster than normal. I can only assume that I had been assertive with Howard because I hated being lied to, though I knew he had no choice. His business was predicated on absolute non-disclosure regarding the treatment of any patient, and a single violation could be irreparably damaging to his reputation.

It was also, I'll admit, that I plainly didn't like him. My ego couldn't compete in his world. It's not that I felt inferior. It was that it galled me how he perceived himself as superior to the rest of mankind and in a pompous manner few would have the nerve to own. I could have laughed, knowing that the beauty of humanity is that every dot along the spectrum of types has to be filled. But I'm human like the next guy—there are certain dots that make the hairs on my skin stand like daggers.

I parked about two blocks from the Howard compound and walked back to a place where I could see the front gate but not be observed. My curiosity, my perennial trouble-maker, was squawking for attention. Was it possible one of his staff disagreed with what they were doing, was about to quit, and didn't care to maintain the code of privacy? Was it possible they might appreciate a couple hundred bucks in exchange for confirming that Stevie Green had been a patient?

"Why not try?" I dared myself.

So I waited. After about half an hour, a woman wearing a nurse's outfit went out through a small gate. She must have been on break because she was walking rapidly. I followed her into a gift shop and noticed her looking at birthday cards. I picked a couple, reading and replacing them. When I came across one that said, "I HATE BIRTHDAYS: GO CELEBRATE WITHOUT ME," I started to laugh, offering me the opening to talk to her.

"Take a look at this one," I said, still chuckling as I handed it to her.

"I think I'll get it," she said in a quirky manner. "It's for my husband. He's the only person I know who would appreciate it...besides you."

"Birthdays do lose their appeal as you get older, don't they?" I knew I was on safe turf because she couldn't have been over thirty.

"You can say that again."

"You from Topeka?" I asked.

"You're not?"

"Passing through on business. Not much here, is there?"

"Not really much left after the big oil boys packed up... 'cept where I work."

"What do you do?"

"I'm a nurse at a place called The Howard Medical Clinic."

"Never heard of it. What do they do?" I asked innocuously.

"The doctor is a famous plastic surgeon," she said proudly.

I decided to play into what I read as a boast.

"Wait...Howard Medical...I think I've read about it," I mentioned matter-of-factly. Then I pondered before proceeding. "That's the place where all the stars and dignitaries come to—"

"You got it. Boobs and butts, noses, eyes and cheeks, lifts and pulls...you name it. You can leave as an unrecognizable person if you want."

"I've heard that too. It's crazy I know, but..." I purposefully stopped myself, hoping she'd take the bait and urge me to complete the thought.

"Nothing is crazy where I work, except most of the patients. But what were you going to say?"

"I think I read it in a magazine or newspaper," I said coolly. "You know, there's all these nutty stories about this singer Stevie Green, and it said he had come to this clinic so he could disappear."

I laughed it off as a good conversation piece, as well as an insane idea. I could see her attitude change abruptly, like a riot policeman raising a defensive shield to take the charge of a rowdy crowd.

"We can't discuss any particular patient," she commented sternly.

"God no, I can imagine," I assured her. "Place like that has a reputation."

"That's the only thing I don't like about the job. I worry if one of us spilled the beans about a case like a Stevie Green...and I'm not saying he was a patient, but since you mentioned it, that's the type of person we see...anyway, Dr. Howard is a strict man. We're warned about what we can and cannot say. We make a lot of money because of that issue and we have great retirement plans that we'd lose if we ever violated the code."

"I don't know who you are and as far as I'm concerned we never talked," I laughed. "Hey, look. Here's another of the same card. We can both get it."

"That'll work."

"Nice talking to you, Ms....don't tell me," I quipped as I walked off.

Stevie Green had been a patient at The Howard Medical Clinic. She might as well have told me. Howard might as well have told me too. The cat was out of the bag. What a vast world Stevie Green had opened for himself within which to build a new identity. Why, where, what—after all this, I'd be a liar to say I hadn't any interest in answers, but I also knew there would never be any. My heart had joined with other fans like Delia, Cooley, and Reuben wishing him well.

The next morning, I left Topeka. I doubted I would be returning to be remodeled by Dr. Howard, though my life had taken so many unexpected twists and turns in the past couple of years that I couldn't dismiss anything. I did know that I was puffing my chest, admiring my skills as a blooming investigator. I liked it.

I needed to call Arnie to inform him about my trip but I wasn't in the mood. I decided to leave it for a later date. I wondered how much Jay Weiner knew but decided that might not be any of my business. The investigative work into the tribal finances was now in first place on my task list. I knew when I arrived home that I would have to address it, but frankly I wasn't looking forward to that job any more than when I first engaged the Stevie Green matter.

At least it was still springtime. With love blossoming right under my nose, it was shaping up to be a dandy summer—more fanciful than I could have dreamed.

14

SURPRISE, SURPRISE

WHEN I ARRIVED HOME, Preeti, Josea, and Souche were playing with Henry Higgins in the front yard. It was adorable—Souche toddling like a leader with the pisher following.

When they saw me, I was greeted the way every man yearns, with lots of endearments. I was immediately parked on a lounge chair and handed Henry. I'm not an expert on dogs, but after having a baby I picked up on the basics quickly. I held the little guy up in the air and watched his short tail wag and his two-inch tongue try to reach half a foot to lick my face. Then, I put him in my lap to pet him and he loved it, showing his appreciation by peeing on my pants. To my amazement, I was informed that the white patch on his buttocks was not a diaper.

It was a good laugh and truthfully I was excited about having this new friend with us. He was cute, a skinny guy with patches of black, grey, and white. Josea informed me that Henry is called a blue roan, but even the genius couldn't explain why he would be referred to as "blue" when there wasn't a hair of that color on his body.

I was hoping, however, that Josea's brain would yield benefits for me in another endeavor. On the plane coming home, I went over the material Len Cloud had passed to me in his workshop. Since Josea had planned and coordinated special commando operations in Israel, I assumed she could help me with the acquisition of data and then the analysis of the information as I began looking into the tribal finances. She had informed me that if there was anything she could help me with she would be available, so I took it upon myself to invite her assistance without discussing it with Len.

What I had learned going through the packet my father-in-law had given me was that the entire finances of the tribe were placed in a trust entitled, *Mescalero Trust*, and handled through Alamogordo Federal Bank. Funds were funneled into the account from a number of enterprises operated by the tribe. They were all under the umbrella of the trust. After normal business operations, an allocation was made from the profit pool to the members. Some earnings were retained for investment and expansion. Those decisions were made on a tribal basis but with responsibility fell primarily on the ten council members. There was a network of existing contracts, mostly based on pledges from projects in operation at the time and there were also legal agreements funded directly from retained earnings for entities under development. At the time I was brought into the investigation, most of the financial affairs were under the categories of forest, natural gas, construction, and maintenance.

It all appeared fairly routine to my untrained accounting mind. Even Josea agreed after reviewing the file, that on the surface everything seemed sensible, organized, and transparent. However, if Len was suggesting corruption, it had to be occurring on a deeper level. We couldn't imagine there were bank records to show Platta withdrawing millions of dollars for his personal use.

What we did reason was that the most likely opportunity for mischief would be with respect to awarding some of the pricier contracts. We had access to the names of the companies operating under agreement in the various projects, but we did not have those files, including the details of how the contracts were bid and awarded. I called Len. He told me he had all the information we needed. In fact, he had kept records going back several years and had them all at his place in "cartons."

The word conjured up the recollection of the walls of Weiner's office. I wasn't looking forward to the task but at least this time I'd have help. When I did drive over to his house to get the materials, I was relieved that what I wanted was contained in only four rather large boxes. I loaded them into my car.

"Don't do a thing with what you uncover until you talk with me first," he said firmly. "Platta can be a mean son-of-a-bitch and I don't want to lose a second son-in-law."

Over the course of the next couple days, Josea and I—often with Henry supervising by foot-printing the documents he thought most important—outlined the material and determined that we needed to look into about fourteen companies that had been or were presently working under contract and then triple that many that had bid on the same opportunities. As we went through the material, looking for procedural irregularities, we concluded that all the contracts were orderly and fairly awarded; the lowest bidder won. The details of what work was to be done for what price was included, but since each of the bidding companies had the same information there was no need to analyze the cost per se.

That was what we considered the first phase in the process. Next, we wanted to examine more details about the companies bidding for the work. Josea raised the question of whether or not there might be favoritism whereby the owners of one company or another were made aware of the competing bids. If so, they would be able to undercut them, making profits later by reducing costs through shoddy workmanship, cheap materials, or by not completing the work as contracted—and then renegotiating additional allocations to do so. She also brought up "tie-ins" or "rigged bidding" whereby the companies competing against one another were in concert, such that they all agreed to come in with high bids, knowing that the one awarded the contract would make a bundle and be able to kick back profits to their cohorts. I started doubting I was going to need Farley after all.

Our plan was to drive to Albuquerque the following day and conduct research on the 40 or more companies that were on the list. We called both the New Mexico Public Regulation Commission and New Mexico Office of Secretary of State. Between the two, they would have registration information for all of the corporations, partnerships, and private companies operating in the state.

Since we planned to leave about ten that morning, I woke up early. As I lay in bed, I realized I needed a mental break. A walk in the woods for an hour I figured would be the perfect remedy to clear my mind. I thought of taking Henry, but the little man wasn't ready for long traipses into the backcountry. I ate a light breakfast and took off.

I had been gone about twenty minutes before I stopped to rest on a large boulder with a jagged face that jetted upward. Standing on the ledge of the boulder, I could scan the area a full one hundred and eighty degrees from my left to right. I picked this exact point because it looked out across to a waterfall about forty feet high.

I loved watching the water freefall into a small pool before lazily wandering along a narrow stream that disappeared under the remains of a fallen oak. It always made me think that in fifty or a hundred years this miracle of nature would still be flowing majestically downward, long after I passed my last breath. Realizing that so many of the objects in nature were superior to me had the effect of relaxing the sense of responsibility I now lugged, similar to Atlas carrying the globe on his shoulders.

I was wearing a tan lightweight top and faded jeans of a similar color. My arms were outstretched horizontally, both resting on a slit in the rock likely representing an era millions of years in the past. My stillness and the blending of my clothing with the earthy background was such that if a hunter were passing he might not have noticed me.

It turned out it wasn't a human that interloped on my position, but instead a massive elk. Though it's classified in the deer family, I'm convinced that any person seeing this animal in the wild could never mistake it for a sweet little doe we might find in a meadow. This fellow was gigantic. His antlers were in full bloom, gorgeous branches shooting upward in a display of vanity and authority.

He rounded the path I had been on, but from the opposite direction. As he turned to negotiate the boulder I was standing on, he stopped, sensing no doubt my presence through scent. His right antler was inches from my face. As he rotated his giant head to the right, he eyed me. I had been told what to do if by chance I ever encountered one of these beasts, but the physical proximity of the two of us was such that I doubted those giving the advice had ever experienced my vulnerable position. Still, I refrained from moving and I bribed instinct with a prayer to avoid making eye contact—I had never been so instructed, but I stopped breathing as well.

All he had to do was move forward a foot and he would have impaled me as the next coming of Christ, trotting off with me hanging from his two treelike appendages until he realized that I was blocking his view, at which time he would toss me ragtag in the brushes. Fortunately, what he did instead was take a deep sniff before proceeding on his way. *Phew, phew, phew.*

When I calmed down, I did what most people do after an experience of this sort, look for the deeper meaning. Was there some reason he was there at that moment? I was certain that my physical therapist hadn't sent him, but if she was responsible, it was probably to get me to see what she had been harping on for months.

I typically went twice a week for sessions. I had imperfectly healed fractures and dislocations from prior trauma in Israel—the therapy helped. Periodically, she'd refer to a plastic skeleton she kept in the corner of the room, pointing out joints, demonstrating how the bones are connected, and then instructing me regarding the manner in which the parts move as the body bends and stretches.

For some reason, she never mentioned the word balance, but in an instant—while the images of my elk buddy were fresh—I realized that symmetry was everything I had been working toward. The skeleton of the human body is heavy and inclined over time, due to gravity, wear and tear on tendons, ligaments, and muscles groups, and of course laziness and poor posture, to compress. Older people commonly shrink.

That elk must have had at least a hundred pounds of antler on his head, and certainly with that weight we'd expect him to be suffering at a minimum from chronic cervical pain. But there was no indication he did. The explanation for his success was evident as I envisioned the positioning of his head—the weight was kept so perfectly distributed that it had no effect.

I straightened my body and tried to feel that precise allocation of weight, starting at the heels and then rising through the back of the thighs, up the rear spine and into the dorsal ribs, all the way to the upper back, neck and frontward to the sternum. Believing for an instant that I had it, I was about to scramble home as quickly as I could. But then I remembered my new therapeutic mentor was traveling along the road leading the same direction I intended to go; I wasn't ready for a second lesson so soon. I waited several minutes before assuming it was safe to leave. It wouldn't be long before I'd confront my second surprise of the morning, a whopper.

There was a clearing about a hundred yards from where my near fatal encounter with the elk took place. I cut across it knowing it was a shortcut, because at the other end the path picked up again. I proceeded about five minutes before coming to a grassy knoll on my right. I had just exited a cluster of tightly knotted aspen trees when I caught out of the corner of my eye what I thought were two humans lying next to one another. Not wanting to startle them, I pulled back a few feet behind the trees to deliberate what to do next.

I decided I could navigate left through the forest and get back on the path further along. If I were quiet I wouldn't disturb what I assumed were two young lovers. I took only a step or two before I was permitted a full view. As I tiptoed between the thicker cover of the trees, I couldn't help but peek to the right…it was Josea; I was sure of it. She was passionately kissing a man lying beneath her, but I couldn't make out the identity of the figure. Not wanting to risk being caught spying, I walked softly deeper into the woods and in a few steps lost sight of them.

Josea had only been in Kuruk a few days and had spent a good deal of time at our home. Sure, I had been away for short periods and didn't know what she had done with her time, but since arriving in Mescalero I hadn't noticed anything unusual. I had to find out whom she was with. The most obvious consideration was Reuben, who I moved immediately into first position.

Since it was only an hour until we were due to leave,

and I knew Josea was always prompt, I was certain she'd be returning shortly along the same trail. I know it was a rotten trick, but I positioned myself so I could not be detected while viewing the direction from which I knew she had to approach. I would have my answer in due time—she'd either come back with her secret lover or, in order to avoid suspicion, separate before getting back to our house. In the event of the latter, he'd lag behind her by several minutes.

I called it perfectly. Josea came into view in fifteen minutes. She was wearing loose fitting cotton blue-and-white check pants with a white top. On her head was a pale yellow bonnet. Her stride was perky, a half-skip cadence. I could see a smile on her face that only a person in sneaky love would wear.

I saw her proceed onto our front yard. I waited. Within minutes, I noticed a gangling male moving through the woods, sauntering gaily. But instead of heading to my house, he took a turn onto a back road that wrapped around a mile before leading to...Kuruk. I was correct. It was Reuben.

Reuben?

Even knowing there was no other logical conclusion, I still couldn't believe my eyes. What had happened? I knew there was fire when they first saw each other but Josea had denied it. Reuben had confided in me essentially that he'd never had a woman and I knew Josea was still damned by her virginity. What a miracle! I couldn't wait to get home and tell Preeti.

Actually, Josea's choice of man threw me into a bit of a quandary. My closest friend, a fellow known to have excellent judgment about his fellow man's character, had repeatedly warned me about not knowing who Reuben was as a person. A woman I adored as a friend and respected immensely was choosing intimacy with that same man. Sadly, I reasoned one had to be wrong. The trouble is that sometimes reason is a fool's pal.

I went through the back door a few minutes after Josea went in. Then, I quickly dressed for our trip. I had only a brief time to tell my wife what I had witnessed. While the disclosure took less than a minute, it took twenty to calm her down. I had to convince her that she couldn't under any circumstance let it be known she was aware of the affair.

During the drive to Albuquerque, I let Josea do most of the talking, wondering if she might bring up the subject. I even joked that I was still working on getting her the right man. She smiled dismissively, as if she appreciated the thought but had no expectation that I'd succeed.

We went first to the Office of Secretary of State. The tan two-story building with white trim had three gold-rimmed glass doors and we proceeded through the center one directly to the Recorder's Office. I assigned myself to examine a lumber contract awarded to Hawk Industries and sent Josea off to inspect the records for a construction job at The Inn, won by Sure Builders.

The records showed that Hawk Industries incorporated in 1984. The president and key stockholder was Martin Lattimer. Ralph Puente, Hank Reeves, and Bob Lake were listed as the principals and officers. The company was in the business of selling forest products. They bought up the rights to acreage and then processed the trees into construction boards, veneers, moldings, doors, and window encasements. The final products were then sold off to retailers.

In this case, there was a grove of 1,500 acres in the northeastern corner of the reservation composed mostly of ponderosa pine and quaking aspen. The contract outlined the removal of the existing growth and replanting of the area with a new crop of similar variety. The winning bid had been for $286,000.

However, this was not a typical we-pay-you-to-do-a-job contract. The tribe was paying nothing. The $286,000 was what Hawk was paying the tribe for the rights to the natural forest materials, to do what they pleased with it as long as the money bid went into the tribe's trust.

The bidding rules were consistent insofar as there always had to be four competitive filings for each contract. If more companies vied for the business, the council usually chose which of the four offers they would entertain based on reputation and experience. In this case, the other three companies were Gold Products, Heaven Land Industries, and Earth, Inc. Their prices to the tribe came in much lower—$179,000, $184,000, and $163,000 respectively—it was logical that Hawk would win out, bringing thousands of additional dollars into the coffers of the Mescalero tribe.

My next task was to check on the principals for the other three companies. I looked up each and made a list of the names. I noticed that Gold Products hadn't been incorporated until a year before the contract was posted. They listed their officers as Hank Reeves, Jesse Wilcox, Bob Lake, and Dean Brightwater.

Heaven Land was not incorporated, but had been registered as a limited partnership, also just a year before the announcement. The general partner was Ralph Puente and the limited partners, a total of ten, included both Bob Lake of Hawk and Jesse Wilcox of Gold.

Lastly, Earth, Inc. incorporated in 1996. Names associated with it were Stan Fastow, the president and main stockholder, Aaron Sky, Dean Brightwater, and Hank Reeves.

I sat and looked at the graph I had jotted down as I contemplated what I had learned about each of the companies. I wasn't sure what to do with what I had uncovered, nor what to make of it, except I knew it stunk. Who were these people that were obviously tied into one another in a crooked alliance?

It took me hours to uncover a frightful determination. I'll spare all the gory details. Most important is that these were names of individuals who had been bidding on jobs for the tribe for the past ten years. They had incorporated numerous entities during that period for the sole purpose of creating a crooked bidding system.

Where the big profits were going in the end I didn't know... yet. However, it was obvious that Len Cloud's aspersions were not vacuous. It crossed my mind at the time that some of these names might not even refer to real people but instead represented dummy names being used to fill in titles.

I would soon discover that my suspicions were far from absurd. A few of the names of people involved were shells to the extent that they knew nothing about forestry and worked in totally different industries. They had no idea they were listed as officers for these bogus companies that were registered and de-registered as casually as one butters a piece of toast. There were also a number of names listed on various entities that would actually prove me frightfully accurate, in that they represented fictitious identities.

I was leaning back in my chair trying to decide what my next step would be when Josea walked up. She was wearing a smug grin. Josea sat down and laughed.

"You're going to love this."

"Josea, you're going to love what I found too," I countered.

She then presented a pattern of bidding for construction contracts nearly identical to what I had found pertaining to forest products—many of the names were duplicated.

How much money could be involved? We both wondered what the answer was going to be to that question but a cursory calculation indicated that it had to be in the several-million-dollar range that had passed hands one way or another illegally during the past decade—just from the few transactions we had uncovered thus far.

I could see the numbers dancing in her mind and her curiosity peaking as the figure grew in size. Josea, who had more contacts in more fields than anyone I knew, couldn't resist calling a friend to see if our assessment might be close. This man referred her to one of his friends who happened to be working at Weyerhaeuser, a giant forest product company. She discussed the details of the contract for $286,000 awarded to Hawk; off the top of his head he calculated the amount of lumber that would be realized and "conservatively" estimated the deal was worth at least a million dollars—we had likely grossly underestimated the scope of fraud committed by these men.

None of this, of course, implicated Platta more than any of the other council members, including Len Cloud. Nor did it rule out responsibility of the entire tribe for not doing due diligence by exploring the history of the bidding companies— the whole damn tribe may have been fools, but my assessment from knowing these people said that was improbable. Regardless of what, if any, knowledge of the criminal activity the tribe had, the schemes used against them were worthy of prosecution.

This was an area where legal jurisdiction would be questionable. Typically, a matter of this sort would be handled internally through the tribal legal system. However, because of the prevalence of the problem and the non-Indian participation, the FBI would have to step in to investigate and then have the State of New Mexico prosecute the guilty parties. Poor Len Cloud. Poor Gabe Kershaw. The latter was going to be a busy man.

The next question was what to do with what we had uncovered. As we drove home, we addressed the point.

"Are you going to tell Mr. Cloud about this when we get back?" Josea asked me.

"There's no rush, is there Josea? This has been going on for years," I proclaimed. I continued by informing her about what had happened at the last council meeting and the building tension regarding the upcoming Puberty Ceremony. She agreed it would be best to wait until after the July Fourth festivities. In the meantime, we would see what else we could uncover on our own in order to seal the proof necessary to bring the guilty parties to justice.

"Mr. Cloud is convinced this Platta is dirty, right?" Josea said, seeking clarification.

"That's what he thinks, but he never told me why or gave me any evidence to support it."

"He may hate the guy, but that's not sufficient to charge him with a crime," Josea reminded both of us.

"That's what I was thinking. My father-in-law and his buddy Walter appear the most dogmatic about tradition. Platta, I can tell you, is the furthest from their attitude of any of the tribe members," I explained based on what I had observed. "It wouldn't be a stretch, given my father-in-law's disdain for Platta, to cloud...a little pun there," I chuckled, "his impression of the man and start to believe he is responsible for acts outside of his authority."

"Let's undress Platta, just in case," Josea bluntly suggested. "I like your father-in-law so I'm giving him the benefit of the doubt until proven otherwise."

"Okay then. We keep this hushed until after we've finished our work and the ceremony has passed," I confirmed. "I guess we're back in business," I joked.

Josea liked the humor, shaking her head and rubbing her hands through her hair. "This is puppy play for us. Simple crime. Nobody gets killed but a few people go to jail—big whoop," she giggled.

"Let's hope nobody gets killed. Len indicated that Platta's a tough character," I enlightened her.

"Huh," she answered cockily. "We know what bad ass characters are like."

"Josea, don't be too cavalier," I warned her. "I want to be around for my wife and little girl."

"I want to get laid," she howled.

"For that we'll have to get you a lover first," I responded, testing to see if her reaction might bring about an admission.

"What if I told you I had one?"

"I'd be a very happy man. Go on, give me something to dance about," I dared her.

"Not yet," she playfully responded. "We have work to take care of first."

It was quiet for a few minutes, the landscape of miles of desert sand tranquilizing our senses. I did wonder why I still hadn't called Arnie and LIVE to inform them about Topeka— I wondered and wondered, but decided nothing. Procrastinating? I wasn't sure. I just wasn't ready to place the call.

I always loved the ride heading out of the desert floor and climbing to higher elevations. This afternoon, I decided to take Highway 380 and then jackknife back on the 70 into Mescalero. I liked to vary the drive, and both ways were about equal in time and distance.

We had just passed the town of Capitan. Off to the left, the prize of the Guadalupe Mountains, Capitan Peak—over 10,000 feet high—had robed herself in a stunning orange dress with varying shades of red and yellow patterning the fringes, the design flowing magically as the sun played peek-a-boo with darkening grey clouds eager to ruin the mistress's party by drenching her gown. The colossal stood atop a massive pyramid-shaped rock foundation and looked out over her domain. Miles of flat red dirt spread out as a fiery ocean protecting this island pearl. Far in her distant view was a highway where she could spy tiny antlike vehicles thrusting themselves like impulses traveling along a nerve.

It was I, along with Josea, in one of those teeny specks of metal. I felt small in the eye of what I considered a giant goddess rising out of the earth's belly. It helped put in perspective that all of the important business of tribal corruption and missing persons could be blown to dust by Ms. Capitan clearing her throat: it was a sobering thought to take home with me. I'm sure I would have been able to sustain it for at least fifteen seconds had I not been passed in rapid succession by first a procession of three police vehicles with activated sirens and a moment later by a longer column of five similar cars and two vans.

Josea gave me one of those what-the-hell-is-going-on looks. I prepared her that we were likely heading into a nasty road collision involving several trucks and cars. I'd seen them a couple of times and they were no party, especially when one of the locals had been drinking and then recklessly declared war on the twisting mountain roads, crapping out and taking several other innocent people along for the ride.

I was wrong. We drove uninterrupted to Hondo where we took a sharp turn west. When we reached Ruidoso I swallowed. It was only ten or twelve miles to Mescalero and there was not much in between. I was getting scared. Call it instinct.

Call it visceral fear. My family was in the locale where too many police vehicles had likely been summoned. That was not a good feeling.

It also didn't settle with me when a few miles past Ruidoso, I saw a roadblock stopping cars from leaving Mescalero. There were more state troopers than I imagined worked for the State of New Mexico—most must have come up from Alamogordo.

Sorry, but I felt like wetting my pants—I had good cause to want to do so.

15

ONE PLUS TWO IS THREE

I HAD FORGOTTEN TO bring my cell phone and Josea's had run out of juice. As a result I was inclined to drive faster to get home, and I would have had the roads not been jammed with law enforcement personnel. When I did finally enter Mescalero, I knew it was very bad. It was worse than very bad, which is tragedy. Off to the side of the road were clusters of people, some I knew by name and others only by sight. I could tell by the hand movements and facial expressions that they were frantic. Some I noticed were streaming tears of lordly supplication.

Josea looked at me but said nothing. I hit the side road leading to my house and floored it, screeching up to an empty home except for Sir Henry poised in the pantry, heedlessly wagging his tail. I stormed through the rest of my domain and found everything was in order. Then it dawned on me. It was Wednesday, one of the days Preeti went to Kuruk to tend to the garden.

It was only a few minutes away. Instead of calling, I jammed the accelerator to the floor and made my way to the restaurant. As I pulled into the lot, I witnessed, along with several other people, my weeping wife and a mimicking baby. I jumped out of the car. I wanted to touch them to be sure they were not illusory figures. Preeti had already gathered up Souche and was on her way to intercept me.

"What happened?" I yelled.

Preeti couldn't talk, moving her mouth and forming words, but without making sound.

"Is your dad okay?" I shouted. "Just nod your head if you can't talk," I added, almost absurdly.

My words must have struck a chord of humor.

"He's fine," she said, simultaneously bobbing as instructed. "We're all fine here."

Then she burst out crying again.

"It's unfair. We're being punished," she managed to groan through the tears. "What did we do?" Then she screeched beseechingly. "Where is White Painted Woman? Where is Jivin? Somebody killed the Shash and Ortega girls. They were just starting their lives, just like Ila."

There were so many sirens off in the distance that it was impossible to determine where they were all coming from. Replicating my speeding car performance, within minutes Len Cloud pulled into the parking lot. He stopped his van next to mine, only a few feet from where we stood. In the front seat next to him was a young girl I recognized, but whose name I couldn't recall.

Len got out of the car and went up to Preeti. He wasn't a demonstrative man, but he hugged his daughter and pulled her head to his shoulder, holding her there. Then he came over to me and embraced me, a first.

"Shitaa, why is Leila with you?" referring to the preteen looking girl still sitting in the vehicle.

"When I heard about the murders I went to get her," Len offered.

Preeti was perplexed by his action, so confused she confronted him on the spot.

"Father, that's Oscar Moon's daughter?" Then she spoke quietly so as to be sure Leila couldn't hear through the closed window. "He's one of Platta's puppets on the board. You're always saying how much you disrespect him. Why would you go to his house?" Then she paused to further contemplate the peculiar situation. "They're all the way up north, the other side of town from you."

Len's face rarely changed form. If there was any visible alteration owing to Preeti's questions, it was a slight tautening of his features.

"I've acted as the spirits spoke to me."

I noticed that as Len responded, he planted his feet almost defiantly on the ground to proclaim the rationality of his action.

"That spirit must have known something nobody else did," Preeti answered, more bemused now than when she began her interrogation.

"Death is a bird of prey now. We must starve his will," Len declared. He often spoke in riddles or with oblique references intentionally leaving ambiguity for a person to dwell on.

He stretched his arms as far as he could horizontally, reaching to eternity. Then he turned side-to-side, looked behind as he rotated his torso almost three hundred sixty degrees. When he was finished, he faced us.

"This is where our people come from. We have been brought famine, war, the White Man, fire, thunder, and rain. All we have to live for is the survival of our People." He stood with his big chest rising like the elk's antlers, confident that with balance he could never be knocked off his pins. "Murder will not end our people."

"I know it won't, Shitaa," Preeti said as she grabbed him by the hand. "I still don't understand what would have told you to go to the Moon house."

Preeti noticed Leila still in the car and motioned her to come out.

"I'm glad you're okay, Leila," Preeti said kindly.

The girl smiled shyly.

"Were you home alone?" Preeti asked.

"My father and mother were both at work, but Mr. Cloud called them when he got to my house."

"We'll take you back after they get home," Preeti offered. She took the girl by the arm. "Come with me. I'll get you something to eat."

The girl had followed Preeti for only a few steps when a figure appeared from near the garden, approaching from the woods behind Kuruk. I couldn't make out who it was at first, but within a second Josea, realizing it was Reuben, spontaneously called out his name. As she did, she seemed to catch herself in an unconscious divulgence, flashing a quick look in my direction. She knew I had picked up on her excitement.

Reuben had been running. He was wearing a sweatshirt and long pants. He climbed over a low wood railing. As he spotted us congregated in the lot, he trotted over.

"What's going on?" he inquired. "I'm hearing sirens all over the place."

"Where were you?" Preeti called out.

"I was out hiking most of the day and I decided to run the last bit," he responded casually.

"With a sweatshirt in this weather?" I admonished, talking down to him like a child.

"Things change," breezed out Reuben's smiling lips. "I want to get into better condition—just general health."

This feeble figure was out exercising, wearing a sweatshirt while it was still warm out—he looked ridiculous to me. Still, I regretted speaking as I did to him, especially now that I knew he and Josea were romantic.

As always, he took no offense. That was one thing about Reuben. He could sag under the force of a self-invented depression but let insults and other petty affronts pass his ego as indifferently as the U. S. Government creates debt. I did sneak a peek at Josea as Reuben spoke, but she planted her eyes downward—she had revealed too much already and wasn't about to satisfy any further curiosity on my part.

It was obvious that Reuben had no idea what had taken place. Preeti broke the short silence, hopelessly calling out to nobody in particular, "What are we going to do?"

I told Reuben what had happened; he never said a word. He turned around and walked straight to Kuruk and then to his room—I suspected it was going to be a slow night at the restaurant anyway.

Len received a call from Leila's father and left to take her home. We went inside the restaurant to figure out what to do next. None of us felt like talking. We knew we were going to have to attend a double funeral in a few days. But worse, we now wondered how many more deaths might occur before the monster was apprehended.

One thing was for sure, Len Cloud was wrong. The killer was not a vagrant, the winds had not puffed away the evil spirit, and the killer would need to be caught in Mescalero. It was time to try and talk with my father-in-law, a discussion I told Kershaw I would have days prior.

Kershaw was right. He needed cooperation from all the members of the tribe. If one murder inspired the agent to the degree it had, three would supercharge the man. The people of Mescalero had to turn for protection to a force greater than what the tribe or Len Cloud could provide.

Preeti remained fixated on her father's strange behavior, in going to get the Moon girl. My wife was convinced that no divine light had guided Len to Leila's home.

We stayed at Kuruk for some time that evening. Lots of tourists visiting at The Inn were not deterred by murder and showed up for a meal at Kuruk before getting slaughtered at the gambling tables at The Inn of The Mountain Gods. It was about seven when we ate. Before leaving, I went into the kitchen to offer an unneeded apology to Reuben for my disrespect. I noticed his right hand was wrapped.

"Reuben, I really feel badly for the way I talked to you."

"Stop treating yourself like you should be a saint," he admonished. "Give yourself license to be human, Zach," he said in the kindest manner.

"I didn't think it was—"

"If you're asking me to forgive you, forget it." He laid his words down like a legal verdict.

"Why won't you?" I chuckled.

"Because I would then be validating that you did something wrong." He looked at me tenderly. "Screw it. You like me. I know that. And you've been there for me when I needed you. That's what counts most."

"Thanks, Reuben."

"No! Thank you, Zach!" His right wrist flicked a pan for one of the chefs, the stir-fry inside flying upward a foot before landing unmolested into the hot skillet. He noticed me watching him. "It's all practice, like being a juggler."

"What happened to your hand?" I assumed he had burned it in the kitchen, and I was going to offer to look at it.

"Like I told Zuma," pointing to one of his assistants, "I sprained it today when I was out hiking; I fell."

"Sorry."

"What's going on here in Mescalero?" Reuben asked dolefully. "Do they have any idea who might have done this?"

"So far, I believe they're making little progress. Things are going to heat up now, though."

"I came here because I thought it would be good for me. I hope I'm not bad luck," Reuben said with signs of the same pitiful tone reminiscent of his prior depressive episode. His grief of still unknown origin hadn't abated entirely, but it had eased. I assumed that the sprouting affair with Josea might have sent the sickly mood on a permanent holiday. Now I feared that because of these latest murders, his despondency would snatch center stage again.

"There, you did nothing wrong yet you're blaming yourself. Just a minute ago you chastised me for doing the same," I conveyed to highlight the contradiction.

"If I could follow my own advice...I'd probably be the only perfect person left on earth. We all know what's right but we can't always do it. I may not think it is right to swat a bug. Still, I do it." Reuben deepened the philosophical bent. "What we do that we believe we shouldn't is what defines us as individuals. What do you think about that?"

"I'm not sure. I'd have to contemplate that one," I said, bemused by the statement.

"Think about it like this. We all do what is right. We follow the Golden Rule, the Ten Commandments, 'do onto others as...' and 'thou shalt not...' but what if every living soul solemnly devoted their lives to those principles...and was faithful to them? What would the world be like?"

"I'll give you my opinion," he continued. "It would be worse than Orwell predicted in his novel, 1984. Every person would be divinable, charitable, gracious, respectful, and honest. Zach, there'd be no hate because there'd be no cause for the feeling, there'd be no crime because there'd be no motive, there'd be no deviation because there'd be unalterable consistency, there'd be no greed because there'd be no victory in possession, there'd be no honor because there'd be nothing to disrespect, and worst of all there'd be no love because without hate there'd be no source for birthing its opposite— I'm not sure there'd be feelings at all.

"Now, are you reading me? We are born out of inconsistency, variability, contradiction, and deviancy. We have no choice but to follow the destiny those unique patterns dictate. If I had romance, a wife, and a child, then that would be fine. But the way I imperfectly handled that based on my personal traits and character would be what defined me as unique. Nobody does it right, but everybody does it different." Reuben raised his voice to emphasize what he perceived as a critical point.

"Likewise, if I remained celibate my whole life, never took a lover, how I conducted myself under that condition is what would distinguish me. Imagine, as a being lacking sexual satisfaction, I might birth myself to a great talent or an imposing monster. But how I behave in either of those outcomes, my irregular way of conducting myself, how I would deviate from the ideal we imagine possible for any state of being, that's what makes me the one-of-a-kind person I am, that's what makes all of us one-of-a-kind people."

As he paused his commentary, Reuben noticed one of the cooks touch his hand to his brow to wipe a bead of sweat. The act was forbidden in the kitchen, the cook trained to use a cloth so as to not risk the body fluid ending up in the food. Reuben ran over to the man.

"I told you twice now not to ever do that," Reuben chastised him.

"What?" the cook said dumbfounded.

"What?" Reuben mimicked the behavior with a mocking tone. "Never touch. That's the last time I'm warning you."

He walked back to me, leaving the man to chew on the reprimand.

"Could I have kindly told him that? Sure. But I'm pissed. If he does it again, I don't want him in my kitchen. Do I feel guilty? Yes. But I'll fight that damn feeling to my death because that shame is what puts me at war with my special self—if I acquiesce to the shame I might end up perfect. There is no honor in remorse."

On one level, his argument was flawless. Yet, on another level, I could see perilous faults. Even more concerning was that he seemed to be contradicting himself. If there was no honor or purpose in remorse, which I understood to be key ingredients in depression, then how could he fall to the depths of despair I witnessed in him? I had to raise the point...and did so without regret.

"Reuben, it all sounds great and much of it I agree with but tell me—"

"Tell you why I get depressed, right?" He completed the thought for me. Then he laughed, almost maniacally. "I don't know. And I warned you not to take my advice."

"You're not playing fair," I charged. "You're a thoughtful man. You have to believe what you just told me. You have to know why you're depressed."

"Maybe I do, but it's not anything I can talk about." He unwrapped the bandage covering his right hand and tried to flex it, grimacing before bracing it again. "No, I can't tell you. I can't burden you in that way."

"How do—"

"Zach, if there was anyone I believed could possibly cope with it, probably you'd be the one," he complimented. "But you're going to have to trust me on this. I know where I deviate, what makes me who I am, but that doesn't mean anyone else has to know or should know."

I noticed his breathing was always amazingly under his conscious domination, but at this moment he sucked in an unusually large volume of air and didn't breathe out for quite some time. When he did continue talking, I wondered how he could hold it for so long, but he seemed unaware of what he had done.

"I will say this. I do believe what I told you," he continued on an exhalation. "Now add this. What we do that defines us as unique, from the most attractive, positive, and wondrous to the most ugly, negative, or evil, can also destroy us. We really have no control over it. Nor do we have influence over how it might devastate other people."

I assumed he had uttered his last words on the subject but I was wrong. After walking around the whole kitchen, checking the progress of the dishes being prepared, he came back to me with the finale, a real knockout punch.

"I should have never come here. These people would be better off without me around."

What the hell was he telling me that he couldn't tell me? And what did it have to do with him still drowning in regret while prescribing a diet of strict abstinence from that reproachful state?

For the first time I wondered if this great chef was like so many artists, a bit off center, perhaps more than a bit. Could he be a smidgen nutty? Might I be better off to define the relationship as strictly business? Hah. Would I be able to, now that he and Josea were big kids playing hot sex games?

I had one other thought. I allowed myself less time than I would allocate to considering a non-anesthetic open-heart surgery before burying it like toxic waste, hopefully never to be dug up for the next fifty thousand years. Could Reuben kill? And was he trying to tell me something in that regard?

Preeti, Josea, and I went home. When we arrived, Len was waiting for us. The front yard was lit up, and circling in the middle in a continuous east, south, west and north pattern was my father-in-law. As we approached, he kept moving but asked us to stop, which we did. All four of us, Preeti, Souche, Josea, and I, were standing close to one another.

As Len paced himself about the perimeter of the imaginary circle he had drawn around us, he seemed to be working his way toward the center. He kept moving, all the while his eyes focusing on our group as if we were herded animals. Finally, he stopped toward the east and looked first to the sky and then toward his assembly.

"My father, my father's father, and a thousand of my fathers have spoken. There will be no more murder."

In one day, there were two firsts for Len. He had hugged me earlier, which he had never done. Now his face revealed a ghostly sorrow, an appearance I had never observed on him. His eyes glazed, as near to tears as I ever thought I would see. He was not defeated, just tortured with pain. I assumed it was for the murdered girls and their families, but it was worse than that.

Len turned to leave, opening the imaginary corral door for the four of us to go into the house so we could try to sleep.

Preeti and I couldn't talk. It was not only that we were so tired that thoughts were scarce. We simply couldn't sort through all that was happening; we wisely decided to let it rest. She did address one thought, her father.

"I feel terrible for my father. Sometimes he comforts himself with wishes, an old man living in a make-believe world."

"Maybe he needs to do that," I suggested.

"I would never say it to him, but I better hope this Kershaw can figure out what has happened." Preeti turned on her side to face me, hard pressed to keep her eyes open. "Can you check the front and back doors again?"

Those were her last words before drifting off.

I lifted myself out of bed and inspected the doors and windows. I didn't have a shotgun but I was considering buying one—I had never even fired a handgun. I returned to bed and tried to think of something to make me laugh. I fell asleep still trying.

16

GRIEF

SURPRISINGLY, DURING THE NEXT few days leading up to the funeral of the two latest murder victims, the community was, at least on the surface, fairly tame. People may have had their arms ready at night but during the daytime I observed nothing but the usual rifles strapped to the interior of the drivers' pickup cabins.

With the exception of anyone with a young daughter who was approaching thirteen, activities resumed normally. Whether it was by design or chance nobody knew, but the three murders had all been girls approaching their thirteenth birthday. They were also three youths who had made no declaration whether or not they would be participating in the Puberty Ceremony.

Nobody wanted to believe that a lunatic was killing girls of that age for the purpose of scaring them into committing to the ceremony, but nobody dismissed that possibility either. Because there were so many girls who had already announced their intent not to participate, who remained unharmed, the argument had less appeal, though murdering a few might have been intended to influence the remainder to fall in line and follow the customs of the tribe.

The prevailing opinion remained as it had been after the first murder, that a stalker or madman who didn't live in the community and who was not Apache was entering the reservation, likely through the surrounding woods, and committing violence. In fact, some of the best trackers in the tribe, men who knew the area intimately, were canvassing the mountains they thought most promising for such a creature to be camping out between kills. Not one person expressed, or was willing to believe, that the killer was home grown and living amongst them. They all concurred that the style of the first murder would preclude an Apache doing the crime, but they still had no details regarding the latest two murders.

The morning after those two tragedies, I went to see Len again at his studio. I called ahead. My intent was to forward the essence of the message Kershaw wanted me to convey. Now that Len's proclamation that the murders would cease was obviously wrong, I thought he might be more amenable to reason. I wanted to make a pitch for him not only to help Kershaw but to also encourage the other tribe members who respected him to do the same.

As I came out of the house, and on my way to my car, I glanced down. In front of me was the most beautiful petal of a flower I'd ever seen. What caught my attention, besides the bright red shade, was its perfect shape and velvety-appearing texture as well as the fact that I didn't recognize the variety—Preeti had planted each of the perennial and annual specimen in our garden and she would refer to them by their given names as if they were old comrades with whom she'd shared both sorrow and joy. The one I was looking at was not one of her buddies.

I bent down to pick up the sample, intending to show it to her. As my hand was about to snatch it, the thing blew forward a couple of feet. I took a few steps toward it. Now standing over the object, I again crouched down to grab the small bloom. Once more it whisked itself just beyond my outstretched hand. Had I not been wearing shoes and socks, I would no doubt have felt on my feet and legs the commander wind under whose dominion the tease operated as it skated along the ground.

After several successive attempts to seize the brilliant treasure, only for it to mindlessly toy with me, a grand gust of wind bullied its way into the garden and blew the petal out of my sight. In the midst of trying to chase it down, I recognized irritation on my part, but when it finally dodged me for good I was able to laugh off the experience.

I would have thought nothing more about it except... except it seemed to be emblematic of my journey to gain full control over my life. On many occasions in the past, I'd perceived all the essential elements that defined the world of Zach Miller to be bundled neatly. But then when I happily closed in on the package, believing I could place a harness around it, that I could demonstrate that I was the ruler of my own fate, it jumped forward, turned its mocking head at me, and then beckoned me to try again. I knew I wasn't being singled out. My experience was not much different than what I had listened to most of humanity moan about, but that tiny red object could have been acting with deliberation—that's what rankled me.

I finally revved up the engine of my old Volvo and in minutes pulled in front of Len Cloud's place. I was surprised to see Kershaw's vehicle. Our timing was near perfect in that the FBI man was just closing the door of his car and about to go to the front of the house. As it happened on my last visit to Len, I noticed him coming out of his workshop. This time he was caught off guard when he saw both of us standing together. His face stiffened. I could see a glare, no doubt Len jumping to the erroneous conclusion that I had set him up, planning all along to bring Kershaw. The FBI man must have read the same script and took the initiative to dispel any doubts Len had about complicity between him and me.

"I need to talk with you Mr. Cloud," Kershaw said before glancing in my direction. "I don't know what your son-in-law is doing here but it's up to you if he listens in."

Len looked at me and with his right hand motioned me to follow him into the studio, Kershaw courteously insisting I go first.

"What is it your FBI wants with me?" Len scowled.

"I have a couple questions for you. I'm giving you a choice here. We can do this friendly like right here or I can take you down to headquarters."

"What do you want to know?" Len grumbled.

"You were the first person at the murder site of Udaya Shash, right?"

"I did call in the murder, correct," Len admitted. "But I wasn't the first one there."

"Then who was?" asked Kershaw with a thread of sarcasm. "The killer?"

"The killer and whomever called me," Len said evasively.

"Might they not be one and the same?" Kershaw posed, not hiding that he was nettled by Len's attitude.

"I don't know anything about that. All I know is somebody told me there was a murder at the west end of the reservation, near the flats. I rushed out there," Len Cloud explained.

"You know about everyone living in Mescalero. You're saying you want me to believe the caller didn't identify himself and you didn't recognize the voice?" Kershaw said indignantly.

"You can believe what you want."

"I don't buy it," Kershaw harshly confronted Len. "And I'll need an explanation why you went over and interceded to get the Moon girl."

"I know the parents both work. With murder happening right then, I rushed out to be sure she—"

"There were several other girls in danger and you did nothing to be sure they were safe?" Kershaw interrupted irately. "Why the Moon girl?"

"Why not?" Len said indifferently.

Kershaw was losing patience. I could see why. Len wouldn't give in a hair. Plus, his behavior on the afternoon of the murders had been highly suspicious. I don't think Kershaw believed Len to be a killer. More likely from Kershaw's perspective, Len might have been a passive accomplice to murder. Or, alternatively, he was a man choosing to maliciously withhold information critical to an investigation Kershaw was increasingly devoted to, and doing so owing to his foolish resentment of the White Man interceding in a tribal matter.

"I'm playing fair and being damn generous with you. I find out you've held back evidence that could lead to an arrest or that you tampered in any way with the crime scene and I'll haul your ass to jail and prosecute the shit out of you," Kershaw said in a most unfriendly manner. "As far as I'm concerned, your attitude has contributed to letting these last two murders happen. Think about that as you're putting out this holier than thou image. Eventually the tribe members are going to figure it out and hold you accountable."

Kershaw turned to leave, stopping to look angrily at me.

"I asked you to talk some sense into this man." Kershaw's consternation was unabashed. "Now might be the time."

Usually Kershaw wore a tan cowboy hat similar to what the country singer Garth Brooks wears—with a short goatee he was a respectable double for the popular artist. It seemed to be his custom to take it off his head when he was indoors but also when conversing with someone outside, as was the case during this discussion. He took his hand to straighten the inner band and slipped it on his head as he marched off.

Len smiled as if he had just got away with a prank.

"He'll learn," Len said derisively. "Little too arrogant for my taste."

"I didn't know someone had called to notify you of the murder," I said to probe deeper.

"Forget it," Len curtly stated. "What brings you out this early? Preeti doing okay, I hope."

"As well as can be expected." I abbreviated my response, eager to address what I considered a more pertinent matter. "Don't you think at this point that with what's going on it would be better to give a hand to Kershaw and his people? What if others die?" I proposed. "Wouldn't you feel you might have been responsible because you contributed toward neutralizing people like Kershaw who were trying to help, people with proven expertise in murder investigations?"

"I promise you there will be no more murders," Len said emphatically.

The absurdity of his position galled me. I identified with the outrage Kershaw had displayed. I lost my temper.

"You issued nearly the same proclamation last time... and you were just as cock sure," my voice leaving no mistake he was frustrating me.

"You are not Apache so you could never understand what I'm saying," Len countered but with no sign of perturbation. "We have been humiliated, degraded, and deceived throughout our dealings with the White Man. There are certain of our affairs we cannot permit them to be involved with or we will lose our identity and no longer be a People."

"But you said yourself that no Mescalero Indian would do this crime as it was committed. So wouldn't that suggest that this is a matter falling outside the rule of the tribe?" I reasoned.

"No sane Mescalero would do this. Yes, I said that," Len proclaimed.

His last sentence nearly drove me over the edge—in my opinion he was guilty of what I call "crazy-making communication," and it riled me. By altering a single word he'd changed his prior position, and worst of all, done so shamelessly.

"Do you realize what you're doing?" I shouted. "First you wholeheartedly propose that the killer couldn't be a Mescalero. None would strangle a young female face-to-face. But then in the next breath, with equal assurance, because you conveniently modified your prior statement by adding the word 'sane', you say it could be a Mescalero tribal member. I don't get it."

Len waited to answer. He shook his head as if he were processing a complex thought.

"That's what I meant when I said you wouldn't understand because you are not an Apache...but let me try to explain." Kindly, and with compassion, he put his arm over my shoulder. "We do not think of a finite position as you would. We might proclaim with certitude what we believe or perceive at any moment in time yet know we are permitted to change our position without embarrassment.

"You have the expectation that an absolute is forever and it's shámeful to back off the position once stated. It's a subtle differential in the wiring of the brain evolved over thousands of years. Most important, it's a mechanism for change. No group of people, Zach, could survive without some process of course correction. To adhere to a position that is no longer tenable is a deadly game.

"It's true one word changed, but I was not aware of it until you brought it to my attention. I believe both statements to be true, each correct at the moment I spoke them."

I knew in my heart that my father-in-law never intended dishonesty or deceit. He had no inhibitions against expressing himself resolutely one moment and modifying his position as new information was presented at another. He was right. I was not a Mescalero. I appreciated that his explanation permitted me to retain the same level of respect I'd always had for him.

"When we go to the Puberty Ceremony this year I'll explain more. Last year, I neglected you. This year, I will treat you as a son. I apologize for not helping you understand us better." Len delivered a slight nod of his head, accompanied by what looked like the Apache brand of a smirk. "You'll know the many masks your wife wears on her face better after the ceremony. Perceiving beneath the disguises of a woman to find her truth is never an easy thing to accomplish, even when you come from the same background."

I trusted Preeti had revealed herself to me, but it wasn't worth debating with her father. More critical to me was wondering if anyone would be in the mood to celebrate this year at the Puberty Ceremony. I think Len sensed what I was thinking.

"Don't worry. The raging water will run its course and soon we will swim in the gentle currents left behind." Len said confidently. "I've been through many storms and you've seen a few too. As long as we are fierce warriors and show no fear, we will endure."

I thought of how I had survived seemingly intolerable conditions in the past, creating voyages to galaxies and planets where I could escape pain and suffering, and then returning to courageously face the despair of my situation. Len was right. We all had to be brave. The problem was there were too many brave chiefs in the kitchen. Kershaw had the proverbial balls of steel and Len's were probably made of titanium.

The next few days were devoted to preparing for the funeral, an event that thankfully passed without any intervening crises. Families huddled together. If the monster responsible for the murders were to strike again, he would have to change his target because no woman would be left alone for weeks.

Very shortly after the funeral, a tribal meeting was called. It seemed at face value to serve no purpose other than to bring the people together and to affirm their commitment to the upcoming ceremony over the Fourth of July. The festivities were approaching rapidly and preparations needed to begin soon. Many speeches were made, mostly short ones and with the standard pattern of council members first, followed by tribal members in the order of elders, more esteemed adults, the general adult population, and then younger people. However, there was one deviation, again having to do with Walter.

It seems the man was on a mission to upset any attempt by the other tribal members to reestablish harmony. He knew that in spite of the tragedies endured by the people, deep faults were running through the tribe. Walter took the position that the murders were an omen of things to come, warning the people that if they didn't heed the message, in this case the one he was preaching, the situation would worsen. Walter sat quietly while each of the council members wishing to speak presented their remarks. When everyone had taken his or her turn, he again violated the prescribed directionality and moved counter-circularity to a microphone.

"I am willing to give my life to save us as a People. Death has descended upon us because we disrespected what we have held sacred since we became a People. It is not too late to mend our ways and make peace with an angry spirit." Walter's eyes were deep set in his broad griddle-flat face, and as he talked the slits gradually closed, seemingly sealing off from the people he wanted to influence.

"Our people, even fifty years ago, would never imagine permitting the girls coming of age not to participate in the Puberty Ceremony. But now we sell the trees that make our land beautiful so that lumber can build homes in far-off places, we sell the gases beneath our earth to heat homes and businesses for people we don't know, we sell rooms, food, and gambling to people from other states and countries—we sell and sell and sell.

"And while we get richer and richer, we find that what we have acquired in exchange for the gifts god has given us is suffering. So what do we do to heal that pain? We sell more so we can attain additional trinkets to relieve the suffering. And now, we are selling the last jewel.

"The question is simple. Should we shoot off fireworks for the tourists and have our girls laugh from the grandstands rather than pay tribute to their people by participating in a rite of passage? We can choose. But it will be the spirits that will judge us...and if deemed necessary, punish us."

Walter left the microphone and walked out of the meeting. Within minutes, Platta dismissed everyone.

Len Cloud rushed out of the room. Preeti and I were in no hurry, and since we had Souche with us, we lingered some time before leaving. By the time we reached the parking area, most everyone was gone. We were about to get into the car when we heard loud voices. Preeti spotted her father with Walter some distance away—across from the council building—standing in a clump of large fir trees. We noticed that they were in a heated discussion. While not inclined to eavesdrop, we couldn't help overhearing what had to be the finale to their encounter, a burst of angry words.

"You've gone too far this time," Len crossly warned.

"You would let us die!" Walter fired back before delivering an insult. "You're the coward!"

"Your mind has been poisoned—"

"My mind is clear as a brook," Walter declared. "I see through the mud and dirt. We have never faced a threat like we do now...and we are about to lose," Walter exhorted.

"Then we will lose fighting like honorable warriors and not disreputable thugs," Len voiced peacefully.

His tonal presentation thrust Walter into a more irksome state. He looked at Len and walked off disgustedly.

We got into the car and left. On the way home, Preeti was upset.

"My father is not himself," she lamented. "And Walter is crazy. He's a dangerous radical."

"Has he always been so extreme?" I asked her.

"I went to school with Walter. He was a hardheaded young man, but what do you know when you're young? I never paid much attention, but in the last year or two I've seen a change." Preeti turned to hand Souche a toy that our baby had dropped on the floor of the back seat. "I've noticed that the men in our tribe go one of two ways in the twenty year range. They either decide they're Apache and adhere stringently to the tradition or they weaken their association with the tribal customs."

"I guess we know where Walter stands."

"I'm not sure," Preeti said in an ominous tone. "Walter seems to be taking it way past my father. For shitaa it's all about the pride of our heritage, but for Walter I see it as a personal conquest. That's frightening."

It had been over a week since my trip to Topeka. Like a dopey cow moseying around the herd, every so often the thought that I needed to call Arnie would wander into my mind—and I'd let it stray away. But finally, I knew it was time to reach him. I waited until after we had lunch. I was able to contact him without leaving a message.

I could hear in his voice that he was irritated I hadn't called before. I used the excuse of the murders in Mescalero and he eased up. He was eager to hear what I had found out, and I conveyed to him every detail of the story, including my conclusion that Stevie Green had gone to the Howard Clinic and been surgically done over into the appearance of another physical being.

I told him I appreciated the opportunity to help out and that I was surprised myself how much I was able to accomplish. I let him know that I assumed I hadn't disappointed the band. Then, I announced that I was finished and they could handle the findings as they saw fit. I paused to appreciate the relief I was experiencing.

"I was going to call you, but it turns out it's just as well I waited. There is one more thing I'll ask you to do and then I swear you can take leave and I'll always be in your debt. Zach, after you get back from Los Angeles—"

"I have no plan to go to L.A. in the near future. In fact, I believe my mother and her husband are coming to visit me soon," I informed him.

"Zach, one last thing. It'll take you a day. When you come home, I'll have a surprise for you."

"I was just thinking how much I yearned to find an ordinary, plain and uneventful life," I pled foolishly.

"It's not your fate to have that. You should have figured that out by now," he chirped.

"I think I'm getting that message."

"Here's the story," Arnie announced. I could hear him unwrapping a piece of gum and then beginning to chew on it. "Whatever we decide to do about Stevie, we have to hash out later. But when we do we want every fact that we can get."

"I understand that."

"Then you'll appreciate why I'm asking you to make this trip. If you doubt that Weiner is being a prick, see if this helps. His personal secretary, Angie—"

"I remember," I interjected. "She was a grim woman, not particularly welcoming to me."

"Like attracts like, they say. The two of them were a duo. Anyway, she was diagnosed recently with colon cancer. Surprised that I'd know? Well, I have ways of keeping an eye on Mr. Weiner. If you want to know what happened, he fired her. Imagine the heartless schmuck, after fifteen years of loyal service."

"Touching story," I quipped. "But what does it have to do with me?"

"How would you feel if someone did that to you? Would you maintain your allegiance to the boss or want to strike out to harm him by whatever means were available to you?"

"I get it. But what can she say regarding Stevie?"

"That's the point, captain. We don't know but want to find out. Since you were around there working, at least she knows you. See what you can get out of her. Hell, she could know where Stevie is. If she seems to need a little incentive to revive her memory, you know the budget."

"How do I find her?" I queried, not trying to conceal that I was chafed by the request.

"I have her address and phone number," Arnie quickly offered. "Got a pencil and paper?"

The next morning I caught an early flight to Los Angeles. She lived in Encino, a community in the San Fernando Valley, the only positive aspect being that I could fly into little Burbank Airport and leave to go home that same afternoon.

When I called her, I was surprised she set no obstacles to me seeing her. She was married. Mr. Mason sat in while I talked with his wife. When I explained that I had questions I wanted to ask about Stevie Green, she laughed as if she should have guessed.

"Stevie Green's band couldn't wait. I would have told them if they called that there was no hurry. I'm not about to die from this," she bristled. "Just be mutilated a bit by the modern day medical machine," she wryly joked.

"I'm sorry. Still, it's great you have that kind of attitude," I complimented. "That will guarantee you safe passage through the healing."

"You're kind. Still, I have a ways to go."

"Can I explain why I'm here?" I asked.

"Stevie Green. You looked at everything there is. I don't think Mr. Weiner held back a smidgeon to be honest. I organized most of that material myself." She punctuated her statement by pointing her left index finger at her heart.

"Okay, but can you recall anything that would suggest Weiner knew more about Stevie than he disclosed?"

"There was nothing out of the ordinary in the office. Obviously, most of our work pertained to Stevie and Jay, all of their partnerships and investments that they had together and separately. You can imagine that was a handful. Mr. Weiner has had a couple of other clients as well. They were also friends of his that he had agreed to help with various legal matters."

"I know I may be on a merry goose chase, but we thought it would be worth checking."

"What about the calls you told me about, dear?" Mr. Mason reminded her.

"I don't think they had anything to do with Green, Les." Ms. Mason deliberated. Then she addressed me. "There was one man who called every single week at about the same time. Weiner made sure he was always there to speak to him. If my boss wasn't there, the man never called."

"Was it a client?"

"No, I don't believe we ever did a bit of business for him."

"Do you recall his name?"

"Let's see. You want the first name or the last?" she smiled.

"Both would be best," I answered greedily.

"The reason I'm laughing is because I never knew if Artanis was a first or last name. He'd just say, 'Artanis for Mr. Weiner, please.' I'd put him through."

I sat silently. Stevie Green was checking in weekly with Weiner, conducting his affairs, instructing his friend on what he needed...and god knows what else. It was amazing what I had discovered and at the same time trivial and inconsequential to my life, and probably anyone else's. Still I had to press the play button, asking more questions.

"Did you ever overhear their conversations?"

"Occasionally I'd listen to Mr. Weiner's side. It could be odd, I'll admit." She paused to organize her thoughts. "I remember one time Weiner seemed a bit annoyed. He told him something to the effect that he needed to 'stop dickin' around' because he was going to get caught. Then another time he seemed to be scolding him. He told him that somebody was on to him and that it was his opinion...Weiner's... that it was too hot where he was and he should move on."

"So this man...what was his name?" I inquired indifferently, not wanting to raise her attention to the fact that the name F. Artanis meant anything to me.

"Artanis."

"Okay, Mr. Artanis. He called weekly. Nobody else kept

in touch with Weiner who might have been serving as an intermediary on behalf of Green?"

"No. Honestly, he's dead. I'm sure of it."

"What proof do you have? The band members, as you know, won't buy anything short of verifiable fact. If you can package up a convincing argument for me that I can take back to them, I think they'd be appreciative."

"It's more than instinct but less than evidence. I knew Weiner well and saw how he moped and wept after Stevie was gone. He lost something important to him."

I thanked her and left. Arnie had insisted I take a town car when I landed in L.A. I had the driver waiting. When I came out of the house, I jumped in and hollered out like a senator to the driver.

"9701 Wilshire. I'm short on time so see what you can do." I tempted him by flipping a twenty-dollar bill over the seat separating us.

I shouldn't have been so generous. He hit the 405 Freeway with a running start and was doing a hundred miles an hour, weaving through traffic like a hustler losing a cop. Thank the Lord I didn't have the nerve to hire one of those daily rate Porsche Turbo deals with driver and make it a hundred-dollar bill, because the expression "scared the shit out of me" nearly became literal—by the time we arrived at my destination I felt ill.

I called ahead to Weiner's office to make sure he was in, but I didn't announce who was calling. I knew my business with him would only take a minute. After that, my only problem would be ordering the driver to return me to the airport in slow motion, which I hoped I could get for free. I took the elevator to the penthouse suite.

I noticed that where Ms. Mason had been previously stationed a buxom blond girl oozing sexiness sat. When I told her I wanted to see Weiner, she politely asked me to be seated. I could see her talking on the line to him. A minute later he came to greet me.

"Miller, why didn't you call?" he said congenially.

"Didn't know I was coming."

"Well, come on down and tell me everything you've found out about my friend." He was ridiculing me. "Once you solve the Stevie Green matter, we'll all sleep peacefully. I trust my records were helpful."

"Actually they were. I'll make this short. Honestly, I don't know why I had to make this visit—"

"Come now. You're being too modest," he chuckled. "You have something to shove in my face. I hope that's where you intend to shove it."

It peeved me that he was right. He had been able to see straight through me. Then I realized he knew before I even came to see him that I had solved the riddle. He knew I was at Howard Medical and that I had taken off to interview Cooley and Delia Spruce—he knew that I had discovered the truth about Stevie Green but that I could do no more with my knowledge than publish it in a cheap gossip magazine. The fact remained it was exactly that, hearsay, and unless I could produce a living being going by the name Stevie Green, I had borscht.

"You look at me like a germ. But what have I done?" Weiner asked, clearly acknowledging a pardonable act. "Do you have people who you love and who love you? Have you ever had a friend in trouble? And if you did, how far would you go to help him?" Weiner steered his commentary by taking a right angle turn. "Really, Miller, you've evolved into a crack investigator." He stopped to make sure his next point drove deep into my heart. "But it's not your thing."

"I rather tend to agree." The words flowed unconsciously. "I'm far more inspired by fantasy."

"Well then, there you have it." His voice was sonorous. "You can end the story any way you choose. I'll be your first reader, I promise. Hell, I'll go further. Put it together and I'll represent you. As far as entertainment attorneys go, you could do worse," he chortled.

Then he did the oddest thing. On his desk was a wooden box I assumed was filled with cigars. He opened it and handed it to me, inviting me to take a sample of its contents. But instead of a smoke it was filled with See's suckers—chocolate, caramel, and peanut butter. This was a different part of Weiner, the pompous asshole humbly offering a treat to his defeated foe.

I had been raised on this brand of sweet delights. I chose caramel. I took it out of the cellophane wrap and put it in my mouth, recalling that Josea had brought me one when she first visited me in Israel. It tasted great as I began sucking on it in front of Jay.

"I might take you up on your offer," I said sincerely to Weiner. "You might find what I do with this story entertaining."

"Fantasy, that's my business too," Weiner smiled. "Who gives a shit about reality anyway? It's for the old and infirmed."

I stood up, knowing that the next time I met with Weiner I'd be toting a copy of my latest novel and hoping he would be charitable enough to help let the rest of mankind see it.

"The little dude," he sang. "The little dude," drawing out the sound as he repeated it.

"What do you mean?"

"That's what most people called Stevie," he smiled. "You didn't know that?"

I shook my head in disbelief. I couldn't shut off the thought. *Stevie Green, the little dude? Jivin is the little dude! Somebody has to be wrong, don't they?* I had one more question. It was none of my business but I couldn't resist.

"I was just curious about your secretary."

"I thought you were the devoted family type," Weiner jested with irony. "She could break up a happy home, couldn't she?"

"No, I'm referring to the one that was here before," I clarified.

"For many years I might add. What about her?" he asked casually.

"What happened to her?"

"I fired her. Why do you ask?" His response was amazingly unaffected.

"What led you to terminate her?"

"Don't tell me you were getting on with her while I was out to lunch." He was enjoying his own humor. "If you insist on knowing, I didn't exactly fire her, unless you consider a two-year severance at full pay termination. She's ill and I told her to get better and not worry about the office—she knows she has her job waiting for the rest of her sweet life." Then with a glisten in his eyes, he devilishly smiled at me. "By the way, what brought you to L.A. today? Surely it wasn't just to let your buddy Jay know what a dick he is."

I said nothing. The joke was on me. Secretary Mason had withheld nothing during her discussion with me. She'd been told by Weiner to be candid; he knew I was coming before I walked off the plane. I eloquently bowed my head, mumbled a couple haphazard comments, and left.

After the ride to his office, I thought better of taking chances, so I promised the driver another twenty-dollar tip if he drove safely—payable upon arrival. The ride back to the valley was slow and gentle. I had plenty of time to digest the day's activities.

No matter what I did, what I experienced, how profound I considered a moment's wisdom, regardless of how sure I was about one thing or another, everything could change on a dime. I could go from wise man to idiot as fast as a train can flip a track and send the lives of hundreds into peril. Again, I reviewed Len Cloud's Apache mentality and determined that it might have some merit.

I detested Weiner. I had wanted to go to his office for no reason other than to let the jerk know that I had made him. I wanted to hate him. Damn it, he ruined the whole thing. Now, he might become my agent? I wanted to throw a thirty-something's tantrum. *Why can't I have things the way I want, if not all the time, at least once in a while?*

17

GUESS WHO'S COMING FOR DINNER

I WAS MENTALLY DRAINED and napped most of the trip on the plane. I picked up my car and started for home. Preeti was there when I called to tell her I had landed. She told me she'd be at Kuruk and that I should meet her there. Because I was tired I objected, telling her I might just take a light dinner at home and wait for her.

She wouldn't have it. She rarely pleaded with me, so I agreed. When I arrived the lot was full, which was not unusual. However, what was not typical was the number of limousines. Often we had one, occasionally two, but not four—I wondered if a dignitary had decided to dine with us, but there were no guards posted, something I had witnessed numerous times.

I went in the back door and noticed Reuben was not in the kitchen but instead his first assistant was calling the plays. Everything seemed to be operating smoothly, and I thought nothing else about it. Then I proceeded to the dining room, and there was my explanation for Preeti's insistence that I meet her at the restaurant.

The entire LIVE band along with Preston, were at a big table with Preeti and Josea. They all clapped, which I thought odd. I was fortunate that the hair I had on my head was thick and dark. I could run my hands through it without it ever looking disheveled. I did so several times, trying to absorb the scene.

I was wearing tan slacks and a burgundy Izod shirt, closer to a golfing outfit than my normal beaten-to-shit blue jeans, t-shirt, and brown moccasins. Preeti had made them for me out of the same material as hers; it was a buffalo hide so thick yet soft the foot feels like it's packed in cotton and cooled with air conditioning.

I shook a bunch of hands with inside, outside, and inverted moves, had my shoulder slapped buddy-style several times, and my neck squeezed. Then I kissed Preeti, followed by Josea. I noticed Josea had altered her apparel and was wearing lightweight and loose-fitting pants and top, not sensual but rather previewing an earthly look. The only times I saw her in dress similar to the black leather attire she'd arrived in was when she took her motorcycle out for a ride, which was less frequent as time passed.

She sat at the table between Sonny Boy and Rudy. Preston had reserved a seat for me between him and Preeti, with Arnie across from us.

I whispered to Preeti for an explanation regarding Reuben's absence in the kitchen. She informed me that earlier in the afternoon he'd taken ill with a stomach virus. He thought it was a twenty-four-hour flu and assumed he'd be back on duty by the next day.

"So you retiring on us now, Zach?" Arnie swatted his words across the table, loud enough for everyone to hear.

"I believe I completed what you asked of me," I gracefully returned his shot.

"What about today? Were you able to get anything out of the secretary?"

"I'm going to make this simple and sweet. Stevie Green is alive. I believe that as strongly as I believe my wife and two closest friends in the world are at this table with me. Where he is, what he is doing, will he ever be discovered, I don't know, don't care, and don't want to think about. Fellows, I'm done," I proclaimed adamantly.

"Just one more thing I was thinking about..." Arnie said contemplatively. "Only kidding! The man is free to raise his family and run what I hear is the best restaurant in the western states. A toast."

He held a glass high in the air. Then Arnie continued with a more earnest tone.

"We really appreciate your efforts."

"I'll drink to that," said Sonny Boy Blue.

Rudy offered similar sentiment, and then some.

"I expressed to you my opinion, Zach, when we first met. I wish Stevie Green the life he's chosen, whatever that is. I learned more from him than anyone I've ever met in the music field, and I've been studying and performing since I was eight years old," Rudy said with obvious reverence. "Stevie had to grow up and go off on his own. To do that he required separation, to not have us need him. I still think a lot of this is our fault for not encouraging him to cut loose long ago. Besides, we're a smash hit on our own."

"If that's how you feel, then it doesn't compute why you've gone to all this trouble to prove something you can't do anything about," Josea countered.

"We're not asking your advice," Arnie replied dismissively. "We'll decide what we want to do."

Arnie's blunt reply was no doubt a gut reaction to the notable derision in Josea's voice. She had never shared with me her views on the subject of searching out Stevie Green once it was determined he was alive, but what I heard her expressing was a near perfect duplication of the attitude so many others had voiced in a more sentimental and charitable manner.

Sonny Boy Blue had no problem with her objection to the task they had hired me to accomplish. Arnie did. By far, he was the most outspoken advocate of not only determining if Stevie was alive but also investing money to find him—who could have known that Reuben's great menu items, which we were about to be served, would be spiced too heavily by the heated debate coming between Arnie and Josea? Arnie had a mind to dig his teeth into my friend.

"I don't know who you are, young lady—"

"I'm Josea Roth and I'm Zach's good friend. That's about all you need to know." She cocked her pistol and aimed at Arnie.

"Well, dear—"

"Goddamn it, if we're going to debate an issue at least let's stick to facts, or opinions we're willing to own...and cut the 'dear' bromides. I don't go down that easily."

"A little sensitive, are we?" Arnie's mockery was evident.

"*We* are not sensitive. You may be, but I'd more aptly call my state...riled. Frankly it offends me when someone uses condescension to try and grab the upper hand in an encounter," Josea stated bluntly. "For years I tolerated it so as to not insult the inferiorities of others, but I'm on sabbatical and that permits me to cut all the crap out of my life."

"You have a right to your opinion about Stevie Green, though I don't really see what business it is of yours," Arnie thrust at her.

Arnie was peeved. While he was still game for a clash, I could tell her you-don't-impress-me-because-you're-a-big-rock-star attitude had backed him up a full twelve-inch foot.

"Seems to me you're the one proposing to make the Stevie Green affair a public show, unless I don't read you correctly." Josea leapt forward, mindless to his apparent retreat. "After all, if you're going to be calling out the nation to find him, then you would want to start by assigning everyone the duty to search their bedroom."

"If you think he'd end up in yours then you might start there. Frankly, I'm doubtful you and he would sack up well," Arnie struck back mean-heartedly.

"You seem to have trouble letting a debate zero in on the relevant subject matter. If I were moderating this discussion, I'd want to have the opponents talk about human traits such as respect, dignity, compassion...and even love." Josea proposed. "This man, Mr. Green, is telling you he doesn't want to be found and you're using a planet of followers who are mostly empty and sad souls seeking relief in an iconic figure as real to them as Buddha, Christ, Muhammad, or Krishna to justify violating his fundamental right to be and to exist on his own terms."

"Oh, I see—"

"I don't think I'm quite finished," Josea cut back at him. "To me, what you're proposing is the worse crime one human can commit toward another. It's one thing to employ my friend to confirm for your own selfish curiosity whether or not the man is alive, but to suggest taking the matter one step further is deplorable."

Josea rested her case momentarily. The waiter was serving the first course. Four additional portions of the meal were coming, and I had to doubt we were going to finish number one before one of the two choked each other—I was sure it was Josea's neck that was about to share the fate of Ila Clearbrook because she was too smart for Arnie, was probably morally correct, but didn't have the grip strength to strangle him first.

"That's bull...shit!" Arnie quickly took her pause as an opportunity to challenge her high-ground virtuosity. "When a man has risen beyond stardom, has become a godly figure to millions, he owes to them an explanation for why he is withdrawing his love. In exchange for the fame and fortune we earn, we incur a great debt to those who hold us in high esteem."

Arnie was enraged, the burning embers of his emotions enticing him toward recklessness. "You want my honest opinion," he shouted. "I think Stevie turned out to be a sad poltroon, a jellyfish lacking the backbone to face himself."

"Let me propose a hypothetical to you," Josea softly suggested. "Stevie Green, your band member, comes to you and says, 'I quit, I want to stop this business and go away. I want my privacy and for you to leave me alone.' Would you graciously respect his wish? If you need time, I stay up late. I typically don't require much sleep."

Arnie did take some time. It was enough, in fact, to indicate that what he was concluding even he didn't like. He was forced to punt.

"I'm not sure. Like you said, it's a hypothetical so it really bears no relationship to reality."

"Wow, talk about cowardly acts of jellyfish," Josea reamed heartlessly. "The fact is, my hypothetical is exactly what you deliberated in real life many times, but as Rudy mentioned, refused to confront. This man didn't just pick up and disappear one day. You guys lived together, knew each other intimately for years, and if you're telling me you had no idea how he felt, you got just what you deserved," she said, a clear attempt to smear his face in hypocrisy.

"It's like a man whose wife disappears and he acts like the victim. How could the sap live with her for years and still have no awareness of what she was feeling and thinking? That's the crime, and to tell you the truth," Josea paused, preparing to insert the mortal spear in the bull's heart, "your persistence with this matter is a perverse attempt to relieve yourself of the responsibility and blame you deserve."

"I don't really need this." Arnie growled. Then he looked at me and continued as he pointed dismissively at Josea, "I'd sincerely enjoy sharing a meal here with you, but only if this thing is in her cage."

Arnie headed for the door. In a minute we heard his limo driving away. The rest of the band called it quits too. I was glad. The ongoing loyalty between them was most important. My only concern was for Preston. I feared he'd get caught in the crossfire and be let go from his job. When I mentioned my concern, he whisked it away like a pest fly.

"Don't worry yourself. They're not that stupid to get rid of me," he boasted mischievously. "Besides, now that my position with LIVE is on my resume, I'd have ten offers before the ink on the termination letter dried." Then Preston announced proudly, "I'm somewhat of a star now in my field."

That evening, I felt relieved that my association with the band had officially ended. I had to get some rest. But as it turned out, the bickering for the evening had a way to go. This time it was Josea and Preston. For some reason, Preston wouldn't let up on Reuben. Now, making matters worse, Josea was carrying on a confidential romance with the man. She hadn't time to unclench her jaw after chewing on Arnie before Preston held out his arm for her to bite. I think the only thing that prevented a full blowout between them was they both knew how precious each of them was separately to me—that's friendship.

"Where's your hot chef, Preeti? Boozing in his room or has somebody figured out he's a pervert and arrested him for the killings around here?" Preston chortled.

"Zach told me you had issues with him," Josea snapped. "Is there something wrong with the man not feeling well?"

"Not a thing. And for the record, I don't have issues with him. I have issues with Zach, Preeti, and Souche, issues like their safety."

"Do you know the man well enough to justify having these concerns?" Josea questioned innocently.

"That's the point, nobody knows who the hell this Reuben fellow is. He doesn't exist. I've checked out every Reuben Zapata living in our country and none are he. There is no public record confirming the guy is alive. My opinion is he's probably a fraud running from a sick past," Preston cried out. "I'll tell you something. That's how these characters are. They build a trust one place or another and then when entirely unsuspected, they begin their spree of crime—then they move on to do it elsewhere. You know the rest, a bunch of naïve suckers are left devastated, wondering what happened."

"I have to ask you again though. What really are you basing these aspersions on? So far listening to you, all I hear is paranoia." Josea spooned a sip of soup. "For god sakes, Preston, it's that type of attitude that leads to people like Hitler gaining power. Why don't we go haul him out of his room and shoot him now so we can be sure he doesn't harm us in the future?"

"You're being ridiculous," Preston shrugged. "What I'm suggesting is that Zach demand background information to establish his identity and if he doesn't produce it, fire him."

"I told you last time we talked that I ordered a tandoori oven because Reuben worked in an Indian restaurant in Seattle," I chimed in.

"Yes, you did. And I was going to inform you tonight that I had Seattle records checked and nothing, not an address, state income tax return, driver's license, not a single piece of data exists to show that Reuben Zapata lived there."

"Oh my," Josea mocked. "Lots of people work briefly in a place and move. That proves nothing."

"I've also had the rosters of every culinary school in the world checked and none in the last twenty years have had a Reuben Zapata as a student," Preston yelled victoriously to Josea.

"Maybe his mother taught him to cook. Give me a break, Preston," Josea said with disgust.

"You don't need to defend the guy, Josea, unless you're screwing him," Preston shouted.

Bingo! Preston had no way to know he had just walloped her a good one.

"The man has demonstrated he's honorable and conscientious. We have no right to ask more of a person than sound character," Josea countered, ignoring his insult.

"Josea, we have a right to protect ourselves. Would you go and marry a man you knew nothing about other than he seemed like a nice guy?"

Josea sneered, intentionally looked away from him before taking another serving of her soup. Simultaneously, a platter of pasta was brought to the table.

"I'm hungry. I'll try to find out more about him. You know I'm pretty good at things like that. Isn't that right, Zach?" Josea chuckled.

That's how the conversation ended. The rest of the food was served and we finished eating. I didn't know what she was going to discover about Reuben, or how, but I couldn't wait to find out. It was my impression that the second encounter with Preston went worse for her than the first with Arnie. She knew Preston had raised a worthy point; she was going to have to address it.

In the meantime, there was still the matter of tribal corruption on the list of things to do. Once I completed my work on that subject, I assumed my life would settle down to a simmer. Little did I know these stories had legs as long as the necks I so admired on skinny girls growing up.

18

PLATTA AND HIS SONS

THE NEXT MORNING, JOSEA and I were due to continue our investigation. I ran over to Kuruk before leaving and found Kershaw enjoying breakfast. I walked to the table where he was sitting to say hello.

"Sit down," he instructed. "You're just the man I wanted to talk to."

"I hope I'm not a suspect," I quipped, realizing too late that this was not the type of witty expression to make to an FBI man.

"If you were you'd know it," he assured me. "But I'm not the type of man to tip my hand. When I make a charge you can bet your momma's bosom that'll be your killer," he asserted. "I had a long talk yesterday with the tribe president, Platta. I'm sure you know him."

I nodded and he went on.

Kershaw shook his head sadly. "That father-in-law of yours doesn't have a lot of friends. Platta calls him and his sidekick, Walter, reactionaries. Lots of conflict on the council, which I'm sure you know more about than I."

"I know Platta and Len Cloud don't see eye-to-eye, but there are many tribe members who also back my father-in-law."

"May be that way. I know from the few people who will talk to me that there are serious problems for these people to address. But that doesn't pertain to me, does it?" He stopped momentarily to set the stage for his next topic. "I'm going to level with you, just in case. I don't buy it myself, but Platta's theory is that in some way your father-in-law and Walter are wrapped up with these murders."

Kershaw sat back, shrugging his shoulders like he was tossing a sizzling question mark into my lap. I smiled at the absurdity, refusing to take his lead.

"He reasons that the two of them would stop at nothing to get the tribe to move in the direction of past customs and traditions. The tribe makes a big deal of their Puberty Ceremony coming up in a few days. Platta told me these girls who were killed were choosing not to participate. It's his belief that these young girls were killed as a warning to the other female members—"

"I have to clarify one point because I'm sure that one of the girls, though I can't recall if it was Nita Ortega or Udaya Shash, had never formally announced whether she was coming to the ceremony. I'm not sure the other two had made a declaration either."

"I appreciate that," Kershaw noted. "It really doesn't matter because I don't buy it about Cloud especially, not yet anyhow. Hell, I can't rule out the motive, but at the same time it doesn't ring true to me either...then again, I'm not an Apache."

"Forget Len Cloud being my wife's father, but does it make any sense that people who solemnly adhere to their Apache Indian heritage would kill their own for no purpose other than to terrorize people into a tradition they may reject in the end regardless?"

"Exactly as I see it." Kershaw agreed. "No, this killer is right under our nose and mocking me. He'll do it again when the time is right and now that our beam is on young girls, he'll change the target. His motive is the kill, plain and pure. Many serial killers have to feed every once in a while to satisfy their appetite for blood, simple as that."

Kershaw had finished eating and dropped a ten-dollar bill on the table. He stood up and grabbed a box of cigarettes from his breast pocket.

"Come on outside for a minute while I fuel up the lungs," he said, motioning me with one hand while the other was holding the smokes.

We walked a short distance to his car. He rested his backside on the fender as he withdrew a lighter from his pant pocket and ignited a single stick. He dragged in a deep breath and exhaled a well-practiced white stream.

"Yeah. We found a piece of Kleenex over by the body of Udaya Shash. Whomever it belonged to must have had a cold. We got enough fluid to make a match when the time comes. Boot marks made perfect indentations at the crime scene— damn sweet of the killer. Gum at the Ila Clearbrook's death scene, too."

Kershaw took another draw, swallowing the fumes of the

after-breakfast-picker-upper several seconds before a near imperceptible residue escaped his mouth.

"Not going to be long before the shit hits the fan here in Mescalero."

The cigarette was only a third smoked and he tossed it on the ground, meticulously squeezing the life out of it with the toe of his right foot boot before reaching down to pick up the butt and deposit it into his coat pocket.

"I'm going on my way now. Lots to do..." his voice trailed off. "That father-in-law of yours is a hard son-of-a-bitch."

I went back to the house. Josea was ready to leave. We were headed back to Albuquerque to finish checking a couple unfinished items. We wanted to see if we could tweeze a few new facts that might bring us closer to a full understanding of the matter of misappropriation of tribal funds, a crime we knew for certain had occurred.

We had decided before leaving that Platta was the obvious suspect, given his influence with tribe members, his official position on the tribal council, and Len's suspicion of him. I briefed Josea on my meeting with Kershaw and in particular his comments about Platta's own suspicions of Len and Walter, none of which seemed to intrigue her. What most interested Josea was Platta's family. She opened a file she had prepared with information we had attained up to that point, along with notes to serve as a roadmap for this day's research.

"Funny you should show this to me," I commented while looking at the sheets of paper. "Your first item on the agenda for today reads, 'Look into personal finances of Platta and significant family members.' That's where I thought we should start too."

We did start there. Our first assignment was to find information about the two sons. The hall of records documented that they both lived in Albuquerque. They were named Gopan and Narsi Platta and in a moment we had their addresses. We also attained Platta's wife's name, Betty, and learned that he had one living brother, the first eye-opening shock...Ralph Puente.

We looked at each other and swallowed what we both knew was potentially explosive. Ralph Puente (we later found out he had a different surname from Platta because they had different fathers) was the general partner of Heaven, LLC and an officer of Hawk. If that were the case, then who were the other officers and limited partners of all the entities we had determined to have gained unfair advantage in the bidding process and who had extorted funds from the tribe?

We had our work cut out for us.

It might be best to present only a few of the discoveries we made, since the full disclosures would require a volume of its own. The information was obtained over the course of several sessions and with the assistance of P. A. Farley—which I'll discuss momentarily.

It turned out Platta's wife was Caucasian. She had no brothers but was extremely close with two cousins, Bob Lake and Jesse Wilcox. Stan Fastow was a very close friend of Platta, and Dean Bridgewater, Aaron Sky, and Martin Lattimer never existed.

In some cases, the companies that were awarded the bloated contracts were in the business they claimed and actually did the work. There were several instances, however, in which the companies were parking lots for funds and the work was subcontracted to legitimate businesses. In all cases, the work was completed but at an enormous premium.

After ascertaining the above, we agreed that next we needed to thoroughly investigate the financial affairs of the Platta family. It wasn't difficult to uncover the fact that the two sons were living high, both dwelling in multi-million dollar estates. Determining where their income was coming from was not as simple a task. In fact, it didn't take long once we began the job to know that we had a problem. It was one thing using public records to sniff out leads. It was another accessing bank records that we had no right to without a subpoena. Josea could break into the computer systems as simply as a mom gives her crying baby milk. But it was an illegal act that might conceivably come back to her, and that was too risky.

It was time to call Farley. He was in his office and invited us to visit. We weren't more than a half-hour away and in no time I was violating Len Cloud's instruction. I felt badly about it but at the same time knew we needed to use the investigator's services if we were going to acquire the evidence we required to confirm that Platta and a number of others were crooks. I had no reason to suspect that the murders were related to the corruption, and hoped they weren't.

The exterior wood stairway creaked as we went to the second floor. His door was partially open. As I pushed it, I saw the backside of Farley standing in the corner as he busily whacked away at his pinball machine. I noticed for the first time a large bald spot about five inches in diameter covering the back portion of the scalp, looking like a flesh-colored kippah—a small cap worn by Jewish people in temple or on the streets if orthodox.

"Sit down," he yelled before a word was spoken informing him of our arrival. He was absorbed in play and didn't turn to greet us.

It took him a couple minutes to finish the game. I assumed all the bells and bongs were signs of him putting up a good score. I further assumed if that were the case, it might put him in a fine mood. I was right. When he finally welcomed us he smiled, his chipped amber tooth an advertisement for dental hygiene. He was dressed in the same outfit as the day I'd met him—it may have been his only suit. He sat at his desk, leaning his head down for a moment before straightening up and addressing us.

"I must have done a bang-up job for you if you're back already."

"I don't know if what I need is possible." I said dubiously.

"Believe me, it is. I could set up the assassination of a prime minister, senator, or bulletproof celebrity if you pay me enough."

"There might be a few politicians we all could do without," I mumbled.

"The only good politicians are dead ones," he bellowed. "But you didn't bring the little lady here to talk about nonsense... and by the way, what is your name, pretty thing?"

"I'm Josea," she answered politely.

Farley squinted his eyes, making a show of his deliberate attempt to recover a loose piece of information floating freely in the universal space of his mind. Then he became animated, suggesting he just snagged the elusive tidbit.

"That's an unusual name, dear," Farley said slyly. "You're not..."

Josea knew where he was going. She reasoned it would be easier to shorten the process for Farley.

Josea's name would frequently be included in the same sentence as Stephen Hawking, the distinguished cosmologist and genius who, sadly, had been stricken with an incurable motor neuron disease, ALS. The average person wouldn't likely perk up at hearing either of their names but anyone aware of the field where science, spirituality, and politics intersected would recognize the name Josea Roth. Farley reached across his desk and picked up a magazine. He thumbed through it, opened to a page, and then offered it to Josea for her to see.

"That's you?" he questioned with astonishment. Farley had made the association that sitting across from him was an esteemed scientific mind; a young lady who had authored over a hundred articles, written several books, and had been a sought-after lecturer around the world.

Josea, after dealing with trauma in Israel, had gone through a shutdown, though not a thorough fracture of her ability to think. Still, even after her spiritual retreat, she needed to escape the demands of a world pressing on her like a migraine. Her audience and fan base were nowhere near that of Stevie Green, but finding a place where she could exist incognito was as urgent to her as she assumed it had been for the musical star Green. Being with Preeti and me offered the escape and privacy she needed to complete her recovery. Now Farley had made her.

"That's me, but I'm here as a customer. I'll have to insist on the same strict standard of confidentiality you offer all your clients," she insistently advised him.

Farley stood and deferentially reached out his hand to shake hers.

"It's an honor, Ms. Roth. You have my undying guarantee."

"Mr. Farley, the reason we're here is that Josea has been helping me look into a matter of possible corruption. We need financial records that are not public, if you understand what I'm saying. It's rather complex and extensive, but I think if we limit it to just a few items to start we'll have sufficient evidence to turn it over to the authorities who will know what to do from there," I explained.

"A little touchy, but son, this is the electronic era. We don't need to crack bank vaults, do we?" he humored. "I doubt we'll ever need safes again—nothing can be locked away. Ms. Roth knows that."

"Of course," Josea answered. "But we want to be discreet."

"Understood, my lady. No use bantering this any longer. Depends on how long it takes and how much I might have to pay the right person to get the information, but if you leave me the same retainer I'll start as soon as you tell me the assignment."

I wrote the check and outlined the information we wanted. Farley scanned it.

"Piece of cake. You're lucky, at most a day or two," he said confidently.

We left and drove directly home. Preeti was waiting. She looked troubled. Josea drifted off to her room to give us time alone.

"I called my father to see if he could come over and watch Souche. I wanted to drive to Ruidoso to shop...he refused," she said ominously. "You know he would never miss a chance to be with Souche."

"Did he tell you why?"

"Said he wasn't well. I've known him my whole life and he's never said he was sick."

"People do come down with an ailment once or twice in their life," I advised. "This may be his first."

"It's the way he sounded. His mood was somber. Several times he repeated to me that he wanted me to be sure not to forget that no Mescalero Apache could have done the killing. 'How can you be certain?' I asked him. 'Because there were only three girls killed.' The odd number convinced him."

Preeti ran to intercept Souche, who was stooping to palm a claret cup cactus, attracted to the half-moon mound with tiny, bright red flowers blooming around the base. The yard was exploding with bush morning glories that had sprung large pink blossoms from their underground tubers. The colors were cheery, inspiring to Souche's curiosity but not enough to lighten Preeti's mood.

"Does it really matter if it was one of us or another race?" she rhetorically pled to the heavens. "Those little girls are dead! What's important is that the killing stop." Preeti then deliberated sharing another thought, one she knew she couldn't keep to herself.

"Zach, I was wondering if the reason my father ran over to get Leila Moon is because he didn't want her to be number four. You know about the number four. To my father, if it stopped with four murders than he might have to face the possibility it could be an Apache who is the killer. He talks like he's getting divine messages sometimes, but it does seem farfetched that he'd know she was an intended victim. You know, Zach, if my father knew someone in the tribe did this, he'd kill the person himself."

"Your father's not a killer. I can't believe he would ever commit that sort of act," I contested.

"I don't believe he is either. But don't you get it?" she pled. She was instructing me further on the Mescalero way. "He'd kill the person who was the murderer so as to avoid shame coming to the tribe—that's the justice my people would demand."

"I understand. But this is the twenty-first century. You think he'd risk spending the rest of his life in jail?"

"Yes," she said emphatically. "He'd give his life for his people. Part of him is not living in any one century. He lives in eternity."

"Let's wait and see what happens. Do you want me to go over and check on him?" I offered.

She signaled affirmatively. I left immediately.

When I arrived at Len Cloud's house I knocked. Then I waited, but he didn't respond. I saw his vehicle and wondered if he might be in the shower. I sat on the steps for ten minutes before knocking a second time. After a short wait he came to the door, holding it cracked partway open.

"Tell Preeti I'm fine. I'm in prayer." He spoke ethereally, as if was waving to Einstein's Theory of Relativity.

He shut the door, leaving me standing on the porch.

19

CORRUPTION,
SAME OLD STORY

TWO DAYS AFTER LEN Cloud refused my attempt to visit, he still hadn't come to see Preeti and Souche, which was unusual for him. He would take his daughter's calls but tell her he was in communion with his fathers and couldn't be disturbed. It upset Preeti each time he'd rebuff her but mostly she kept perspective. If her father needed to work through something that huge, she could be sympathetic and give him the space he needed.

Then when least expected, the phone rang. I answered. Len asked if he could come to our home. Of course, I said yes. When I told Preeti he was on his way, she breathed a sigh of relief.

"He must have been with Jivin. How foolish of me."

That was her way of saying he had gone to the "Big Spirit" and found peace. Len arrived shortly after calling. He seemed his normal self.

"Zach. How's that matter I asked you to look into coming along?"

"It's more complicated than I thought. I'll need added time but as soon as I know anything I'll call you," I answered vaguely to stall the matter.

"That's fine. Take the days or months you need to do it right."

"Shitaa, I saw Gloria Chicory at the market yesterday. She mentioned Walter hasn't called her for a couple of days."

"Crazy kid! Probably took off hunting," he responded dismissively.

"Would he go alone?" asked Preeti.

"I've warned him it's not a good idea but he's like a disobedient son. He'll be back," Len grunted. "You can be sure of that." Then he threw in an afterthought. "If he's not here by the Puberty Ceremony, start worrying." Len ended the discussion with a *that-kid* snicker.

"The ceremony is just a few days from now," said Preeti.

Len nodded and then left to look in on his only grandchild while she napped. Often he'd sit in her room while she slept and he wouldn't move, as if he were governing her sleep.

I had shared every detail of my investigation of Platta, et al, with Preeti. She only made one summary comment, "Doesn't surprise me but it's going to be chaos around here again. Zach, can you hold off doing anything until after the fourth?"

I assured her the statute of limitations would not run out, informing her I had already decided to postpone owing to that very point. Further, I informed her that when the corruption was out in the open, it would be adjudicated through a state court.

My phone rang while we were talking. "It's Farley," I informed Preeti as I took the cell into my office.

"This time you're going to have to pay big," he crowed.

"Why?"

"Lots of billable hours," he chuckled. "You'll see. In fact, I think you better come down here so we can talk in person," Farley suggested. "If this is going where I see it, some ass is going to fry. You free today?"

"Sure. I'll check with Josea but I'm positive we can be there by early afternoon."

"I'll be here all day and into the night. Just got a sweet job for a hotel," he said merrily.

I went to find Josea but she wasn't in the house. When I asked Preeti if she knew her whereabouts, she lifted her eyebrow to tell me she assumed the young lovers were out together. I informed her that it was important I find Josea, but that I didn't want to risk discovering them together. Preeti reminded me it wasn't a concern because Reuben wouldn't miss being at the restaurant by eleven for the delivery of his new tandoori oven.

Preeti was right. Josea and I were able to make it to Farley's office by one thirty.

"Kids, the reason I wanted you to come in is I don't think you want me to email or fax this information. Take a look at what we have. Not particularly sophisticated but you'd be surprised, most graft isn't. Blue collar crooks are not known to be the brightest people...they are the most religious," Farley reported without a smile.

"Most religious?" I giggled, looking at Josea to share the comedy.

"You're a bright man but there's a stone side of you," Farley kindly insulted me. "They trust that nobody will ever look into what they do, that nobody will ever find them out. They operate with high levels of faith. Get it? They're stupid."

"What stupid things did these people do?" I questioned him.

"About every one I've seen. I don't care who is part of this deal or what you do with the information I'm giving you, but let me tell you there's enough here to earn people some serious jail time. Take a look."

Farley had diagrammed a simple outline showing how money was moved. Each of the entities we had asked him to investigate would take a portion of the funds received either in payment from the tribal account or advanced from the proceeds of ballooned transactions—from underbidding the purchase of rights, such as the lumber deal—and transfer them to a conglomerate account entitled "Neptune." Farley suggested the name was chosen because the planet is the furthest from earth and therefore least likely to be detected. In Farley's words, "Even in their attempt to be smart, they were idiots."

Platta controlled Neptune, having sole discretion. The other entities, all the corporations and partnerships run by relatives, friends, and fictitious parties, had already enjoyed their share of the booty. Platta personally had, over the last few years, invested an amount Farley estimated to be several million in properties throughout the State of New Mexico, all in his wife's name. Farley had listed for us each of the purchases. He'd also documented how the transfer of funds for the down payments of each piece of land, office building, or commercial property was handled.

As far as the sons went, Gopan, living in the larger of the mini-mansions, had retired from good investments, the best of investments—the type where you risk nothing of your own. He and his brother were both receiving revenue on a monthly basis from rental properties that had been bought with funds transferred from the same Neptune account.

Their homes were also purchased with money taken from the generosity of this inexhaustible fund, courtesy of the Mescalero tribe. Narsi, a son who must have been second-class to his older brother—owing to his mansion being much smaller—had been a teacher for all of one year, taking very early retirement when it became apparent that the flow of income from Neptune would eclipse the salary of even a thirty-year district superintendent.

Farley's detailed findings went far beyond these initial points. That is, the dates of funds coming into and out of the account, the sources from which they came or to which they were distributed were meticulously documented. If the rule is "follow the money," Farley's eyes were green after this assignment.

When Josea asked what was next, I told her nothing until after the Puberty Ceremony, at which time I knew the cow dung would be hitting the proverbial fan. What I didn't know was that the volume of feces would be so vast that the tribe would be able to add manure to their lineup of profitable businesses.

20

THE TANDOORI DINNER INVITATION

WITH THE FOURTH OF July weekend quickly approaching, we spent the next few days preparing food for the ceremony. It was one time that owning a restaurant was disadvantageous. In addition to the normal demands of preparing meals for hundreds of people a day, Reuben and his staff, under Preeti's supervision, were readying dozens of sweet Indian breads (a traditional recipe that Preeti agreed to modify to Reuben's recommendation), sunflower cakes and pots of green chili. It was a sacred tradition for the Mescalero people to demonstrate their generosity by giving.

In addition to arranging food for the festival, we were getting ready for a full house of visitors. My mother and her husband were coming for the celebration—our home was buzzing with excitement. My mom adored both Preeti and Josea, each in their own way filling her latent wish to have had a daughter. Both, in turn, reciprocated the adoration. They would be arriving the following afternoon, Monday.

On that Sunday evening as the dinner service was settling down, Reuben asked if he could talk with me. I assumed he was exhausted and needed to take a few days off since we would be closing during the ceremony. Instead, he said he had an inspiration owing to the arrival of the new tandoori oven. He had created a few new dishes and figured what better audience to test them on than all of us. Since we would be closed Monday, he wondered if he might invite us all to his premiere Indian dinner.

I accepted Reuben's offer for us to act as guinea pigs for his new dishes, something I had done many times before. He was so excited he couldn't resist previewing the menu, most of which I had no frame of reference for since I rarely dined in Indian restaurants. Thus, when he called out that he would be serving sweet potato samosas and hot onion pakoda as appetizers with naan garlic bread, tandoori skewered prime rib and prawns in tamarind sauce as main dishes, masala dal and channa cabbage as sides, and mango mousse for dessert, all I could say was, "I'll look forward to it, but truthfully only the mango mousse sounds vaguely familiar." He assured me it would be a feast worthy of a king's celebration. He wasn't kidding, except no kings showed up.

I was looking forward to time with my mother, but I also wanted to let her meet Reuben so I could ask her opinion of him. This dinner would serve as the perfect opportunity. I had talked with her regarding Preston's concerns, and she had heard a mouthful from my friend as well. She was another person I knew to have sharp antennae. If her picture of

Reuben also blurred, I would be more inclined to push in the direction Preston was suggesting.

Early the following morning, my mother and Nasir called to let us know they had spent the night across the Arizona border in Gallop, New Mexico and assumed they would arrive near noon. It was all coming together nicely. The Puberty Ceremony and Fourth of July would be spent with my family and Josea. There would be entertaining fireworks commemorating both the American and Mescalero culture—I anticipated that there would also be a second display of fireworks beginning after the weekend, for which there would be no cause for celebrating. The sparks about to fly would be from hot embers singeing corrupt Mescalero officials.

Preeti had received a call from Walter's cousin informing her that Walter still had not shown up. My wife tried to comfort her by assuring the woman that Walter would be back in time for the ceremony, now only a couple of days away. Still, she expressed to me that it seemed odd he would disappear without a word, and for such a long period of time.

When she called her father to see if, by chance, he had heard from Walter, he told her he hadn't but in the back of his mind recalled Walter saying he was taking a trip and would be back on time. Again, he reminded her that this was not the first time he had left unannounced and that he was a grown man. Preeti wasn't satisfied. She agitated on the issue all that day.

It was almost exactly noon when my mother, Kaye Miller, and her husband, Nasir, pulled into the driveway. We all went out to greet them and my mother froze. The look of joy was unimaginable, but also overwhelming. I think she didn't know how to handle it, a rare moment for the lady. She was looking at her son, daughter-in-law, first and only grandchild, and a young woman she cared for like a daughter. Whom would she hug first?

She found a clever way of handling her dilemma. She motioned for each of us to come to her and she hugged the living daylights out of all of us together. Then to complete the chain, she grabbed Nasir by the arm and pulled him in. But her first words were to Preeti.

"I'm sorry, Preeti, for your sadness. I told you the other day on the phone I was going to stay until everything was settled here, and I mean it. I'll help with Souche and do whatever you need." She looked lovingly at her daughter-in-law. "It breaks my heart what you have been through." She solo-hugged Preeti, me, and then finally, Josea. She left the little one for last. She lifted her up, embraced her tightly, and after close inspection of her beautiful features, she handed Souche to Nasir.

"Take her. She's your grandchild too."

Kaye Miller had met her husband—now my stepfather—while in Israel working passionately to find evidence that would validate a plot against the Israelis, one the Israelis refused to believe when I informed them of it. Nasir had been a well-known and respected journalist in the Middle East who for the most part had retired after bonding with my mother. The couple married shortly after I returned home.

It was really perfect having all of us together. Preeti was notably sad, and my mother hovered over her gently but not intrusively. I notified everyone that we would be having dinner at Kuruk and explained the circumstances. Comically, I prepared the group who were soon to be subjects of a Reuben-experiment by letting them know they might want to bring Rolaids if they weren't used to food on the hot side.

We spent the afternoon hanging around the house talking. The time passed quickly, and in what seemed like a moment, we were on our way to the feast. When we arrived at the restaurant, I counted the place settings—seven. I quickly calculated that with Preeti, Souche, and myself, plus my mother and Nasir, and finally Josea, we were at six. Did Reuben miscount? Or, I wondered, was there going to be a seventh surprise guest?

It turned out to be the latter. It never dawned on me who it would be Reuben had set the added place for...Reuben! Every time he had tested new menu items on people in the past, he assembled them at the table and took special interest in serving his own preparations. This time he sat down with us, promptly making an announcement.

"Just this once I'm changing the game plan. I have Dolly and Isha here to serve, and Bueno's in the kitchen. I want to test these dishes out with everyone else—it's a special night."

Reuben raised a cup of wine. The glasses in front of each of us had been filled before we sat.

"I hope this will be a most joyous dinner for all of you. It will be for me," he slyly added.

I tagged on to his line. "I thought Reuben was going to cry if I refused the tandoori oven so that's why he's so happy."

"Wait until you taste the food. Then you'll see if your investment has been worthwhile," Reuben bantered.

"It's already worth it. What you've done for Kuruk is priceless." I raised my glass a second time to toast him. "To Samosas, Pakodas—to you."

My last words coincided with a platter of the most beautiful brown breaded and fried onion fritters being brought to the table. I had never had pakodas, but Nasir knew what they were. After tasting the first one, he immediately deduced that Reuben was no joke in the kitchen. Nasir had traveled extensively throughout the world during a career spanning three decades. He had eaten in the finest restaurants.

"I don't believe I ever told you, Zach, but my first post for Al Jazeera was in their bureau in Delhi, India." Then he addressed Reuben. "I've had onion pakoda in many restaurants but I can tell you these are the best. What did you do?"

Reuben grinned. "I use a mango puree with sifted flour and add just a sprinkle of cayenne. Then I use peanut oil for the frying. I believe it's the choice of oil with the mango that sets the flavor."

By now the second appetizer was being placed on the table. Nasir snatched one before the platter hit the surface. He took a generous bite and savored it like a wine connoisseur.

"The dough. Magnificent! Reuben, you must ask us to dinner more often," Nasir complimented.

Preeti was quiet and Kaye Miller tried to draw her out.

"Preeti, tomorrow we'll take Souche for the day, if it's okay," she offered. "Sometimes a day to yourself can help."

"Thanks. Of course, you'll take her. Souche would love that. But I don't think it's time I need." Preeti was not a person to withhold how she felt. "We are a close people here. I'm not an Apache in the way my father is, but I am devoted to my heritage and the faith of my people. Things are terrible, as you know, and now a man we all know well is missing."

"We don't know for certain that he's missing," I corrected.

"Zach, we don't...but be sensible. It's been days now," she stated, the peculiarity of the circumstance boding unfavorably for Walter in her opinion.

"But your father said he's done this before and he'll be here for the Puberty Ceremony," Josea reminded her.

"He won't be here. Walter has met a bear," Preeti proclaimed.

"Are you saying he's dead, Preeti?" my mom asked.

Preeti nodded agreement.

"How do you know?" I posed curiously.

"The heart knows, my love. Death is still descending on our land. I pray White Painted Woman will come to visit the Puberty Ceremony. Then she can help turn us back to harmony as the circle demands. But I think it will take even more this time."

I had not heard Preeti in the past speak much about her tribal beliefs, but that was changing.

"Walter was trying to fight off death by defying it. The bravest of warriors cannot win that battle," she posited.

The table was quiet. If Reuben had been planning an eating experience of laughter and joy, he had just been bonged on the head by a wild pitch. Still, the discussion had a ways to go.

"After the Fourth, we will send a search party of the best trackers. They will bring back his body," Preeti said with certainty. "At the ceremony, we will bargain with the devil to end the murdering."

I waited until she paused, sensing after a few seconds of silence that Preeti had completed the prognosticating. Instead, she continued.

"Kaye, Nasir, Josea, Reuben, in a few days you will be part of the most sacred ceremony of my people. There will be thousands of guests who come from different cultures and backgrounds to watch something they don't understand. I would like to share with all of you a few points because during the ceremony this year I will be praying."

They all sat and stared like pupils waiting for the professor's lecture.

"As humans we face no greater threat than that of the unknown, for it brings with it the potential of chaos. My son, Jivin, could see into the future, but for most of us it is only on a rare occasion when we are in possession of such vision. All we know for certain is that the future will bring change.

"But there is a location we call time, and when the future is beckoning us to say goodbye to the past there is a space between where we were and where we are going. That is the precise zone separating the death of the past and the birth of the future. That gap between seems to us in our normal perception to be so tiny so as to not be distinguishable, so that the two dimensions of past and future are in fact one. But that is not true.

"Actually, the separation between what has happened in the past and what will take place in the future can be expanded tremendously. Certain people can step between the two realms, use their spirit to widen the gap even further, and stop the imperceptible flow that makes dimensions of time and space inseparable. From that position, they can guide the process of change to avoid chaos.

"My people are facing what seems like an endless chiasm. To survive we must have help from a great spirit. Everything you will see at the Puberty Ceremony is symbolic of the act of bringing ordered change."

Preeti glanced out toward all of us, noticing she had not lost any of our attention.

"My father will dance, but it will be the spirit of Libaye, the boy clown, the paradox—what Jivin personified to his people—that will bring healing. Too many people have tried to impose their personal wills to either keep the people in the past unchanged or move them to the future unharnessed from their history. That's why there has been murder."

The table was silent. Preeti was wandering into new territory, her soul lit. Her father warned me she was an Apache at heart, and I was being presented indisputable proof. I loved the force and depth of vision being borne out of her, much like she birthed our child. My worry was that her expectations would be disappointed. Desperation is parent to hope and hope is a sucker's bet. Preeti was not a foolish lady, but I could see the despair toying unmercifully with her will.

After she finished her short lesson, she looked refreshed. Her spirits also seemed cleansed.

"Reuben, I've been talking and keeping everyone from enjoying the feast you've prepared. I hope you'll accept my apology," Preeti appealed to our host.

"I've suffered too watching what has happened over the past few weeks," Reuben responded. "I like to think of this as home. To see the peace and beauty of Mescalero harmed hurts me also." He looked with sincerity at his boss. "Your words are far more important than the meal. You have no need to apologize to me."

"Then let's test out the treats," Josea sung out.

We did. Reuben had a number of suppliers for each of the foods he required in preparing his dishes. His meat vendor was in Kansas and he had the beef flown in daily. If what he received wasn't up to his standard, it went back. Reuben had the reputation of fastidiousness by the companies sending products to Kuruk. On occasion, I'd get an angry call from one of the suppliers regarding a return, but I would always support my chef. I knew in the end it had to do with customer satisfaction. That's what kept us in business.

That said, where he came up with the idea of blister-packed prime rib bathed for forty-eight hours in a wet steam and then served as melt-in-the-mouth skewers I hadn't a clue, but it was a hit. The prawns were what Reuben called tens, meaning there were ten to the pound. They were large, crunchy, and with a taste sensation that would make chefs bow—the man had a gift. We would soon find out he actually had two of them.

When we finished the main courses and several side dishes, Reuben had us sit for a moment. Presumably, he went to check something in the kitchen. We appreciated the break to digest and relax. If I were a cigar man, this would have been the perfect time to light up.

Reuben came back sporting a grin on his face. Had Preston been present he would have called it a "shit-eating grin." The man had something else to bestow on us other than the meal. He couldn't wait to share his second present of the evening. None of us knew what to expect and were further baffled when instead of taking his seat between Preeti and my mother, he picked up his glass of wine and moved to position himself behind Josea.

"I have a special announcement to make. I know this will come as unexpected to most of you." He smiled at Josea, who did the same back to him. "Josea and I are engaged."

If I could I would leave about a hundred pages blank right here, because that's how long the silence lasted before Josea broke it.

"Well, are we going to celebrate or sit here looking at each other?" she whooped. She took a healthy gulp of her wine and kissed Reuben. "We were hoping that announcing it now would be a good omen for the upcoming tribal festivities. We'll wait until just after to get married," she added giddily.

I still hadn't said a word.

"Zach," Josea called out. "Do you remember how long you knew Preeti before you decided you would marry her?"

"About that long?" I answered with intentional vagueness.

"How long is that?" Josea persisted with the questioning.

"As long as it took when you first saw Reuben the other day," I teased.

Josea giggled and grabbed Reuben by the scruff to draw him in for a kiss.

"Got you on this one, didn't I Zach?" she said proudly.

"Not really," I said indifferently. "I would have never said anything but since you've gone public I'll admit I saw the two of you the other morning out in the woods."

"You stinker," Josea said playfully. "And you said nothing?"

"I was waiting for you."

"And you Preeti. You knew also?" Josea asked.

"Zach and I have no secrets."

Josea was off guard, but only for a moment. "We're getting married. Did you figure that out? We even had..." she stopped for a laugh. "Did you figure that out?"

It was actually a great way to end the evening. After we finished the celebration, we were ready to go home. Preeti and I gathered up our little daughter, who'd slept on the floor throughout the announcement. We assumed the big child, Josea, was coming home too. But as happens for all parents, things change—we were to have one extra bedroom empty that night.

"I'm sleeping here with Reuben," Josea informed us.

As for what this new arrangement meant to our lives, to Kuruk, we would have to wait for the answer from the dancers traversing the chiasm between the Shadow World and the Real World. For now, all we presumed was that soon after the Puberty Ceremony we would be attending a wedding.

On the way home, I solicited my mother's opinion, especially regarding Reuben. I wanted to see if it coincided or collided with that of Preston.

"Mom, any impressions of Reuben?"

"As far as I'm concerned the man is gold. One might question what a fellow of his mind is doing as a chef, but as far as I'm concerned all it means is that he has a dominant artistic side and uses that great mind in the service of creativity."

"And you Nasir?" I inquired.

"Let me just tell you, Zach, if you're worried about Josea she's going to be a happy lady."

Souche was in her car seat between Nasir and my mother, sleeping like an angel. Timed to my mom's last words, she made a gurgling sound.

"Is little Souche joining the conversation?" Preeti asked from the front.

"No, actually I think she passed gas," my mom responded with a sniff.

On that note, I cracked open my window.

21

THE PUBERTY CEREMONY

THERE WERE NO ADDED murders. The number had remained an odd three.

For now, at least, the ceremony could go forward with the belief that the killing had passed like a mysterious plague; the assumption that no Mescalero Apache was involved prevailed. It mattered not that there was no rational foundation for the comfort that had been peddled similar to forged art amongst the tribe members. There was fresh optimism permeating the beginning of the event; that's all that mattered.

For days prior to the opening of the festivities, a physical transformation could be seen throughout the mesa where the ceremony would take place. The roads were also busier than normal. Dust circled and settled every which direction as cars, vans, and trucks hauled people, equipment, and supplies to the reservation.

Relatives living in other cities in New Mexico or out of state began to arrive. They took vacation time to coincide with the Puberty Ceremony and to be with the rest of their families. Structures were being set in place. The central area of the mesa was being fenced off so that the space within it could be allocated in the traditional rigid manner. It had to be partitioned with separate locations for the girls going through the ceremony, their families, the singers, dancers, and musicians. The head singer occupied the center area inside the fenced space. There was also a temporary structure called the Holy Lodge.

During the first day of the four-day-and-four-night ceremony, Len Cloud sat for a time with Josea, Reuben, and me—Preeti was going to be singing and at that time was busy preparing for her function. When he showed up, it was the first time I had seen him out of uniform. He was wearing cutoff jeans frayed at the bottoms. His torso was painted with two figures, an arrow and a rifle. On his head was a beanie cap of red and black with several buttons sewn around the perimeter. He looked ridiculous. I might have laughed except I didn't dare offend him.

Sticking out of the beanie was a large blue-and-yellow feather waving in the light breeze. He said nothing about his appearance. Both Josea and Reuben looked stupefied, but neither risked saying a word either—besides, they were so gaga in love it made no difference to them.

Len pointed to the lodge to give us some perspective.

"It's called the Holy Lodge. There are twelve specially selected poles holding it up. I harvested each of them. The four foundational pieces are called the Grandfathers. See them?" he asked to be sure we were paying attention. "Those four poles are of particular importance. The first to be set is in the east. It coincides with the first day, the day of Creation, and represents the Power of Life.

"The second is placed in the south. With the Creation complete, we must now have the Power to grow. We need rain and sun. The third is moved to the westerly location. It represents the third day of Creation and the Power to endure. What purpose is there in life if we cannot continue to participate in its endlessness?

"Zach knows this but you two don't. You'll notice the circle moves from the east and around to the south, west, north, and back easterly. This is the Circle of Life and must not be challenged without terrible consequence." Len looked at me, knowing that I was also thinking about Walter, who still had not made his appearance. "If you look carefully at how the area is laid out, and then how the various ceremonies and activities are conducted, you'll notice they always follow this prescribed circular path.

"As you no doubt figured out, the fourth pole is assigned the northerly location and stands for the Power of completion and respect to The Creation. There is symbolic significance to everything you've seen and will see during these four days." Len stopped to choose his next words exactingly. "Sadly, there are an increasing number of exceptions, as some of our people are willing to give the guests what they want rather than what we stand for. You see, there are Apache people who are now more interested in wealth than tradition, but in the next few days we will try to resolve our differences."

Len took a deep breath, ceasing his lesson. He then stood to leave. He offered no explanation for why he was going. It would not be until the final day that he would return to embellish further for us. In fact, even Preeti refused to discuss with me the clothing her father wore. Each day, he put together a different outfit suitable for a Halloween contest of the absurd.

It was the fourth day when everything built to a crescendo. The tempo of the music intensified and the dance presentations increased in speed, volume, and oddity. Len Cloud had been one of the first performers, sharing his piece with three other dancers—a perfect foursome. He moved in the most ungraceful fashion—totally incongruous to the other partners. In fact, each appeared to be moving to different rhythms and beats, influenced by alternating instructions.

They were each dressed as foolishly as Len; actually the others might have exceeded his nonsensicalness. One, in particular, caught my attention, a man wearing what appeared to be diapers with a bra-like apparatus around his breasts—it was not his mother's clothing he was experimenting with, unless the poor lady had the chest of a slide rule. None of us had a clue what was going on until an hour later when Len, now garbed in his usual outfit, came to sit with us.

"It was very hard today—I tried with all my heart, but I am not Libaye like my grandson was."

Len's hardened face had a perpetual look of sadness—it had been visible for days.

"What's a Libaye?" Reuben posed the obvious question.

"If you have time to pay attention I will tell you."

Len stared at Josea and Reuben.

"Of course, we do," Josea quickly assured him.

"Paying attention is the rarest talent. By paying attention, the Shadow World and the Real World can become one or be separated by great measures of time and space. If you can pay attention you are a great person. Jivin always said that the only difference between him and the rest of us was that he had the power of unmitigated attention." Len looked my way. "He could make you pay attention if he wanted, couldn't he?"

I smirked, knowing where my father-in-law was headed.

"Yes. But I couldn't stay there and I'm not sure now I can go back," I answered.

"Okay. So I will ask if all of you can pay the closest attention you can," he compromised, aware that his first request of total attention would likely not be satisfied by any of us. "We have the Shadow World, which is our world, one of illusion, change, a world of phantoms of the mind and hidden meanings. We also have the Real World, the world of potential, power, space, and truth.

"Most people live their whole lives in the Shadow World. It's not bad. For most humans, it is good."

"Why?" Josea asked.

"Because to traverse from the Shadow World to the Real World is dangerous and frightening."

"I think we have something close to that in my religion, Judaism. I have studied an ancient line of inquiry collected in a body of works called Kabbalah. It deals with the mystical aspect of Rabbinic Judaism. It's the esoteric teaching of the relationship between what we see as an external and mysterious

Creation on the one hand and the mortal and finite universe of the Creator on the other," Josea rattled off as easy as a little girl reciting her ABC's.

"Yes, it is close. I think the wise men in any culture have had to address these matters. We Mescalero are greatly concerned with esoteric issues. Our forefathers approached them as secrets only a few chosen ones knew about. Their emphasis was on how we could use the Power to traverse between the two realms."

"So the scary part is going there—by paying attention?" Josea questioned.

"Yes. We are not all prepared to make the journey. We must be able to cross back and forth between the two realms. Only then can a person provide healing for their people. There are no rules for when one is suspended between the two worlds. If one ventures there but lacks the proper Power, he may be lost forever someplace in the time and space warp between the two worlds."

"I suppose what you're saying is that one cannot really will themselves to go," Reuben wondered.

"I don't know. I'm not an authority on that subject because truthfully I'm not sure I've gone. But I assume a great force in the universe tells the earth being it's time and that they can do it. Then they go," Len calculated.

More than the rest of our group of outsiders, Josea was obsessed with the bizarre costumes. She had several times casually commented between us on the outlandish outfits worn by Len and several other tribe members. I knew she couldn't quash her curiosity in spite of the fact that Preeti had refused to even address the question when she posed it to her.

"What about the weird clothing and outfitting?" Josea stopped to deliberate. "Let me guess. It has something to do with making it a game?"

Len said nothing for a moment. Then he looked at me.

"Little one with the big brain. Isn't that what you called her?"

I recalled Jivin using that exact phrase to describe Josea, but I didn't see what difference it made as to who used the reference. I sent an affirmative nod to him.

"That's fairly close. You see we believe Libaye, the clown, can loop back and forth, positioning himself for periods of time in the World of Games with No Rules. So we dance the clown. Truthfully, though, most of us are not going to make the journey. Personally, it's an act of fertilization, the rest of us helping the boy clown, the Power, to make the trip and thereby help his people."

"The boy clown?" popped out of Reuben.

"We believe the boy has more Power than all the grown men together," Len continued. "He will be the one who can help people see through the window that will show them who they are and offer a passageway into their potential, the Power of the People. So when the boy dances, we watch. He may paint a dove on his chest and a dagger on his backside and dance between the worlds to help us reconcile between violence and peace.

"Most important is that we must make progress and at the same time retain our culture. How can we do this when one force is pulling us away from what is known and another dragging us toward something unrealized? The vision for cultural change comes from the clown. His magic is that in the end there will be transition, but it will seem like everything is the same."

"That is beautiful. I feel that. It's an amazing concept," Reuben expressed enthusiastically. "It's real...but magical at the same time. It's resolution of differences. It's overcoming feelings of hate and enmity, but without conscious awareness. Is that what I'm hearing, or is it my imagination playing with wishful thoughts?"

"I've never heard it said like that." Len was taken by the keen interpretation. "Reuben, you are a wise man. You could be a Mescalero," Len joked, though he seemed to be doing so in earnest.

"I doubt that. But I could be a cook for the Mescalero," Reuben quirkily answered. Then he posed a question to Len. "I understand what is being addressed here, but why is it called the Puberty Ceremony?"

"The girls being inducted into the ceremony walk the land for four days. After that, they have earned the symbol of influence, the eagle feather, and they are no longer girls. That's when our cultural heroine, White Painted Woman, enters their soul."

The crowd around us was applauding an act, but we were somber in our silence. None of us wanted to mention murder, but three less girls had survived for White Painted Woman to circulate about the population to keep the tribe vibrant. Len addressed the point for us.

"We have had death lately but we will survive that. What we cannot survive is loss of our heritage and way of life. Look around you," Len suggested. "Can you 'pay attention' to the deep meaning of this ceremony when you are distracted by banners, fireworks, advertisements, and displays of modern music?"

"Of course, you can," Reuben insisted. "If you can dance the clown between the two world realms, you can embrace the future without giving up the past."

Len appeared to be touched by Reuben's astuteness. "You are a Mescalero." Then he followed the compliment with a gem of a statement. "Too skinny to be a warrior...but you have the wisdom of Old Man Thunder."

The festivities ended at dusk. Len had already dismissed himself from us to take care of other responsibilities he had for the ceremony. The huge crowd dissipated rather quickly, leaving a residue mostly of locals and participants. The three of us were still talking when I noticed a vehicle pull up with another right behind it. I recognized the first as belonging to Gabe Kershaw. He hopped out while another agent sitting shotgun followed him. From the second vehicle, two other plain-clothed men exited and marched a few feet behind Kershaw.

Len Cloud was talking to Platta at the time. Their conversation did not seem friendly. It was interrupted when Kershaw appeared. He communicated with the two men for a minute or two. Then I noticed Len turn his body clockwise to scan around him. When he came to us, he stopped and pointed.

Kershaw followed the line of Len's extended index finger. I assumed he wanted to talk with me. I had no idea what could be so urgent that he'd come out at night, especially at precisely the time the ceremony was ending. Kershaw began striding in our direction. So forceful and authoritative was his movement that the other three agents seemed as if they were being dragged behind him by an invisible force. Josea and Reuben had their backs to them the whole time and didn't witness any of what I did.

It all happened so fast I really couldn't process what was going on. I do know Josea was screaming while the agents stood guard like mastiffs.

"You have a right to remain silent. Anything you say or do—"

The words made no sense...until Josea and I were left standing while Reuben, with his hands cuffed behind his back, was led off by the four men.

Josea ran after the men, screaming threats in their faces so invectively I had to pull her off for fear they'd arrest her too. As they loaded Reuben in the car, I stood holding Josea, who was wailing like she'd lost a child. She never saw Reuben mouthing pitifully, "I'm sorry."

I saw his lips form the words. I was sorry too. But what was he sorry about? He might have been angered, insulted, embarrassed, or indignant...but sorry?

He didn't ask a question like, "What did I do?" He didn't argue, "You're making a mistake, you have no right to do this!"

No. All he said was, "I'm sorry."

It peeved me. My first thought was of Preston and his barrage of not-so-mild admonitions about Reuben. I had no idea what the charges would be but knew intuitively it couldn't be failure to appear for an outstanding traffic violation. Equally wacko was the prospect of an arrest for forgetting to file his income tax returns for the past decade—hell, if the Secretary of the Treasury could get away with tax evasion, what penalty could Reuben be facing? No, it wasn't tax evasion or a ticket for rolling through a stop sign. The mystery was solved for all of us in short order.

"He's been charged with murder of the Clearbrook, Ortega, and Shash girls," Len informed us.

Josea was inconsolable, crying hysterically when she heard the word murder associated with her beau. Then, as if her team just lost the first game in a seven-game series, she calmed herself. She was ready for battle.

"It's a bunch of shit. It's like reverse discrimination," she defiantly protested. "Reuben couldn't damage a flea."

Preeti had heard the news and came rushing over, setting off a second round of tears for Josea. She kept muttering loony exclamations like, "I'll defend him to my death." "They set him up." "They don't know who he is."

As she protested the injustice of the charges, I muttered to myself that it might turn out none of us knew who he was— or what he was capable of doing.

I prayed all the way home. I'm less a fan of supplication then diarrhea, but still I dreamed it was all a mistake...please, please, please I recall rehearsing as I looked at my friend sobbing in my wife's arms.

My mother and Nasir had left the ceremony hours before us to relieve the babysitter. They were playing with Souche in the living room when we came in.

"What happened?" Kaye cried out, horrified by the shroud of agony covering Josea's face.

Josea ran up to her and continued sobbing while my mother held her. I eyed my mom as she looked at me for an answer. When I told her, she held Josea at arms' length, grasping her shoulders.

"Now you tell me, dear, is he innocent?" she demanded.

Josea nodded her head to indicate he was.

"Then we will fight this. If we could get Zach out of that mess in Israel, this should be a breeze for us," she said confidently.

The FBI had brought charges against Reuben. They had been investigating for weeks and must have amassed extensive evidence. Not to mention that Josea was in love—for the first time—and that's not typically the most rational state from which to pass judgment on one's partner. Yet there the two of them were, convincing each other of his innocence.

Walter was a no-show for the entire ceremony. That meant White Painted Woman had not restored peace and harmony.

The upside was that Reuben—if proven to be the killer—was in jail and the murders would be over for good. The downside was that if Walter didn't come to the ceremony, it was guaranteed he'd run into trouble, serious life-threatening trouble. There was no other explanation because had he been arrested, his cousin and Len would have been called to the rescue.

There were only two possibilities. The first was that he had been killed. Either he'd run afoul with the wrong person or persons or, while hunting, he had been attacked by a bear and mutilated—the latter highly unlikely in that Walter was one of the most knowledgeable about the local terrain and wildlife. The second possibility was that he had run for his life because he was the one who had killed the girls—and somebody knew it. This was also highly unlikely now that Reuben had been arrested and nobody had suggested Walter as a suspect.

It was still fairly early when we arrived home. Preeti assured me she would settle things down in the house. She asked if I'd go to her father's place and talk to him regarding what they were going to do about Walter.

I agreed. Truthfully, though, I had my own agenda to address before visiting my father-in-law.

22

MY FIRST FEDERAL OFFENSE

I DROVE TO KURUK. By the time I arrived, it was dark and eerie. The FBI was nowhere in sight. I presumed they'd already swept Reuben's room or would swoop down again the following morning to double check.

With only diffused moonlight, I keyed open the back door. Not wanting to arouse suspicion in the event somebody was watching, once inside, I took a flashlight and used it to make my way through Reuben's living quarters. As I beamed the light around a space I had lived in and knew intimately, I noticed that my focus was more on what was missing than what was present.

There was not a single photograph or keepsake to suggest the man had a past. Where were the people who were or had been precious to him? Other than a lone photograph recently taken of Josea, there was nothing intimate. He was an authentic minimalist. He had minimal clothing, minimal possessions of a personal nature, and minimal materials indicating interests or hobbies.

I made an inspection of his cottage but found nothing I thought important. I was certain that the FBI had to have already taken any evidence they wanted. I sat on the sofa, appreciating the darkness and silence. I couldn't help thinking back on the afternoon of the first murder when Reuben came back bruised and Preeti ministered to his wounds. Then like tattlers, more thoughts dashed at me to participate in the prosecution of Reuben.

After the second and third murders, it was Reuben who curiously showed up from an all-day hike, alleging to have been running to get in shape while wearing a sweatshirt on a hot afternoon. Then when he was informed about the murders, he walked away without a word.

There was more. Reuben had sunk into a funk just after the first murder. Then when I talked to him, he went so far as to pronounce his innocence to the crime more as an interrogatory than declaratory statement. I battled to dismiss the pesky thoughts, squashing them downward into my psyche.

Before I left, I had to satisfy the curiosity that had inspired me to enter his room. Under a floorboard in the bedroom was an empty space. It was no bigger than a loaf of bread. I had shown it to Reuben when he moved in, telling him it was a good place to leave a valuable. We never discussed it again; there was no reason to have done so.

I was certain that unless the FBI literally tore the structure apart, they wouldn't have found it. With my flashlight illuminating, I went into the bedroom and opened the closet door. Carefully, I lifted the plank. After removing it, I noticed that the only items were a number of recent phone bills. Didn't seem like much, but instinctively I stuffed them into my pocket.

I replaced the piece of wood. As I did, I wondered if it wouldn't be worthwhile to check the calls he'd made. Was it possible that some of the numbers would repeat, offering a clue about family or friends? Anyone knowing my past would have questioned how I hadn't learned my lesson about snooping—but I hadn't—the urge was an untamable beast sure to get me into trouble. I did deliberate putting the phone bills back and playing fair, but sometimes playing fair is boring. Besides, if doing it on the up-and-up was the game, why the hell was I there in the first place?

I snuck out of the cottage like an amnesic burglar ignorant of having robbed his own house. I reached into my pocket and felt the phone bills, hesitating to take them out because I was aware I was committing a crime by tampering with evidence. I walked straight to my car and left for my father-in-law's home.

When I arrived, Len acted as if he'd been expecting me. We sat across from one another on two matching wood frame chairs.

"I suppose you have news for me?"

"About what?"

"This business with Platta. What did you find out?" he asked pointedly.

"I didn't want to brief you until I finished. Unfortunately, with the Stevie Green matter and then helping Preeti get ready for the ceremony, I haven't given it the attention it deserves," I explained apologetically. "My plan is to pick up the ball now that I'll have time. I think I'll have it completed in a couple weeks," I said to buy myself the maximum time I thought I could justify.

"That's fine. Believe me, the rascal Platta is as safe where he is as Reuben. The murderer is in jail," Len said with disgust.

I felt irked by his quick conviction of Reuben but said nothing.

"He's probably dead," Len voiced. He spoke void of any sign of emotion.

"I don't know who you're talking about."

"Walter," Len said casually.

"For some reason, his cousin has been leaning on Preeti. She's got a lot she's trying to cope with right now."

"I'll call the cousin and notify her," Len volunteered.

"Notify her of what?" I questioned, wondering how he could pronounce him dead when there was no proof that was the case.

"Tell you what," he said as if we were negotiating a contract. "I'll put a group of people together and go out tomorrow to find his remains."

"What about Kershaw? Shouldn't he be notified? In all fairness, what if there's a mistake and Walter is the killer? We can't dismiss the probability that he took off to escape arrest."

"Kershaw knows he's missing but it's not his jurisdiction. Sure, Walter was a tad unbalanced but not a killer. When all the facts come out you'll see that it couldn't have been an Apache—I told you that."

"You said it couldn't be a 'sane' Apache," I reminded him of his revised conclusion.

"Now it's clear that it's not any Apache."

"Okay, but Len, isn't Kershaw going to look for Walter?"

"Put Kershaw out in those mountains and he wouldn't be able to locate his balls," Len shrugged, a gesture suggesting I was a buffoon to even raise the possibility of the agent knowing how to find a missing person on Apache land. "We'll locate Walter."

Based on past experience, I knew Len could be mistaken— from my point of view Kershaw had a damn good chance of finding Walter, and an even greater one of finding his testicles. Still, I knew Len would take off to try and discover what had happened to Walter.

"What evidence do they have against Reuben? Do you know things that haven't been announced yet?"

"Zach, wait. It will all come out and you'll see he's guilty," Len stated as fact. "Smart kid. It's too bad. I liked him too."

"I believe we should let him have a trial first before we convict him, don't you?" I responded with irritation.

"The White Man needs trials so he can play with facts like acts in a circus." Len closed his eyes. "He's guilty."

I would say that evening was the first time I felt revulsion for the man. I went home with rage in my veins. I would join forces with Josea Roth and Kaye Miller to defend Reuben Zapata against what I wanted to be a "false" charge of murder. Len Cloud, regardless of his great power of perception, needed to be taught a lesson in humility.

23

KERSHAW'S LAST MEAL AND THE SEARCH FOR WALTER

THE ARREST AND ASSUMED guilt on the part of Reuben had far-reaching repercussions, filling the spectrum from inconsequential to grave. On the lighter side, my first call after arriving at Kuruk the morning following the disaster with Reuben was from an angry Jill Radcliff, the personal secretary to the governor. She was "obviously" cancelling the invitation for Reuben Zapata to cook at the state leader's home—she was so testy with me one might have thought I committed the murders.

A most surprising development had to do with my staff at the restaurant. I assumed that as everyone arrived for work there would be chaos. It was my job to hold hands with the people I knew would be devastated. As expected, the workers were in disarray; there was lots of crying, disbelief, and disillusionment.

It's one thing to read about a serial killer and how that person held down a job, had a family, went to church, and volunteered for community activities. It's another thing to be one of those people who actually had a direct relationship with that person now assumed to be a cold, killing monster.

I told everyone that if they felt they couldn't handle their duties at work that day they could leave. I even offered to pay for the shift regardless. I also suggested bringing in a psychologist to talk with them. I was shocked at the way they pulled together. Not one staff member would consider leaving. Collectively and individually they expressed appreciation for the offer of outside professional assistance but trusted that they could deal with it among themselves. Within moments, we all kicked into gear and breakfast was served without a glitch.

I assumed the kitchen staff was going to take greater attention. With Reuben out of the picture, I anticipated having to make major changes. Soeze would prove to be amazingly valuable. In fact, before I arrived she had already outlined the calls she planned to make to some of the top restaurants in Albuquerque and began exploring possibilities as far away as Los Angeles, San Francisco, and New York. She also placed a call to a friend in Texas who was in the restaurant business to research a replacement for Reuben.

I had another idea that dawned on me as she and I strategized the issue. Why not temporarily promote Reuben's key assistant, let the rest of the staff continue their duties, and take our time before hiring a chef who might want to bring in a different philosophy? We already had a great reputation doing what we did. Plus, all the recipes Reuben had developed he kept on the computer. There were hundreds to choose from because he was constantly revising the menu. We would have no problem making seasonal changes for the next two years; our customers would never tire of the fine food. Besides, a miracle could happen and bring Reuben back to us. Soeze agreed—we didn't need to panic. Thus, we put the talent search on a slow burner.

I was about to leave when Kershaw came in for breakfast. Had he arrived a minute later, I would have missed him. I nearly physically ran into him as he entered. He insisted that I sit and chat.

"Didn't know if you'd be open but I wanted to get in what may be my last meal here for a while," he informed me. "We're wrapping up."

"I assumed you would be soon."

"Sorry about all this. What's going to happen with the restaurant without Reuben?" he asked considerately.

"We were just discussing it. We'll be okay, at least for now." I assured him. "Besides, let's not convict Reuben before he's even tried."

"He'll be indicted," Kershaw said matter-of-factly. "He'll be tried. And my bet is when it's over he'll be happy that some years ago they abolished the death penalty here in New Mexico." The agent ended his statement, flashing an odd twinkle of the right eye.

"He's going to have his fiancé and my mother on his side," I mentioned. "That's not a bad team to have in your corner, especially when they believe you're innocent."

"The regular, Mr. Kershaw?" the waitress asked, by now his order a formality.

"Thanks, Molly. But since this may be my last breakfast here for god knows how long, I'll take some of that thick organic bacon with my eggs." He seemed in a playful mood. He gestured to Molly with a naughty pucker. "I'm deserving of a splurge today."

"I'll get your coffee, sir," she assured him with an extra pat on the shoulder. "Zach, anything for you?"

I signaled that I was fine.

"When I first started with the bureau I worked serial cases for about four years. These killers are not all the same like some people insist on portraying them. In fact, the only thing that binds them into a class of their own is that they are all vicious animals. Do you know why they do what they do?" He aimed the question with his eyes to be sure I knew we were on his turf. "They like it. They need it. They can live normal lives like Reuben, fooling everyone they associate with, because they are normal...until they get hungry...and then their appetite is insatiable."

I recalled Reuben talking about deviations and how they define us. At that time, had my chef been hinting to me that he had a whopper of an eccentricity? Had he been informing me that he was a part-time serial murderer?

There was a coffee mug in front of Kershaw; he took a tiny packet of Stevia sweetener out of his pocket.

"The wife's a health nut. I should be ashamed, but the truth is I'm happy to sneak a side of bacon behind her back," he grinned before returning to the topic of serial killers. "That fiancé of his wouldn't ever know that the man she's sleeping with, and wanting to raise her kids with, is creeping off once in a while to do a kill. Believe me, she's a lot better off to get the pain over with now."

"Well, I'm not drawing any conclusions until it's over," I assured him.

"You'll be at the various proceedings, I'm sure. So we'll be able to talk more after the evidence is presented," he said with contrition. Then he shook his head in resignation. "It's surely going to change your mind. I'm sorry. There are sickos in the world. It's not easy to come to grips with the fact that you've been duped by one."

I guess I was like so many other people under similar circumstances. I had shoveled a hole in the sand just deep enough to bury my head. Why couldn't there be a happy ending, the waking from a bad dream to a miracle?

"The only one who might come out of this like a prince—I'll get into it in a moment—is that father-in-law of yours," Kershaw said resentfully. "And I'm stressing the word 'might.'"

"How is that?"

"We'll clear out of here. That's all he wanted from the beginning...and that the killer not be one of his own," Kershaw spit out. "I'm a good listener and I study the people I deal with. The pride issue for Cloud is as transparent as a bad magician's trick. If the killer had proved to be an Apache, I think the lunatic would have killed him himself."

"It was very important to Len Cloud, I know, that it wasn't a Mescalero Apache. Can't you understand why and appreciate it?"

"Oh, I understand it all right. But you don't endanger the lives of others because you *wish* something to be one way or another. Hell, I wish my mother wasn't suffering from severe Alzheimer's, but I'm not leaving her to babysit my kids because I want her condition to be different."

"He does get a bit extreme—"

"There's more. I don't want to alarm you, but your wife needs to be prepared." Kershaw was deliberative, seeming unsure how to proceed. "The real issue I wanted to talk to you about is what's been gnawing at me since the last two murders. Turning the tribe against me, all the foolishness he was involved with, is the work of an ignorant old man. But what may be criminal is his behavior pertaining to the day of the last two murders."

"I don't think Len Cloud would do anything criminal," I stated. "But like you said, to protect the honor of his people he might refuse to talk."

"He'll talk. That's the point your wife needs to be prepared for. I've already put in my reports, detailing exactly what I understood to have occurred at each of the murder scenes. The prosecutor will put him up as a witness and the judge is going to shit his pants when your father-in-law tells this outlandish story about getting a call from someone telling him there was a murder but that he had no idea who contacted him."

"We can't be sure he did know who was calling."

"Even his daughter doesn't believe him. You heard that," Kershaw nailed the point in. "Here's the problem. Reuben, the killer, was not going to place a call to Len Cloud. He'd be the last person Reuben would have tried to reach. But...what if there was a witness? And what if the witness didn't want to get involved but knew that of all the people who would intervene quickly, it would be Cloud. So, he called him.

"You understand what I'm getting at?" Kershaw stopped to check the logical progression of his thoughts. "There may be a living witness to a murder and your father-in-law is withholding evidence that may be critical in the prosecution of the case."

"Taking your line of thinking one step further," I suggested, "what if the killer isn't Reuben and my father-in-law knows it but is protecting the real killer because the man is Apache?"

"I like your heart," Kershaw laughed. "If it's someone other than Reuben, we have a doozie of a situation here. But you're right. The *defense* is going to want to know what Len Cloud does."

Kershaw's breakfast arrived. The first thing he did was put a stick of bacon to his mouth and chew the end like a mischievous child. He looked up at me, waving the thin brown flag of defiance. "You should try it some time."

"We get this bacon from England...pretty outstanding."

"Here's the other issue that could land Len Cloud in the crapper," Kershaw continued, putting a forkful of eggs in his mouth in a well-mannered style. "I've talked to a lot of people around here and there were many young girls out alone on their way home from school or practice that afternoon, any of which could have been another victim. Several were within a short distance of where Len Cloud was at the time. But he chose to go across town to pick up the Moon girl, daughter of a family he doesn't get on with?"

I swallowed without a plate of food in front of me. All I could do was shake my head, lacking a defense for his seemingly odd behavior.

"What Len Cloud should understand better than anyone on the reservation, since he is the equivalent of an attorney, is that because he's on Indian land does not exempt him from the laws of the United States of America," Kershaw affirmatively charged.

"I really don't have answers for any of this," I lamented. Then I changed the subject. "I noticed you went back to Reuben's room. Find anything there?"

"I'll tell you this. What we needed from his room we gathered before we arrested him, that's all I can say."

"I'm sure you know that Walter Chicory disappeared," I mentioned to change the subject.

"No official report has been filed by the council. As far as I'm concerned, let the tribe deal with it," Kershaw dismissed with a wave of his now naked fork.

When I arrived home, Preeti informed me that her father had put together a team of the best trackers. They had left early that morning to find "the remains" of Walter. Nasir had driven Josea and my mother down to Albuquerque because Josea wanted to purchase legal books—she was already studying what role she might play in a team of lawyers defending Reuben and he hadn't even had an arraignment. Thankfully, she also had the good sense while in the big city to interview prospective criminal defense attorneys.

It was a blessing for Preeti and me to have some time alone with Souche. We spent it relaxing as best we could under the circumstances. It was late afternoon before we were descended upon. Josea, my mother, and Nasir, as well as the returning tracker, Len, all arrived at the same time.

Len had just walked in. Preeti wasted no time initiating the interrogation of her father.

"Shitaa, what happened?"

Len Cloud shook his head in defeat.

"We found nothing," he stated flatly.

The man looked troubled. He was still sweating, which I rarely witnessed, and he seemed dehydrated. Preeti was so distressed that she paid no attention to her father's compromised appearance.

"What are you going to do?" Preeti pled. "You know the country around here as well as anyone. You have to go out again," she insisted.

By now, the others had arrived. Len went into the kitchen for a glass of water. I noticed him leaning over the sink, washing water over the back of his neck, indifferent to wetting his shirt. He loitered in the same stance for several seconds, resting his aging body. The rest of us gathered in the living room, Josea taking the floor.

"Zach, I settled on this guy Sam Ashton to handle the initial phase of representing Reuben. He'll be at Las Cruces tomorrow where they're holding Reuben and conducting the arraignment," Josea reported in a businesslike manner. "I wouldn't have faith in the man if we had to go to trial but he'll work to get Reuben out on bail. Then we'll have this nonsense dismissed by the grand jury, if it even gets there," she said confidently.

"We'll be going with you, you know that?" I informed her.

She took a deep breath, her eyes squinting that familiar look she had when she was about to make war with forces as powerful as gods.

"If I have to, I'll fly in Bernard Goldman from New York to handle this," she continued while shuffling through papers. "We have no idea what the evidence is at this point, but I can't imagine what it could be. Still, I want to be prepared for anything."

Bernard Goldman was considered to be the modern version of Melvin Belli, the criminal defense guru of my mother's generation. With the tech world in full bloom, Goldman was a man rising to the level of myth. He had defended the most publicly followed murder cases of the last decade and had a reputation of only defending innocent clients. The facts in one of his cases were so obviously conclusive of a conviction that when the jury found the accused innocent, Goldman smirked with the confidence of a man who not only seemed capable of walking on water but who had just accomplished it for millions on YouTube.

I knew money was not an issue for Josea. Her style of living was always frugal and she commanded large salaries for the positions she held. Still, I had concern just how deep she could go in advancing money for legal fees. When I questioned her, she looked at me like I was goofy.

"Zach, the money is not an issue. I'm going to get married." Then she rolled her eyes and simpered. "Haven't I waited long enough?"

This was not going to be easy. In my opinion, there was a heaping tablespoon of irrational exuberance that might sour the wow-all-is-going-to-work-out-wonderful expectation drink she was brewing—the sad reality was Reuben Zapata just might be guilty. She had dismissed that possibility. Then to make the situation worse, my mother was egging her on.

"Josea, we'll all be dancing at the wedding," she assured her. "In the meantime, we'll go down there tomorrow and I'm sure Reuben will be with us tomorrow night."

I looked at Preeti. I could tell she was of the same mind as I was, wondering if she was watching a Loony Tunes cartoon. Len Cloud came in from the kitchen and sat down, Josea jumping on the opportunity to grill him.

"Did you find out anything about Walter?" Josea addressed Len Cloud.

He shook his head, reaffirming what he had just told Preeti.

"This is really important because Walter might have run for fear of being caught," Josea posited a point I had already considered.

Len had no response, almost ignoring her.

"Mr. Cloud. Is there anything you know that might help?" While he remained mute, she forged forward with her next question. "Somebody called you that afternoon. This might be critical to Reuben if he has to put up a defense."

Len still said nothing. Josea looked to Preeti for help, knowing that Len's daughter was dubious about what he had conveyed regarding that afternoon. I had not even talked to her about what Kershaw had warned, not wanting to burden her with more worry before it became a necessity. Now Josea was forcing a point that was sure to be pivotal if this went to the grand jury, and even to trial.

"Father, we all know how you feel about honor, about protecting the tribe, but would you let a man pay for a crime he was not guilty of because you don't like the truth?" Preeti asked.

"Daughter, I don't want to ruin the party, but this man in jail is a murderer. When the evidence is presented, you'll be of a different opinion," Len said wearily.

He stood up and walked out. We heard his truck start up. As he drove off, the breeze delivered a gust of gaseous fumes through the open windows. Things were about to ignite.

24

THE ARRAIGNMENT

WHEN WE ARRIVED IN Las Cruces, one of the seats of the Federal District Court of New Mexico, I was taken aback by the physical structure. The locals referred to it as the "new" courthouse and they had every right to use the designation. The architecture was more fitting for a design center you would find in Los Angeles than a building conducting legal proceedings for the state.

Yet perhaps they had it right. The façade was modernist to the extent it was composed of flat walls of concrete distinguished by offset colors ranging from tans and browns to bright yellow and blue. The structure was composed of several modular sections, their depth and perspective coming from counterbalanced lengths, widths, and heights. These discrete compartments conveyed weight and power, the force of law jurisprudence. It was an announcement that justice would be dished out without sympathy or deviation from the formal rule of law.

That morning the sunrise put on a lightshow. The few small blue areas visible in the horizon were deepened in color by an explosion of red, orange, yellow, and purple blasts of light. They shot out from afar and then arced toward earth as if they were being fired from giant hoses used to water the sky and earth beneath it.

We parked and walked into the lobby. Sam Ashton met us. He was a man in his sixties. He exuded confidence, the type who had seen and dealt with it all. His short, portly body suggested an indolence that was in sharp contrast to his disciplined style of legal practice. He struck me as a man not inclined to sugarcoat a nasty outlook, yet at the same time he made it clear that he would be the lawyer to affect the best outcome in a proceeding.

He greeted Josea with familiarity. Then with a bit more formality, he welcomed Nasir and my mother. Josea introduced me and he politely shook my hand.

"I'll be meeting with Reuben in a few minutes. I'm sure he'll be pleading not guilty, so what's going to happen after that is the judge...I already checked and Judge Vernon Winkler will be hearing the matter...will announce the charges and then ask for a plea. The matter of bail will then be addressed and also whether or not we'll go to a preliminary hearing.

"I know this judge very well. That doesn't mean he'll favor me one inch, but I can tell you he's a fair man. He may call the prosecuting attorney assigned to the case and me to the bench. It's possible we'll have a preliminary hearing and if so I know I'll be able to expedite that as well as the grand jury hearing, if we go there.

"If you'll trust me here, I'll handle this first phase. I want to see how much information I can get regarding what we're even dealing with and then report back so you can decide where you want to go next."

"What are the chances of bail and if so how much do you think it will be?" Josea asked.

"As I told you yesterday, it's hard for me to tell before I understand what Reuben is facing. The fact that he's not living here with family and has no firm, long-standing attachments locally will make bail harder to get because he'll be considered a high risk to jump," Ashton explained. "Then, if the judge determines that the charges seem to have merit it'll be all the more unlikely."

Ashton noticed disappointment on Josea's face and tried to be encouraging.

"That doesn't mean we won't walk out of here with Reuben. We're getting ahead of ourselves," his voice trailed off to slow down the expectations. "No use fishing in the dark. I'm going to see Reuben now. I'll see you all in court."

Minutes later, we took our seats in Winkler's house and waited. It wasn't long before Reuben Zapata, handcuffed, was led into the courtroom. I'm not sure what I expected but it was not what I perceived from a man accused of triple murder. There was no sign of regret, remorse, fear, defiance, cockiness, or sadness; there was the closest to nothingness I had ever seen on a human face. Reuben had abandoned the carnal prison of his body and mentally taken off to a distant world, allowing the proceeding to unfold in his absence.

In that sort of mindset, I wondered what, if anything, he talked to Ashton about. Had he returned to what Len Cloud called the Shadow World to advocate on his own behalf? I recalled that my father-in-law had complimented Reuben by calling him a Mescalero before knowing he was suspected of murder. Was it possible that Reuben had taken the lessons from the Puberty Ceremony and was playing the clown, dancing merrily in a state somewhere between the two worlds? He wasn't laughing, but he wasn't crying either.

He never glanced our way. I could see it pained Josea terribly. I imagined her telepathically trying to reach out to him. Sadly, he displayed no sign of receiving her vibes.

Judge Winkler read the charges, three counts of murder. It was horrid even hearing the words in the context of a courtroom, because for the first time I believed this was real, even to Josea. Then he asked for a plea by Reuben, at which time Ashton stood.

"Your Honor, my client refuses to enter a plea."

In disbelief, Josea rose up and yelled to Reuben.

"Reuben, what are you doing? Reuben I love you."

If getting his attention was the goal, she failed. Reuben showed no indication that he had heard her, but Judge Winkler had, and he sternly admonished Josea. He let her know there would be no second outburst. Then, he addressed the legal matter.

"The court will enter the plea of not guilty on behalf of the defendant," he pronounced indifferently.

Next the issue of bail was raised. The judge asked the prosecutor if he had any information to be taken into consideration before he ruled on the point. In response, the prosecutor requested permission to approach the bench. It was agreed, the judge asking Ashton to join them. They conferred for quite some time before the two attorneys went back to their chairs.

"No bail. The accused will remain under custody until the preliminary hearing. I'll set that for...next Wednesday. Is that agreeable to everyone?"

Neither attorney entered an objection. The proceeding ended. Reuben was led out of court. Still, he never glanced in our direction.

We met afterward with Ashton. As he described it, the picture was not pretty. There was no question the case would go to a grand jury, and from there, in his opinion, to trial. Reuben had refused to even talk with Ashton and thus the judge was legally forced to enter a plea for him.

Ashton commented on Reuben's mental state, similar to my prior observation. He said he had never had a client so void of will and so detached from the gravity of the situation he faced. It wasn't that Reuben was thumbing his finger at the matter. Worse, he refused to acknowledge it.

"The prosecution shared a few facts with me. That's why I didn't debate bail," Ashton explained. "Besides, the state of mind Reuben appeared to be in would have cautioned the judge against granting bail—he would have ruled against it based on mental capacity, for sure."

"What did you find out?" Josea asked urgently.

"It was vague. They offered no specifics yet but did allude to the fact that evidence had been gathered at the crime scenes that placed Reuben at those locations—they claim to have biological…genetic proof. There's more." Ashton said almost apologetically. "They have witnesses who've stated that on the dates of both murders Reuben appeared with some sort of minor injuries."

"Zach already told me about that," Josea shot out. "Those were nothing."

"I was also told all three girls were killed in an identical manner. There was frontal manual strangulation. I noticed Mr. Zapata isn't a particularly large or powerful man—"

"Mr. Ashton, does he look like he could murder a hamster?" Josea retorted without comical intent.

"Unfortunately, I've tried enough of these cases to know that when it comes to murder, knowledge and speed are far more critical than strength, Ms. Roth."

"That's just great," Josea frowned. "Let's dismiss any possibility of his innocence."

"I'm not removing defenses, but I'm certainly not going to argue ones I can't uphold. Now, I'm not about to say the prosecution has a slam-dunk deal because that is never the case. If we're going to fight, we'll fight them tooth and nail," Ashton exclaimed. "But we're going to need his cooperation."

"Can I see him?" Josea asked. "I think I can talk to him." She looked at me in the most obtuse manner. It was apparent she had something to tell me but was pained that she couldn't. "I know him differently than anyone else does."

I hoped so. I was rehearsing one more time the scenes as I recalled them both afternoons when the murders occurred. He was a mess after the first. Then, not only had his behavior been odd after the second but also he had sprained his right hand. It seemed to me that was not a good injury to have when you're a gangling weakling suspected of having strangled two young girls. Now Ashton was talking about incriminating evidence of a biological nature at the crime scenes. It didn't seem like a positive day in court.

"I hope he'll agree to see you, Ms. Roth. He's in a very strange state," Ashton reiterated to her.

"Tell him I know who he is," she told the counselor. "That I will always know him. You have to be precise and tell him that exactly," Josea emphasized.

"I'll see if I can arrange it. I'll call you tomorrow. In the meantime, let me poke around and see what I can find out before next week." Ashton paused a moment. "I don't want a word mentioned about what I told you regarding evidence. I have my own channels to find out information and it's not to our advantage to have any of them dry up."

"When will we get the reports...officially?" Josea asked.

"We could have passed on the preliminary hearing and gone directly to the grand jury. I know most people want to bring these matters to closure as quickly as they can, but in this case it's to our advantage to use the preliminary hearing to get a better picture of what the prosecution is holding. There will be witnesses called and it could get testy, but it's worth the effort."

I was aware that both Preeti and I had ministered to Reuben the afternoons of the murders. It was also known that our staff had seen his condition—at least one was already volunteering as a witness. I wanted to know if Preeti and I might be called.

"What you're saying is that even my wife and I could be asked to testify?"

"No doubt. I'd be surprised if you aren't. You see they want this to go to the grand jury. If they do a lot of the work now, it's easier down the line. Plus, they take no risk of the judge tossing out the case at the hearing—clearly that's not going to happen unless some extraordinary evidence proving Reuben's innocence is presented to the judge."

"So my father could be called as well?" Pretti asked tentatively.

"From what you tell me, I doubt it. He's not going to be a cooperative witness for the prosecution or us right now. However, and I'm sorry to say this Mrs. Miller because this could become a touchy issue for you, our side will have no choice but to call him if this goes to trial," Ashton informed her.

Pretti stood quietly, knowing it was going to happen and fearing the consequence for her father.

Ashton had business at his office and left. As we were walking, I couldn't help wondering where the money would come from to handle the legal bills. I knew my mom adored Josea, and she had a good deal of wealth. Still, I doubted she'd offer to help with the financial burden. I thought it might be a good time to raise the topic.

"Josea. I can't imagine Reuben having the money to pay for his legal bills. What are you going to do?" I asked harmlessly.

"Zach, I know lots of people; money will not be a problem."

Then she giggled. "Don't worry, I'm not going to need anything from any of you except love."

"I wasn't worried you'd ask me for money, Josea. To fund this, you'd be better off looking for a venture capital investor."

"I'm having a hard time getting you on board to have faith in Reuben," she said, stunning me with her accurate perception.

"I'm being protective of you...I know you don't think you need it, but you do. I want nothing more than for this to work like a fairytale—"

"But you never believed in them, did he, Kaye?" posing a rhetorical question to my mother. "Even after the way you ended up with Preeti, you still don't believe," she said with a stern face. "You're a tough one, Zacchaeus Miller." Finally she smiled. "But I still love you."

"It's not that I don't believe. I just don't know what or when to believe."

"Poor boy," she teased. "Actually I don't either most of the time. But I do when it comes to this man, Reuben, I do. You'll see."

I sure hoped so.

The next morning, Ashton called and asked to talk to Josea. We all stopped in our tracks to listen to the one-sided conversation. Finally, she hung up the phone.

"I'm going back to the courthouse tomorrow morning at eleven to see Reuben." She smiled proudly. "See, I told you he'd hear me."

"Josea, I can tell when you have a secret and won't tell me," Preeti called out.

"I'm in love, okay? Now you have my secret."

That ended the discussion.

He was such a nice guy. How could he be a killer? I ruminated on this point endlessly. In the meantime, I began planning an undercover sleuth operation to see if I might get closer to an answer on my own. My efforts were going to leave me breathless.

25

THE PHONE CALL

THE NEXT MORNING OUR little troop, sans Preeti, took off again for Las Cruces. My wife needed time with Souche, worrying her daughter might forget to call her by the name "Mommy."

It was only a little over an hour's drive to the courthouse. Josea was excited to make the trip. I was preoccupied with preparing to tie up a couple of loose threads that had been dangling like temptations in front of the "analyze this" compartment of the left hemisphere of my brain.

I suspected everything I was eager to explore, and more, would be dug out of Reuben's past as the inevitable trial proceeded. But I saw no damage in getting a running start. The phone bills were the more nebulous of the two items I had on my radar. What I expected to find was really nothing. But then, why did I go to the trouble of taking them and then leave them alluringly in their envelopes sitting on my desk?

When we arrived, Josea leaped out of the car and took off. I told my mother and Nasir that I had a couple of projects to take care of and if they didn't mind I would meet them in an hour at the car. I stopped at an Internet bar to do my business.

I decided to start with the more concrete piece of information pertaining to Reuben, specifically his social security number. It was the only piece of personal information I had taken from him when he was hired. As was the case with every other employee, the payroll service took deductions and deposited them against the various social security numbers.

I never thought of checking the background of any of my employees. I had no reason to do so. If there was a problem, I felt confident that the sole surviving efficient quasi-official branch of our government, the Internal Revenue Service, would discover it. Still, I wanted to double-check his just in case. I'm sure Farley would have discovered in thirty seconds what it took me most of the hour to find. Reuben's social security number was valid, conformed with his legal name, but...curiously the number did not make sense temporally in that the date of issuance of his identification number did not conform to his age.

There was nothing incriminating, however, about that single fact. There are situations where foreigners don't take out social security cards in America until after they enter the country and then begin to earn money—a forty-year-old person may have a social security number that was released back into the system when they were thirty-nine or forty. I put the issue aside and turned to the phone bills, which I had never opened.

I took them out of their respective envelopes and put them down on the table. There were few, very few, numbers that he had called. But as I perused these limited items, my eyes began to shoot out of my head. I stared at the bill, locked in a state of awe for what seemed like an eternity.

I wasn't going to laugh. I wasn't going to scream. I was going to place a call. I opened my cell and punched in the ten digits of the area code and phone number that was repeated several times on Reuben's statement. It rang and the voice on the other end spoke to me. Then I answered.

"Hi, this is Zach Miller."

The female voice on the line responded back with a question I immediately answered.

"Yes. Tell him I'm calling from 306-227-4218." I slowly enunciated each number.

I waited only about as long as it takes to run a red light.

"We need to talk," I voiced insistently.

"Funny damn joke. I wish you'd stop testing fate," the man retorted impatiently.

"I wish I could," I said to him. "But this is Zach Miller."

The man must have stopped breathing because there was a deathly silence on the other end that lasted for quite some time.

A few minutes later, I was walking the several blocks back to the courthouse. By chance I met up with my mother and Nasir who were returning as well.

"Zach, what happened? You look white," my mom asked with alarm as she stared at me.

"I just need to talk to Josea. I'll be fine," I tried to say reassuringly.

"Just take care of yourself, son. That's the most important thing. This will all get sorted out."

"I know," I responded as I picked up the pace.

When we arrived, Josea had just walked out to the front of the building and had a smile on her face. I doubted she would after we talked.

"I have to speak to you, alone," I said abruptly. "Mom, Nasir, can we meet you here in a half hour? Please, it's nothing concerning you."

They kindly took off without pumping me for an explanation. I reached for Josea's arm and led her around the side of the building to an isolated bench.

"I'm going to ask you something. Before you answer I need you to remember who I am. I'd never lie to you, you know that, right?" I posed rhetorically. "Are you carrying a very, very deep secret that you want to tell me?" I asked flatly. "If so, is it something you know would break a trust if you disclosed it—but you know it may have to be breached in the end anyway?"

Josea's eyes widened. "It's too big. I might be the only person who knows," she said frightfully.

"You're not the only one," I assured her.

She looked curiously at me.

"Who else?" she gasped.

"I'll tell you later."

"No! Now, Zach," she pled assertively.

So I told her.

"That I knew," she said smiling. "But that's it—there is nobody else."

"I'm sure that's true." I was as certain as I could be. Then I added. "I am going to have to tell Preeti. You know that, Josea."

She nodded. Still, I could see her mind diving into primordial chambers where ancient accounts held record to betrayal and unfaithfulness not yet conceived, with consequences disastrous to kings, princes, and whole civilizations.

"You know Preeti. She'd give her life before double-crossing a friend," I assured her. "She's a lot like her father."

Josea really had no choice and knew it. It was my wife and I'd have nothing between us that might later cause resentment. Besides, I trusted Preeti and realized I might need her for advice down the line.

"Tell me how you figured it out, please," she begged, content to leave the subject of Pretti's reliability.

I explained to her about the phone bills and the call I'd placed, knowing we had much bigger problems to address.

"We better figure out what to do soon," I stated with urgency. Still, before that I had to ask how her meeting went. "Tell me what Reuben said."

"He's innocent," she said bluntly.

"Josea, he doesn't get a free pass for murder just because you say he couldn't do it. Then if he is, he better start giving us something to work with."

"That's the problem. He doesn't know how to defend himself. The reason he wouldn't enter a plea was because he assumed...well you know...he'd still be found guilty."

"Let's go way out on the limb and assume he's innocent. Now, if that is the case then the evidence against him has to be false, right?" I proceeded methodically. "So our job will be to refute it."

"Right, but we don't have a lot of time. If he believes the game is up, he'll never let himself live to face the consequences."

That afternoon, shortly after we arrived home, as Ashton warned us might be the case, Preeti and I received our subpoenas to appear as witnesses on behalf of the prosecution. We had no choice but to comply. We also had no inclination not to, other than the unpleasantness of going into a courtroom to provide information that could help convict Reuben.

We had nothing to hide. Objectively analyzing the instances we knew we would be questioned about, we had no reason to consider that either of our testimonies would be strong evidence against him. Josea, of course, wasn't pleased about us appearing, period. She had no choice but to understand.

"I'm sure you didn't get a subpoena to appear for the preliminary hearing for Reuben?" Preeti asked when Len Cloud came by our home later.

"Why would I? I haven't a thing to say," he responded resolutely. "They can call me all they want but I'm not testifying in their hearings."

"Stop being stubborn, father. You know you have to if they call you," Preeti retorted to his obstinacy.

"The man's as guilty as that child is innocent," Len proclaimed, pointing to Souche, who was tracing imaginary patterns in the rug while Henry Higgins, stationed next to her, was practicing to be the first dog in history to perfect a full summersault. "Truth speaks only one tongue, but lies have a thousand languages."

Josea walked out of the room. No doubt she wanted to dip her single tongue in hot water lest she speak a truth Len Cloud would consider disrespectful.

The next few days were quiet, but not tranquil. Josea was eager to get to work but really had no direction. She was like a power station with nobody drawing her energy. The pacing, grunting, and moodiness were nearly unbearable to be around.

On the morning we were to attend Reuben's preliminary hearing, an unrecognizable vehicle pulled up in front of the house. I was finishing my grooming. It was Preeti who spotted it first. She came running into the bathroom to inform me.

"A black limousine just pulled up," she said curiously.

I calmly picked up my wallet and stuffed it into my back pocket. Then I started to button my shirt.

"You know what this is?" she asserted more than asked. "It has to do with Reuben or—"

"Reuben. Right. I'll explain in a minute."

I went out of my room. By the time I reached the living room, Josea was looking out the window. I motioned for her to wait. I walked out the front door and up to the back window on the driver's side of the car. Preeti and Josea were without a doubt watching for any sign that would reveal the mystery. I'm sure they both witnessed a hand reach out to shake with me.

"I haven't said anything yet. Give me five minutes and we'll be out," I informed the man.

I was about to go back inside but before taking a step I surveyed the area around my house.

"You couldn't have been followed?" I checked with him.

"No way," he said absolutely. "But I did call the New York Times and Time Magazine," he quipped.

I went inside, not acknowledging his humor. Two of the most important people in my life were waiting eagerly. I had intentionally kept a secret from them—I'd wanted to avoid being bombarded with questions I couldn't answer during the days before the man in the limo arrived. Now I would break the news. It took me only a brief moment and my explanation was completed. Both Preeti and Josea were standing with their with mouths wide open.

"That's it, ladies. Now the number is four. There are four of us, one for each season one for each direction along the circle of life, right Preeti?" I stated proudly. "Let's hope it never gets past that because it could become a lot bigger number in a blink."

We came out of the house and the driver jumped out to open both of the rear doors for us. I made the formal introductions and off we went to Reuben Zapata's preliminary hearing.

"It's good to have friends during times of need, isn't it?" the man conversed. "It's also good to have all the money in the world at your disposal when you're charged with murder."

"I'm concerned about this," Josea expressed. "It could backfire if he interprets it that I have betrayed him and everyone knows."

"Can you get a message to him so he's prepared?" the stranger asked.

"I'll ask Ashton how we can do it," Josea responded.

"Good," the man said obligingly. "You know, Josea, I'll do anything to help...anything." Then he intentionally gazed out the window to mitigate the impact of his statement. "But what if...just what if he's guilty?"

"I'd have to think you know him fairly well. Do you really believe that?" Josea snidely posed.

"Do I know him? Do I know Reuben Zapata?" he countered, turning back to face Josea. "Do we really know any man?" he whispered. "But I'll tell you, my heart will be broken if it's true."

We sat silently in the car. When we arrived, I opened the glass partition separating us from the driver.

"Would you mind dropping us off up the block and waiting there?" I instructed.

He drove straight past the building about a block. I doubted the Las Cruces courthouse had many limousines delivering witnesses for a case. I didn't want to arouse attention.

"Good thinking," the other man said agreeably. "All we need is the local press digging into who I am and what I'm doing here."

We walked the short distance and entered unmolested into the building. Ashton was waiting. I introduced the man to my right as Mr. Bennett, explaining he was a family friend who was coming to offer support. It was only half of a lie, though the big half.

"Be prepared folks; it could get testy. You understand the purpose of this procedure?" Ashton began a brief explanation. "If they have evidence that the judge concludes will not hold up in trial, or that the manner in which the evidence was collected has been prejudiced, the judge may determine it be thrown out and drop the charges immediately." Ashton took a moment before offering the next moralistic addendum. "That's good for society if he's innocent, but if guilty... regardless, I couldn't get any other information about what they have. They're guarding it like a virgin.

"Now look. The prosecution is desperate to make this case. The whole community of Mescalero and most of the southern half of the state has already convicted Reuben. It could be a terrible failure for them if the state blows this case. We'll try to use that to our advantage."

"You'll be calling no witnesses, I presume," Mr. Bennett asked.

"Who can I call?" Ashton responded. "I don't know what you've been told but thus far Reuben won't even talk to me. We had to let the court enter his plea."

Mr. Bennett shook his head in dismay.

"This is open to the public so be prepared for lots of interested parties," Ashton prepped us. "In fact, let's get in there now so you can all get seated."

We went in. The room was already half full. However, there were four seats in the front row waiting for us—how Ashton calculated four I don't know, but perhaps he had dealt with the Apache people enough to know that three might have been perceived as a bad omen.

As we sat, Mr. Bennett queried Josea about Ashton.

"We'll have to deal with representation if this goes on," he announced.

"I've already called Bernard Goldman. I met him when I was in law school," Josea answered.

"I didn't know you had a legal background."

"Harvard—not criminal so I'm brushing up. I was very close with Professor Randolph and through him I became acquainted with Mr. Goldman."

"Good. So if need be we'll bring Goldman in with whatever team he wants," he spoke authoritatively. "It's not a bad idea to have a local like Ashton stay on, would you say?"

"This is likely a fruitless discussion. Reuben will end it on his own terms if this goes on and on. I'm sure of it," Josea said solemnly.

There was no time to dwell on her prognostication. Reuben was led into the room. By this time every seat was filled. He had his head down and was notably depressed. Ashton sat next to him and whispered in his ear. I assumed it was what Josea had asked him to tell Reuben, about the parties present to support him. But he didn't look around the room at first.

Then, for a fleeting second, he peeked out from his face-hung-down position and instead of stopping to make eye contact with Josea he fixed on Mr. Bennett. A look of alarm spread across Reuben's face.

Finally, the judge entered. He was announced as the Honorable Judge Vernon Winkler. The proceeding began with the prosecution. Two of our staff, a waitress, Tess Crossbow, and a maintenance worker, Jesse Spring, were called, along with Preeti and me, to testify about Reuben's condition and behavior on the two afternoons of the murders.

Most of the emphasis was on Reuben's appearance and the unusualness of his behavior. There were also two witnesses, who'd worked for Reuben in the kitchen, who testified regarding the hand injury evident on the evening of the second and third murders—I was also questioned on that point.

This was the beginning of what proved to be a procession of incriminating evidence that had been amassed mostly through the efforts of Kershaw and his agents. The first "piece" of physical evidence entered was an actual stick of chewed gum, determined to be Wrigley's Spearmint. It was noted that the saliva matched that of Reuben. In addition, when his quarters were searched, an entire box of that exact brand was found. The staff in the kitchen had been interviewed and concurred he religiously chewed gum and only Wrigley's Spearmint flavor. I also knew this to be true, but it was not brought up when I was called to testify.

The next item was a piece of Kleenex found at the scene of the third murder. It had been tested in a laboratory, and when compared to body fluids from Reuben Zapata, confirmed to 99.9999 percent that there was a match. There was also mention of boot marks at the scene of the second murder. The indentations had been preserved due to a kindly climatic condition that afternoon. It was determined that the sole print matched the type of boots Reuben was known to wear, but when his room was searched the used boots were missing. Another pair of boots still in the box that had never been worn was in the closet. These had a different pattern on the soles.

It was the contention of the prosecutor that Reuben had intentionally destroyed the old pair, knowing they might incriminate him. He also argued that Reuben planned to replace the discarded pair and had bought the new one with foresight and deliberation. He simply hadn't had the occasion to use them yet and thus they remained stored away. Furthermore, the prosecutor contended that the Kleenex likely fell haphazardly out of a pocket and the gum was a careless oversight committed during the chaos of murder.

The state representative also portrayed Reuben as a wanderer, a man roaming into town with no past and no prior connection with any local people. He had gone about building a trust with many new friends for the sole purpose of falling under the radar of suspicion while he committed unthinkable crimes of violence. There were various other items the prosecutor referred to at the time of the hearing that had not been fully developed. He promised, however, that by the time of trial his team would be able to complete a perfect replay of the events leading up to and including the murders committed by Reuben Zapata.

Ashton had warned us that he suspected this was going to the grand jury. He made no attempt to lead it elsewhere. He had no grounds to argue the matter with the judge. No doubt he planned to use the period between the present proceeding and the time of the grand jury hearing to refute the prosecution's case. There were no procedural violations for Ashton to use to argue for dismissal.

The only positive thing now was that we did have a good deal of time, and access to Reuben. We hoped we could convince him to assist with his own defense. The key problem was that there were things Reuben didn't want his attorney to know—four was the maximum number of people he could tolerate knowing his secret; maybe he was an Apache.

Before being led out of the room, Reuben glanced in our direction again. He made eye contact one more time with the gentlemen I'd assigned the name Mr. Bennett. As he was turning away from us, he made his only attempt at communication. He shrugged as if to say, "I fucked up." It sure looked like it.

On the way out, Mr. Bennett flopped his head downward. A moment later, he looked up at us.

"This is not good. They have evidence packaged by the FBI as sanitary as tampons," he said despondently. "The only thing I see is the premise that he was set up, but how do you legitimize that one?"

None of us had on-the-spot answers. Ashton met us outside. The first thing he told us was that he had very good relations with the U. S. officials where Reuben was being held and as long as we were respectful he could provide direct access to Reuben for interrogating him in preparation for the grand jury process. Josea asked when she could meet alone with him. Ashton promised he could arrange it within a couple of days. She had already informed the attorney that she had been licensed in New York, California, and Massachusetts but never practiced. Still, he could put her on his list of investigators working the case.

On the way home, it was a somber scene. There was very little talking. Nobody wanted to dwell on how bleak things looked.

We're told it's out of chaos that order is born. We're also told it's out of hopelessness that miracles are delivered on the wings of angels. I know each of us was signaling despair. The question was whether or not an angel was reading us and about to make a mercy flight to Mescalero.

26

DROPPING A BOMB

EVIDENTLY AT THE TIME when Reuben had shared with Josea his little giant secret, it was known only by the stranger, Mr. Bennett. Even with Josea, Reuben had dispensed with details of the how and why pertaining to his concealment. He wasn't ready to make a full disclosure to her but vowed that in time he would. He only wanted her to know the overall truth because he loved her. He promised that she was the first and only female being he would love.

Josea's goal for the next meeting with Reuben was to take a tape recorder so she could later transcribe a permanent record of the interview. She didn't know how worthwhile the information might prove to be, but she valued details and wanted volumes of them to search for clues. So on the morning she was going to interview Reuben, she packed the device—a digital machine with a backup just in case of an electronic glitch. She was able to sit with her "client" in a comfortable room that contained a desk.

When she came home that evening, she was exhausted. A dark shade of gloom had dropped over her. She said nothing about the meeting. Instead, she went directly to her room and didn't come out for an hour. When she did, she made an announcement.

"I'll let you listen and you can draw your own conclusions," she said to Preeti and me.

Then she played Reuben Zapata's verbatim statement.

I was raised in a Jewish home. My parents were Sephardic Jews. I remember myself as being a quiet boy, a bit introverted. My interest was not in science like my father, who was a physicist. I was drawn to the arts. My parents never unfairly judged this inclination on my part. To the contrary, both my mother and father respected the arts, especially classical music. Thus, when I showed interest and ability in that direction, they provided every opportunity imaginable.

We were not rich, but we were not poor either. My mother had a stroke when I was quite young but over time made a fair recovery. Still, while she had been trained as a pharmacist, she never worked again. But the real problem was that neither my father nor mother seemed to have anything in their life other than me. It may sound like an ideal situation, an only child whose parents doted over him and would deliver any of his wishes. It was far from it. As a result, I developed a massive case of guilt.

It seemed like everything I did was measured in terms of what I was giving back to them as opposed to what I wanted or what inspired me. So, while I excelled in my studies and practices, I became increasingly sad. I hesitate using the word depressed but in fairness that might best describe how I felt much of the time.

I could have never shared this with them or for that matter with anyone else. To do so, in my mind, was to disappoint my parents. So instead I became a prodigal child whose ego was fed from the venomous fangs of guilt.

So it went—I don't need to tell you—all through my career everybody I associated with became an object for which I had to suffer pain like a martyr in order to satisfy the beastly shame trying to claw me to death. I wanted to run away, but similar to a whipped child, I needed the punishment more than I was willing to admit.

Both my parents died tragically and simultaneously in a plane crash. That was the beginning. As you can understand, I was far less devastated than I imagined I would be—and I'll admit that innumerable times during my teen and adult life I had rehearsed their passing from this earth; the obvious interpretation being I wished their death as a means to free myself from the ownership I granted them over my life. There are times when classic psychoanalytic theory can be accurate and I would insist that this sad statement is true.

Obviously, I had grown to hate and resent them. After they died, I was left with the dirty task of tying up their affairs. It was the first time that I physically looked at their possessions. I realized in the process of going through their personal affairs that I knew almost nothing about them. I had lived more as an interloper in their lives than an integral part. I really wasn't a player; I was an object.

I finally came across a box containing documents. I wasn't seeking their money, but having an opportunity to peer into their thoughts, to know something about them appealed to me.

I found more than I'd bargained for. You see, it turns out I had been adopted. I had never been informed of this critical piece of information pertaining to my personal identity and resented the fact as soon as the discovery was made.

It turns out my father had worked for the U. S. Atomic Energy Commission in Albuquerque, New Mexico at the time. A baby had been abandoned and come up for adoption. My parents took the leap. I was only a few days old when I was provided a home and family. How blessedly convenient it was for them (pardon my pitiful emotions) that my skin tended toward the dark side and wouldn't raise concern if I were a Jew of southern European extraction. Anyway, after the adoption, my father had a job opportunity in California and off the young family went.

It was the details of the adoption that interested me. At least I thought I might have the right to know what had happened to my biological parents. I went to Albuquerque to begin researching who they might be. To make a long journey short, I never found either of them. But what I did come across was the knowledge that I had been left on the steps of the adoption center in the early morning hours just before they opened on a Monday morning. I wasn't even a day old and greeted the staff with a cry of hunger—I think I must have voiced that sound a million times since then but never knew what I was screeching.

Other than the basket I lay in, and the blanket covering me, I had but one possession, a note. It was that single item that brought me to Mescalero—that brought me home. What did it say? "Born in Mescalero on June 15, 1971." (You must excuse these weepy outbursts but my history still pains me.)

As a result of my own investigations, I already knew the next statement he proclaimed. Still, hearing it spoken aloud exploded like a bomb in my mind.

I don't know what, if any, name my biological mother or father had for me but my adoptive parents named me Stevie Green.

The three of us bawled like ninnies. Preeti and I looked imploringly at Josea. We wanted an explanation of how it would end. We wanted a declaration of innocence. We demanded it. Hell, I demanded it.

"So what are we to take from this?" I rammed at Josea. "That he had a part of him that split off, a sick character dissipating the intolerable hate through sport murdering?"

"He isn't finished," is all Josea offered as she pressed a button restarting Stevie Green's voice.

So now you know it was not by chance that I ended up in Mescalero. From the beginning, from when I first hatched the plan to escape from Stevie Green, it was my intent to come home and explore my roots. It was symbolic to me that the last concert Stevie Green would ever do should take place in Albuquerque, New Mexico.

It came to me shortly after my parents died, and subsequent to me discovering my past identity, that I had created a monster of a life. My career weighed on me like ancient metal battle armor. I couldn't comprehend how fans could devote more attention to me than their lovers, parents, spouses, and even their children. My band members were dragging me down. I could no longer create in an environment where I felt progressively more responsible for them, as well as for the millions of strangers that meant absolutely nothing to me. In fact, there was nothing left that had value to me.

Of course, suicide rose quickly to the top of a list of options to terminate the torture. But then I decided I could leave Stevie Green like a bad dream. I had unlimited funds with which to do whatever I wanted. I also had the undying loyalty of Jay, similar to what you (Josea) have with Zach. By the way, it was odd seeing Jay show up with all of you in court. (Laughter by Reuben) Jay must have crapped in his pants when Zach called him using my number and letting him know he'd found me.

Anyway much of what happened immediately after the concert at Isotope, Zach cleverly figured out—and I compliment his acumen to put it all together. Believe me, I apologize for any deceit on my part toward Zach and Preeti, but as you can imagine it was unavoidable. Besides, even though I knew what Zach was uncovering about Stevie Green, it really made no difference because I firmly believed he would never find the man who really no longer existed. I'll admit it was thrilling watching him expose my disappearance.

I actually spent months in Topeka being redesigned into the appearance you see before you. Dr. Howard was a prick of a man but a master surgeon with ethics as elastic as his greed for money. After I left his clinic, I became Reuben Zapata—I had acquired all the necessary documentation for that identity previously. I felt that I left Stevie Green when I exited the stage in Albuquerque, taking on my interim identity as F. Artanis.

(Laughter) I loved playing games with letters and numbers. It used to drive Jay crazy, but Frank Sinatra had always been *my inspiration to be the best, and when I came up with LIVE I was in a megalomaniacal stage of my evolution, playing with despair by sticking my tongue out at it.*

My first stop, Josea, after leaving Topeka, was Atlanta, where I attended a small city college that had a few culinary courses. I stayed there just long enough to get the basics down. Then I came back to California and by a quirk ended up in Napa Valley. It was there that I had the opportunity to be a kitchen aide at Le Fleur restaurant. By chance, the founder and chef, Tomas Wipsey, was there for two weeks. That's when I learned how to run a real kitchen.

I did work in an Indian restaurant in Seattle for a short time. That was just before I finally came to Mescalero. I wanted to develop the art of cooking before I came home. It worked out perfectly that the job opened up at Kuruk at the precise time when I ventured home.

I loved everything about Mescalero and believed I would never leave. For the first time in my life, I started to feel like a living person, like myself. I loved the work, loved being with Zach and Preeti, and I loved watching Souche grow. But I was lonely. Imagine, I'm the most famous rock star in the world, some say in history, women crawling around day and night, and never once had I had a sexual experience.

It was the same story that had been all my life. I wanted love and didn't have it. I was afraid of sex and never tried it. Then you (Josea) came along, and the second I saw you I knew you were the one. At last the torture of loneliness would end. How did I know that it had been the same for you, that you had never found intimacy? Did I see it in your eyes? I have no answer, but there was magic in looking at you and that enchanted me.

So now look how it turned out. Is it too late for me? What is going to happen to me? (Silence) Am I guilty? I know you want to know. The problem is Reuben Zapata will never be tried. You see, before that happens, everything I'm telling you will come out, one way or another, and I'll be known as Stevie Green.

"How would anybody ever know?" Josea interjected a query.

You'll see. Before it was only Jay. Now I chose to share it with you. But Zach and then Preeti were added to the list. How long do you think it will be before more people put it together? I will take just one nurse at The Howard Clinic who happens to see that the newly designed Reuben Zapata, whom she knew as Stevie Green, is on trial for murder. How long will it take for her to decide that the few extra bucks Howard gives his staff for not disclosing the identities of clients is chump change compared to what the story is worth to the press. With my picture plastered on the front of papers, and the history of serial murderer Reuben Zapata coming out for millions to read, it won't be a week before somebody puts it together.

Hidden away here in my safe world of Mescalero, I've had huge odds in my favor to never be identified, even if I lived to a hundred...but not now. So I have to tell you that I can't let that happen. I will not go back to Stevie Green. The only way to avoid that is to end the existence of Reuben Zapata.

Josea. Let me ask you. Would you believe me if I told you I was innocent? With my history, what I'm telling you now about me, would you ever trust that there isn't a part of me that is so damaged and twisted, I can only contend with it through hate? If there were that part of me, would I even know it? Would I be able to tell the truth to myself or would the monster operate as an independent being within the ego system of what I know as I?

So, in fairness, how could you not have doubt? Can I dispute the evidence they've uncovered? If I stand up and tell them I've been set up, then they would want to know by whom and for what reason. I can't do that. I, Reuben Zapata, more than anyone needs the proof. But I'm sorry, my love, if it's not to be. I will not subject you to Stevie Green. Should that killer be alive inside Reuben Zapata then I will have to bear responsibility for the heinous crimes committed by him. (Silence) Honestly, you would be a fool not to question my ability to be truthful, and you are the furthest from ignorant of any person I have ever met.

The way I'll end this is to say I came here to find myself. That's always a risky enterprise. One never knows what they'll discover once the search of self begins. I want to die here and be buried in Mescalero.

Josea pressed the stop button and the room fell silent.

"He never said he was innocent," I lamented.

"I know," Josea admitted. "Later, I asked him several times and he flat out refused to answer. All he would say was, 'I could never satisfy the question for you. I'm sorry. I love you and it pains me that I can't give you the peace of mind you would like—I'm so confused I can't even give it to myself.'"

"He's right," I affirmed for Josea. "What if it wasn't Reuben? What if he never put the angry, lonely, and victimized Stevie Green to rest and that killer lives as an isolated entity within the man you love? " I then highlighted what she had to hear herself. "Listen to the tape again. That's what he's claiming as a possibility that even he wouldn't be able to confirm or dispute."

"Don't be crazy!" Josea barked at me as she started to walk out.

"Josea, stop it," Preeti called out. "Zach is not going to stop helping with this until it's over, one way or the other. You know that. What he's saying, and he's right, is that only the truth will prevail and provide the answer we all need to know...including Reuben."

"The question is where do we go from here?" I posed. "We need a plan."

"One thing I want to do is have Ashton obtain from the prosecutor the coroner's report on Ila Clearbrook," Josea suggested. "I know Reuben mentioned to you, and he told me also, about the women for whom he helped change a tire that afternoon. If the time of death corresponds to when he was helping her, or is close to that time, at least we've started to raise doubts."

"I don't recall him saying anything about the vehicle except it was a pickup, right Preeti?"

"That's all he said at the time."

"I mentioned it to him and he said he thought it was a black truck but it was hard to tell. I understand that. They all look filthy here," Josea snickered. "He said he thought it was a Ford or Chevy, but aren't most of them? Anyway, what I was thinking is we run an ad asking for information. If we put it in all the local papers and the Albuquerque Daily, we might by some outside chance get a hit."

"Unlikely you'll get it on the news but what about the Internet too?" Preeti suggested.

"Yes. I'll look into that as well," Josea responded.

"Good. Now we have two things to do. Also, just for the hell of it, can Ashton get a sample of the saliva on the gum and the fluid on the Kleenex and have a preliminary test done?" I posed. "I'm sure there could be a mistake."

"Why couldn't somebody have dropped those clues at the sites to implicate Reuben?" Josea said, returning to an old theme.

It wasn't impossible but the likelihood seemed so remote I chose not to respond.

I did know that we were in a fix. Reuben Zapata would never go to trial and risk having to face the charges as Stevie Green.

27

THE GREEN TOYOTA PICKUP

THE NEXT FEW DAYS were quiet. Josea was frustrated. She was a mental machine assigned the project of repairing a glitch in a system but had no template for how it operated. She kept staring, studying, trying to discern what to do. It went on for hours at a time, and we could see her smashing brain pulses with mental hammers, nearly losing the most precious tool she possessed, her capacity for reason.

Preeti and I tried to distract her. I'd call her from Kuruk, asking her to come over and assist with one project or another just to get her mind off the endless track she was traveling. She always complied, but I could tell her head was in a cell in Las Cruces.

Then, on the fourth day after placing the ad, she received an email from a woman who identified herself as Beth.

"I have information about the tire repair you advertised about," is all it said. Josea wrote her back. She asked if she could meet with her as soon as possible. The women responded that

she would like to but was scared. The second response by Josea was brief.

"*So am I. We are talking about saving a life. I need your help.*"

The woman finally emailed a response agreeing to meet with Josea. She stipulated the condition that her husband could never find out. She lived in Tularosa, only a few miles west along the highway to Alamogordo. She proposed meeting Josea at a fast food joint at eleven in the morning the next day. Beth said she'd be standing by her green Toyota pickup in the parking area.

Josea asked me to come along. When we arrived, we spotted her immediately. She was an enormous woman, grossly overweight. Her jet-black hair was stringy and dropped shaggily down to the shoulder line. She was wearing a pastel floral-patterned dress that reminded me of what my mother called a "moo moo." It looked like it had been purchased in a shop selling Hawaiian products. It hung loosely by two thinly braided shoulder straps and the only skin it revealed were the rolls of blubber bubbling off the shoulders, down onto the arms, and then separately in the calf areas.

She saw us enter the lot and Josea pointed toward her. We parked and the obese lady lumbered over to us. I noticed as soon as we were standing next to her that her face was puffy and without makeup. The features were nicely proportioned. It was easy to see that at one point in her life, when she'd been a few hundred pounds lighter, she most likely had been a sweet looking woman. She seemed scared, like she was committing a violation.

"I'm Beth," she said timidly.

"I'm Josea Roth and this is my friend, Zach Miller," Josea said kindly. "Do you know of the Kuruk restaurant in Mescalero?" Josea asked her.

"No...I mean yes, but we don't go out like that," she responded, sounding like a low-class Oklahoma transplant.

"Zach and his wife, Preeti, own it and their chef, Reuben Zapata, is in trouble. You may be able to help," Josea informed her.

Beth's discomfort increased. She seemed poised to leave, as if she had made a mistake by coming.

"I read about it in the paper," she whispered, hushing her voice for no reason other than to impress upon us that it might be dangerous if anyone were to overhear her. "He was such a nice man. That's why I called. But I can't go to court or nothing like that." Her fright level was rising like a thermometer stuck into a baking roast.

"No. No. Let's not even think about that," Josea said in an attempt to ease her concern. "All we need to know now is what happened."

"You see my husband doesn't like me talking to other men. So if he found out I had a flat and didn't call him..." She broke into a display of histrionic tears, her voice squeaking. "If I had called him with a flat he would have been real cruel to me so I let the man help me. I can't let my husband find out I lied to him."

Josea looked at me, her eyes registering a mixture of disgust and pity.

"I understand. But for now, can you just answer a few questions?"

"I'll try, miss."

"Do you recall about what time it was when he helped you?" Josea asked.

"I can tell you exactly," she responded excitedly. "Yes, it was four-fifteen in the afternoon. My husband sent me out to pick up a part he needed to fix his truck. I left the store and the clock said five after. I was out just past Ruidoso, and I imagine when I broke down it was west of Ruidoso Downs and a little east of Mescalero...that's right for sure."

"How long did he spend with you fixing the tire?" Josea fired at her. I could tell she was trying to keep the woman talking so she didn't drop back into the state of fright.

"Twenty minutes. I'm sure of that because I came home about twenty minutes later than Clay—that's my husband—expected me." Beth giggled quietly, as if sharing a deep secret with the two of us. "I told a fib. I told him I had to wait for the part."

It was comforting to know that Reuben would kill himself before trial, because the thought of trying to get this lady to testify horrified me. I was motivated, however, to pump her like a lever to get everything out of her, because I assumed we might never get a second chance. Josea seemed unsure what she was going to ask next, so I jumped in.

"I'm curious about something. When he came up to where you were stuck, how did he look?"

"Oh, my, terrible. I felt so bad for that tiny little man," she said with animation. "He was all bruised and torn up. I asked him what had happened." She stopped to consider. "What did he say? Well, let me see … hmm … he said … he just said it was nothing and he'd be fine. He really never told me."

"I can imagine it took a lot of courage for you to meet with us," Josea complimented.

Her words appeared to frighten the lady more than comfort her. "Really, I have to go. I can't be away too long," she said with a deep breath as she turned to leave.

"Wait, please. If I need anything else can I email you?" Josea urgently appealed.

Beth paused to draw in closer to us, speaking in a muted voice. "Clay doesn't know I have the email. So sure, you can contact me anytime."

She waddled toward her car, not even turning to acknowledge our thanks. There was no need for either of us to discuss the tragic condition of this woman's life. She made me think of babies, newborns. They're fresh, ready to take on the world. Along the way, they're whittled like a block of wood. The fortunate retain the texture, fiber, strength, grain, and beauty of the original object. Others lose their will, heart, grace, confidence, courage, faith, and even their passion. There is nothing to judge. This woman had lost more than most.

But Josea was right. She did have courage. She had met with us.

In our gallant attempt to preoccupy Josea with activities when she couldn't directly involve herself on Reuben's behalf, we scheduled outings. Preeti would take Souche out to the park or a class for moms and tots and invite Josea to come along. On this particular evening she had planned a movie and drive down to Alamogordo for dinner: anything to keep busy. Len Cloud was scheduled to sit for his granddaughter.

He arrived about four thirty and we were ready to leave. Len asked if I had a minute to talk before we took off. We sat on the porch, a cool wind whipped up intent on putting to rest a warm summer day.

"Everything going okay for you at the restaurant without the kid there?" he asked, referring to Reuben.

"I'm awed how everyone has stepped it up. We're doing amazingly well. Our volume is about the same," I answered.

"This matter with Platta," he continued. "I know there's been a lot—"

"I've been negligent. I admit it," I interrupted.

"You're busy. I probably shouldn't have imposed on you. Really, I didn't know whom to turn to. I felt you could conduct the inquiry best."

"I promise you I have it close to complete. Like any matter of this sort, partial answers can be misleading and I would prefer finalizing everything before we talk," I offered as a compromise.

"That's fine." Then he sat mute. Len Cloud seemed stuck in a mental gear.

"What is it?" I tried to urge him to talk.

"Walter. Reuben. They both upset me," he divulged.

"We're doing what we can for Reuben," I offered.

Len tightened his lips, drawing his mouth nearly inside out. "I wish I could make it all right." Then he stood abruptly.

"You don't know how this has upset me. I can't fix it," he strangely reiterated.

I had no idea what he believed he could have done. I also felt badly that in his aging he was being tormented by circumstances he had no control over. Yet even more, I was puzzled by the shift in attitude regarding Reuben. Before he had written the man off as guilty—and seemed to have done so without sorrow.

"It's odd. The older I get the more I seem to regret things. I loved Preeti's mom. She was a beautiful lady. Just...she died too early. I had another love before..."

He never completed the sentence.

"Have a nice time out," he said graciously. "And, Zach, try to help your friend, Josea, let this go. We'll all be happier."

He went back inside. A moment later Preeti and Josea came out. Driving down the hill, I reflected on what seemed like an odd conversation with Len Cloud. The man had a lot he wasn't willing to talk about. How could I have known that what he was tiptoeing up to was fact that unless redacted from his personal history would leave his heirs debating his legend between hero and hangman?

28

BLAME IN ON THE BABYSITTER

WE ARRIVED HOME ABOUT eleven. Souche was asleep on Len Cloud's lap. Little Henry Higgins would have otherwise been assigned to his quarters in the pantry, but owing to having touched the heart of Grandpa, we found him lying by Len's feet when we entered. Our little pet innocently lifted his head to the sound of the door opening. After struggling to his feet, he trotted over so we could all love him up.

Len was in a reclined pose, dead to the world—quite a babysitter. We put down our things, and even with a few cute yelps by Sir Henry, neither of the two woke. In fact, Preeti took our daughter out of her father's arms without arousing him. If we had crime in Mescalero, which we no longer did since the tragedies of this tale, a robbery could have taken place in our home and the two occupants would have awakened in the morning unaware of the intrusion.

"Zach," Josea admonished as she dropped her purse on the dining room table, "Reuben's transcript is sitting here."

"I was reading it again," I casually commented. "Let me have it and I'll put it away in the office."

I collected the several pages along with some notes I had taken and carried them into my room. I'd had a small safe installed in the floor of the closet that was sunk in a slab of concrete. I kept important papers there. When I hung up my pants, I took a moment to open it and put Reuben's statement inside, reproving myself for my negligence in leaving it out; it wasn't the type of document I'd want to lose during a burglary.

It took me only a short time to brush my teeth and take care of the other little functions I did to prepare for sleep. As I lay in bed waiting for Preeti, who kept her skin immaculately fresh and youthful with a several-course treatment of lotions each evening, I began drifting into a half-sleep state. Often when I had similar experiences, it would be a reverie from my horrors in Israel that commanded my unconsciousness. Typically, the images served to harshly whip me back to full awareness with my heart accelerating and my body covered in sweat.

This evening, I had sunk deeper into my imagination and was in a total dream state by the time Preeti called out from the bathroom. She was letting me know that she was nearly ready for bed, but the interruption permitted me to fully grasp the content of my nightmare.

I had never dreamed of Preeti's father, but surely it was he who was the lead character in this scene. He was hovering above us and had taken the likeness of a giant prehistoric bird of prey—I couldn't identify the parties who were with me, but

I knew I was not alone. Len's face was human, except for his mouth, which was a beak the size of a football, with a sharp, bright fiery point. The overall image of the features of the face was blurred—all I could make out from the impression was that it defined him as a heartless hunter.

His wings spanned several feet, and as he held himself in place like a helicopter, the waving limbs blew us into a shiver. We huddled out of fright, anticipating that one of us was to be his next meal. I recall his eye intent on me in particular. He blinked as the wings drew back, a gesture confirming that he had picked his victim. But before he lurched down at me, his face contorted into a gruesome grimace. A second later his immense body fell, covering all of us with a hot, oily material that had an aroma reminding me of a rancid turpentine tree sap.

We all tried to escape, but as if we were in a tangle of lines and ropes spun by a gigantic spider, we couldn't free ourselves. The odor turned increasingly noxious and we were gasping for fresh air. I thought that I was about to pass out when Preeti called out to me from the bathroom. Her voice is what had awakened me from the unpleasantness.

It took me an hour to fall off to a more tranquil rest. I didn't awake until early the next morning. We were brought to consciousness not by Souche, as would have been the normal call to duty, but rather by a call from Len Cloud.

After we'd arrived home the night before, we did manage to wake him. He insisted on driving back to his place to sleep. In the morning when he called, he was suffering a terrible fever and told Preeti he had been up all night. There was no thermometer in his place, but he said he felt he was burning up and couldn't get out of bed. Preeti put herself together and ran over to look after him. It wasn't until much later in the afternoon when she was able to ease him to sleep.

Preeti came charging into the house. It was clear she was distressed.

"I can't take any more of this, Zach. Every time I turn around, it's another crisis," she cried out. "All I want is for the three of us to have our life back. Don't you think all this is affecting Souche?" she hollered at me in a tone she rarely used.

She carried on for quite a while. I could well understand that her father was plainly the proverbial straw breaking the camel's back.

"Can't the man just be sick? Does it have to be a doom and gloom deal? He acts like he's dying," she said exhaustedly. "I was just starting to sleep, to get to where I could be at peace with Jivin having left. Then it's business, death and murder... now illness. It's insanity, Zach. I'm telling you, Stevie Green may have had the right idea...leave it all behind and disappear," she spewed out irritably.

I let her storm her way through the feelings. I wasn't surprised she'd come to a breaking point; her father being the catalyst was far from shocking. After all, Len was her father and mother. The thought of losing him was ghastly to her. Of course, it was going to happen and she knew that, but not now, on top of everything else.

"He's talking nonsense." She angrily called out to me. "Here's what he said. All in broken pieces of sentences."

"How could I ever see...it was in the future? The spirits played games with my soul...it was a joke...it was cruel. What choice did I have? Had I known everything ahead of time... worse...it would have been worse. Is this being stuck between worlds? I don't know if I can come back. I can't understand how this happened."

She described him rattling on. He was burning up from fever.

"Zach," she screeched, "talk to him, please. I can't make any sense of the man."

"I'll get right over there, Preeti. We'll get through this." The platitude sounded good and I hoped it would reassure her.

I left without another word. I had no more to say. The pressure was wearing on both of us.

Len's house was dark. I noticed he had closed the shades. I knocked several times without an answer. Finally he came to the door and cracked it open, shielding me from entering. His eyes glistened from fever. He had a deathly appearance. The room stunk. It awakened my olfactory sense to the dream I'd had the night before.

He looked at me pathetically.

"The buzzards are flying over me. I must face them alone."

He shut the door. I knew it would be rude to push the matter, so I left.

Over the course of the next two days, his condition remained unchanged. Preeti called regularly, but he refused to let her see him. He also objected adamantly to her entreat that he allow a doctor to treat him. Preeti could tell his voice was weakening and commented to me that this is how he would die, like a Mescalero warrior who went off alone to make his passage to the Land of Eternal Peace. She was distraught. I knew the only thing keeping her in the game was Souche.

The morning of the third day of his illness, I went to Kuruk. I was surprised when Gabe Kershaw showed up. For the past week, he and his troops had been nowhere to be seen. It was a pleasant relief to the community.

As he walked in, he asked the waitress if I was there. She found me and informed me that he wanted a moment to speak. Of course, I went immediately. When he saw me, he smiled, rose from his seat, and shook hands with me. He asked if I would sit down, motioning with his left hand as he used the right to remove his hat and toss it on the seat next to him.

He ordered oatmeal with raisins and milk, whole-wheat toast, fresh-squeezed orange juice, and coffee. It was a departure from the breakfast I had seen him routinely choose.

"That's a pretty healthy breakfast. What happened to your usual?" I joked.

"We'll get to that in a moment," he said elusively. "I went to see your father-in-law several times in the last couple days but he wouldn't answer."

"He's been very ill and won't see anyone, even his daughter," I informed him.

"Sorry to hear it. But he's still one of the most stubborn old coots I've ever come across."

"He can be a handful," I concurred. "He's gotten to me on a couple of occasions. So, what did you want to talk to him about, or shouldn't I ask?"

"No, you should ask. In fact, I planned after I talked to him to sit down with you anyway." Kershaw unwittingly bore down on his teeth as he pulled back his lips. "This is a nasty business. Every detail means something and lives can be lost over a mistake."

"I'm sure it can take a toll after a while," I commiserated.

Kershaw's eye narrowed; there was something important his mind was conjuring and he had to make a performance out of delivering it.

"Can't leave a stone unturned," he winked. "Funny thing that's bothered me about the murder scene of Udaya Shash. You went to the preliminary hearing so you know about the Kleenex. It's not going to break his case, but the prosecutor does have a problem with that piece of evidence."

"What?" I asked impatiently.

"Don't get too excited because I don't imagine it'll change too much with all the other incriminating evidence." Kershaw paused. "Damndest thing, though. When I got there, lying about a foot from the girl's body was the Kleenex. It had been a very mild and calm afternoon, less wind than a mouse breathing. So it's not surprising the light tissue wouldn't have moved, right?"

"I'm sure," I said perfunctorily, eager for him to get on with the point.

"So, if you were the killer and you accidentally dropped it or it fell out of your pocket during the kill, chances are it would have laid right there for us to find. You with me, Zach?"

"Yes. It makes perfect sense."

"To begin with, you wouldn't have known it dropped. Then, logically, you would have had no concern if the wind kicked up all of a sudden, which happens out there all the time. So let me ask you if you can figure this out, because it's been poking at me ever since I discovered it. How and why was that Kleenex laying under a small rock?"

Kershaw sat back as if he'd just positioned a rook on a chessboard and was awaiting my move.

"It was under a rock?" I said with astonishment.

"Little fucker didn't walk. Would have taken a small twister to move that stone. If that happened, the Kleenex would have blown far from the body before the rock had a chance to stop it."

Kershaw remained poised, leaning his weight back in his chair.

"Your father-in-law was the first person on the scene. I wanted to ask him if by chance he'd noticed the rock on top of the Kleenex. Could he have kicked a stone and it landed on the Kleenex? Beats the hell out of me what happened there. Crime scenes, Zach, they're tricky," Kershaw said in an ominous manner.

"It's something for Reuben. It raises a question about one piece of evidence and it offers weight to the argument that he was set up," I suggested.

"I wish you luck. That nice lady friend of yours is going to have a hard time of it once he's convicted," he said offhandedly. "There's a pile of facts against him. There's no way what I'm telling you alone is going to change his fate. But I want you to know I documented what I found so it is entered into evidence. Of course, I didn't comment on the questions I'm raising with you pertaining to how the items appeared at the scene. Also, I did have the rock tested for prints or any sign of human fluid, but it was clean."

"We'll take what we can get at this point."

"Came by also because I wanted to let you know I'm leaving the area. I've been reassigned."

"I hope it's a promotion."

"Oh, it is. But I'm not taking it," he said with another wink, this time adding a note of merriment. "Decided I'm leaving the agency—too much death. Too many assholes like my boss—he has a hard-on for me so long he could frighten a whore."

"What will you do?" I queried him.

"Going west. My brother is a restaurateur, pretty successful one in fact, in Los Angeles, your hometown. He's looking to open his own restaurant, a unique concept. If he can pull it off, he wants me to come in with him."

"You'll have to get a new hat," I joked.

"I thought those Bel Air billionaires might like a cowboy maître d' seating them," he smiled back. "Fact is, I told him about Kuruk and he actually came to eat here a couple weeks ago. I didn't want to tell you because I thought you'd feel compelled to give him a halfer."

"I would have comped him."

"What my brother and I talked about was approaching you...and your wife of course...about opening a Kuruk there in L. A. Zach, he's well-connected and respected in his field. He has several prospective backers. Anyway, we wanted to explore buying a franchise."

I couldn't help laughing. The thought of a network of Kuruks in all the major cities of America was everything I least wanted. To my taste, we were rich with what we had. From the beginning, I had never aspired to be a businessman. My answer to him proved the point that I was not entrepreneurial material.

"I'll make you a deal. If that tip you gave me about the Kleenex pans out and in the end we get Reuben freed, you can have the franchise free of charge for the whole damn country," I promised.

"If I would have known that beforehand, I'd have thrown the Kleenex in the trash and shoved the chewing gum in my mouth to see if it still had life," he said stone-faced.

I stared back, unable to discern if he was being truthful.

"Zach, I was kidding," he smiled, amazed at my gullibility. "If I wanted to go on the take, I might have made a fortune when I was working drug enforcement. No, I'm one of those less fortunate jerks with a bulletproof set of ethics; that assures me a lifetime of hard work—and then I'll die."

"Then you'll be there to comp a meal at the L. A. Kuruk when Preeti and I come to eat?" I smiled.

"I hope we will all be partners and make a fortune."

Kershaw picked up his hat and stood. He dropped his card on the table with his personal cell number clearly written on it.

"Let me know if we have a deal."

Later that morning, Preeti called. Her voice was elevated. She hurriedly announced that her father had made a breakthrough. The fever finally capitulated to Len Cloud's obstinacy. She asked if I could go to his house. He told her he wanted to talk in private, only with me. He stressed to her that it was urgent.

When I arrived the curtains had been pulled up, allowing the noon sun to shine rays through the south facing living room windows. He opened the front door as I was getting out of the car. I walked toward him and he reached out to squeeze my hand, dispelling any doubts I might have had about him regaining his strength. He was typically strong as a bear, and if he didn't pay attention, he could grip a man's hand to the point of hurt. I was about to say "ouch," but he eased up.

I can't say he was the same old Len Cloud. He looked as if he had gone through a battle for his life. His demeanor was serious. The meeting had an agenda and I could tell he wasn't looking forward to it.

He had prepared a pot of coffee and had water boiling for tea. We went into the kitchen. He and I poured our preferred drinks. I followed him into the living area where we sat. He faced me while I positioned myself in a chair looking out the large living room window toward the front of his house. I was gazing at the garden, preparing for him to speak. I lifted my cup to take a sip of the hot tea. All of a sudden, the hugest bird I've ever seen in my life landed on the arm of the old wooden bench stationed next to a fir tree in his front yard.

I almost dropped the cup. As I gazed at the feathered creature, it reminded me—in larger proportion—of the wood piece Len had shown me that Preeti carved during her youth. Without a doubt, the living specimen was staring back at me—Len's admonition that I might meet it someday had come true.

At the same instant, I recalled Preeti's wood carving, the interloper staring at me drew me back to the recent dream I'd had the of a phantom beast dwelling in my unconscious. At once, I realized that the monster peering at me in reality was in truth reminiscent of the bird in my nightmare. I was so overtaken by the likeness that I couldn't speak at that moment to signal Len; he began talking but I couldn't hear a word he was saying.

I remembered that the beak of the bird I had dreamt about was partially obscured to me, but after this real-life version landed in front of me, the image came into crystal clarity. It was bright yellow and the full white head of the bird made the color stand out all the more brilliantly. The face was wise, old, prescient, and bold. The eyes of this living specimen remained honed in on me—no mistake. It reduced me to an admixed state of fright and exhilaration. The body was black and what I'll ignorantly call the fuselage had to be two or three feet long, with a sleek powerful chest.

After a moment of transfixing me with its sharp vision, it partially spread its beak as if to speak to me before gaping at me frightfully. Then, seemingly to intimidate me, it lifted its wings—I noticed they had a span of at least eight feet. There was also a tail feather that plumed a pure white color and matched the face perfectly. I could see the talons grasping the wood perch with enough force to crush its prey. While gripping the arm of the bench, it began waving its wings up and down in a show of authority.

My voice muscles unknotted. I shouted. "Look!"

I pointed, my heart pumping both from the appearance of the beastly creature I had witnessed in my dream as well as the sheer awesomeness of its beautiful replica in living color. Len turned around and stared. He stayed in the same position looking at the bird, but I could tell the eyes of the intruder remained focused on me, ignoring Len entirely. Then, in an instant, it lurched off the wood platform and flew across the yard. It ventured westward, hovering over a grove of Blue Spruce trees before disappearing out of my sight.

I still couldn't talk, but Len could.

"Do you see why we wear feathers?" Len asked calmly. I was still without power to respond. "It's the American Bald Eagle. God has given him the authority and we as a People only have empowerment when we wear his feather. The supremacy of man is always conditional on forces greater than us. The Eagle reminds us of our duty to, and dependence on, nature."

"I dreamt of that exact bird a few nights ago," I said excitedly. "It was the night you took ill."

"I'm not surprised," Len Cloud said contemplatively. "I've called on him many times over the past few days."

"I've never seen anything like that bird before," I couldn't help repeating several times.

The image of the eyes was irrepressible, the...authority.

"He knows you now. He'll be back to see you," Len instructed me.

Then as if nothing had happened, he backtracked his speech from the beginning.

"I'll get right to it," Len said businesslike. "I've made my decision about what I want to do. For three days since this came to my attention, I've counseled with the Gods of our people. All I ever wanted was for us to live as our ancestors did. I'm not a fool. I knew all along that our cultural heritage would be challenged. That was fine with me. I knew we could adapt and still maintain the glory of what our fathers taught us.

"We have a magnificent history. There could be no greater pain for me than to think that the world would be left without what we have learned through the centuries, millenniums, and perhaps hundreds of thousands of years we have had Our Spirit guiding us."

Len Cloud took a sip of his coffee and looked mournfully at me. He shook his head. He was anticipating the horror he was about to drop my way, to pour over me like the burning greasy substance the eagle coated on me in my dream.

"What I have to say to you, my son, I will never speak again. I have talked for the last three days with Death, but I was rejected. If you want to call for my end, I will understand. I'll offer no objection," he said with a sense of resignation.

"But I have done only for the good of my people. I had no choice to do otherwise unless I acted in defiance of my elders. I would suggest that nobody, not even Preeti, your devoted wife, Josea, your faithful friend, or Reuben, your honorable friend, ever hear the words I am going to speak."

Len went on without hesitation. He had resolved his tragic role in the affairs of the last several weeks.

"You wonder what happened to Walter Chicory. The whole tribe can't find closure to his disappearance. They conclude that he fell into the hands of evil, either killed by animals he was hunting or by humans of ill intent. They are wrong. It is I who killed him. At this moment, he lies in a grave that appears to be of his own construction, but I will get to that in a moment.

"I have no regrets for what I did. I already mentioned to you my concerns about Walter, his meanness and how it might shame me in the end. Well, he had gone crazy. I had foolishly refused to face it. After the council meeting you attended, when he intentionally defied the circle of life, I still rejected what I knew to be true. I wrote off his behavior as a wayward but well-intended prank to wake up his people to the dangers they were ignoring.

"I talked to him like a son to reason with him that what he had done was not the correct approach. I told him that our forefathers would not approve of what he did and that he had to have more faith in the force of running water. He listened and said nothing at first. Later, he called me a pigeon, and after that a coward."

Len had prepared his confession but was weary from the near fatal illness. I thought several times he might pass out, but on each occasion he found strength to continue.

"Zach, after the first murder of Ila Clearbrook, I was convinced of what I told you, that it was a vagrant. I could not conceive that an Apache would take the life of another of his people by facing them eye-to-eye like a shameless beast. I was wrong. Had I listened to the Gods speaking truth to me, I would have seen it.

"It wasn't until the day of the last two killings that I figured it out...it was Walter. He had gone totally insane with his obsession to save his people. He was going to kill four girls to teach the tribe a lesson that the Puberty Ceremony must be attended by all the qualified girls. Of course it was nuts, but Walter had wandered deep into the Land of Evil."

"Then why did he kill in the fashion he did?" I couldn't help interrupting. "What difference did it make if he had shot them?"

"He was crazy, but still wily. He had the same pride of his people as I. It would have killed him to have anyone believe a Mescalero Apache committed the crimes. He knew the manner he chose to kill would lead us to the conclusion that the White Man or another outsider who was not a warrior had done it. He even played dumb when I first told him why it couldn't be a Mescalero. He knew all along what I was telling him," Len Cloud shrugged, an exclamation point to his failure to accurately read young Walter.

"Let me go on. Sometime after he killed Nita Ortega, the second murder, he called me. He sounded deranged. He told me whom he had killed. He told me where the body was. Then he told me he was at the flats west of town and had also just killed Udaya. It hit me at that moment that he had committed the murders following the traditional circle: Ila was in the east, Nita in the south, and Udaya in the west.

There was no doubt he had to complete the pattern by killing number four and doing it in the north.

"It had to be the Moon girl because there were very few families living in that area and she was the only one I could think of immediately who was eligible for the Puberty Ceremony. So I took off for her home and got there before Walter was able to slay her.

"I never got to the crime scene of Udaya but I did call it in. Whatever evidence was found at those scenes was the work of Walter. He had no regard for Reuben. Your chef and friend was an outsider, like you. The only difference was that you were exempt because of your marriage to Preeti.

"Walter went into Reuben's quarters and the restaurant to steal the items he planted at the crime scenes. You know the rest of what happened that afternoon and subsequently. I knew Walter had to find a fourth to kill—"

"I don't understand that," I interrupted again. "If he didn't want it to appear that the murderer was an Apache, why finish the circle and end it with the number four?"

"There are times when one is compelled to do something that is outside their conscious control; he had to complete the circle. As I said, he was crazy. How could he be consistent and predictable, even to himself? He couldn't."

Len was far from finished. I was just beginning to gag over what he'd just confided in me—he had killed another man.

"After that day, I watched Walter like an infant to avoid giving him the opportunity to kill again," Len said with a sad shake of the head. "He was rarely out of my sight from the time just after the third kill until after the council meeting and until I had the opportunity to kill him. I refrained from passing judgment on him for what he had done. I didn't want him to suspect I disagreed. But he was guilty. I knew that the penalty of my people would be death. I had no choice but to execute justice."

"But you let Reuben take the blame!" I shouted desperately.

Len sat quietly while facing my outburst. He looked more deeply troubled than at any time during his confessional.

"I'm getting to that," he said in a slow and muted voice. Then he waited for what seemed an eternity before continuing with an account that would have me working overtime to fully absorb.

"I despise the invasion of outsiders to our homeland. I don't have a hatred for the White Man. I respect all people, but I don't want the customs, laws, and traditions of our people to be compromised by others who have no respect or appreciation for the way we think and live.

"I knew that Kershaw's investigation might go on for months, longer, even years, until he had an answer as to who had killed the girls. I didn't look forward to them being around, but what could I do? I knew they would never find Walter.

"Zach. How was I to inform them that it was Walter who was the killer? As I told you, if it were an Apache it would be devastating to my people. Believe me, I was not afraid of the punishment I would have received by the White Man's law for what I did. But it was the same problem...justice had to be dispensed by our customs and laws, not theirs.

"I chose to leave it alone, let the investigation come to a simmer. There would be no resolution for my people, but that was better than knowing Walter was a maniacal killer. The problem was I had no idea Kershaw was collecting evidence that would implicate anyone, let alone Reuben. After the arrest was made, I felt a sense of horror. I again confided with the fathers of my people and it was decided that history provided the context for me to remain silent—that was what we determined to be the appropriate conclusion," Len said, raising his arms to indicate it was a decision made by a collective unconscious body.

"You have to appreciate the injustices my people have endured at the hands of the Europeans first and then the Americans. We have paid with thousands of lives. The sacrifice of one life in exchange for the terrible tragedies that had occurred was an unfortunate but acceptable solution. So I said nothing. I was going to let the White Man's justice settle the matter."

"Then why are you telling me all this now?" I posed with the highest imaginable degree of confusion.

This seemed to be the point he was not looking forward to in his admission. Never had I seen a man in front of my eyes turn from dark skin to a shade of ash, as if he had aged another twenty years in the tick of a second. His eyes now performed a feat that I had never witnessed before; they began to water. His face also contorted so that his features concurrently sunk inward. He then buried the shame within his cupped hands.

"Reuben is my son!" He yelled a hideous sound of agony. "He's my boy. He's the child I thought would never come back to me."

I wondered for only a brief instant if Len Cloud had joined Walter as a loon bird. But no, I quickly dismissed that thought. My father-in-law was speaking truth. It was the pain of discovering that his flesh and blood was rotting in jail that had caused the rupture in his soul. He was at a loss for answering what to do; that's what had nearly killed him.

"What makes you think that—that he is your son?" I questioned with total befuddlement.

"The other night when I babysat Souche. You left papers out. I happened to glance at them and…I kept reading. It all came together."

I couldn't understand what he was talking about. He was blind to the difference between Stevie Green and Stevie Wonder. What could the disclosure of Stevie being Reuben mean to him? I didn't have to ask.

"After I finished reading, I put the papers back and fell asleep. I convinced myself it was a strange coincidence, or even a dream, and I dismissed it as such. After you came home and I finally woke up, the thought was pounding like a heartbeat in my head, as if each pulse was a deathblow. I was up the rest of the evening looking at old papers I had saved in a box in my closet. In the morning I made a call, and after that, I knew for certain.

"Zach, we all have specters in our past. Perhaps it is for that reason my ancestors called where we live the Shadow World. Parts of our personal history don't appeal to us and we try to dodge them similar to evading daunting omens. But destiny likes to play the role of trickster, digging up buried acts of shame and forcing us to own them.

"When I was a young brave, I had an affair with a white woman. It was a short episode in my life. She was pregnant after only one union between us," Len reposed. He paused for a couple deep breaths, the moment allowing the point to settle on me. "I wanted to do the proper thing and did. I supported her and vowed to uphold my honor by marrying her. She kept refusing. Still, she stayed in the area. Nobody knew of the affair. But as the pregnancy progressed, I pressed more insistently for us to marry. I had told her I wanted to raise my child, but she wanted no part of me. A day before she was due, she disappeared." Len's eyes closed gently.

"I searched for her but could never find her. She hadn't told me where she came from. When I finally went into the apartment where she had been living, I found nothing except proof that all along she had given me a fake name. It was then I realized I might forever long to see the child I'd fathered.

"I've never mentioned this to anyone. I suspect now it will have to come out and I'll accept the consequence." He now revisited me by gazing into my eyes. "By the way, she left on June 14, 1971 and the baby would have been born, as Reuben states, on June 15, 1971. I called the adoption agency myself and they had no other information about the mother or father. What Reuben wrote is true—*Born in Mescalero*. You see, I was right all along," Len proclaimed, but without arrogance.

He paused again. I knew I was being requested to ask the question.

"How is it that you were correct?"

"My boy is a Mescalero Apache," Len Cloud stated proudly. "He's a stringy thing, isn't he? But he is a warrior at heart."

I had to agree. As I thought about it, Stevie-Reuben, whatever name he took, was a tough character.

"You have a son who could definitely qualify as a singer for next year's Puberty Ceremony," I added, not sure what else to say.

"He reminds me of my grandson. He and Jivin both have immense powers."

"They do share a lot in common," I agreed, recalling in particular the odd coincidence when Jay Weiner mentioned that Stevie was also referred to as "the little dude" and those occasions when Preeti mused about a likeness between Jivin and Reuben.

"We have to get him out of jail and freed of the false charges," Len voiced.

Len Cloud was the same human being at that moment that he had been days earlier when he was ready to watch Reuben face charges of triple murder, and likely spend the rest of his living days incarcerated. But now this same life was one that belonged to his own flesh and blood, and he was willing to fight to free him. I could see the matter from his perspective, and even concur he had acted justly, but it still disturbed me.

"I have to ask you something else," I addressed to Len. "I'm not trying to be disrespectful. You told me you had conferred with your fathers and decided Reuben taking the charge of murder was acceptable justice. Yet now that you know he is your blood son, you're violating the wisdom bestowed on you."

"You're missing the point. He is now a Mescalero. He is one of us. I have to fight, even die, for him," Len answered.

I knew there was something huge to be learned about the human condition from what had just happened, but I wasn't going to have the opportunity right then to figure out what—if I ever could.

"I've already taken care of what I can to help settle this," Len explained. "In the middle of the night, I went to where I buried Walter. The earliest recorded stories of our people—and of course similarly for just about every culture—attest to the fact that under certain conditions old men who know they are dying, or other men who believe they have done wrong and deserve death, will facilitate their own passing.

"I know of a method used by men who don't want to be eaten by the animals but prefer a sort of casket. They dig an underground chamber with a small opening. Then they use a large fur or piece of material and pile it as heavy as they can with soil. As they climb into the cave, they drag the dirt over the opening and then pull the item inward so that the full volume of soil falls into the opening, covering the hole and protecting their remains. Usually, they have a rifle to end their life before they run out of oxygen."

"Sounds gruesome," I commented.

"Death must always be honorable and dignified. These men spared the people they loved the pain of a last few days of suffering or the prolonged injury caused by knowing that a loved one has been put to death most ingloriously.

"I prepared a typewritten admission by Walter. It states his sorrow for doing what he did to Reuben and so on. I shot Walter with his rifle when I killed him. So when I dug the grave, I put him inside and set the rifle to suggest he shot himself.

"Tomorrow, Zach, I will take out another tracking team and this time I'll be sure his grave is discovered. Once that happens, you should be able to go to Kershaw or whomever and get the charges dropped."

I sat for a long time. Len knew I was overwhelmed and gave me as long as needed to digest the mass of material he had heaped on me.

"I'm sorry to pester you with more questions, but some things make no sense to me." I was pleading more than asking. "If you were going to let Reuben take the punishment that rightly belonged to Walter because of the shame it would have put on the tribe, then how can you now devastate them with Walter's written admission of guilt?"

Len Cloud laughed. He laughed and laughed and reminded me of Jivin when he would clown.

"They'll have to get over it."

"They have to get over it? They'll have to get over it!" I repeated like a dummy.

"Zach, what could I do?" Len admitted. "What is right at one moment may not be at the next. We have to be able to alter our stance as the conditions dictate. Often we have no authority over what the changes will be. We're little things on this planet. Gaining Reuben for my people might offset the suffering of losing Walter. Judge me as you wish."

"One little thing, right?" I posed to him. "It all started with one little thing—the girl, Reuben's mother."

"Yes. I was lonely and foolish. She was a tease...a tiny, scrawny one like Reuben, as I recall. I was weak."

"How old were you?"

"Thirty-five," Len calculated. "I had never found my love and became desperate. I was drinking at the time. That's no excuse, but you don't always make the best decision when you're intoxicated—I've never drunk since."

I wanted to think I was one of the lucky ones. My father, I had learned previously, was killed pursuing his passion as part of a military operation; he had not been on the right side of luck. Len Cloud ran out of luck and was facing a life-threatening crisis because of a moment's indiscretion. The list could go on and on. As I proceeded with examples of bad luck, I knew I'd had my share too. Nobody can make it through without sooner or later paying for taking a random and innocent wrong turn.

"Stevie Green is Preeti's half-brother, my new brother-in-law," I whispered at last. "One little thing! It's huge."

"No." Len corrected, nearly giving me a heart attack.

"What do you mean, no?"

"*Reuben Cloud* is Preeti's half-brother," Len Cloud smiled. "I believe Stevie Green is gone forever. Stevie Green," he paused to consider, "is not an Apache sounding name."

"Right."

"I'm sorry for what I have put in your heart. There was no choice but to bring you into this. This will be difficult for you.

You will never be able to tell even your wife that you know who killed Walter. I'm presuming you won't bring the truth out to your authorities. But if you do, I promise I will never mention that I discussed with you whether or not you should, nor will I hold it against you if you turn me in."

I knew there was no option. What was I going to do, have my wife's father, the grandfather of my child, the father of Reuben, put in jail for the rest of his life for doing justice for his people, for acting in accordance with a set of laws that he and his tribe had held sacred for centuries?

"You understand," Len emphasized, "that you can't let on a word of this until we return with Walter's body tomorrow."

I shook my head, bundling the full gamut of human emotion into a simple gesture. Len stood up and came over to where I sat. He pulled my head into his chest and held me tight and close.

"We are bound now in the deepest way two souls can be together. I will rest some day in the Eternal World knowing this story will die with you. The gods are already laughing."

I left my father-in-law alone, recovering and in reasonable spirits. I was going to have an impatient and uncomfortable day until he returned with what remained of Walter.

At least I had every reason to believe a happy ending was coming. But the gods did indeed love comedy—what other tricks were going to be played out first?

29

KERSHAW'S FRANCHISE

I KNEW PREETI WOULD be waiting for me and eager to hear every word that her father had spoken. This would be the first time, and I prayed the last, she wasn't going to get the truth.

As soon as I saw my wife, I explained to her that her father was much better, was terribly remorseful over having his daughter worry during an otherwise sad time, and that he had been deeply troubled over Walter. I also let her know of his plan to take out another search party in the morning. She wasn't keen on him taking off so quickly after his illness but understood there was no use trying to change the old boy's mind.

Later in the afternoon, Josea came home. She had been feverishly thrusting herself into Kuruk, serving tables and helping in the kitchen. It was a place to work off her energy without harming herself or anyone else, to sublimate her grief in hard work, and to contemplate what she was going to do next.

After she settled in, she looked over to where I was sitting.

I stood up. I carefully avoided any sign she might perceive that I knew something and was holding out on her. I did hug her. Then I whispered with more confidence than I should have.

"It's going to be okay. I know it."

She looked up at me with her eyes bathed in liquid.

"Don't do that, Zach. No false hope, please."

I shut up and embraced her again. She had more to say.

"I talked to Jay Weiner today," she disclosed. "I called him to see if he had any ideas. He said he was about to call us. He thought I should get in touch with Bernard Goldman now rather than wait. Obviously we could only tell him a portion of the story, but he felt Goldman should be in on it from the beginning. His opinion was that Goldman had to know that we might only have until the indictment or shortly afterwards before Reuben takes matters into his own hands."

"I agree. We should get him out here as soon as he can come."

My hope was it would be a moot issue by the time he would be able to make the trip. Still, I had to refrain from saying anything that might raise suspicions.

"It's two hours later in New York but I might still reach him today."

Josea wandered out of the room to place the call and I held my breath for tomorrow.

My mother and Nasir had settled into the perfect guests during a time of crisis. They made themselves scarce, taking Souche for sightseeing trips to White Sands National Monument, Albuquerque and even overnight to Santa Fe and Taos.

We couldn't have asked for more. They arrived home from a shorter outing to the market and to buy some toys for Souche and Henry just after Josea came in and had placed the call to New York. When they saw Josea walk into the living area with a smile on her face, it signaled a positive event.

"I love to see that hopeful look on you, Josea," my mother told her.

"Bernard Goldman is flying out tomorrow," she said gleefully. "Maybe now we'll get some action."

I had no idea what miracle she expected from the man. But what did it matter? Reuben Zapata could comfortably afford the first class airfare and fee for a planeload of top New York lawyers from pocket change. He may have been rotting in jail but his estate was growing richer by the hour.

The evening passed. The next morning everyone went about his or her business. It was close to eleven when Len Cloud pulled into the driveway of our home. Quite the actor, he played his role impeccably. He came into the living room.

"I think you all might be interested in this," he announced with a piece of paper in his hand. "We found Walter, dead. It appears he took his own life."

Nobody said a word and he continued.

"This is a letter he left with his body." Len was waving the document. "You may want to read this, Josea." He handed it to her.

Her mouth gradually opened to allow a long inhalation of shock to her lungs. It produced a slow spread of energy through her venous system, as if power grids were being activated one at a time while each of the organs was enervated. It all culminated in an ear-piercing shout of exhilaration that may have been heard by Reuben in his cell.

"Yes!" her arm reached high to the heavens. "He's coming home and I'm getting married."

At this point, the others did not know the content of the cheery suicide admission statement. After a moment, she actually composed herself enough to read it out loud. When she finished sharing the note Len's hand had typed, there was shared joy by everyone. I, in particular, jumped up and down with excitement, for obvious reasons.

Then, after only a few minutes, I noticed Preeti walk into the kitchen alone—she was in tears.

"I know what you're thinking," I expressed. I had anticipated that she would be upset over Walter being the killer but was relieved she'd put it aside long enough to share Josea's excitement.

"I went to school with him. He was like a son to my father. I can't believe it's true," she lamented.

I hugged her for a few moments before she insisted we go back with everyone else so as to not ruin the experience. We agreed to talk more about it afterwards. Weeks later, Preeti could still be heard expressing her disbelief and grief.

None of the group present in our living room had a clue about the rest of the treats coming their way. It looked like it was going to be one happy family.

It turned out it was not a bad thing having Goldman come in on the case, even with the admission by Walter. Fortunately when the grave was found, there were five men present and they would all serve as witness to the fact that the letter had been there, including how Walter had stolen from Reuben the Kleenex, boots, and gum, and that Walter had built his grave and killed himself inside it.

But that would not be enough to get the prosecutor to drop the charges on behalf of the government. Willy Woodcrest, the U. S. prosecutor, was no dummy. He smelled a rat. He just didn't know where the stench was coming from. The problem was he didn't want to stop looking.

After Goldman arrived, he and Ashton met. Thankfully, they got along well. Based on the extraordinary circumstance, they called for a special hearing in private with Woodcrest and Judge Winkler. Goldman and Ashton together had enough muscle to move the judge. That afternoon the meeting took place.

Goldman hardly looked the part of the smoothest criminal defense attorney in the country. He had an appearance closer to a pit bull named Jawbreaker than a St. Bernard puppy named Beethoven. If he was going to win over a jury, it was going to be by terror rather than tenderness. He appeared to be the last person you would want to represent you in a trial. Even though he was Jewish, he could have doubled for Luca Brasi in the Godfather. If looks could kill...

The funny thing about him—it was all exterior, superficial impression. And that may have been his magic—set the stage for your victims to believe they're going to be shot in the chest and then kiss them on the keppele (endearing Yiddish word for a baby's head I learned in Israel). By the time the trial ends, the jury is so happy to be alive they'll go along with whatever the boss says—I had a lot of confidence in Goldman from the beginning.

Goldman and Ashton took the position that since five men witnessed the letter, it had to be valid. At a minimum, it should be sufficient to get Reuben out on bail. They also argued that they had a right based on this new fingding to see all the evidence and supporting documentation.

Woodcrest countered, wisely, that the evidence against Reuben was so overwhelming that it couldn't be dismissed based on the unsigned admission. In fact, he raised the obvious question of why this man would scribe an admission in the first place. He surmised that there had been wrongdoing on the part of the advocates of Reuben Zapata.

Then, he went so far as to raise the "idiotic" question of why a man would bury himself, never expecting to be found, but take an admission letter with him to his grave. It wasn't a dumb thought. The attorneys countered that Walter was crazy. Not a bad rebuttal.

What was accomplished from the meeting with the judge, however, was that Reuben's attorneys came away with full details regarding the evidence. This included all commentary by Kershaw pertaining to the Kleenex being miraculously positioned by a stone securing its movement—I could embellish to our counselors later on the doubts this raised in the agent's mind.

Furthermore, it was agreed that before the grand jury would be handed the matter, Reuben's attorneys would have full access to the physical body of Walter and all of his belongings. This meant also that there would be a diligent search made of Walter's dwelling by a neutral investigator.

Goldman took a suite at The Inn. It was arranged that Ashton would do the same. No other associates were called in at this stage because the two attorneys thought they might find some new piece of evidence on their own. It looked to them like the case was now teetering and with one or two more items it might come crashing to the ground.

After reviewing the prosecutor's material, Goldman noticed reference to several casted prints taken from the indentations made by the boots presumed to belong to the killer. He knew the treads were identical to the boots Reuben wore and that a pair had been missing according to the defendant.

Goldman had Len Cloud drive him and Ashton, Josea and me, to the scene of the murder where the impressions had been made. Woodcrest balked at him taking the original casts and had copies made. They were carefully wrapped and placed in a suitcase.

When we arrived at the scene, Goldman took the suitcase and we walked to the exact spot where, according to Kershaw's notes, the impressions were taken. He placed each down in the sequential order of footsteps. The soil had been moist on the afternoon of the murder and was composed of a clayish material. It made for excellent casting.

"The prosecutor questioned the reason why Walter would take an admission letter with him into a grave he never expected to be discovered." I recited the concern to Len as we were standing together.

"What does it matter what he thinks?" Len mocked, kicking his boot into the dirt, creating a deep indenture. "Five men will testify it was there," Len added breezily. "Besides, a man has to make a formal admission before his God. We can argue that's how Walter adhered to his sacred Apache heritage."

He then glanced at Goldman. The attorney was pressing each cast into the ground so as to simulate the steps the murderer made. He was particularly vigilant about the elevations and angles. In fact, he brought a construction level with him to be sure they were at the perfect simulation of what had occurred as the killer walked those few paces.

Now Goldman took precise pictures from every angle. When he finished he opened the suitcase, readying to pack up.

"You want to tell us now what you brought all of us here to see?" Josea asked.

"No" Goldman responded playfully. "I wanted Sam to get some billing in on the case. I don't know where our client gets his money but I'm told fees are no object." Goldman smirked cunningly at Josea.

"Ms. Roth, he's playing with you. Usually we use investigators to do this type of work—" Ashton was explaining when interrupted.

"I used to be one myself before I went into law. I love doing this sort of work," Goldman interjected.

Ignoring Goldman, Ashton continued. "What he's looking at is the gait of the killer. No different than a car. If it's out of alignment, the tires track inward or outward in a distinct manner. If it's a tiny deviation it may not prove much, but if it's large it could make or break a case," Ashton explained.

"Sam's got it," Goldman confirmed. "What I'm looking at is a nasty case of supination."

"Of what?" I asked meekly.

"Same as under-pronation, Zach. The foot hits the ground on the lateral side of the heel and then as it transfers weight from the heel to the metatarsus, the foot doesn't roll far enough toward the neutral or medial position," Goldman pointed out. "Look at this," he said as he stood over one of the casts he had set in the ground.

"Excessive weight is borne on the fifth metatarsal, the outside of the foot. The person who made these marks doesn't absorb shock correctly as the body weight comes down on the feet. We might expect that sooner or later alignment problems will develop in the knees and hips in particular," Goldman lectured like an orthopedist.

"What we'll do next is take a look at Walter's body. We want to get his shoe size and compare it to Reuben's. We'll also want to get Walter's medical records," Ashton added. "Let's see if we get lucky."

Walter rarely went to a doctor but a physician in Alamogordo, Dr. Benny Huerta, had been the family practitioner since Walter was born. His records were received in only a day. As fate would have it, referenced early in Walter's life was a foot abnormality and subsequent referral to a podiatrist in Albuquerque, Dr. Brian Shaw.

Attained with equal ease, Shaw's records were a giant plus to the defense of Reuben Zapata. Indeed, Walter was born with an abnormality of the feet, a severe under-pronator. He wore a size nine-and-a-half shoe.

It turned out that Reuben wore the exact same size. Goldman and Ashton arranged to have Reuben taken under supervision of the court to the site of the murder where the casts were taken. He then put on the boots that were found on Walter's feet when he was brought in by the search party. He took several steps and then a court appointed investigator made impressions of each of the indentations.

The results were indisputable. Reuben walked with an almost perfect gait, no evidence of either under- or over-pronating. Furthermore, Goldman and Ashton had already had a scientific review of the soil performed. Their objective was to determine based on the depth of the impressions made by the killer what would be the approximate weight of the person wearing the boots.

It was the conclusion of the laboratory where the tests were run that the man would weigh between two hundred twenty and two hundred forty pounds. Walter weighed two hundred fifty-three as per his last medical visit for the flu several months prior to the date of the murders—a sure heavyweight.

Reuben? The scrawny thing weighed in at one hundred twenty-six pounds and would have been a perfect feather-weight boxer except the man lacked the speed, power, and will to have succeeded in any sport.

Walter had written in the admission letter (penned for him by his mentor, Len Cloud) that he had stolen the boots, Kleenex, and gum. It was easily determined by numerous witnesses that anyone might have picked up a piece of Reuben's chewed gum from the kitchen at Kuruk. It was further reported that during the time Reuben was nursing a cold, Walter could have taken the Kleenex as well.

As each fact was placed in order, it became apparent to Woodcrest that his case had fallen apart. What did he really have left? That Reuben had come back from hikes and health improvement outings on the afternoons of the murders? That he fell and was injured concomitant with the tragedies?

Woodcrest was also made aware of Reuben helping to change the tire of the heavyset woman, Beth. Sure the time-frame during which he assisted her did not clear him of potentially being at the murder site earlier, but there was a nagging question that the jury would likely judge in Reuben's favor. Why stop and help a stranger if you just committed murder? Woodcrest also had to factor in that the Kleenex had been pinned in place by a stone. It presented as an obvious giveaway that the scene had been orchestrated to at least raise suspicion about Reuben's involvement.

As the findings of Goldman and Ashton were being reported piece-by-piece to Josea, she was calculating that it couldn't be more than a few days before Woodcrest would throw in the towel and concur that Walter legitimately wrote the letter and committed the crimes.

It was a Thursday afternoon when Goldman called, telling us the prosecutor's office wanted counsel for Reuben Zapata to meet at his office that afternoon. Preeti, Josea, and I quickly raced to The Inn where Reuben's lawyers were waiting in the front. We drove to Las Cruces to Woodcrest's office. He only invited in Ashton and Goldman. The three of us waited outside. A half-hour later, Reuben's attorneys came out smiling.

"We'll be meeting with Judge Winkler when he gets back to his office. If he has no objection...the United States is dropping all charges."

Josea broke into a sob. Preeti and I had to use all of our joyous energy to contain her. Goldman and Ashton acted like they had just chipped from off the green and the ball had rolled into the hole.

"Damn good job, if I don't say so myself," Goldman bragged to Ashton.

"Seems to me this Walter did our work for us," Ashton countered humbly.

Goldman came closer to Ashton, whispering so only the four of us could hear.

"Walter didn't write that note."

"What are you talking about?" Josea queried.

"Didn't you notice in the medical records where the doctor's early reports comment that Walter was a slow learner... he had problems with reading and writing?" Goldman responded.

"Oh my, that's right," Josea exhorted.

"When the search of his dwelling was done, I noticed there were no books. I also looked at a couple written pieces I'm sure were his. The writing was nearly illegible, with lots of spelling and language errors," Goldman added.

"The admission letter Josea read was grammatically perfect and the phrasing really not the way Walter talked," Preeti noted.

"That doesn't mean Walter couldn't have had someone type the letter for him and still have committed the crimes," I banally piped in.

"That's exactly what he did," Goldman asserted. "But he either had an accomplice or someone who wanted to spill a bag of beans they knew would free an innocent Reuben."

I turned to my wife who stood on my right. I noticed her creamy dark Mescalero Apache skin whitening as the circuits of her mind churned like a computer. She had to be calculating an answer she had already considered. I poked her with my foot and she looked up at me.

"I love you. Be happy for Josea now, okay?"

She nodded her head and forced a smile.

"I hope we're not about to wrap this up and leave a second murderer out on the loose to come back later and terrorize these or some other people," Ashton expressed with concern.

"Sam, I doubt that. Our conscience can be at ease," Goldman said respectfully. "You know as well as I do that all of the murders were done by the same set of hands. No, the person who wrote the note had a peripheral role, probably no more than an aid to Walter's supplication to God for forgiveness."

Josea, it seemed, could have cared less. Her only concern was getting Reuben out of the cell so he'd soon be swooshing in his sweet baby's arms.

"Can we call Reuben and let him know?" she asked.

"Let's not do anything before we see Judge Winkler," Ashton cautioned. "I hope to Christ he doesn't pick up on any of these peculiarities himself and delay the release."

"Unlikely," Goldman retorted. "That's not his role. I think it's really no more than a rubber stamp now."

"How did Woodcrest miss what you're saying about the letter and Walter not being able to compose it?" I tossed the question out to whoever could answer.

"My guess would be he did know," Ashton responded. "You see Woodcrest understands the people in southern New Mexico and especially the tribal groups. He's very sensitive to their plight and appreciates what they've been through. What's to be gained by raising a question that would only cause more embarrassment? It's clear, Reuben, the accused, is innocent and that's all he is being asked to address at this point."

"I agree, Sam," Goldman offered. "I might add that there's even more to his motivation. I had my people get some background on Woodcrest. He's known as an earnest prosecutor but like so many in his position he has his eye on political aspirations down the line. The last thing he wants to do is to prosecute cases with a high probability of failure. He'd much prefer a case falling apart in its infancy than risking embarrassment down the line, especially in a high profile matter where he has to go up against probably two of the best attorneys he's ever faced. It's not advantageous in a campaign, say for example, for the governor to have the record show you recently had your mug speared in muck."

"Good point. He placed no obstacles in our way, did he?" Ashton gloated.

"So it will end here?" my practical wife, disinterested in the legal assumptions, stated more than inquired. "I wish I could thank Mr. Woodcrest—he's right to let it go."

Shortly, we were all walking to the courthouse to meet with the judge. The attorneys for the defense and prosecution went in. Twenty minutes later, Reuben was ordered released from prison.

We were taken to a waiting area. It took about a half-hour before he was escorted to us. His first stop was Josea. Puddles of tears were released; they're probably still using suction machines to clean up the mess.

All along I had been communicating with Jay Weiner to keep him abreast of our work to get Stevie out of jail. While everyone was celebrating, I took a second to separate off from the group and call him. It totally shocked me when he started to cry. He's the last man I would have expected to respond in that matter, but admittedly I had misread him terribly from the start.

He thanked me endlessly for taking the time to let him know and told me to have Reuben call him when he got settled. He couldn't resist a light humored comment at the end.

"And don't forget to tell him he made over seventeen million dollars in the last month."

I assured Jay he would hear from an emotionally confused, but wealthier, Reuben shortly. Before walking back to join the others, I had one other call to make. I searched in my wallet and took out a card, punching in the numbers on my cell.

"This is Agent Kershaw," the voice identified itself.

"Zach Miller," I informed him bluntly.

"I was waiting for your call," he snapped out.

"My call?" I chuckled. "What do you mean?"

"I'm waiting for you to give me my franchise."

"Well, you'll be thrilled to know that Reuben has just been released."

"Indeed I am. I knew you were a man of your word."

"You're misreading me. It's just that I don't want to get on the wrong side of an FBI agent," I quipped.

"Ex-FBI agent, Zach."

"You're serious about this restaurant business," I muttered.

"We already have a location on Rodeo Drive in Beverly Hills. We're going first class. I told you we have a big backer," Kershaw said excitedly.

"You said you had several prospective backers," I retorted.

"No. Just one."

"Who is it that's putting up the money?" I had an irrepressible urge to delve where I had no right to go.

"Can't discuss it...a silent investor," he responded to my query.

That's all Kershaw would say. Still the point stuck in my immediate consciousness like a phone that wouldn't stop ringing. I'd have to return to it later.

"Okay. You'll get your franchise," I assured him. "But if you wouldn't mind, I recall the last time we talked that you assured me I could 'bet my momma's bosom' whomever you charged, in this case Reuben, would be convicted and sentenced to life," I poked at him.

"So, what about it?" Kershaw responded heedlessly. "That was then and now is now."

Sounded like Len Cloud to me.

"And while we're on the subject of things not making sense, it makes none that you'd be expecting me to call if you had wagered that Reuben would be convicted."

"It makes perfect sense," Kershaw responded casually.

"But if Reuben's fate went as you predicted, you never would have received a call from me," I said intentionally to reiterate the point.

"How about we leave it like this? I had a hunch," he proposed mysteriously.

"A man of your training doesn't change his mind unless he has cause for doing so." I persisted in soliciting an explanation. "What did you learn after we talked?"

"This is as far as I'll go on the subject...for your protection," he stressed. "It wasn't so much what I learned as what I knew that I never spoke to anyone about and assumed nobody else would discover."

"But they did discover it?" I pushed, knowing I was trespassing beyond the limit he had just set.

"Let's get back to the franchise deal."

Kershaw was not going to be nagged to discuss the subject further.

"It'll take a bit of time because I've never been a franchisor before."

"We'll get the lawyers to draw it up in no time," he said, sounding like a real businessman rather than an agent of the FBI. "Zach, I know you offered me the franchise rights for the whole country, free, but that's not the way I do business. All I want now is this restaurant in Beverly Hills...and we're going to pay royalties for it. Then when we expand to different locations, we'll pay for that too."

"Make it a buck as far as we're concerned," I answered nonchalantly.

"You're going to be a wealthy man when Kuruk's open around the world," Kershaw confidently informed me.

"I'm wealthy now! What more do I need?"

I felt like I was pleading with him not to send buckets full of wealth my way.

"Reuben will cooperate with the menus and consulting with my brother as we get started?"

"I promise you, he will."

We hung up. It all seemed so effortless. Kuruk literally built itself. Now it was possibly going to grow into a chain of exclusive restaurants located in the largest cities throughout the world.

I knew what was coming next. Len Cloud was about to gather his family. Wow! He had disclosures to make that were going to change forever the dynamics between these people—including myself. We were about to have a scene that television would have paid a bundle to broadcast as a reality show—only this tale was the real deal.

30

FAMILY TIME

REUBEN HAD NEVER BEEN anyone other than Reuben to us, so there was really little adjustment to make. Rarely during the couple of days after he arrived back at Kuruk did we discuss Stevie Green, and those occasions were only when he brought it up to me. Reuben resumed his life in the same home he had occupied before the arrest. It was the same home Preeti had lived in with Jivin, then briefly with Jivin and me. Josea was with her man continuously, but they refrained from talking about the future.

Reuben was content to immediately step back into the kitchen. At the same time, I noticed Josea spending more time writing—what she was working on she wouldn't reveal. Within two days, however, we were all settling into a comfortable routine. Josea and Reuben were scheduled to be married later that week, and my mother wouldn't miss staying until after the ceremony.

Throughout these two days, Preeti pestered me with questions about the letter found with Walter and his admission of guilt. Had her father authored it? She must have asked me at least a hundred times. I kept telling her it was pointless to deliberate, because he would go to his grave without ever telling a soul. She knew that to be the case, yet she still wouldn't let it go.

Also during that time, I was obsessed with a hunch I felt as compelled to pursue as Preeti did her unanswered question. I was being as foolish believing I'd ever get to the truth, as I knew she was being.

The question was simple. Had issues arisen for Kershaw that raised questions regarding the alleged guilt of Reuben, but he couldn't convey them formally in his role as an agent? If so, did he find a way to mention them to someone (Josea, Goldman, or Ashton) and by stepping out to do so indirectly assist in Reuben's release? Then, if that were the case, did the information get back to Reuben, and in turn to Jay Weiner—who was writing the checks—such that in the end the "big backer" for Kershaw became Reuben's estate?

I deliberated on my best chance for closure. The attorneys would never divulge it to me even if they trusted I wouldn't say anything. Jay Weiner might say something revealing, but I could count on no more than an innuendo intended to leave me in doubt. I didn't want to take a chance on causing any further strain to Reuben by raising the topic with him.

That left Josea, the one I surmised would be the most probable of the group to give me an answer. I knew she hated to withhold anything from me, and her ability to keep secrets was only a tad better than Souche's. I met her at Kuruk. I intentionally brought Henry with me. I thought it might loosen her up since her good friend, who was never really intended to be anything other than Souche's puppy, was becoming a preteen gentleman. He was growing up, but not out. He had the cutest skinny body and his hair was short and soft. Sometimes I shamefully fought with my daughter about who was going to hold Henry.

It was between mealtimes. I was comfortable in bringing my buddy in with me. He was able to jump up on the padded seat with only a light push on the buttock. Josea sat across from us.

"I told you about Kershaw and the franchise deal," I began. "He mentioned to me that he had a big backer. In fairness, the first time we talked he said his brother thought he had several people with money to get him started, but when we last talked it all came down to one person. When I questioned him about who was putting up the money, he refused to answer."

"He probably didn't want to make a disclosure of something that is confidential," Josea responded.

"Sure, that might be. But I have a bothersome thought I can't put away," I mentioned to set the stage for the next more direct query. "Josea, is there something that happened...that I don't know about? Is it Reuben funding the venture?"

She looked at me like a poker player sizing up another player's bluff.

"Zach," she zeroed her gaze on me. "Did Len Cloud kill Walter?"

Her question floored me. She turned the table on me. There was no way I would respond with the truthful answer to her even if she presented me with irrefutable evidence proving she knew—which I didn't believe she had.

"If you knew the answer to that question you might not want to tell me, because it might leave me to deal with something painful, and regardless, with no reward in the end, right? It would have nothing to do with trust. It would be about love. Sometimes we demonstrate love by staying mute on a subject and by protecting another person from unnecessary suffering or confusion."

"I understand," I said quietly.

"Drop it, my dear friend," she entreated.

I gestured that I would.

"Is that a promise?"

"Okay," I surrendered.

I surmised that most likely Kershaw hadn't done anything illegal or unethical. He might have shared with her "impressions." In fact, it was my thought that the information about Walter's deficient reading and writing skills really came from him. From there it went through Josea, and finally to Goldman. It sounded logical to me. But what did it really matter if as a result of the agent's goodwill Reuben instructed Jay Weiner to fund his venture? Nothing.

It was on the third day after Reuben's release when Preeti received a call from her father, requesting a get together. When he specified that he only wanted his daughter and me, Reuben and Josea in attendance, she thought it peculiar. She didn't question him, but raised the point to me. I faked bemusement but I knew what was coming. Preeti and the others were in for the shock of a lifetime.

He thought it would be easier if we all met at his house. After dinner, the four of us took off. Len Cloud greeted everyone calmly, inviting us to sit. He gazed from one of us to another, as if inspecting the toes and fingers on his new-born infant. I noticed the three of them getting uncomfortable as my father-in-law unintentionally drew out the event. It was Preeti who broke the silence.

"Shitaa, you're worrying me," she said impatiently. "Why did you call us together?"

Len Cloud smiled adoringly at his daughter.

"You have always hated surprises, my dear," Len reminisced. "I must impose on you this evening because I have a few of them for you and the others."

"If you're sick, I can't hear it now," Preeti shot out imploringly at him.

"No, I'm well, I think. But I have a story to tell," Len revealed. "Please sit and I'll disclose everything. But I must ask each of you to say nothing until I tell you I have finished. Is that agreed?"

He waited for the four of us to each commit to his terms.

Len then repeated the story he had told me days earlier, with the obvious exception of his role in the disappearance, and then discovery, of Walter.

"Now as you see, for all of us in this room the associations are forever changed," Len smiled. "Preeti, you now have Reuben as your half-brother, and of course, Reuben, Preeti will be the sister you never had. Zach is your brother-in-law. Josea, Preeti will be your sister-in-law and I your father-in-law once you and Reuben marry—and Zach will be your brother-in-law.

"There's more," he said as he looked at Reuben. "You now know you have Apache blood running through your heart. I joked at the Puberty Ceremony that you were Mescalero and my greatest joy is to now be able to say it is true in every sense. If you wish, you may change your name one more time, to Reuben Cloud."

Len now paused to give Reuben ample time to absorb his new name. Then he glanced compassionately toward him and continued.

"I know what I'm telling you will not be easy to accept. I want you to understand that there was nothing I could have done to change the course of events. The woman who birthed you, Reuben, I had no way of finding her after she fled. Every clue she left was a deceit. I had no way of knowing what happened to you. My only hope was that whatever had happened, someday the winds would shift and you would be blown into my life. I now feel whole for the first time in all these years. I can pass in peace to the Eternal World when I'm called."

Len Cloud then stood up and kissed and hugged each of us, beginning with Preeti, then Reuben, followed by me, and lastly Josea.

"I'm finished," he said bluntly as he sat down.

Reuben stood and went over to his father, sitting on the edge of a small table. He leaned forward and positioned himself close enough to speak in Len's ear. But what he had to say was no secret to any of us; he spoke with a full voice.

"You read the story I wrote for Josea while I was in jail. If that information were to be made public it might endanger my life. If not that, it would for sure cheat me of what is now most precious to me, my privacy. I have to ask you to keep this a secret," he began. "Throughout my whole life, I also never felt whole. At no time did I have a sense of belonging with the people who raised me. My life was filled with fantasies of going home. It was a theme continually laced through my music."

"You must have been a great artist," Len Cloud said to his son.

"He's modest," Josea interrupted. "He was beyond great. He was the greatest."

"I hope now you will let me teach you the songs of our people. I hope you will create new songs to tell our story. Then, at the next Puberty Ceremony you may sing and dance, just as my grandson did," Len said with sad eyes. "I'm sorry you never met him. He was as extraordinary a person as Josea says you are."

"Josea and I have already discussed plans for music. I'll tell you about it later," Reuben responded. "I'm happy I came home."

Reuben reached out to his newly found father and embraced him. "I want to know you well."

Len Cloud stood. "All of you leave now. I'm getting old and need to sleep more." Then he laughed. "And I want to be rested for the wedding."

We left, four souls now bonded for life by more than our devotion, friendship, admiration, and respect. We were a family. I couldn't wait to get home—my mother was going to love this story.

31

WEDDING BELLS

THERE WAS NO REASON TO delay wedding plans as far as Josea and Reuben were concerned. The following Saturday evening would be the date. Surprisingly, the guest list was large. Josea's family would be coming. Friends and family in Mescalero were invited, and Jay Weiner would be coming in from Los Angeles. Preston was flying in from...I had no idea where he was working that week. They wanted to host it at Kuruk, so we announced we were closing the restaurant for the evening.

While Preeti was frantically racing to help set up for the event, it didn't stop her from pursuing the confrontation with me. I anticipated it would eventually happen. We were in the front yard watching Souche play.

"Zach, will you tell me the truth?" she posed.

"Our marriage rests on me never doing anything other than that."

"My father talks to you now. I know he confides in you. It happens when men get older. They need to get things off their chest."

How she knew this I had no idea, nor did I know that it was true, but she seemed confident.

"Did he ever tell you he wrote that letter? You know, the one they found that Walter supposedly wrote," she asked pointedly.

"What do you mean 'supposedly?'" I queried.

"Zach, I told you I went to school with Walter. He was close to illiterate."

"Really? Well, your dad never said a word to me about it, if he did."

It was a stinkin' lousy deceit. I felt like a crumbled cake.

Preeti looked up at me and with the gentlest touch drew my face to hers, whispering in my ear.

"Sweetheart. Sometimes we have to keep a secret."

Talk about being humbled. She took my hand and led me to where our daughter was bending over to dig with a toy in a sandbox next to Henry, who was also plowing sand—the two small butts adorably sticking out like a matching pair of buns while the hands and paws were on their way to China.

"Isn't she beautiful?" Preeti commented to change the subject.

I was certain by then that she had figured it out—her father had punished Walter. She knew the man as well as anyone. Still, she wasn't about to judge her father. She was Apache down to her inner cell structure. She knew how the elders of the tribe for thousands of years past would have ordered Walter's fate. It was exactly as I knew her father had settled it.

She also knew that I withheld truth from her. Still, she elevated me to higher esteem for doing so. She never perceived what I had done as a breach of our trust. Instead, I had followed the authority of the Eagle. It was an amazing experience and she was an amazing person.

Two days later, on a Thursday evening, I was at Kuruk. I received a surprise guest for dinner. State Trooper Corbin walked in with his wife, Gayle. I was in my office when one of the waitresses came to ask if I had a minute because one of the diners wanted to say hello. I came out and there he was, already seated next to his wife, a woman who looked like a midget next to her husband.

When he saw me he offered a warm grin and stood up—he was larger than I recalled. He took my hand and in his giant warm grip, I wondered if I'd ever find it again. He introduced me to his wife and asked me to sit.

"Gayleen loved the food so much I promised I was going to bring her back. Don't worry, we're not here for a freebie," he laughed. "That Cooley is quite a nut job, isn't he?"

"I didn't really see that part of him," I responded kindly.

"Still believes in that Stevie Green story," Corbin chuckled. "Damn fool, at least."

"He was off target about Green, that's for sure," I said, putting the matter to rest.

"Sorry how it all ended up about those girls who were killed," he said sympathetically. "Hope your wife is okay."

"She's getting over it. It has been hard on everyone around here," I informed him.

"Gayleen and her people are the same way, right darling?"

"I just couldn't believe Walter Chicory could do such evil," Gayleen responded in disbelief. "I knew his cousin. She's real sick now."

"I try to explain to her that it don't much matter if you're a Caucasian or Indian, you can be a killer," Corbin directed to me. "She just can't accept it."

"I wonder if refusing to accept it is exactly what will keep it from happening again. Is it possible in some crazy way that by believing it can happen we endorse it, but by disbelieving it we can suppress it?"

"That's a little deep for me," Corbin responded. "I know I've seen killers born out of every damn circumstance and there will always be a world with sick souls. Don't make a difference if they're red-, white- or yellow-skinned, they can murder."

He was right. I envied his ability to perform mental reductions on complex matters and then find peace in the answers. I'd probably still be debating the point while doing my now-I-lay-me-down-to-sleep prayer with Souche. Kindly, Corbin interrupted my jealousy.

"Hey, the wife looked up Kuruk on the Internet before we left. It seems your chef has a new Creole menu. How is it?"

"If you'll let me, I'll take care of ordering for you. I think you'll be pleased," I assured him.

We chatted a bit longer and then I placed an order for them. I refused to let him pay. After they left, Soeze heartlessly chewed me out—the lady needed a husband.

On the evening of the wedding, Kuruk looked more like a floral shop than a dining room. The place was buzzing. Len Cloud, at the request of Josea and Reuben, arranged for a municipal judge from Alamogordo to perform the service. About an hour before they were to be married, Jay Weiner arrived. Reuben was nervously talking with a couple of guests when he came in.

The two stared at each other, but as had been agreed prior, they made no public display of their relationship. Jay Weiner was introduced as a friend of mine, and it would not be until shortly after his arrival that I would be able to get him and Reuben alone in my office. I left the two to talk in private.

The timing was perfect. Preston arrived within minutes. I was excited to see my best friend. I had already told him every part of the story I was able to share.

"You have no idea how glad I am to have been at least partially wrong about Reuben," Preston mentioned.

"Sorry, Preston. I think it's one of those rare occasions when you were more wrong than right," I teased him.

"He's no murderer, thankfully. But does Josea know what his life was all about before he arrived here at Mescalero? Because he didn't commit murder does not change that he might have—"

"Tell Josea after the ceremony that you're happy for her and apologize for your negativity about her husband," I advised him. "Everything you would want to know she knows. It's not my business to talk about it, but I promise he's a solid guy."

"If you say so, it's good enough for me." He paused to continue processing his perceptions. "I still can't get past the fact that something alarmed me about him...something told me he was not a straight shooter."

"I'll tell you one thing, Preston, but only if you agree to drop it forever."

"Go ahead because I gather this is one of those trust deals you're not going to break, even for me."

"You're right on that account. Also you're right that there was something in his past that he was concealing. It was big. But it was not dangerous, criminal, harmful, or evil. He's a great person," I assured my worrisome friend.

"Thank god for that. I just wanted you to be safe."

Preston couldn't contain the paternal instinct that was beginning to pop out of him like measles. If I could get him married off and into the journey of parenthood, he'd finally be able to apportion some of that concern more appropriately toward a wife and child. Still, I always appreciated how he looked after me. At the same time, I couldn't forget that ironically it was he who always, unintentionally and unconsciously, found a way to whipsaw my life in one direction and another—and he wasn't through.

"I wanted to mention something to you while we have a chance to talk," he said with that excitation that alerted me it might be better to change the topic.

"Oh, no, Preston," I bellowed. "Don't you think you've got me into enough trouble with your stories?"

"Look how rich your life has been because of me," he bragged.

"I'll admit I am becoming wealthy, but my plan now is to

do a little writing, run Kuruk, and be with my family—Preeti is talking about another child, and you know how that goes."

"Just listen to me. You met my cousin, Stacy, the one who is a political analyst in D.C."

"I remember her."

"Her best friend is a woman who is the lead criminal investigator for the Metropolitan Police Department of Washington, D.C.—"

I went down on my knees, a silly pleading gesture to get him to stop.

"No, listen to me. This is really something." He proceeded. He was so earnest that there wasn't even a chuckle as he offered his hand to bring me back to my feet. "She's got a story that she wants to write based on a real murder spree—"

Then he took out his cell phone. "Here's her picture."

I glanced at a very attractive brunette, about our age.

"Tell her to call me. I'll instruct her on what she needs to read to know how to write a novel," I offered.

"She's already tried to write it. She says she can't. I told her about you, and she wants to come and tell you about it," Preston informed me without a shred of disgrace.

It was about this time Preston started to rev up his pitch. It was the same one he'd used to entice me to meet the mystic "little dude" who sent me to Israel, where I was almost killed. It was also the identical tease that resulted in me running around the country chasing a man who was living and working every day within feet of me. Preston could make life exciting, I'll grant him that.

"Zach, I told her about The Inn and she made a reservation... but it's not until next month."

"Let me think about it. Right now I have a wedding to attend."

"She says she's got everything documented. Stacy says she's one of the most remarkable women she's ever met," Preston said, keeping up the promo.

I couldn't help busting up in laughter.

"Yeah, tell her to call me," I remarked casually, changing my attitude to coincide with the delicious thought I was nurturing.

"You won't regret it. It's supposed to be a one-of-a-kind, unimaginable story. Exactly what you like," Preston continued.

As we finished our talk, Preeti signaled me that we were about to begin the ceremony. The music started and in a flash the two lovebirds were man and wife.

We danced. We ate. We laughed. We celebrated. We partied.

It was the father of all fathers, Father Time, who ultimately brought the evening to a close.

EPILOGUE

SO MUCH TRAUMA, DRAMA, uncertainty, mystery; so much planning, preparation, excitement; so much fantasy, anticipation, wishing—and then in a matter of moments time warps experience to a mere memory that over time fades to no more than a faint series of images. The wedding was over. My story, *Mescalero Blood*, was completed.

I had seen Stevie Green's last concert. Then the world wept. I searched in the hopes of drying their tears. But what did I discover? That Stevie Green had never existed. He had been a figment of his and everyone else's imagination. The shell referred to as Stevie Green had been mislabeled coming off the shelf.

His real name was Reuben Cloud. He had been born the first child, a son, of my father-in-law. He was the half-brother of my wife. He was my brother-in-law, the husband of my dear friend, uncle to my only child, a master chef, and a musical genius—and I had the honor of attending his wedding.

As I reflected on the story, it seemed so simple. Life's force works its magic through birth and death, while destiny and free will dual endlessly for ownership of the events and experiences between the two states. As humans, we pray for predictability to bring security while at the same time recklessly gamble away the props we've labored to construct for our shelter and safety.

Peace? It has to be found in a slivery dimension where time and space appears to us as one, a gap where in truth few brave souls visit occasionally between the Shadow World and the Real World. All the music that Stevie Green had created, the hopes and dreams stimulated by his lyrics and sounds, were no more than one being's wish to find the courage to journey where man rarely had the attention span to travel.

Stevie Green had been a tortured soul. He had been blindly leading a flock of equally suffering beings—all destined to drop weightlessly off the end of an inevitable cliff. As they flopped over the precipice, they would hit bottom, most landing on clouds of elastic flinging them back again so they could once more live in a world of shadow and darkness.

That's the human condition we all face, one where on the rebound we find new Stevie Greens. The question is, how many of mankind's trampoline jumpers might wake, pay attention, and peek into that elusive space between, where instead of a Stevie Green they might discover...their own being.

Peace?

Two days after the wedding I met with Len Cloud. I brought a folder detailing everything I had uncovered about the tribal fraud, but without disclosing Josea or Farley's roles. He looked it over and said nothing for some time. I could tell he really didn't know what to do.

"I'm an old man," he stated. "I don't know if I can live through what this will do to my people," he shared sorrowfully. Holding out the folder he continued. "This is worse than I imagined."

His eyes were droopy. It was terrible timing. At last his life seemed aligned—he had his son—and now this. He didn't have the heart to deal with the matter, nor did he have the will to drop it and allow the fleecing to continue.

"Can I help?" I asked.

He said nothing. I took that as an affirmative.

"I have a suggestion. See what you think," I proposed. "It might be sort of a compromise between the White Man's way and the Mescalero way."

Len smiled. I believe he appreciated my tact.

"Let's handle this privately. No state prosecutors coming to the reservation. No shame to the people. No disclosures."

"Yes, I see where you're going," Len slowly delivered his words.

"I could go to Platta and tell him everything. I could let him know that no information will be disclosed publicly if the theft stops. Then we insist that as much money as we can find from the guilty parties be returned in the form of gifts to the tribe," I proposed.

"It'll be a bit tricky because they'll have to turn over their personal accounting and have it audited," I informed him. "Houses and properties will have to be sold by many individuals and some will be left financially destitute. Believe me, Josea can handle that part. It will take time to get it all sorted out, but in the end we can accomplish more than having it handled through the courts, and cheaper."

Then we sat a bit longer, ruminating on my proposal before I added provisions. "We'll also have to insist that Platta resign his position on the council and cease to have any involvement in tribal matters. He'll have no choice. Otherwise, it'll be jail for him and both of his sons. His kids will have to get jobs...but that's better than jail also."

So it was agreed. During the following several months, innumerable private meetings were held to sort out the details of returning assets to the tribe. Farley was called in as well. He proved to be a great asset. I surmised as time went on that we were making progress.

Then things began to unravel. Lawyers suddenly appeared to represent the guilty parties, their admissions retracted. So many fingers started to point in so many different directions that the playing field began to look like a pile of tossed toothpicks. All of a sudden, there were no parties that had committed wrongdoing; even Platta was defending himself.

That's when I learned a sad but worthy lesson: it's not wise to deal straight with crooked shooters. The matter of tribal crime had a long way to play out; the weasels had used the time to build fortresses to defend themselves. In the end, it turned out precisely as I'd hoped it wouldn't. Once again the tribe would be looking for White Painted Lady.

During this period of time when I was trying to resolve the matter of tribal corruption, three other developments were taking place. The first was that I was going to have my second child. Preeti was pregnant and it seemed to revive Len Cloud's spirit. He distanced himself from the nasty corruption business as much as possible.

"Now you'll have two children too," he joyously repeated to me each time we talked. Family was really all he wanted to deal with at this stage of his life.

The second item had to do with Kershaw. He had been in touch at least weekly for one thing or another. Recently he had called to let us know that Kuruk, Beverly Hills was set to open March fifteenth, just two months away. I was going to be papa to two restaurants as well as a big shot franchisor. No doubt my relationship with Kershaw had a future.

The last matter pertained to Reuben and Josea. It took place about two months after the wedding. Reuben had continued as chef of Kuruk. In his spare time, he and Josea worked on a project together that the two of them refused to discuss with me. Then one afternoon, they asked if we might talk.

"If it's okay with you, we want to build another structure on the property," Josea proposed.

"What for?" I asked, at the same time calculating that because we had several acres of land, getting the permits wouldn't be a problem.

"What if people coming to Kuruk could not only have a meal but also take in a night at the theatre?" Reuben explained. "What do I have to spend my money on otherwise?" he laughed, knowing he was worth hundreds of millions.

"Who will put on the productions?" I asked.

"We're writing musicals. It's what we've been doing together," Josea revealed.

"After all is said and done, I still want to do something musically," Reuben noted enthusiastically. "No more than a hundred seats. I never want this to go further than right here in Mescalero," he added emphatically.

As it turned out, two structures were built. The first was a theater with 135 seats. The second was a dormitory-like facility to house the artists and personnel associated with the theatre productions.

The first performance opened shortly after Kuruk, Beverly Hills went into operation. It was called *Wrapped*, a melodious hip-hoppy piece about a struggling singer and musician who concocted a ridiculous but loving scheme to push his family away. Because he blamed himself for all of his musical failures, he concluded that he'd deprived them of what he had always promised to provide.

The production was sold out from opening night; it kept up that pace while Reuben and Josea began working on a second piece entitled, *Misty's Place*.

A month after the opening of *Wrapped*, a man sitting in the front row identified himself to Reuben as Max Freestone, a Broadway producer who'd flown in from New York solely to see the show. He wanted to discuss further development of the piece with the plan of taking it to Broadway. I recall overhearing the short conversation.

"So what do you think, Mr. Cloud?"

"I don't mean this disrespectfully, Mr. Freestone. But go back to New York and don't ever come here again," Reuben said without room for negotiation.

I noticed Freestone twitch his left eye nervously before walking away from a rebuff he'd never anticipated and likely never previously experienced.

An attractive woman, about thirty-five years of age, was waiting to talk to me while I eavesdropped on Reuben's conversation with Freestone. She wore tenseness like battle fatigue, but an air of confidence wistfully announced she would survive.

"You're Zach Miller?" she asked.

"Yes, I am," certain she was the same person whose picture Preston had shown me on his cell phone.

"I know it's been months since your friend Preston mentioned me to you," she said impassively. "I've not been up to it but I'm getting closer to being ready."

I stared at her long brunette hair, which meticulously dropped downward like a smooth waterfall. Her face was pretty, but I could tell she had been suffering inwardly.

"My name is Nadine Street. I'd like you to help me with my story."

From Kuruk! Ah Jivin. How could I have ever doubted you?

Upcoming Novels by Dennis A Nehamen

Crushing Steel

The Greatest American Outlaw

Musicball

Crushing Dreams

To Protect The Guilty

Misty's Place

The Making of A Madman

Juliette

Dogma i

ABOUT THE AUTHOR

Dennis A Nehamen, Ph.D. is a forensic and clinical psychologist who has authored novels, screenplays and musical books, including the award-winning musical *Wrapped*. Published novels to date include the first two books of *The Zach Miller Adventure Series, Mistaken Enemy* and *Insatiable Hate*. He lives in Los Angeles with his wife and has two adult children.

www.ingramcontent.com/pod-product-compliance
Lightning Source LLC
Chambersburg PA
CBHW030541260626
47157CB00006B/2142